I0676303

THE
HARBINGER

WRITTEN BY
CHRISTOPHER HUNTINGFORD

The intent of this book is to offer information of a general nature to help the reader attain insight on the concepts and systems developed by the author. All stories, accounts and otherwise are based on the author's personal experience and recollection of events. This includes acknowledgements of various people, companies and otherwise who are mentioned within the content for the sole purpose of sharing the author's personal accounts and interpretations.

Published by Christopher Huntingford

www.HarbingerChronicles

Printed in the United States of America

Book Cover Design by Dan Fowler
Editing by Kimberly Cantrell
Interior Design by Dan Fowler

Library of Congress
Cataloging-in-Publication Data
Huntingford, Christopher.

Harbinger Chronicles: The Harbinger

Christopher Huntingford -- 1st Edition
ISBN-13: 978-0615871905
(The Harbinger)
ISBN-10: 0615871909

DEDICATED TO:

W.R.H.

Once learned, anything is possible.

Courage is that which propels us forward.

Take the road less traveled.

Seize every moment.

Embrace your humanity and know you are not alone.

Persevere.

Be unflinching.

Patience and Kindness.

Play to win and play to learn.

You will learn more in defeat than in victory.

And finally,

Defeat the darkness.

PROLOGUE

The sun had barely passed the halfway mark in the sky as a hooded figure stepped into the cluttered campsite. The cloudless sky shined down upon the camps inhabitants while they scurried about their business. They paid just enough heed to the stranger and stayed out of his path.

The man took stock of the campsite and its dwellers. It was dingy and each person looked to have worn the campsite on their garments. The man pulled his robe above his ankles, as if to show his contempt for their living conditions, and made his way through the site. He walked over the rubbish and pots that had been carelessly strewn over the ground. Finally, he made his way to his destination; the main structure that was made from little more than animal hides and branches. He meant to enter but was stopped by a trio of old women who had been quietly watching him since he had entered their campsite.

"Hold there," they cried out in unison. "What is your business with us?"

"I seek someone. I was told I could find her here." He waited, impatiently tapping his foot, as they circled around him.

"We think not," one old crone replied. "We do not

receive many visitors."

"No," the second hag agreed. "It is as if fate brought you to our camp."

"Yes," hissed the last woman. Her hair was nearly gone and her eyes gleamed with a fierce orange hue.

"I like his cloak, sisters," she whined as she touched his cloak. "Come on, help me to it."

"Sisters?" The hooded figure asked. "Are you the maidservants of Azrael that are so widely known?"

The women looked at each other uneasily and their noses twitched at the mention of the name.

"That's a legend! To say that is to pronounce your own death sentence," the crone snarled. They backed away slowly and fidgeted from one foot to the next.

"Come now," he said soothingly. "The sisters are infamous according to tradition, and talented beyond compare. They have the ability to peer into the future. It is stated only they can create an elixir so undetectable to a man that he will drink it unknowingly while they control his very thoughts and mind. It is even said that they can control his very moment of death."

"These sisters are..." he continued slowly, "legendary."

"To speak of them is forbidden!" The patchy-haired woman's eye twitched and her skin moved as if a pebble was being smoothed under her skin. It ran down her neck and she blinked twice. Her eyes lost their orange glow.

"Who forbids speaking of such legends?" His voice snarled with such contempt that the campsite shook.

"The Lords of Alveus." They retreated away from the man in a vain attempt to return to their work.

"I am the lord of Alveus and that makes me your master, my sisters!" He placed his hands out in front of him with their palms outstretched. "Come and swear your allegiance."

"We take no masters," the oldest one said. "But I will take your cloak." The skin of all three women rippled and each sister's eyes glowed different colors.

The crone produced two daggers and whipped them at high speed towards the man. She produced a third from behind her head and it followed closely behind. The hag stretched her hand forward and immediately an iron pot flew to the man's left side. The patchy haired one shut her eyes and the man felt a presence inside of his mind.

"Stand still," the voice ordered him and his body snapped rigidly to obey.

The daggers were an arms-length away when his mind alerted him to the imminent danger.

"Enough!" he shouted. With full concentration he pushed the voice back from his mind and into the unsuspecting sister's head. He lifted his hands up and froze the knives and pot in the air. They dropped harmlessly to the ground. With a wave of his other hand, three roots of nearby trees were unearthed and whipped their roots around each sister's throat.

The old women clutched at their throats, but there was little they could do. Every twitch of a muscle brought increased tightness and shortness of breath. The man chuckled as he moved his fingers back and forth, as if he choked them with his own hand.

"What do you want with us?" A low guttural voice snarled at him from the tent's shadows.

"Come out where I can see you," he commanded. "It's alright, I won't hurt you."

An elderly blind woman emerged into the daylight and poked about with her cane. She wore the same rags as the sisters and looked every bit decrepit.

"I take it you are not kingdom folk. Your aura says

so much more."

"Never mind my aura; I am in need of your service."

"Release the sisters, and I will help you."

The man opened his hands and the branches released them. The roots slowly uncoiled from their captives and retreated back into the ground from whence they came. The three hags cowered and rubbed their throats. They quietly gnashed their teeth and retreated behind an old wagon.

"Who are you, that you should trouble us so? Let me touch you," she asked. She held out her hand in the stranger's direction. Although she inched closer towards him, he stayed put. He held his hand up and waited until she was close enough to touch.

He grabbed her hand and a rush of wind began to move through the campsite. She held on tightly and as she stood her ground, faint specks of color began to collect in her eyes. With each drop of color, she gained back a tiny bit of her sight.

With his other hand, the stranger removed his hood and revealed his face. The woman gasped at the figure that took form in front of her.

"My Lord!" she exclaimed and dropped to her knees. He released her hand and the drops of color in her eyes disappeared.

"How may I serve you?"

"I seek a sign." His gaze fell upon a rabbit that nibbled a patch of grass nearby. With a flick of his wrist, one of the tree roots seized the rabbit, as if it were a snake that had caught the poor beast, and carried the rabbit to him.

The man took hold of the rabbit's ears and placed it inside the witch's hand. He produced a jeweled dagger and placed it in her other hand.

"You are the soothsayer," he commented. "Tell me

what the signs say."

The witch held the struggling rabbit to the ground and lifted up the dagger. With one stroke she cleanly sliced the belly of the rabbit in half. After a yelp and a faint attempt to escape, the rabbit lay in its own blood. The witch thrust her bony fingers inside the rabbit and felt inside to reach the organ.

"The future presents itself," she whispered. "The liver is good. Fate smiles upon you, my Lord. When you kill him, everything will be yours."

"It is time then," he mused. "It is time to put my plans into motion. The kingdom will pay for their sins, and when the time comes, all will be set back as it was."

"What would you have me to do?" the soothsayer asked.

"I, too, have seen the future," he said and pulled his hood back over his head. "In time, a young man will fall into our clutches. He will be wearing the armor. When he does…"

"Yes?" she cried eagerly?

"Go and tell Nicodemus to wait for him. When he finally has the traveler in his hands, you will kill him where he stands."

"As you wish. You have me and my sister's oaths of service." They knelt on their hands and knees in a show of fealty.

"If we are successful, I will restore you to your rightful placc, and you will have much more power than you can possibly imagine." The man grinned evilly and turned his back to the campsite. "Before I am finished, I will see them all beg for death."

CHAPTER I

"Alex! Wake up!"

Alexander Wolfield opened and rubbed his eyes vigorously to adjust to the bright sun. "Really, Sofia, you could have been gentler in waking me." He glared at his sister and stifled a yawn.

"If I'd have been courteous, everyone would have been talking about you for weeks."

"What does that mean?" Alex sat up and began brushing off the sand that his clothes had collected.

"For starters, one of the king's sons is sleeping in plain view of everyone in the city, on the beach no less. Lastly, you talk in your sleep. People will begin to think you're a sorcerer in a trance." She offered her hand to him to pull him off the sand.

He refused her hand and lay back down on the sand.

"For starters," he retorted, "This sand is the softest I have ever felt and it feels wonderful to have the sun's warmth on me as the water laps onto the shore. It soothes me."

"If it soothes you, why do you thrash so?"

"It's those dreams I have." Alexander looked

towards the fishermen mending nets and his eyes caught a black beast moving quickly towards them.

"Can you remember this one?"

"No," Alexander sighed. "I never remember anything more than shadows." He looked away from the fishermen and towards the horizon. "I don't like the feeling it leaves me. I'm always unsettled and whatever it is feels like it comes closer to me."

Sofia knelt down beside Alexander and grabbed his hands.

"Let's not focus on shadows, my brother. Let us focus on our birthday, and that we shall have many gifts to enjoy!" She pulled him up and brushed the sand off of her dress. She was too busy to notice what Alexander was watching.

The black beast had found the fisherman's catch and chewed through several fish before the fishermen caught on to what was happening to their livelihood. When they did, they immediately started after the animal. Startled, the animal grabbed another fish and ran in Alexander's direction with the fishermen in pursuit.

"We need to be off to make ready for Edward's arrival," Sofia commanded as she brushed sand off of him. "This could be the first day that you and I make an appearance without something going wrong."

"Too late," Alex stated. "Keira!"

"You brought your dog?!" Sofia shrieked. "What were you thinking?"

Sofia caught sight of Alexander's large black dog as she streaked down the shoreline and was followed by three fishermen who cursed angrily. The dog raced through a busy area where fishermen and net-menders worked and paid no heed to man or his work. With destruction in her wake, she bounded in the sibling's direction. She made her way to Sofia who quickly lost her balance and fell onto the sand as she tried to impede the dog's escape. Alexander dropped to his knees as he wrapped his arms around the dog's neck. She pulled and pulled against his weight, and managed to carry him six feet before she finally lay down and licked his face.

"Now you've done it," Alexander muttered and stood up to face the angry mob. Several fisherman and their wives expressed the grievances towards the prince. Their livelihood was ruined and their day's work wouldn't feed anyone. That dog had spoiled the fish!

"She should be punished proper!" one man shouted and raised a stick over his head as if he meant to be the one to do it.

The smile disappeared from Keira's lips and her tail stood up straight in the air. Her eyes focused squarely on the peasant and she gave a short menacing growl. Her hair stood on edge and she pawed at the sand. The crowd gave space quickly and moved back several feet.

"There, there," Alexander said as he smoothed Keira's ruffled hair. "No one is going to hurt you. They were just playing with you. After all you are the prince's dog, and no one," he took great care with his words, "will ever lift a finger to you." Keira's demeanor changed and she smiled once again and wagged her tail energetically.

"On behalf of my pup, I extend my apologies to you good people. I assure you the Crown will be generous in its compensation for your losses." He removed a small pouch from his belt and tossed it towards the group. "Let us not be so quick to punish one who has such a zest for life." He motioned to Keira to follow him. He passed among them and the peasants bowed their heads respectfully.

Sofia was not one to go quietly. She stomped after Alexander and was much aggrieved.

"Will you toss money at me too, or will you extend me an apology?" she demanded.

"We need to hurry to the dock. Edward's ship is on the horizon." He pointed towards a silhouette that had entered the port and flew the countries banners.

"Don't change the subject. Look at you!"

"Look at me? Look at you! You're a mess!" he responded.

"Argh!" she shrieked. "This is your fault. I promised mother we would both be decent and presentable to greet Edward."

"That was your promise. It wasn't mine," he said. "Honestly Sofia, when are you ever presentable? You spend more time riding and fighting than I do! If the Queen wanted us presentable she should have made us stay in the castle where it's quite safe from dirt and other scandalous goings-on." He stopped and gingerly dusted the sand off of the sleeves of her dress.

"Better?" he asked.

"NO!" she hissed back. "What if Edward has brought a Prince with him? Or someone even more important?"

"He went to negotiate a trade arrangement with the Atreides. I visited there a few years ago. You can trust me when I say there are no Princes worth your look, unless you deign marrying a prince who doubles the weight of their gold with his belly. Ah yes," he continued in a mocking tone, "Sofia the Fair and Xoros the Fat. That's what they call him, you know, but not to his face. Such a promising couple, perhaps he could give you a bit of a plumping."

Alexander cupped his hands over his eyes and peered to the horizon. "I see it," he pointed. "Edward's galley is heavy laden and bends the waterline below the ocean. Your Highness, your portly mate awaits your love!"

"Quiet!" Sofia turned red and quickened her pace. "You are absolutely the worst brother I have, twin or not."

Alexander feigned an injured air and placed his hand over his heart. "Keira, I do believe that my sister insults me. Her worst brother? Really? What do you think?"

Keira wagged her tail and barked in response.

"Even your dog agrees with me. Hurry up, Edward is nearing the shore."

As Alexander and Sofia made their way onto the pier, they were joined by Baron Iden Morgan and his retainers. Baron Iden was sharply dressed as he wore the finest silks that came to trade in his city of Brookehaven.

"Your highnesses," he said gregariously. "Many blessings to you both. I look forward to visiting Middlebrooke for the celebration."

"You are very kind," Sofia replied. "My brother and I look forward to seeing all of our father's friends. I have to commend you on your clothing. The fabric is absolutely stunning."

"Do you like it my lady?" he asked with a mixture of haughtiness and humility. "Being a Baron of a seaport allows me the ability to sample the finest that this world has to offer. Any merchant wanting to trade in Alveus must first go through Brookehaven, and it is my responsibility," he sniffed, "to ensure that the quality of each good traded is good enough to sit in the hall of His Majesty."

"It is good to know that you have His Majesty's best interest at heart and not your pocketbook as others seem to have," Sofia replied with a placid tone. If her intent had been to stick a knife into the Baron, she would have hit her mark true. She smiled politely and walked towards the edge of the dock where sailors shouted at one another to help Edward's galley dock.

"I am happy your sister still holds such a fine

opinion of me," the Baron whispered to Alexander sarcastically. "Perhaps my gift to her will at least satiate her for a time."

"How is my ship?" Alexander asked as he wished to avoid an awkward conversation.

"It is in perfect condition," the Baron answered. "I have my best men inspect its seaworthiness every month. We have it in dry dock currently to inspect the hull."

Their conversation was swallowed by the commotion of the townspeople who were on the dock. Whispers of "Prince Edward" danced about in the air and people thronged about to catch a glimpse. The Baron shouted for the people to make way as he and his guard moved to greet the Prince.

"Welcome back to Brookehaven, My Lord," the Baron trumpeted. "We thank God for your safe return to the house of Alveus." His soldiers saluted and cleared a path through the throng so that Edward and his men could pass through undisturbed.

From the boat, Edward stepped forward onto the dock and a cheer arose from the crowd. Edward brushed his dark locks out of his face and waved to the crowd. The Baron's men held firm as the crowd pushed forward. Edward smiled and stretched his large frame so that his tunic rose up enough on his stomach; exposing his muscular frame. Several girls in the crowd swooned and nearly fainted, which caused the crowd to only become more excited.

Sofia rolled her eyes at him and shook her head. Alexander estimated she was the only girl on the dock not under his spell. If Edward had given the word, he could have driven the crowd to do horrible acts of atrocity in his name. If the Crown Prince had said another word, the crowd might have torn the clothes from his back just for a scent of him. Thankfully, Edward had a good heart, and evil thoughts never entered his mind. Unfortunately, he did cause a scene wherever he went.

"Baron Iden Morgan of Brookehaven," Edward called out with his deep voice. "I thank you and your city for a most heartwarming welcome. You are a most favored city with the Royal Family."

The Baron bowed respectfully and bid that Edward should follow. Before anyone responded, a little girl ran towards him. She was no more than eight years old, and as the Baron was dressed in the cities' finest, she was dressed in its worst. Her unkempt hair and dirty face suggested that a harsher hidden living condition existed in Alveus' finest city.

The city watch sprang into action. Each man turned around and pushed the crowd back violently. For fear of an assassination several others jumped between the girl and Edward and pointed their swords at her. Sofia was pushed towards Edward and she protested they stop.

Edward yelled above the chaos and ordered that everyone stop immediately. Every man and woman on the dock, with or without a weapon, held perfectly still. Edward and Sofia pushed through to the little girl, who now trembled with fear.

"Little girl, what is your name?" Edward said it so kindly that you would have thought it was his own child that he addressed.

"Andromeda, me lord." She avoided eye contact with him directly and Alexander wondered what she had thought she could accomplish by running out in the first place.

"You have caused quite a commotion, Andromeda," Edward smiled. "Such a pretty name too. A big name, for such a small girl."

"Yes sir. No sir. I am big enough; I look after my baby brother."

"You do?" Sofia asked in surprise. "What does your mother do?"

"She sells flowers. Want to buy one?" Alexander was amused by the young girl's cheekiness. The townsfolk took after their Baron and sought a coin in every interaction.

"Of course we do," Sofia said pleasantly. "Where is she?"

The little girl pointed towards the back of the crowd and ran to her mother. With much pulling and hesitation the girl finally produced her mother before Sofia and Edward. She was young too, and couldn't have been older than twenty-five. She was a bit haggard in her appearance, as if the dirt of twenty-five years had never been washed away. She carried a small wicker basket that had a few stems sticking out from it.

"Come here please," Sofia asked soothingly. "Your daughter is very brave."

"Yes, she is quite a handful, me lady," the woman said as she bowed. "I ask your forgiveness."

Edward chuckled at the situation. "There is nothing to worry about. She wanted to sell us some flowers. Could you show us what you have?"

"Aye." She opened her wicker basket and brought out a beautiful flower with white petals.

"That is a beautiful flower," Sofia said with a mixture of awe and curiosity. "I have never seen a flower like this? What do you call it?"

"It is a lily, me lady. It is a rare flower around these parts, but I have met someone who can grow them."

"It is the most beautiful flower I have ever seen. I will take all that you have and pay you a more than fair price. Alexander, can you pay her please?"

Sofia took the wicker basket from the mother, while Alexander walked over to pay her. He produced two gold coins from his pouch and offered them to her. She reached out to take them from Alexander when he caught sight of her finger nails. For a dirty, disheveled flower peddler, her nails were quite clean. Once their hands made contact, he grabbed her hand for a second. They made eye contact and he glanced down at her hands. She stiffened for a moment, her eyes unsure.

"Alexander!" Sofia demanded. "Just give her the coins!"

He released her hand and she again thanked Sofia and Edward for their generosity. The crowd murmured in approval and cheered loudly for Edward and Sofia's kindness. The procession finally started moving again, just enough for Sofia to make a remark to the Baron.

"Baron Iden, it seems not everyone dresses in silk in Brookehaven." Sofia's tongue was especially sharp when it addressed the welfare of the kingdom's people, regardless of station. "I hope that when Edward becomes King, he finds a way to ensure that all kingdom folk enjoy the prosperity of the land's richest kingdom."

Baron Iden Morgan said nothing, but the look of being chastised by Sofia was neither pleasant nor invited. Edward noticed as well.

"Sofia, your criticism of our host is unwarranted."

"Thank you, my lord," Baron Iden exhaled. The Baron's feathers had been ruffled and his brow furrowed, as a man whose authority was never challenged, he was not accustomed to being chastised, even by royalty.

"After all, we don't have to wait for me to be King to address issues of corruption. When peasants are being cheated, then the Crown is being cheated their tax money.

A peasant with no money is of no value, so it's imperative that corruption-"and he looked directly at the Baron, "cease immediately."

"You are quite right," the Baron groveled. "As Baron of the richest city in Alveus, I could not accomplish that without everyone contributing to the Crown."

Sofia rolled her eyes and stayed silent. The party made its way through the streets of Brookehaven to the river docks. The docks on the Alveus River held several barges, including the Royal Barge, which offered a different mode of transportation to the capital rather than horses. The nobility preferred this method of travel as they were able to seek refuge from the sun underneath the barge's canopies as well as from saddle sores.

They continued to pass through the stalls of merchants and traders who shouted their wares to passersby. They paid little heed to the nobility that walked among them, instead choosing to talk up their merchandise. Sofia clutched her basket of lilies tightly, and the soldiers continued to walk with them, to ensure the royals were not molested.

"Will you need an escort, my lord?" Baron Iden asked above the din. "I can send twenty men with you to ensure safe passage to Middlebrooke."

"Thank you, no," Edward answered with confidence. "I have my guard with me. That should be more than enough for any problems we encounter."

"As you wish sir, but I feel that I will double the men pulling the oxen then, since your safety is my responsibility." Baron Iden pointed towards the oxen that were prepared to move the barge upstream. On each side of the river stood four oxen, tied to a rope that was then tied to the barge. The oxen, and the men that cared for them, were responsible to pull the barge upstream. The current of the

Alvean River was consistent, and never pushed more than what the oxen were able to handle.

The siblings and Edward's twelve guards entered the barge and took their seats while Baron Idren's servants finished loading Edward's personal effects. Baron Idren assigned a few more men with the oxen and waved courteously as they slowly made way to the castle of Middlebrooke.

CHAPTER II

Alexander had come downstream on the Royal Barge, and was quite content to be taken back to Middlebrooke in the same fashion. It was equipped with luxurious comforts, from cushions and pillows to the finest fruits and delicacies the kingdom had to offer. Being as it was unseasonably warm that day, the party retreated underneath the largest canopy for protection from the sun.

The men of Edward's guard took positions around the deck and stayed alert as each man watched the shores for any sort of suspicious action. Their armor glistened in the sunlight, and it looked like the gold Lions crest on their breastplates came to life. They were known as the most fearsome warriors in the kingdom, even more so than the Kings Guard. Edward had recruited many of the men from other kingdoms, as he never felt bound by tradition to choose his own people. As a result, he had the choicest and strongest warriors from all the lands.

Keira had found a shaded spot and stared deep into the water. She barked and wagged her tail at the sight of every large fish. If not for the occasional reprimand from Alexander, she might very well have jumped into the river in search of an extra meal.

When Edward was satisfied that all protection was in order, he joined Sofia and Alexander under the canopy.

"How are your flowers Sofia?" he teased. "Are they worth the gold you spent?"

"They are beautiful, brother, and I do not mind the price I paid if it were to spare a little girl having her throat slit." Sofia never cared much for the ten year gap in their age, or Edwards elevated station. She reminded everyone frequently that she gave no notice of anyone's station.

"Spirited littlegirl," Edward mused. "I should like very much to have a daughter like her. She reminds me of one I have known for eighteen years." He turned his eyes to Alexander, his blue eyes twinkling with mischief. "For the life of me I will never know how two people can be born the same day, yet be so completely different."

"What do you mean?" Alexander asked.

"You both are similar in height and frame. You share the same curly yellow hair and the same eyes. But, you have yet to say a word to me upon my return while your sister has not stopped slighting me."

"Forgive me your Highness," Alexander stated flatly. "Many welcome returns to Alveus. I hope you are well and that your trade efforts were successful. May your reign as King be great and glorious."

Edward ignored Alexander's tone but continued badgering him instead. "I wager you could not be pried away from your books and studies to come to Brookehaven. I wager your sister prodded and poked you until you agreed. And yet you have traveled a great deal, and your sister has never traveled outside of our kingdom's borders."

"Not true," Alexander replied with an injured air. "I

have been thinking about taking a journey recently so it fit within my plans to get out of the castle. Besides, I love the ocean. It offers unlimited possibilities."

"And lastly," Edward concluded, "We get to the root of it. My brother, fourth son of King Magnus, with life at his beck and call wants to sail away and never be heard from again and my sister will not be persuaded to be betrothed."

"To a fat pompous drunk?" Sofia snapped in reply. "I won't be a pawn for anyone, even you, Edward." She crossed her arms and bit her lip to avoid further response but she still could not stop herself. "I would love to hear an explanation of what you thought you were doing at the dock."

"Whatever do you mean?" Edward asked with a hint of sincerity.

"Your display of preening in front of the crowd! Becoming King is a privilege and not a reason for ostentatiousness."

Edward closed his eyes and sighed deeply. "Sofia, do you understand how much weight my shoulders carry? Our father has advanced in years, and the time is coming when there will be a new king sitting on the throne. I must do all I can to unite the people, instill loyalty, and create frenzied support from every corner of the kingdom. If that involves me giving a display of ostentatiousness at one time or another then I will gladly do it. Flattery is preferable to assassinations and war, which is what we will have if the populace does not flock to my banner."

It was true, Alexander agreed with his brother silently. He had seen much change in Edward's face in the last year. Edward constantly journeyed about from kingdom to kingdom as both emissary and face of the future of Alveus. Who could fault him for having some fun with it?

"But maybe if you lacked an appearance of enjoying it so much," Alexander weighed in.

"What? You have commentary on my actions as well?" Edward widened his eyes and leaned forward.

Alexander shook his head no, and offered a meager explanation. "It just seemed like a lot."

"Because I am to be King or because you...," Edward leaned in closer to Alexander and dropped his voice down. "Want what I have?"

Alexander was caught off-guard by the question. What did Edward mean and why did he ask this?

"I see envy in your eyes, my brother. You want the Crown for yourself. You want the people cheering and expressing their adoration for you, don't you?" Edward deliberately tried to provoke a response from Alexander, but he remained silent.

"Stop it Edward," Sofia interrupted. "You have no right to say that."

"I am the Crown Prince, and that gives me the right to ferret out treachery," Edward said firmly. "I want to know from my brother what he desires most. Does he want to run because he is afraid that he will stop at nothing to take the Crown for himself?"

"I don't want your stupid Crown!" Alexander shouted. "I don't want anything to do with being King. You are the oldest brother and by law that makes you the successor to father."

"Would you die for that statement?" Edward kept putting Alexander on the spot with his questions. Alexander shifted uncomfortably in his chair and wished he was elsewhere.

This is why, Alexander thought, I want to be free of this damn kingdom and its politics.

"Death seems rather final," Alexander stated dryly.

"A man with convictions would give up his life for them without asking why. He would not hesitate and he would carry himself with passion for his lord." Edwards tone had changed as if he were a teacher correcting a stubborn child.

"Enough!" Alexander was beside himself with irritation. "What would you have me do? Should I swear my oath of fealty now as we sit on this barge? Would you knight me and send me on a quest to prove my loyalty? How can you question me like this? Have I ever given you reason to doubt my support?" Alexander stood up and shook off Sofia's attempt to grab him by the hand. "Just leave me alone."

Alexander walked to the back of the barge so that he could be out of sight from his siblings. He was irritated and angry with his older brother. Edward often scolded at him, and Alexander never understood why.

He treats me more like a son than my own father, Alexander mused. It had always been that way. Edward had taken a liking to Alexander as a child and was the first one to correct him, in everything. He functioned less like a mentor some days, and more like a task master sent to break his back.

Still, Alexander respected Edward as no other man alive could be compared to him. He was the greatest swordsman in the realm and a cunning linguist politician. People naturally threw themselves and their affections toward his great stature. Alexander was always nearby, in his brother's large handsome shadow.

Alexander's thoughts were interrupted by his brother's boots. Edward stood behind him now, and hovered over him like a hen with her chicks.

"Our sister feels that I should apologize to you."

Edward sounded like a man who had been chastised, and Alexander could sympathize with that feeling.

"Go on then," Alexander retorted.

"I apologize for questioning your loyalty." Edward sat down beside his brother and offered a handshake which Alexander took after a brief thought.

"I know what I said was harsh," he continued, "but hopefully you can understand why I said what I did. You had a look of envy in your eye."

"I did not," Alexander insisted.

"Alex," Edward soothed, "It is human nature to have a fleeting eye, but it all depends on if you act on it or not." Edward raised his hand to stop Alexander's objection. "Any man, if offered the Crown, would take it. Maybe you are right, maybe you would not dream of it, but I saw your eyes at the dock when the people cheered for me. Would you deny to me that you were not jealous of me at that moment?"

Alexander bowed his head. "I don't care about platitudes and the love showered upon me by crowds, but...," and his words turned wistful, "it would be nice to be acknowledged for the good that I do. Receive praise for kind words. Is that too much to ask?"

Edward smiled and put his arm around his brother. "No Alex, it isn't too much. But when you start seeking validation in place of your own self-confidence, you will seek happiness in pleasing others, and that is what no prince should consider."

"Do you know my first thoughts when Father announced I would be his heir? I wondered if I would ever be able to trust a single soul. It birthed a sense of paranoia within me. I see demons in the shadows where there weren't before. I have spies reporting to me from all cities and castles in the kingdom. You are right not to want the crown; it is nothing but stress, where your decisions could ruin the lives of one hundred or even fifty thousand people."

"We could sail off together," Alexander offered. "My ship is in good repair."

"I would never shrink from duty. As Princes of Alveus, we do what needs to be done. If platitudes are what you seek than let my words weigh more than ten thousand voices raised from a city. Alexander, you have the makings of a fine King, and I know whatever you put your mind to and settle at, you will be successful. Now come, let us see what your sister has found so interesting."

Edward motioned to Sofia who was peering off to the eastern side of the riverbanks. "What do you see that is so fascinating?" he asked.

"It's what I don't see," she replied nervously. "When we floated by yesterday this embankment was filled with livestock eating and drinking their fill."

"Herdsmen are always moving," Alexander offered, "But to Sofia's point there is always some sort of activity near the embankment. It's the easiest way for animals to draw water for at least three miles." Together they surveyed the changing terrain. In less than a mile the terrain changed and sloped upwards. This would slow the oxen down and all of the men on the shore would be too focused to notice anything peculiar.

"Alexander," Edward said. "Put your mind in that of a bandit. How would you strike at a barge?"

"We are two miles away from a watch tower. The hill creates an excellent disruption to its sight. With a small band I would take command of the oxen. Then I would fire arrows into the barge until they either surrendered or were dead."

"I would do the same," Edward concurred.

"We are heavily armed and have your guard as an escort. Bandits would not dare attack us!" Sofia's tone grew increasingly worried.

"We are heavily armed," Edward agreed. "Except Alexander, who seems to have no need for his sword." He gave Alexander a look of disapproval, and Alexander immediately made his way under the canopy and fetched his sword. He grumbled a bit about Edward's tyranny, but kept it under his breath.

"Kenric." Edward called his chief guardsman to his side. "Flag the men. Bring the barge to the east side of the bank. Alexander and four of my men will disembark and patrol the shore."

Kenric removed his helmet and shouted at the four men assigned to each oxen on the banks of the river. He used his helmet to indicate what Edward wanted. The ox masters waved back that they acknowledged and understood. The men on the west side of the bank slackened the rope on their side, and the men on the eastern side pulled the barge closer to the shores.

Alexander prepared to jump onto dry land but stopped in curiosity. The other men of Edward's guards did not hesitate and they jumped to the bank and waited for Alexander.

"What are you waiting for?" Edward asked.

"The water level is receding!" Alexander jumped out of the barge to investigate. Edward and Sofia looked down at the water and they agreed that the flow of water had slowed down and the water level had dropped, almost to the point that the barge would rest on the river bottom within a few moments. They looked quizzically at each other for they knew not what to say.

The silence was immediately broken by Kenric. "Traitors!" he shouted and pointed behind the oxen. Just then, the man responsible for tying the rope to the oxen fell dead, an arrow protruding from his chest.

"Shields!" Edward shouted to his men. Each man brought his shield above his head while Kenric brought his over Edward and Sofia. The thud of arrows hitting the men's shields echoed along the bank.

"Keira!" Alexander shouted. He looked for her and found that one of Edward's men had collared her and clung to her behind his shield.

"Alex!" Edward shouted. "Secure the rope!"

The three men left with the oxen were in a precarious position between the oxen, the rope, and the bandits. Several men with axes appeared behind the archers and they began running towards the oxen.

"Come on then," Alexander shouted to the four guardsmen who stood with him. "Defend the oxen." Alexander and the four guards jumped over the side and were surprised when the water level was just below their knees. This was fortunate as the guards armor would weigh them down and drown them if the river level had not receded.

"Shields!" Edward shouted, as another hail of arrows fell upon the barge. "Kenric, I should not want to stay here." Kenric nodded and his men crept to side of the barge closest to the shore.

The fight stopped for everyone when the combatants heard the sound of rushing water. Everyone looked upriver and the mystery why the water level had gone down was clear. A large wave rushed their barge, as if someone had dammed the river. Alexander and the four men in the river ran as fast as they could to get to shore before the water swept them away. As soon as the last man reached the land, the barge was hit with enough rushing force to quickly knock it backwards one hundred and fifty feet. The rope that had been dropped now threatened to slip away.

With the barge in trouble, the fight on the shore resumed. One of the remaining ox masters grabbed the rope and tied it quickly around the oxen's yoke. The bandits reached the oxen just as he finished and made short work of him and the others. Their axes cut through the men as if they were never there.

Alexander and the guardsmen made it to the oxen with their swords drawn and engaged their assailants. The men's swords clashed with the bandits' axes and each man parried and lunged to get the advantage of the other. The few criminals who had stayed back with their short bows fired directly into the melee, with little regard for their own men. Alexander had no shield so he was forced to take cover behind a fallen tree. His pause gave one of the attackers enough time to pass him by and slice through the rope that connected the barge to the oxen.

The lack of resistance from the rope combined with the force of the wave sent the barge careening. On the other side of the river the ox masters held the rope to reduce the strain on their oxen.

"Alex!" Sofia screamed. Alexander surveyed the situation. The bandits had already begun their retreat and they ran to their well hidden horses. Without a second thought Alexander sheathed his sword and dove into the river in pursuit of the rope. As he dove in he noticed the water level dropping again, almost allowing him to walk through the river. The barge had swung almost completely to the west side of the bank and become grounded so that the passengers could safely jump onto the land.

"Everyone to the riverbank!" Edward ordered and he and his men jumped clear. The familiar sound of rushing water alerted Alexander to his peril.

"Sofia! What are you doing?" he asked

incredulously. Sofia had not jumped off with the men and had run back into the canopied area, followed by Keira.

"Not without my lilies!" she shouted back. "I paid good gold coins for these." She grabbed the flowers as Alexander stared in disbelief. He saw the rope thirty feet ahead of him and glanced back to the rushing water. He ran as fast as he could to the rope but the oncoming water overtook him and the barge at the same moment. Alexander stretched out his hand to the cord and grabbed it. The force of the water hit the barge so hard that the oxen's legs nearly buckled. Their strained and groaning gave Alexander worry that they would not last long. Edward and his remaining guardsmen ran to help the ox masters with the ropes and the overburdened beasts.

Alexander fought to keep his head above the current. He choked and coughed up the water from his lungs. "Hang on Sofia!" he shouted as he dove underwater. He held his breath while digging his hands into the bottom of the riverbed and pulled his way across. He made it to the other side, poked his head above water, and gasp for breath.

Alexander was shocked that Edward had been ambushed on his side of the embankment and his men were in a melee for their lives. Fortunately, his guards wore their iron breastplates and helmets, which protected them from glancing blows. Furthermore, they were taller and stronger than their numerous bandit foes and their swords crashed through the bandits as if they swatted flies.

Alexander raced up the bank to the oxen. With assistance from the other four guardsmen, he tied the rope to the yoke and drove the oxen forward. The river current had calmed enough so the barge had stabilized. Edward and his men had taken their side of the river easily and the remaining bandits had fled. Sofia sat on the barge, head buried in her hands, and with Keira's head resting upon her lap.

Alexander walked down the shore so that he was directly adjacent to the barge.

"Are your flowers well, Sofia?" he mocked. "Are they safe?" Sofia lifted her head to reply, but the dark figure approaching behind him changed her thoughts.

"Behind you!" she shouted in alarm.

Alexander whirled around and found himself face to face with an axe wielding bandit. The man glared at him menacingly and raised his weapon to kill him. Alexander went to pull the sword from his sheathe, but discovered he had lost it in the water. His enemy's lips curled into a smile.

"Time to die young prince," he said smugly. With nowhere to run, Alexander braced himself for the lethal cut.

May this death be quick, he thought.

He felt a whoosh by his ear, and the sound of life expiring. Alexander opened his eyes and was surprised to see the bandit fall to his knees, an arrow stuck in his chest. The prince turned his head and acknowledged Sofia, who held the bow that saved his life.

He pried the axe from the dead man's hands and threw it in the river. The four guardsmen came over to ensure he was intact.

One clasped his shoulders and said, "It seems as though your sister has killed more men than you." The other men on the shore snickered a bit as they wiped their blades with the blood of their victims.

Alexander wanted to say something vicious in reply, but he bit his tongue and held it in. He helped pull the ropes to position the barge again midstream, for it would be left to them to be the ox masters until reaching the capital.

It wasn't long after the situation had stabilized, that several riders appeared before them. They were dressed in armor, and Alexander found them a welcome sight. The main rider was a captain from the watch-fort that stood halfway between Brookehaven and Middlebrooke. He and his men were scouring the riverbank, looking for the source of the river's strange behavior. They had seen nothing but Alexander explained the events of the afternoon.

Edward decided that they would rest at the watch-fort that night and should have an escort to the capital that next day. Typically the watch-forts were nothing more than a tower and a few huts with a small stable. This watch-fort stood next to a barracks and included a large stable. These buildings were surrounded by a wooden wall and a small group of sturdy little houses. This was one of two on the Alveus River that was growing into a village.

Outside of the wooden walls, a ferry to cross the river had been established, although it was more of a log raft with a man to guide it. Peasant and noble alike who wished to cross the river without heading to the cities used the ferry. A small inn and tavern had sprung up, as well as livestock pens and vegetable gardens. There were oxen on both sides of the river that provided trade barges with fresh oxen on their journeys.

Alexander was relieved to have made it to the watch-fort. His feet, finally dry, were tired. He had not had to walk quite so much, as he preferred riding. Driving the tired stubborn oxen was even more draining, and pulling the barge towards the river was a manual labor that was never required of princes.

The remaining men of the watch-fort rushed forward and assisted with removing everyone's personal effects into the fort. This ensured that no one would be tempted to risk their lives and steal gold or other goods.

"Your Highness," the captain bowed to Edward, "Our watch-fort welcomes you and your men. We are at your service."

"Thank you Captain," Edward replied. "Your assistance has been invaluable. Send one of your riders to the capital and let them know that we have been delayed. Also, how stocked are you for food? I am sure that my men are tired and eager for a good meal after today's events."

"Of course, My Lord." We will purchase meat and vegetables for your Highnesses from the villagers and perhaps the tavern master can be persuaded to fix the meal. I am hopeful that his cooking would be better than what any of us can provide."

"Dear Captain," Sofia interjected. "Is there fresh water about that I may have?"

Each man of the watch-fort ran with their cups to the water barrels. With much pushing and shouting, each man attempted to have his cup filled. Once they accomplished that feat, they attempted to turn and run to Sofia. Each attempt ended with their water spilled, either by a trip or a well-placed elbow. Tempers began to flare among the men, and the Captain rushed forward immediately with his sword drawn, brandishing his men for the mockery that they had placed upon themselves in front of the heir.

"Dogs!" the Captain shouted. He was so angry he spit as he shouted, with spittle clinging to his well-groomed beard. "Are you the King's soldiers or men running about trying to show their manhood? This is a Princess and as such will have nothing to do with the lot of you! Attention!"

Each man snapped to attention, fearing the wrath of their Captain more than the public embarrassment they had just brought to their watch-fort.

"If I had a half a mind, I'd flay the lot of you and replace you with the lot outside. Fighting over water like dogs on a bone!" He motioned to the oldest grey-bearded man as the one allowed to retrieve the Princess' water.

The older man retrieved the water and bowed to one knee as he presented the cup to Sofia. Edward and Alexander exchanged knowing glances, as if they both wanted to ask, can you believe this?

"Thank you noble knight," Sofia said cheerfully as she took a long drink. "Your kindness is appreciated." She handed him back his cup and he ran back into position with a huge smile on his face.

"Shall we talk ostentatious displays over dinner tonight?" Edward asked.

"I am not responsible," Sofia shrugged. "I merely asked for water to cool myself down."

"Like Helena, you have a face prone to drive wars between nations." Both Sofia and Alexander said nothing in reply, so Edward continued his point. "Helena of Dormont, so beautiful and ravishing, was a sweet girl and betrothed to her nation's enemy's first son. Only she was so enchanting that it was said that every man who set eyes upon her fell in love instantly. She had suitors from all over the world. I believe father might have been one as well."

"Yes," Edward chuckled. "Father was young once too, but he did love mother."

"So what happened to Helena?" Sofia was extremely curious.

"Have you ever heard of Dormont outside of a history text?" Alexander and Sofia shook their heads that they had not.

"Helena's beauty was so captivating that one of Dormont's young nobles became so obsessed with her, he defied his elders. Helena was to marry and cement the peace, and save her people. But this noble, Xeros of Lestrobe, put himself before all others. In his obsession, he went to her to make love to her. To her credit, she resisted, and he forced himself to her. The same beauty that would have saved her people was now their undoing. When the Narensi discovered what had happened, they were relentless. They put to death every man, woman, and child from Dormont and Lestrobe. Xeros fled, but they found him. What happened to him, they left that out of the history texts."

"I am not that beautiful," Sofia remarked. "Your tales are an exaggeration."

"Possibly," Edward agreed, "But beautiful nonetheless." Your name is on the tip of every prince in every kingdom, which is why it benefits the world to have you married within a year."

Sofia opened her mouth in protest, but Edward held his hand up with authority. "You are a princess of the realm. While you are my sister and I love you unconditionally, I must make the decision that benefits my people the best. Now come, it looks as if the Captain has been able to prepare our accommodations."

Sofia's mood was dampened during the evening and Alexander did his best to cheer her up. The villagers had contributed a lamb and vegetables, and while the food wasn't king-fare, it was nominally tasty and more importantly, filling. Keira had a place on the floor near Alexander, and she contently gnawed on a lamb shank. What little ale the watch-fort soldiers had was provided to the visitors, and Edward's men drank every drop.

Edward was lost in thought through much of the dinner and said very little, except in the direction of his chief guard, Kenric. His shield bearer had been the very first man selected for Edward's guard. He was extraordinarily gifted in tactics, and Edward often held his counsel on the small details within battles.

"Tell me Kenric, what think you of today? I cannot

make sense of it." Edward swished the ale in his cup and finished it in one swallow.

"They were not bandits, and that's a fact," Kenric replied.

"How do you know that?" Alexander asked. He was keen on learning as much information as possible from this able warrior.

"For starters, they flanked us. They attacked us from both sides of the river. And they had archers. They meant to pin us down until they cut the oxen loose."

"But the water? How did they stop the river from flowing?"

Edward wrinkled his nose. "That is something I have no answer for. The answers I do have though are a planned ambush, which means that someone was after our deaths. More than likely mine, because I am the heir to the kingdom."

"But it could mean something else." Kenric whispered as he talked.

"What?" Alexander asked inquisitively.

"Not this again," Edward sighed. "You'll have Alexander believing in old superstitions and seeing shadows behind every tree."

"What about the water then. Who could do that? There are sorcerers afoot, I can feel it."

Alexander was surprised that the large hulking warrior could give such excellent counsel yet mention a sorcerer with the very next breath. Edward shook his head in disagreement.

"They were wiped out in the conquest. There has been only one sighting in the last hundred years, and I can assure you that he is very much dead. When we arrive at the castle I will send our men out to patrol the countryside. I am sure that the answers are out there, we will just need to ferret them out."

Alexander glanced over to Sofia, who had picked at her food the entire evening. "If you don't eat they will not find us very gracious guests." She ignored his attempt at conversation and politely excused herself from the table. Alexander also excused himself and followed her out the door.

"Sofia!" he called after her.

"What do you want Alex?"

"You have been silent all evening-"

She cut him off quickly. "Our brother has told me that I am a gift from the family and that I will be used to barter like meat at a market. I am no more important than the lamb we ate tonight. Edward would put me on a plate and dress me up for the highest bidder. It's not fair." She stamped her foot and pouted.

"Ironic isn't it," Alexander responded. "Every villager would want to be us, but they have such freedom over who they can marry, what crops they can grow, and even where to live."

"So, what if I don't want to?" Sofia asked. "What if I say that Helena was a fool? She died because she a man defiled her when she tried to her duty for her people. What if I choose my own husband?"

"Sofia," Alexander tried to soothe her feelings. "Edward won't put you in a situation with someone horrible. He is still our brother."

"What would you do?" Sofia asked. "What would you do if you wanted to do something for the right reasons but couldn't because the King told you that you had to do what he wanted; for the good of the realm?"

"I would just sail away," Alexander said half-heartedly. He knew it was an empty promise, but he said it anyway.

Sofia saw right through it. "No you wouldn't Alex. I have known you every day of your life. You always say you will go off on your own, but I think you would have done it by now if that was what you really wanted. Good night Alex. Thank you for listening." She gave him a kiss on the cheek and a hug that he didn't immediately respond to. She smiled at him and left him standing there.

She was right. There was never a reason for him to stay in Middlebrooke, but never enough force compelling enough for him to leave. He felt that he needed to stay. He had an obligation, but hadn't come to understand why.

CHAPTER III

When they awoke early the next morning, they found an Alveun military escort ready to guide them. Fresh horses had been dispatched for the siblings and Edward's men. The soldiers who gave up their horses to the bodyguard were dispatched to guard the oxen and barge.

They made their way out of the watch-fort in procession, two by two, with Edward at the front and his banner man beside him. The soldiers from the watch-fort tried the best they could to sit in the tower, so that they might catch a prolonged glimpse of Sofia. The peasants who had settled outside the watch-fort took rest from their daily chores and gawked at the procession. It was not an everyday occurrence for them to see their country's future, or any of the King's other progeny.

The road to Middlebrooke was far less eventful and they were happier for it. For a moment, Alexander found his brother behind the serious eyes, and they laughed about stories from their youth. They took turns teasing each other, then teased Sofia together, and felt the sting of Sofia's teasing together. The frivolity was muted when they came a few miles of Middlebrooke's stone walls.

Two centuries of independence had helped shape Alveus into one of the most influential and prosperous kingdoms in their known world. The first king, Magnus the Conqueror, established his capital at the center of the kingdom. He named his stronghold Middlebrooke and it was here that two hundred years of his family had lived and died.

Behind the walls, the citadel was located centrally between the northern and southern gates and astonished visitors in size and power. The city's thick stone walls, iron gates, and eight ballista towers increased its firepower and made it a formidable foe to attack. The defenses were guaranteed to incur heavy losses on any attacking army. If an attacking army did break the wall, they would find themselves having to assault the citadel whose walls protected the keep and the royal palace, home to the royal family.

The procession galloped through the main gate and its guards saluted them as they went by. They made their way through the streets and as the banner man passed a person they immediately bowed out of respect for Edward. Alexander guessed that Edward's charm and charisma were again getting the better of him. Alexander gave Sofia a knowing glance, but she rolled her eyes and said very little. Keira ran ahead of the horses and made her way into the citadel. She looked for her kennel and found meat in her bowl which she then gobbled up quickly.

The pages waited outside for the horsemen. As each man arrived in the citadel they handed their reigns to the page and dismounted from their horses. Once dismounted, they made their way up the stone path to the Royal Palace. The Royal Palace had once been a Great Hall, but each King had added to it, and by now it had established its own identity as a castle within a castle. It had its own towers and its own garden, and it was topped off by a battlement. It was built to be a family's last stand against its enemies, and a showing of the Alveun resolve.

The men that escorted the siblings into Middlebrooke quickly bowed towards the Palace, and moved on to their billets. From the great door, an elderly man with hair as white as doves made his appearance into the sunlight. His beard curled and sat firm on his chest, and the breeze did not sway it.

"My children," he called out. "I am glad to see you safe." A woman his age appeared beside him.

She managed a sigh of relief and hurried to greet them. She gave each one of them a kiss on the cheek and then hugged them. When she hugged Alexander it seemed very awkward for him. He did not appreciate public shows of affection and would have preferred the typical speech.

"Long live the King and Queen," Edward finally stated, which seemed to bring his mother back to the present. "I have returned home from my journey, and I request the doors of Alveus are opened to me."

King Magnus smiled and laughed heartily. He slapped his side and walked towards Edward with open arms. They were near the same size, with the old King an inch or two taller. Neither lacked for confidence in their gait, and each of them oozed self-assurance.

"What a damn fool question! But I suppose tradition is tradition. The halls of Alveus are open to you, Edward Wolfield." His smile and mirth turned dark in an instant as another thought crept into his mind. "What is this about you being attacked by bandits?"

"They were well-organized and well-armed. I cannot say they were merely bandits in search of gold and silver. They seemed to serve a darker purpose."

"And how many of them did you cut down?" the

King asked.

"All told, there were fifteen that were not able to flee back to their masters. Sofia placed an arrow in one that tried to kill Alexander."

The King turned to Sofia, his mouth open in astonishment. The Queen gasped and shook her head in disapproval.

"My daughter killed a man in battle? She is a warrior princess now!" He chuckled. "It will be interesting to see what kingdoms will pay us a visit once the bards sing about her courageousness. And you saved Alexander's life?"

"Yes father," she said. "He had lost his sword-"

"Lost his sword?!" the King exclaimed. "How does one lose their sword in battle?"

"He saved Sofia's life," Edward explained. "That's the part that matters. Father, if you do not mind, we would like to recover from our journey and get some much needed rest. Spending a night in a watch-fort is not an ideal circumstance."

The Queen took a queue from the King's nod. "Manfred will ensure the servants attend to your needs post-haste." She waved her hand to the elderly gentleman who now stood in the doorway. He bowed his head and disappeared back into the shadows of the Great Hall. "The celebration for your eighteenth birthday will go on as planned. Nobles have been arriving from the corners of our kingdom since yesterday. I am sure that all will enjoy the festivities."

"The Crown has spared no expense for the twins," Magnus agreed. "Tomorrow will long be a day to remember."

The family went their separate ways while Alexander headed to his room. He went through the Great Hall, which was being set up for the next night's festivities.

All of the castle servants ran about moving tables and chairs and preparing colorful decorations. As he went along, Alexander focused on trying to find a particular face. He ignored Keira's entreats to play, and mindlessly patted her head. When he ascended the spiral stone staircase and reached his room he immediately undressed. Since the incident on the river, his clothes looked more of a peasant's finest than a king's son. He had just tied his pants drawstring when the door opened and the object of his earlier search wandered in.

"Oh I apologize for the intrusion, My Lord," the young girl said. "The Queen sent me to gather your dirty clothes." She backed out of the doorway.

"No, um, wait. It's quite alright," he fumbled. He quickly put his shirt on and gathered his dirty clothes. "I have my clothes right here."

The servant examined the clothing, her green eyes peering from behind her long dark curly hair. Alexander couldn't bring himself to stop staring at her. He had been infatuated with her the moment she stepped into service at the castle. Her petite frame and slender curves were the objects of many a dream that he cared not to wake from.

"It would seem as if you have had an interesting journey to Brookehaven. Your shirt seems to be more of a rag than a fine tunic." She smiled sweetly at him and he seized upon the opportunity for a conversation.

"Yes, we were ambushed!" he said excitedly. "We were set upon by thirty marauders, and they were trying to kill the ox handlers so that the barge would lose control and possibly drown us. I jumped to the riverbank and singlehandedly engaged them, with no armor! When my brother's men finally arrived to help, I had to dive into the water after a loose rope, and I was able to secure it to keep my brother and sister from going under the water."

Alexander stopped rambling and looked for any signs of the young servant girl being impressed.

Her eyes twinkled with mischief. "Is that where the Prince lost his sword?"

Alexander quickly changed the subject. "Angelica, you look..." his voice trailed off for he could not find any other words. She gave him an odd look and took the clothes from his grasp.

"Amazing," he finally finished.

"Amazing?" she laughed. "I am covered in ash and smell as though I have worked with the animals. Surely you have better things to do than mock the servant girl. I expect your brother Mattias to have words for me, but not you."

"I do not mock you," Alexander protested. "You have a rare beauty that one is hard pressed to find. It matters not if you are covered in dirt; your beauty finds a way to shine through."

Angelica blushed and allowed herself a smile. "That may be what you mean, but why tell me? Do you wish to make love to me behind the doors as a trophy, and then discard me when you find someone new?" The smile faded as quickly as it had come.

"Never," Alexander said emphatically. "I would like to walk with you and talk to you. I have seen you going in and out of doors, carrying on your work and my heart does ache just to be in your company."

"Prince, you shouldn't say such things. It is not in my station to be an object of anything more than fleeting desire to you." Angelica brushed her curly hair away from her face. "I am a servant girl and you are a Lord and neither shall they meet."

"You would rather see me pine and give you stories of my bravery until I can win your affection?" The mood had changed awkward, and Alexander's heart ached. He wanted to grab her and kiss her, but knew if he did, he would be like any other noble that takes what isn't theirs.

"No," Angelica said softly as she turned to leave the room. "You should never tell stories of your bravery. Especially when all the servants know that your sister fared better in combat. I will see your clothes washed and mended and have your tunic for the festival tomorrow night prepared for you."

Alexander watched her figure out the door, and then buried his head in his hands. There was no sense leaving his room now, for if the servants knew his other brothers would hear about it too. He settled down on his bed and stared at the ceiling. Keira hopped up on the bed and lay next to him, so he patted her head until he fell asleep. His last thoughts were of Angelica's lips and f he kissed them, what was the worst that could happen?

Even though he fell asleep earlier than usual, his body was exhausted and he continued to sleep until his body refused to sleep another moment. With a general lack of interest in the day, he opened one eye lazily and peered out towards a small window. The window that he looked through was nothing more than a small slit between stones in the wall but it showed him enough of the outside world, and let the sunlight in. The sun shone brightly through his window, and lit up his room. There were no clouds in sight for it was another perfect summer day in the Kingdom of Alveus. He felt the wind blowing a cool breeze into his room and he responded by covering his head with his sheepskin blanket.

"I really should get up", he thought, "but it's my birthday. I get to sleep late on my birthday. After all, being a prince has some privilege!" The riverbank events were a distant memory already, and he decided if someone made an issue out of it, he would laugh it off.

Alexander perceived sleeping as his only vice. On most days, he felt justified with sleeping; after all, no one did as much as he did in a day. Nearly every day of the year he studied with monks, practiced swordsmanship, horsemanship, and followed whatever princely duties were required of him and every night he fell asleep exhausted. He had lived this life since he was ten years old, and his trip to Brookehaven had been a nice break in the monotony.

Alexander long wished that he was destined for greatness. In what capacity, he had not yet come to terms with. He often imagined himself leading glorious charges into battle or discovering new and exciting lands. Before the new dreams had started, his imagination was the one place where he controlled everything that could come to pass. Today was the day he realized the unlimited potential of his dreams. Not only was today his birthday, but it was official ascent into manhood.

The kingdom of Alveus considered the age of eighteen to be an important turning point in a young prince's life. They were no longer allowed the luxury of laziness like small children. They were expected to join the army in some capacity, and carry themselves with a nobleness and maturity they previously lacked.

The first step of being inducted into the army was the choosing of his bodyguard. This group of men were assigned to guard the Prince, protect him, and if need be, sacrifice their life. Tradition had always held that the strongest and most courageous warriors were put through a series of trials, although Edward had partially departed from tradition and selected foreigners into his guard. Twelve men were selected to serve the Prince, and a nickname would be selected, typically from the most ferocious animals. There was untold prestige in having a bodyguard and the selection of the right name did wonders for a royal's popularity with the people.

Since he was a small boy, Alexander had always been awed at the impressive pageantry of his father's and now Edward's guards. They were armed with the finest weapons of the age, and trained themselves with incredible ferocity and precision in their movements. Any thief or warrior would be forced to reconsider their decision to do the King harm. Alexander also noted that he found extreme pleasure in the notion that others would follow his orders for a change, regardless that he was the youngest son.

He had almost fallen back to sleep when he was interrupted by clumsy whispers outside of his room. The ommands from a girl's voice had riled a dog into frenzy. The dog's nails scraped against the floor as it unsuccessfully tried to gain traction on the stone floor. Alexander knew what was coming and he quickly curled into a ball and hid under his sheepskin blanket. Within seconds Keira charged inside his room and leaped upon his bed. The dog snarled playfully and grabbed the blanket with her teeth. Alexander attempted to push her off the bed but she could not be moved. The dog weighed too much to simply lift if it did not want to be lifted. Alexander struggled to move from under his dog, but it was to no avail.

"Get off of me dog!" Alexander shouted. He hated to wake up like this and he had a feeling he knew who sent the dog in. There was only one other person that Keira heeded.

The dog didn't listen and instead waved its tail furiously as it bounced on the bed excitedly and barked challenges to play.

"Stop it! Get off me, Keira!"

A loud giggle erupted from his doorway. Alexander peered out from under his blanket to see Edward and Sofia grinning widely.

"Alright, alright, I'm up!" He rolled out from under his blanket and sat on the edge of the bed.

"Thanks for that," he growled. He took Keira's face in his hands and shook it and laughed as she opened her mouth and let her tongue hang out. "I'll tend to you later, dog." Keira panted and licked his face happily.

"You've been in bed far too long," Edward scolded. "We have many things to do today. Time does not stop for us." Edward prided himself on being precise with his time and practicality.

Alexander shut his eyes good-naturedly and pretended to wave Edward away. When he re-opened his eyes he saw that Edward had not moved from the doorway. Edward's black hair fluttered in the breeze; and even in his silence he exuded an aura of strength and confidence. Edward moved his arms in an upward motion as if to silently command Alexander to rise from his bed. Had he wanted, Edward's massive frame could have easily lifted the bed and tossed Alexander onto the floor.

"Alright," Alexander said. "I'm up. I'll be down in a moment. Let me grab my clothes."

"I thank you for moving on with life," Edward feigned sarcastically. "Father was asking if you have settled on a name for your guard."

"I was thinking of the Lions," Alexander grinned and looked in Edward's direction for approval.

"That's a wonderful name Alex. It's too bad that I've already named my guard that." Alexander poked at Edward, but Edward was too clever for that. "What's the name of the animal that sleeps all day Sofia?"

Sofia's face grew pale as she stammered over her answer. Her soft blue eyes widened and she stammered in response.

"I...ummm...cows?" Edward and Alexander stared at her incredulously as she bit her nails and trained her eyes on the ceiling.

"Cows sleep all day?" Edward asked in genuine confusion. "I wasn't aware of this. Someone should let the farmers know, or let mother know that her only daughter has rewritten the laws of science. Come now Alex, be serious....what name have you chosen?"

"I was thinking of the Dragons," he reluctantly offered.

"Dragons aren't real. They are tales that mothers tell their children. Everyone knows that." Edwards blue eyes darkened and he sighed as he spoke. "What's the point of naming your guard after mythological beasts? Everyone will think you don't take your role seriously. Father is going to ask you if he sees you, please....please humor him. Pick wolves or something with sharp teeth."

"Dragons have sharp teeth," Alexander argued.

"No they don't because they aren't real, so be a good brother and come up with a name that will inspire the respect of the peasantry."

"Speaking of the people, how are things?" Alexander asked to steer the topic from him.

"Well enough," Edward replied, "The harvest is again expected to be bountiful, and our coffers are filled enough to perhaps invest in building a few more castles. Our population is growing faster than our structures."

"Sounds exciting," Alexander teased. "When will you be launching your grand campaign of conquest you promised when you were twelve?"

"I launched it when I was thirteen, remember?" Edward chuckled. "If I remember correctly we conquered the stables and part of a castle wall. That was a grand game we played, but war is a game for children, not for princes."

"Alexander," Sofia added, "You have given your brother the lecture!"

"It's no lecture," Edward said. "Besides, if we really were to widen our gaze, it would be to the north or the east. I do not see the north as much of a campaign, there is nothing there but thieves and a raggedy barbarian tribe. If we expanded east, we would find ourselves in a costly war. It is far better to take care of our own and make Alveus lead other nations in leaving this wretched darkness and into an enlightened age of science."

"Listen to Edward," Alexander said in awe. "He certainly has the vision of a great statesman. Should we start building your statue now? Or should we wait?"

"I will let you touch my hand if you like," Edward said. "You might get more than just a touch of greatness."

They shared a laugh together and Edward left the room while Sofia stayed behind to talk with her twin.

"Are you excited about today?" she asked. Her face beamed with a mixture of pride and excitement for her own day as well as his.

"It's alright, I suppose." Alexander downplayed the excitement in everything. There was no sense to be excited until the moment arrived.

"Oh come on," she went on. "Today you get your own set of guards! Isn't that exciting? I'd love that." Sofia had dreamt of a military career as a warrior princess since she was six years old. There was no precedent of a woman having ruled Alveus, so she lived vicariously through Alexander. She made him teach her everything he learned, especially the art of hand to hand fighting. She had become quick and nimble on her feet, and with a dagger in her hands she was especially dangerous.

Alexander smiled at her. Her hair was extremely disheveled and her face was red from exertion.

"What have you been doing this morning?" he asked.

"Edward showed me how to use a bow while riding and shooting at targets! It was FANTASTIC." Sofia's enthusiasm was contagious.

"Oh did you? How did that fair?"

"It was great until…" she began to move about the room talking excitedly. "It was great and I was just getting the hang of it and then that dog of yours….yes that one….came out of nowhere and started nipping at the horses' hind legs. Well, the horse rears up and I landed on the ground."

"Which is why you chose to wake me up. To tell me all of this." He laughed at his sister's sullied pants.

"Here now," he commented as he inspected the torn trousers, "these are my pants. Why are you not wearing a dress and why have you torn my pants?"

"I do not have any pants of my own," she reminded him. "Mother would never agree to that."

"Well since you cannot ride like a lady, I guess you could not dismount a horse like one," he chuckled.

"It's not funny. I could have been hurt. And since it was the cause of that dog of yours, I would have had father make you my butler for a month."

"Oh you would?" Alexander grinned. "You might die of starvation if I had to wait on you. I can barely take care of myself."

"Ugh, I know. You're absolutely hopeless." She eyed him for a moment as he made little effort to change any of his clothes. He stopped and stared out of the small window in the wall.

Sofia took notice of the plain state that his room was in.

"Alex, when will you let me decorate your room?"

"Never," he chuckled.

"Please Alex. It's uninteresting and devoid of any color."

"Are you saying that I am uninteresting and devoid of any color?" He splashed water on his face from a bowl in his room.

"Stop mocking me." Her tone had an injured air. "Here, I brought a lily. It's my way of saying thank you for saving me."

"The way the story seems to be going is that you saved me while I hid behind your skirt. Very well, you can decorate the room when I leave." Alex leaned his head against the slit in the wall and kept his eye on a small barge that unloaded at the dock of Middlebrooke.

"Not this again," Sofia sighed. She picked up Alexander's sheepskin and shook the dust from it.

"We turn eighteen today Sofia. It is time for me to make my way."

"Where are you going then?" She stood next to Alexander and placed her chin on his shoulder. She looked out across the city to the barge. "Why are you in such a hurry for something that will not happen?"

"It will happen," Alexander said firmly. "I am going to leave very soon."

"Where will you go?" she whispered.

"Out there; beyond the horizon," he answered and pointed mindlessly to the distance. "There's more to life than what is here in this castle."

"I wish for you to be happy where you are," she said sweetly and hugged her arms around him tightly. "Enjoy this moment for you will not turn eighteen again and neither will I!"

"You enjoy it," Alexander said. "Then come with me."

"Mother would never allow it. She barely tolerates

me stealing my brother's pants." Sofia said sadly. "I am a prisoner in this castle as much as you are. Soon I will be married off to an ogre, and have little ogre children." She backed away from Alexander and studied his appearance.

"You're not wearing that today are you?"

"I will not be wearing those pants," he said lightly and pointed at Sofia's torn pants.

"Alex, be serious!"

"Sofia, these are my night clothes. It looks as if Angelica has set my clothes out for me." He pointed to a chair in the corner of the room that had his tunic.

"Well get a move on. Men are already assembling at the field. You know how your bothers are when you are late." She paced impatiently. A stranger might have mistaken her as the one who was receiving a bodyguard.

"Are you coming then?"

"I don't know. Mother's been insufferable all morning. She tried to stop me from riding. Said it wasn't dignified for a lady to shoot an arrow from a horse's saddle and said I should be making myself beautiful for all the princes and noblemen that will be at the Great Hall tonight." She made a sweeping gesture with her hands. "If princes can't accept the fact that I am a better rider than they are, then they can just look at someone else, like Elsie from the Burrows."

Elsie from the Burrows was the daughter of a noble in the eastern part of the kingdom. While not as powerful as any of the town Barons, they still owned large tracts of land and several hundred peasants worked their lands for protection. Elsie was a childhood friend and her name was continually linked as a suitable marriage for Edward. Alexander and Sofia had whispered many jokes at her expense and mocked her when they were children.

"Old frog face? I'd rather look at you covered in

mud and feathers I think. And that's only because you're as handsome as I am."

"Oh am I? And who'll be coming to the Hall to court you then?" Sofia's nose was starting to crinkle. This was the sign that she was absolutely begging for a fight that she was sure to win. Alexander decided a war of wits with her after waking up was not the way to start his day.

"Tell you what Sofie. Go and hide from mother, and meet us later. You won't miss much."

"Can I take part in the events? I'm sure I'd make a better guard than half of them. I'm a much better archer than most of our men. Oh, did you hear? Most of our soldiers are lazy and susceptible to bribery! That was exciting news I overheard. At least if I tried to kill you I'd do it to your face."

"That's very comforting Sofia," he said with feigned hurt. "You'd like to kill me to get to the throne?"

"Oh yes, because Father gave you the crown last night. You're so close to being King!"

Sofia laughed heartily and so did Alexander. As Alexander was the youngest, he was last to the crown and was the least likely to be assassinated.

"Oh Alex, you are my favorite brother." She hugged him tightly until he gasped for air.

"More favorite than perfect Edward?" The hug loosened and she backed away. Sofia looked into Alexander's eyes.

"You are turning into a great man Alex. Don't underestimate yourself. Be who you are and be happy to be that person. I am happy with whom you are, and I'll always stand with you. I love you, Alex!"

Alexander rolled his eyes in mock disdain but stopped when he caught sight of Sofia's face. Her eyes began to darken and her brows furrowed into a tight glare.

"I love you too, Sofia." The tenderness of the moment made him uncomfortable. His upbringing had taught him to ignore emotions; none of the men of the family were particularly equipped to deal with sensitive matters that required a soft approach. Sofia's constant interaction with Alexander forced him to be more sensitive than his brothers, and he suffered their teasing constantly.

Sofia's eyes lightened and a smile crept back on her face but a shrill voice interrupted the tender moment. It was their mother, Queen Caroline, and she called for Sofia from the courtyard.

"Ahhh.....there's mother. Keep the lilies, while I hide! I'll try to get to the field as soon as I can." With that, Sofia and her wild hair quickly disappeared from Alex's room.

Alexander turned his attention back to the window and looked down towards the city. From his window he saw the market place and the vendors as they bustled and tried to sell their goods. Beyond the market were the abbey, the armory, the muster field, the walls, the gate, and then the rest of the known world. The fields to the west had turned a perfect golden brown as the wheat was being harvested. He turned his attention to the barges sailing towards the city on the Alveus River. Alexander wanted desperately to go beyond the walls. He enjoyed the wide open space, and the freedom to ride forever without restraint.

For Alexander, every thought ended with the horizon. That's all he ever wanted. He wanted to go to the horizon and continue to follow it. What was beyond? What did princes in other kingdoms do? How did they live? These were questions that Alexander had since he was a boy, and now, with his eighteenth birthday, he wanted his questions answered.

Alexander craned his neck to gain sight of the barge on the Alveun River. The barge that had docked now floated lazily downstream in the direction of Middlebrooke. Alexander assumed it was a trading barge from the kingdom's northern city of Edgebrooke. Eventually the barge would leave Middlebrooke and follow the river as it flowed past the east wall and continued south towards the port city of Brookehaven.

The river was considered crucial to the kingdom's continued success and health due to the amount of barges that transported gold and silver from the northern mines. The locals were so enamored of the river, they named the kingdom Alveus.

Alexander bored with the timid pace of the barge and looked into the beautiful blue sky. It was a brilliant sight that he never tired of looking at. The sun shone magnificently and the quiet breeze gently lifted some strands of his blonde hair. He closed his eyes, took a deep breath, and stretched his arms out and yawned loudly. Summer prepared to give way to autumn, which made it just a bit cooler, but equally as serene.

In any other kingdom, Alexander Wolfield would have been welcomed as a brilliant king. Although he only turned eighteen that day, he was already exceptionally gifted in academics and military tactics. He was also remarkably pious and charitable for one within the royal bloodline. In many circles of the kingdom, peasants and nobles alike looked upon him with respect, but he would never be king, and that never truly bothered him.

Alexander wished to be more like Edward. When he was a child he followed after his oldest brother everywhere and desperately sought his approval. This isn't to say that Alexander thought living in Edward's shadow was unfortunate. Edward was innately a good person and followed most of the traditions and customs of his people. But Alexander found out at a very early age that anything he did would be measured against Edward's achievements.

When Alexander was thirteen, he left the castle without informing anyone. After two days of solitary living in the forest he successfully hunted and killed a magnificent stag that he had stalked for an entire day.

He returned to the castle with his prize and presented the stag for dinner while the King commented with his favorite tale of how Edward had killed a boar with a dagger at age twelve. Edwards' achievements cast a long shadow that all of his brothers suffered in and Alexander long desired to leave that shadow. Now that Alexander turned eighteen he entertained thoughts of other passions that could be pursued.

Their father had declared Edward the heir five years ago, and Alexander agreed wholeheartedly with his father's decision. There would be no throne in his future. He had considered entering the clergy and becoming a Knight of the Church. That worked well with his piety and desire to help the poor. It was either that or become a soldier. Alexander had not yet fought in a real battle, but just like wanting to avoid any real responsibility through the crown, he wanted to avoid the responsibility of commanding hundreds of men into battle. Whatever he decided, he wanted it to be soon, and he wanted to forge his own identity apart from his family.

A cold sensation on his leg jolted him from his thoughts and back into the moment. Keira's wet nose nudged him out of his daydream. It was if she, too, reminded him of his responsibilities.

He had owned Keira since she was puppy. One day his mother took him to the port of Brookehaven to purchase some of the fine imports that traders brought from other kingdoms. A commotion had incurred from a small puppy that ruined a fine set of freshly cut geese. The Frisian trader that caught her was going to hurl the dog into the ocean, but Alexander intervened and had Queen Caroline purchase the mischievous puppy. Generously and without hesitation, Queen Caroline also paid the trader for the ruined geese. Since that day, Keira rarely left his side. Whenever Alexander rode into the country, he could always count on two companions: his dog and his sister. As Keira grew, she bore a striking similarity to the war dogs of ancient armies. They were monstrously tall, swift, and adept at using their weight to bring down their victims on the battlefields and ripping their throats quickly.

"Alright Dog," he smiled. "Let us go have some excitement." He grabbed the lilies that Sofia had given him and made his way to the Great Hall with Keira following.

He quietly made his way downstairs and looked around for Angelica. She was busy arranging the tableware for the night's celebration. He found himself staring longingly at her figure, but spurred himself to action.

"Milady," he crooned sweetly.

"My Lord," she responded politely. She didn't make eye contact with him and continued to set the table.

"I have been thinking about you." He felt that he would bare his soul to her in hopes that she might see his earnestness.

"Why would a Prince think about a maid? He should be thinking about Princesses and battles. Those are princely things; just like I think about doing your laundry and setting your place at the table."

"So you do think about me?" He asked inquisitively.

She smiled but refused to answer it. "The story doesn't end happily ever after for either of us if you keep pursuing this."

"It can and it will," Alexander said firmly. "Talk to me tonight, please, after the celebration."

She sighed and nodded her head in surrender. His heart skipped a beat from his unexpected success.

"Here," he said as he pulled the lilies out from behind his back. "A token of my affection for you."

Her eyes widened and she gasped. "My Lord, where did you get these?"

"A woman sold them to us in Brookehaven. Have you seen these before? They are called lilies, and my sister swears by them."

"I have seen them before," she replied. "Once upon a time. You should go, before anyone sees us. Please."

Alexander nodded his head in agreement. "Tonight," he said and she scurried back into the kitchens and left him standing all alone. Or so he thought. A shadow caught his attention and he found his other brother Calimus sitting alone.

"Brilliant brother," Calimus muttered, "Giving the servant girl flowers. Maybe she will polish your armor a bit harder than usual."

"Yes," Alexander replied, "and this would be the fifth straight day that I find you sitting by yourself with a flagon of ale. It's a bit early for drink, is it not?"

"It is not," Calimus retorted. "What else does a Prince have to do these days?" He stood up and kicked the bench behind him which caused several servants to run out from the kitchen, but one sharp look from Calimus sent them back into their duties. He was a few inches taller than Alexander, but his poor posture often caused observers to assume they were the same height. He had gained considerable weight in the last year due to his heavy drinking, but kept his non-descript appearance to himself and the taverns he frequented.

Calimus's hair was unkempt, his face unshaven and heavily weathered for a young man who ventured infrequently into the sun. Still, he fancied himself a ladies' man and had quite a bit of success in seducing the young maids about the court.

Alexander shook his head sadly and paused as a feeling of dread swept over him as Calimus's presence was replaced by the commanding presence of his father, King Magnus IX. Although advanced in years, King Magnus still strode through his halls erect and without difficulty. Alexander's brothers had inherited their larger frames from King Magnus as there were few men that could stand tall and look the King directly in the eyes. Although age caught up to him, he aged better than all, and his silver hair and beard were envied by men half his age.

The old king ventured quietly through the hall towards Alexander and for a moment it seemed as if the King passed by without a word, but as soon as Alexander breathed a sigh of relief, his father spoke.

"So, today you will choose your guard?" He looked genuinely disinterested in the answer.

"Yes, father," Alexander replied respectfully.

"Have you selected a name?"

"Yes I have father," Alexander beamed. "A name that inspires fear and greatness. My bodyguard will be known as the Dragons."

"Dragons?" King Magnus stroked his white beard and his brow furrowed in disappointment. "Dragons are not real. Who is inspired or frightened by a mythological beast with scales? Your two worthy brothers chose a name of majesty and power. Edward chose the lion, a symbol of royalty and power. Mattias chose panthers, powerful beasts that are full of cunning. Yet, you have chosen a beast that does not exist."

Alexander stood quietly and said nothing. He dared not disagree with his father.

"It was only a thought," he said meekly. "I have not decided yet."

"In my youth," the King scolded, "Our bodyguards meant something. The men you selected had no fear of death and lusted after glory and fame. When we went to war, we carried our banners that represented exactly who we were in battle. If my soldiers saw me carrying a dragon..." his voice trailed off and he scoffed at the idea.

"Bodyguards now are just pomp and pretty men that drill all day to impress young ladies. Only Edward and Mattias have ever seen real combat, and the enemies we fight now are little better than farmers with pitchforks. When your grandfather," Magnus nodded and bowed his head in deep affection. "When your grandfather and I rode out to war in the Shadowlands, many of the men we went with died. We would have died too, if not for the strength and loyalty of our men."

Alexander was intrigued with the one word his father rarely spoke, and even rarer, explained. "Father, what happened in the Shadowlands?"

"Death," he spoke solemnly. "Death and all of its hellions came for us. When they failed at killing us, they started to play tricks on our minds. They conjured up a jester's tricks, and soon our men turned on each other, thinking that each man had the devil inside of him. There were no strange beasts and there were no pixies or fairies. There was only steel and each one of our swords was covered in blood. When your grandfather had breathed his last breath, his last words to me were 'Kill them all.' And that's just what we did, and we left none alive."

"Who were you fighting?"

"Death and its pale riders." Magnus looked as if he

had entered a trance, and in that trance and been taken back to that battlefield over fifty years ago. His eyelid fluttered and he mumbled a bit, and Alexander strained to hear him speak.

"Father, who was the enemy?"

Magnus looked at his son for a moment. "You take after your grandfather," he complimented. That was the first time in a while that Alexander remembered receiving a kind word. "Who we fought doesn't matter. They passed from the archives of history much like a dream." Magnus recovered his countenance and stood tall and defiant.

"Dreams are the elixir of the weak. We hold everything that is true and tangible and that is how our family rules in strength. We are Kings. Let my words weigh heavily inside that mind of yours. You will make a selection by tonight's feast, regardless if they will amount to little more than peacocks on parade."

The King left Alexander alone in the Great Hall for a moment. Alexander grabbed a few morsels of bread and fruit that had already been prepared to eat throughout the day, and thought about the stories his father never told him. The Shadowlands particularly intrigued Alexander, because the only living survivor that he knew was his father, and the King never revealed what happened. Even Queen Caroline was ignorant of these events, and the chronicles referred to it as the last Great War that secured the kingdom's standing, but with the price of many men's lives in Alveus, including his grandfather's.

CHAPTER IV

Alexander took a shortcut through the Royal Stables. It was the quickest way to the muster field even though it was the least pungent. Fortunately, for his sense of smell, the horses had been taken out of the stalls earlier that day by the stable boys and out to the fields to run while only a few hands stayed behind to ensure each stall was cleaned and fresh hay was being laid in the stalls.

The familiar smell took Alexander back to his childhood days when he was required to learn the care and grooming of horses. He loved horses, but he hated having to care for the entire stable. He pitied the poor stable boys for he knew there was more to their grueling work than what it seemed. It eventually would be a fair trade, for in exchange for their labor, each boy received horsemanship lessons from one of the kingdom's best knights, and within a few years, they would be inducted into the cavalry, the part of the army that received the highest prestige.

Once outside the stalls, Alexander was only a few yards away from the activity at the muster field and he could see that a crowd of townsfolk had already gathered. Alexander made his way through the crowd carefully. Most of the townsfolk were unaware of his presence until he passed in front of them. The selection of a guard was an important occasion and the villagers reveled at an opportunity to watch the soldiers in action, especially the children that clambered on the small walls that surrounded the field.

There were fifty warriors that were already working with wooden spears and swords. Several of them had broken off the main group and were practicing parrying. It was common place for the soldiers to practice, and the promise of being chosen for such an honored assignment as part a prince's bodyguard excited the men in attendance. Anticipation filled the air and the clack of the wooden swords striking each other was louder and more prevalent than in a normal drill.

The standard Alveun soldier was well paid and well fed. They were one of a handful of kingdoms that afforded a standing professional army instead of relying on trained farmers and their pitchforks. Each soldier carried a weapon (sword or spear), a shield, and leather armor. The King and princes, generals, and any noble that served in the army were equipped with armor forged from iron, as they could afford it.

The soldiers were drilled endlessly, practicing formations, speed, and tactics in order to maintain their dominance on the battlefield. Each male member of the royal family was considered part of the army, and therefore required to serve in its ranks. The King was the exception, as he would have already served in the army as prince. If the King was disinclined to lead the army, he could promote a handful of Generals to serve him, or if there was a Crown Prince who showed tremendous leadership, he would be appointed General.

Edward had already arrived at the field and practiced

his melee footwork. He was dressed in full battle armor, with his brilliant breastplate glistening in the sun. With two hands he gripped his favored weapon, the broadsword, and pointed at five of the closest soldiers and barked orders at them. He ordered the five men to stand around him in a circle and they quickly obeyed without hesitation. He had each one of them attack in sequence as he spun about deflecting their blows. Alexander briefly paused and watched his brother's practice intently.

Edward, now in his late twenties, had devoted much of his life to the pursuit of perfection with the sword. Most of the soldiers stopped what they were doing to marvel at Edward's perfection. Alexander felt a brief twinge of jealousy for his brother's skill. The fluidity and ease of the swordplay was like a choreographed folk dance. Not one soldier could touch Edward. Not that anyone would if they saw the opportunity. It was a certain death sentence to strike a member of the royal family.

The sight of another brother elicited a heavy sigh from Alexander. Mattias, the fiery second son of the King, had arrived at the field and as he passed between the villagers they quickly made a path and bowed their head in respect. Edward had invited Mattias to lend his input and he was also dressed in his armor as he wished to practice swords with the men. His disdain of the proceedings was evident as he neglected to cover a sneer when he spotted Alexander.

With his functioning eye, he glared at any villager that did not bow their head fast enough to his liking and punished them for their dawdling. The patch won him no support amongst the peasantry and instead increased their distrust of him. He also chose to be frequently unshaven and often neglected to bathe. His distaste of taking care of his own hygiene had caused his brown hair to be coarse and matted, and he was very rarely without armor during the day. He was the shortest of the brothers and it seemed to drive his aggression as he always hated looking up at anyone.

The only part of Matthias's personality that was welcomed was now on display for the population to see. Alexander had doubts about the men who served in the Alveun army, for their loyalty seemed to shift occasionally behind Mattias. He was one of them, and they embraced him as their own.

Several swift sword movements from Mattias brought forth cheers from the men. While the King held their loyalty by title, and Edward held their respect through birth and experience, Mattias won out on sheer audacity and personal ambition.

Alexander and Mattias hated each other since childhood. Alexander was never quite sure why Mattias hated him, but he was quite sure why he hated Mattias. The hatred between the two became evident from the time that Alexander was eight and Mattias was eleven. Mattias broke Alexander's nose after a game of chess ended in defeat.

Mattias was a braggart and loved to be superior in everything when he was a child. When Alexander had grown a fondness for chess, Mattias decided he too needed to be superior in chess. In a brief game, Alexander delivered such a resounding defeat to Mattias and humiliated him in front of his brothers who gathered to watch. The manner in which he had lost pushed Mattias into a fit of rage and he swung a hardened fist at Alexander.

As Alexander reflected upon it, he surmised that the ending with a bloody nose was the bad ending but the rest of it was brilliant. He felt a sense of arrogance of a certain mastery of Mattias after that day and the two of them continued to prick each other's personalities.

Alexander generally regarded Mattias as cruel and insolent and made it a habit to always stand facing him, and reminded himself to never turn his back in Mattias's presence. One could never be too ready for the unpredictability that was Mattias Wolfield.

Mattias was always prepared for a fight no matter the odds. He had already proven his mettle in battle and as the story went, he led the final charge of horsemen that broke the enemy lines and inflicted great losses among them. This one act inspired the army and had elevated Mattias to a legendary status among the soldiers.

Alexander suspected that, although Mattias was never to his liking, something in Mattias had changed since childhood. He had always been cruel to people and pets around him, but there was something unmistakable in his eyes now; an unquenchable desire to shed blood. Alexander felt very fortunate that it was Edward who was born first, and not Mattias. It was impossible to predict what Mattias would have done for the throne. For now, he preferred to keep the uneasy peace between Mattias and himself, as there was no need for any conflict between the two of them. The question of the throne was settled with Edward so they generally held their own interests, separate from each other.

Edward was the first that noticed Alexander's arrival. He flipped his long dark locks away from his face and his blue eyes twinkled merrily.

"Alex! It's about time! Now we can get started, eh Mattias?"

Mattias looked at Edward and shrugged his powerful shoulders in casual disregard. He held his massive sword in the air and slammed it into the soft earth. For a brief moment it wobbled but eventually came to a stop. Mattias looked directly at Alexander through his cold grey eyes.

"Tie up your mutt and let's get on with it."

Edward tossed a wooden sword at Alexander who deftly caught it midair and grinned. He motioned for Keira to follow him over to a metal stake sticking up from the ground. It was typically meant to keep a horse from running away, but today there were no horses.

"I'm sorry girl," Alexander said as Keira whimpered softly. "We don't need you getting in anyone's way today. You'll be safer here." As Alexander finished tying her up, Edward stepped up on a small wooden platform and addressed the soldiers.

"Gentlemen!" Edward shouted. "As you well know it is Prince Alexander's eighteenth birthday. As is custom in our kingdom, each male prince choose a special bodyguard of twelve of our kingdom's finest warriors. You are regarded as the finest soldiers in our regiments. Twelve of you will be chosen and as a reward of being chosen, and as a special incentive, you will receive ten gold coins as a gift for your loyalty from your king."

"THE KING!" All the men shouted in unison as they lifted their swords and spears in the air. Excited chatter passed through the crowd. Ten gold coins was a more than an incentive for them to do their best.

Edward and Mattias made their way through the soldiers and directed men to different areas of the field. One corner held archery, another for sword, and the third was reserved for foot races. Each course was designed to measure their quickness, strength, and accuracy.

The expectation for a member of the royal bodyguard was simple. You fought and died when necessary for the one you protected. If your lord fell in battle, there was no point in returning home. The shame would be too great to bear. You would be ostracized as a coward, and you would spend the rest of your days hiding from everyone's eyes. No one would take pity on you…if other soldiers saw you they might spit on you or worse, kill you in the most brutal of ways.

To offset the dangers, the rewards for being in the bodyguard were incomprehensible. Every member of the bodyguard received a specially designed and fitted armor. The breast plate and back were forged of the highest quality iron with leather fittings for increased flexibility. This type of armor provided more protection than the typical soldiers' leather armor and therefore helped them last in battle longer than any other soldier. Each soldier received a horse, cared for at the royal stables, was taught to split an apple from the back of a horse at three hundred paces with a bow and arrow, and received a substantial upgrade in their monthly pay. All of this was provided to them by the royal treasury.

As the men excitedly hurried off to their assigned tasks a single horse and rider appeared. Alexander laughed when he saw that it was Sofia that drew closer for she rode like the devil and the closer she came, the more difficult it became to discern her hair from the horses mane. Disheveled and dirty, she fit in with the other soldiers on dirt alone.

"Hello Sofia. Glad to see you could make it," Alexander chided. "I suppose troubling you for a bath is out of a question."

Sofia ignored Alexander's jest. "Have you begun? Please tell me it hasn't started." Sofia feigned with mock disappointment.

"I am happy you found a dress to wear for this occasion and not my pants." Sofia had chosen a yellow dress that allowed her legs the maximum space allowed to be able to mount and dismount her horse freely.

"I tried on some pants but they were very tight. Why are your pants tight?"

"I do not want to alarm you," Alexander said dryly, "But there has been talk that the fair Princess Sofia has gained girth as she ages."

"Are you suggesting that I am fat?" she hissed.

"I am not suggesting anything," Alexander said straight faced, "But if you could fit in my pants yesterday and not today then perhaps the rumors are true."

"I fit in your pants this morning! How can I not fit in them now?" Sofia's face reddened with anger.

"I am not a physician, Sofia, but my best guess would be the amount of haute cakes you eat in a sitting. It's very unladylike."

"And what rumors?" She hissed demonstratively.

Edward interrupted their banter and clucked his tongue at Sofia. "Sofia, you know Mother has been looking for you all day."

"Mother should keep looking; she obviously isn't looking in the right places." Sofia glared at Alexander who just turned his head and bit his lip so not to laugh.

Edward rolled his eyes and shook his head, but Alexander found his sister's cheekiness to be extraordinarily funny. His aura of cheerfulness was quickly ended by the serious business at hand. A snarling Mattias was enough to destroy the mood at a festival.

"I'm not here for my health. Either let's get this done or let's go home," Mattias growled. He turned away and walked towards the men who saluted him as he walked past.

Edward presented Alexander with a leather parchment and a knife. "Put a mark near any man's name that impresses you."

Edward jogged off in Mattias's direction so together they directed the men through different drills. Sofia and Alexander watched and conferred over every arrow and every footrace.

"That one," Sofia declared. "Harold from Fallbrooke. He's a hefty fellow."

"Great with a sword," Alexander said. The two watched as Harold shuffled his way through a footrace with a slender man. The weight Harold carried presented great difficulty. He didn't run very fast. Alexander thought a skinnier person would walk just as slowly. Needless to say, Harold barely finished the race.

"That's true. He's probably the fastest person here at mealtimes. He's probably great with a cow too. He might have his way with it if you gave him a knife. He might eat you. What do you think? Would he break a horse in half? Or do we have a giant horse?" Sofia at first started to whisper, but quickly lost all sense of who stood near her, and her remarks inspired chuckles in the crowd.

"Sofia that's horrible. I need good swordsmen. That giant of a man can crush any man's skull with his fists. Imagine if he held a two-handed broadsword. I bet he could hold his own against father in his prime."

"Crush a man with his fists, crush a horse with his girth…I'll tell you what, if you ever need to flee, just leave him behind. It's not like you'd have a choice. Maybe if you brought two oxen and a horse to carry him places by wagon. Do we have a chariot in the stable?" Sofia tried desperately not to laugh at her own cleverness. When she couldn't contain it anymore, the sharp look in Mattias's eye got her to think twice about any other comments.

Her silence lasted as long as a piece of meat at a mealtime with Keira. "He's as big as a dragon. Maybe he can breathe fire. Now you have a real dragon at last!" Sofia lost her focus and doubled over in laughter as Alexander resisted the temptation to gently nudge her off of the bench they sat on.

Edward called his men to rest as he and Mattias went over to discuss the results with Alexander.

"So Alexander," Edward wondered aloud. "What do you think? Have you made your selections?"

Alexander presented his ideas on who he thought would make the best fit. Sofia immediately disagreed on half of them and presented what was wrong with them and made alternative suggestions. Edward also countered until the three of them were throwing useless words about. The three of them continued to quarrel, neither made any impact on the others thoughts.

Mattias had stayed quiet and was now just holding his head in his hands. His frustration built much to the pleasure of Alexander.

"Away with you sister," he snarled and waved his hand back towards the Palace. "This is men's work. Go and find some knitting."

"If this is men's work, where are the men? You promised twelve of the finest soldiers. I see peasants and thieves." Sofia countered.

"These are the finest soldiers in the regiment. How dare you disrespect them! I have heard enough of your mocking today." Mattias spat angrily. "Why are you here? Do you still speak for Alexander? Or have I confused again who's the Prince?"

Mattias's last comment inflamed Alexander's senses. He moved closer to Mattias as his teeth clenched. He took each step very deliberately and refused to take his eyes off Mattias.

"If you have something to say to me then say it." He said it quietly and under his breath for he wished not to make a scene in front of the people.

Edward tried to defuse the situation, but it was hopeless. Mattias baited Alexander, and like a fish,

Alexander was quick to take the bait. Years of frustration and torment at Mattias's hands had made Alexander extremely sensitive towards his brothers' comments. This sensitivity heightened his aggression in tense situations between them.

"I'll put it to you then. This is YOUR guard not your sister's. You weigh too heavily on her words. Show us a Prince and not a wet rag."

"Better my counsel than treacherous thoughts," Sofia challenged. She directly accused Mattias of desiring to succeed their father. This was a dangerous gambit. To accuse one of treason within the royal family without cause was equally as devastating of plotting treachery.

"Treacherous thoughts? That is my plan to waste my words and actions on the ingratitude of my useless brother. Chide away if you must useless nag." Mattias backed away from Sofia and looked to return to the warriors who had gathered together and anxiously watched the argument. They looked favorably upon him again, for ripping into Sofia about her words regarding them.

What if, for one moment, Mattias wanted everything for himself, Alexander thought.

"Tie away your apron strings from this one," he sneered over his shoulder to Alexander. "Or at least wear a matching dress to the Feast."

"Mattias, hold your tongue," Edward ordered in frustration.

Alexander gripped the wooden sword in his hand and moved even closer towards Mattias. He wanted to strike at him with the sword and be done with the argument once and for all. He wouldn't hurt him too badly. Just punch him as hard as possible in the mouth.

"Why not give the sword to Sofia, for we have heard about her prowess in battle!" Mattias continued his public mockery of Alexander by raising his voice so that the soldiers and the ever increasing peasant crowd would hang on his every word. "Let her continue to fight your battles. Or maybe we can find a real sword for you to use, to see if you know how to use it against a man." Some of the men let out a slight laugh but quickly stopped for fear of discovery. Alexander was incensed that these soldiers held interest in their conflict when they were supposed to be his bodyguard. His disdain for the soldiers deepened as did his contempt for Mattias.

"At least she doesn't kill a peasant and call herself a great warrior for it," Alexander snarled. If Mattias humiliated him in front of the soldiers, than Alexander would gladly return the favor.

"That's enough Alexander!" Edward warned. He turned to confront Alexander and blocked his advance towards Mattias.

Mattias had no more patience for a war of words and as soon as Edward turned his body to block Alexander, Mattias struck first. He threw his fist squarely into Alexander's cheek. Alexander buckled from the weight of the punch and stumbled back. Sofia shrieked in rage and quickly raced to Mattias, ready to bury her fists into him. Alexander had no doubt that Mattias would see no moral issue with hitting Sofia. Edward felt the same for as Alexander stumbled backwards from Mattias's punch, Edward quickly turned and threw his arms around Sofia. He lifted her off of the ground and carried her away from Mattias.

There were several chuckles amongst the ranks as Alexander struggled to get on his feet. Keira gnawed at her rope, trying to help her master. Her sharp teeth glimmered in the sunlight. She wanted desperately to tear Mattias apart. Mattias wisely looked behind him and ensured Keira was still tied to the metal stake.

Mattias unclipped his belt and let his scabbard fall to the ground. He balled up his fists and looked at Alexander who had blood streaming out of his nose.

"Come on Alexander!" he taunted. "Isn't this what you've always wanted?"

Alexander quickly regained his footing and lunged his body into Mattias's stomach. He felt the air leave Mattias's stomach but then felt the weight of Mattias's elbow crashing down into his back. Alexander yelped with pain and stumbled down onto one knee.

Alexander quickly managed to hook Mattias's arm with his own and flipped him onto his back, Mattias would not let go so easily and brought Alexander down to the ground with him. Alexander tried to keep his leverage and keep Mattias on the ground. He swung at Mattias's face, but missed. Alexander felt his grip weaken. As strong as Alexander thought he was, Mattias was admittedly stronger because of his height advantage and his experience. Each of the brothers looked for an opportunity to deliver a powerful blow but neither of them could leverage their bodies and all the blows they struck glanced off the other. Alexander reached his hand towards Mattias's face and he ripped the eye patch off of Mattias's head which revealed his blind eye. Mattias screamed in rage and in a fury flipped Alexander over onto his back and punched Alexander rapidly. Alexander threw his hands over his face to protect himself, but the punches came in to quickly to block. Several punches struck his forehead and he did his best to push Mattias off of him, but his efforts to strike Mattias were to no avail.

Edward finally let go of Sofia and rushed to break up the fight. When he reached them he grabbed Mattias by his ear. Mattias roared with anger but he could not do anything more because if he struck Edward it was tantamount to treason and an immediate death sentence for the one who did it. Mattias had no choice and allowed Edward to pull him off. He walked over to his eye patch and placed it back over his eye. Sofia rushed in front of Alexander and was trying to hold him back from any further fighting. Alexander had blood streaming down his face and nose. She tried to soothe him but he was too furious and he would not look at her. He trembled with rage.

"Stop it now!" Edward commanded. "I am done with this incessant bickering between you two." He softened his tone to a whisper as he grabbed them both by the shoulders. "I love you both, and whatever you two think about one another, you need to keep that behind the citadel walls. Your nonsense has no place in front of our people. None. The next one of you that brings shame on us in front of our people will be dealt with by me personally. Do you understand me?"

He looked at Alexander disapprovingly but Alexander looked at the soldiers. They were huddled together and whispered while they glanced in his direction. He felt mocked. Not one of these men could be trusted to be HIS men. Alexander shook himself free of Edward's grasp and walked towards Sofia's horse.

"Alex," Edward called out. "Where are you going?"

"I'm done. I'm going to the abbey."

"Alex....please," Sofia pleaded. "Your face is bleeding, your shirt is torn. Stay here and let me fix you up."

"You heard what he said to me didn't you? That I let you fight my battles? Just let me alone. Please." The hurt in Alexander's voice was sincere. Edward walked back towards him.

"What about the bodyguard?" Edward asked.

"What about them? I can tell where their loyalties lie. I don't need that kind of loyalty. I'll find my own men and I'll do it my way." Alexander glared at Mattias and his brother returned the glare with equal venom. Never had Alexander felt this rage before, but he wanted to take his sword up and kill his brother.

"I'm sorry Edward," he said with sincerity. "I know what I should be doing. I just can't right now. You can handle father for me, can't you?"

"Yes Alex," Edward said softly. "I'll talk to father. Just give me your word you'll stay away from Mattias."

Alexander leaned down and whispered.

"You can have my word. But that's twice he's made me bleed. There won't be a third time. The next time, we cross swords. You know as well as I do that he's cruel, and he's a murderer."

Edward shook his head. "You don't know that. Events happen in battle. You can lose yourself in the moment."

"So that's makes it all okay? We are noble sons of Wolfield. Surely we should expect more from ourselves or raise our standards. Please see that Keira makes it to the kennels."

Edward nodded his agreement so Alexander turned his horse into the direction of the church and rode through the crowd with the sting of humiliation and defeat seared into his mind.

CHAPTER V

Alexander was relieved when he finally arrived at the abbey and could leave the embarrassment of the day's events behind him. Of all the buildings that Alexander had visited in Middlebrooke, the abbey was the newest, and it always gave Alexander a feeling of peace to be in its shadow.

The abbey itself had been built within the last century and replaced a small chapel that had been originally constructed with the laying of Middlebrooke. The Abbey rivaled the Royal Palace for beauty and was considered the second most beautiful building in Alveus, but that depended on who you talked with and how much faith was a factor in their life. For Alexander, this abbey functioned as a second home and at times he spent more time at the Abbey then the citadel.

As Alexander pushed through the solid oak doors he found himself captivated by the monks while they sang their midday prayers. He always loved the harmony of the chants, for him there was something very simple and spiritual about it. He briefly kneeled, faced the giant wooden crucifix in front of him, and made the required sign of the cross.

Alexander learned quickly that the religious offices demanded respect from all social classes but nowhere was it more examined than among the nobility. To receive the perception of agnostic was to undermine the prevailing theory of divine right. God gave the nobles their power to rule, and in turn their public support encouraged the local priests to keep the peasantry in line. From the abbey's rectory the priests administered impressive oratories that inspired the peasantry to greater heights of servitude and endearment towards their masters. But should any priest feel mistreated or ignored by their villages patron, or worse yet, by the King, then the priests sermons would include great passion of how the divine right to rule had been revoked by God, and how God's people need to stand in fury and be the judgment against the heathen ruler.

This chess game between clergy and nobility had endured through the centuries. The stakes were countless lives of peasants that were discarded during these power struggles. With the advent of Magnus IX, the royalty had finally realized the power of the clergy; they became more pious in appearance and attendance at the masses. With the exception of the one Peasant Revolt the uneasy détente prospered.

Queen Caroline was adamant in her beliefs and she saw to it that Alexander and Sofia were instructed in every tenet of their faith. Alexander was instructed to show respect and pray constantly, and this he did in full view of the people.

After he bowed his head his silence in front of the cross, he attempted to push the previous activities from his mind. He focused quietly and took several calming breaths. Father Malachius warned against giving into anger, it would lead to bitterness and hate and these were qualities that were despised in a Prince of Alveus.

After he took one final breath and composed himself, Alexander moved through the sanctuary in search of Father Malachius.

Alexander thought back to his youth to ensure that he released his anger towards Mattias. When he was younger he frequently crept into the abbey's garden and hid in the small trees in order to enjoy the sounds of the monk's songs. Father Malachius, the abbey's head priest, eventually spotted the intruder, but instead of chasing him out of the church grounds he kindly offered to tutor him. King Magnus declined the Father's initial offer to tutor Alexander but Queen Caroline insisted on it. His mother was excited at the opportunity of her favored son being taught by a scholar from the Church who would have access to all of the Church's learning. King Magnus was convinced to relent and Alexander became the priest's apprentice. Alexander attended lessons at the abbey every day for six years.

His lessons stretched his knowledge past most scholars in the kingdom for Father Malachius apprenticed him to the different masters in the kingdom and had him work those apprenticeships in order to understand every part of the kingdom.

His apprenticeships included working with a blacksmith, metal smith, the head of the Royal Stables, a farmer, a merchant, and of course, with Father Malachius himself. The smiths taught him much about manufacturing swords and spears. Alexander soon mastered the ability of crafting a sword. Although he loved being able to fashion the weapon of war, it was not his favorite apprenticeship. He did however; make friends with some of the other children that worked for the blacksmith. It was the first time Alexander held friends that were outside of his station.

Many afternoons he played war with the children of the village, and he led them into their imagined battles. They were awestruck that he was the Prince. He was immensely popular, and he never needed to prod them into his service. They obeyed readily, and their presence helped develop his cordial personality but fueled his desire to reach for the horizon. New learning motivated him and the thought that an opportunity lay on the horizon to know more than anyone else and to meet new friends and have new experiences helped him along towards his final goal: to leave Alveus altogether.

A community of miners lived near the blacksmith that Alexander apprenticed with. He also worked for them for a time, and learned the process of mining. Alexander lost interest quickly in mining for gold and left his apprenticeship to play with the other children. When Father Malachius learned of this behavior he quickly removed him from the apprenticeship and sent him to the Royal Stables.

The Stables taught him horsemanship and the importance of caring for horses. When he was fourteen, he was given a beautiful black foal that he named Zeus, and his primary apprenticeship at the Royal Stables was to learn the care and maintenance for his horse. As Zeus grew bigger, Alexander frequently rode him to his apprenticeships and forged a tight bond with his horse.

Alexander found his favorite apprenticeship was when he worked with the merchants in Brookehaven. He loved sailing to the ports of other countries. His mother, the Queen, came from a foreign country, and he enjoyed visiting his mother's country and got to know its people very well. He loved sailing so much that he had his own boat commissioned and constructed in the event he wanted to sail down the coast.

Learning with Father Malachius was enjoyable

although he was very strict. On one occasion the priest had Alexander copy an entire parchment of works because Alexander was late for a lesson. Alexander didn't mind, mostly because he learned while he wrote. He also shared these learning's with Sofia, who was never far behind him in thirsting to learn new ideas.

His final apprenticeship was the most difficult for him to absorb. Father Malachius sent him off to a warrior-monastery in the eastern mountains for six months. It was here that the secrecy of combat and stealth were taught to him. It was at this monastery that assassins were trained. When Alexander asked Father Malachius why monks would be trained in this art, rather than spending their time to learn the sacred texts, Father Malachius would always answer, that sometimes all it took was for one man to put a dagger into the heart of evil. It was the church's responsibility to have that one prepared.

For six months, he was put through trials that many soldiers would never know. He walked on burning coals, hiked up and down a mountain with thirty pounds of rocks held in a satchel, and lived by himself in the wilderness for a week where he was given neither food nor water. He survived through his wits and was forced to forage for his own food, water, and shelter. Finally, most of the days at the monastery were spent in silence because the drills demanded meditation and complete focus.

When his time at the monastery was completed, Alexander had mastered the techniques of silence associated with being an assassin. The same premise applied to a human. Alexander learned to kill with archery, dagger, sword, spear, or his bare hands. He knew that if he had his sword at the riverbank, he would have killed that bandit, not Sofia. It continued to chafe him that he lost his sword, and still lacked a replacement.

Alexander finally spotted his revered teacher, Father Malachius. The Father was dressed in his colorful priestly robes, and his focus was lost upon the murals through silent meditation. His slightly bald head was a constant source of amusement for Alexander, as well as his slightly portly figure. Still, with a sword in his hand, Father Malachius became an imposing figure.

"Father Malachius," he smiled and greeted his teacher with a slight bow of the head. "How are you today?"

The priest turned and smiled. "Alexander, my son, many blessings on your birthday."

"Thank you, sir. It's good of you to remember."

"And yet, you look a little worse for the wear today?" The priest motioned to his face.

The memories of his scuffle with Mattias reanimated in his mind and he realized he neglected to clean himself before entering the abbey.

"Oh this? I had a disagreement with Mattias today."

"Ah. Yes. Mattias.....Well, let's not focus on him. Let's get you cleaned up instead." Father Malachius poured water into a small basin. Alexander cupped his hands and splashed water on his face. The water washed away the dried blood from his face and left a small cut just above his eye.

"There's the face of a prince," Father Malachius jested. Alexander smiled politely. "So, tell me, how did you select your protectors today?"

Alexander stayed silent for he feared the searing rebukes that would undoubtedly arrive from everyone.

"I didn't trust them, Father," he blurted out. "It just didn't feel right. I felt like they were more loyal to Mattias than to me. I want to be able to trust them with my life. I do not feel like I can trust a professional soldier."

"That's very wise, Alexander. You listened to your heart and did the right thing, not the smart thing. Trust is an important virtue in a prince. But the ability to trust…who can a Prince trust these days?"

"It does not matter anyway," Alexander sighed and wiped the remaining droplets of water from his face. "I do not need protection from anyone in this world except my family. I live in the world's most uninteresting kingdom. They hold nothing of value for scientific pursuits or new learning; it's only gold, silver, and the weapons of war. Father Malachius, would you believe my sister thinks that a cow sleeps all day? Although she was being humorous, I will wager most of the nobility share that opinion!"

"Alexander, it is a sin to gamble," Father Malachius said with a sharp tone. "Why even suggest such a thing? For you to say it is the same as condoning that type of behavior."

"I am sorry, my Father," Alexander replied and knelt before the Cross. He made the sign of the Cross out of respect as he had done a hundred times before. He whispered a Hail Mary and when he was finished he stood back up and faced Father Malachius.

"I am sorry to have spoken strongly to you, my son, for what you said is nothing more than a dust speck in a sandstorm. When a man loses control of his tongue, he loses control of his soul."

"Yes Father," Alexander nodded in absent agreement. His respect for Father Malachius ran deep, but there always seemed one last thing for Alexander to engage within himself.

Ah well, Alexander thought, at least he recognizes the things I do well.

He did not notice Father Malachius had moved towards a side wall under the rectory. On the wall was a torch-holder and nothing else. He made eye contact with Father Malachius as he reached up and pulled the torch-holder down.

"Come with me Alexander. I have something to show you." Father Malachius pushed on the wall and it swung open and revealed a lighted passage.

In the six years he visited the Abbey, Alexander had never known this secret passage existed. When he was younger, he used to sneak through the abbey and create a few of his own hiding spots with which to surprise the monks.

"Father Malachius?" he queried with a feeling of nervousness. "What?"

"I will explain," his mentor responded. "For now, follow me."

Alexander entered the secret doorway cautiously. Together they climbed down a windy stairwell that seemed to take them directly under the abbey. Father Malachius continued to question Alexander's search for a bodyguard.

"So tell me, what will you do now? It is not fitting for a Prince not to have a bodyguard. It is prestige, it is honor!"

"I've never been one for prestige, Father." In truth Alexander liked to avoid the topic altogether.

"True," he smiled. "Prestige doesn't make a man, his actions make the man. Besides it is all myths and legends. It's about what people believe or choose not to believe."

Alexander's conscience began to lay on him. "Father, can you tell me. Are you absolutely sure that the stories about Mattias are true? How can we be so sure?"

The priest sighed. "I know your feelings in this matter. He's your brother. You never want to believe the ones closest to you are capable of such actions. But yes, I know this is true and to be fact. The poor monk who served that village barely escaped with his life. It was with some effort because Mattias would not want anyone who served the church being able to come back with this story. He was a good monk, and although he may have had his faults, he had nothing to gain in lying to me. There's a lesson in that Alexander. You see the lies in the one who has the most to gain....or the most to lose. Would Mattias lose favor amongst the people if the truth were known and accepted? What would the monk have gained by lying? There was nothing to be gained. I would stake my life on that truth."

Alexander felt incredibly conflicted. He knew the truth, but the acceptance of this truth was incredibly painful, no matter how much he disliked Mattias.

"Listen to me Alexander. You've told me the stories of Mattias in his youth. You know his cruelty, you've felt his temper. Stay away from him....or at least; never turn your back on him. There are much greater dangers to worry about in this land."

Alexander arched his eyebrows in disbelief at the priest. Father Malachius noticed Alexander's bemused look and frowned.

Alexander followed Father Malachius quietly and as the priest passed the last step, he noticed a dark room lay before him. A lone torch flickered faintly in the darkness and Alexander could not see anything other than what the faint light allowed.

"What is this place?" Alexander was unsure of what lay before him. He hated complete darkness of night, and avoided rooms without a torch or any light.

"A room of books and parchments. It is here where we safely keep the history of Alveus." The priest waved the torch in front of him slowly and Alexander saw the faint outline of desks and shelves in the darkness.

"The history of Alveus? Everyone knows the history

of our kingdom so why would you put them in a secret room?" Alexander remembered his childhood and the library in which he was taught to read and write. There were plenty of books placed there, so why a secret room?

"Alexander," the priest smiled condescendingly, "There is what you're taught and then there is everything else. It's not for you to know….at this time. What is for you to know is what the abbey would like to present you on your eighteenth birthday. In celebration of you becoming a man."

Alexander smiled broadly at the thought of a gift and immediately forgot about the room and its contents. The priest lit another two torches against a wall and light penetrated the darkness and Alexander beheld a large wooden table covered by a long cloth. The cloth was a deep burgundy and was decorated with an emblem of the head of a gryphon which held a large white cross in its beak. Father Malachius took the exquisite cloth and removed it from the table which revealed a beautifully crafted turquoise suit of armor. The crafted image of a gryphon matched both breastplate and shield and was made of gold.

Alexander was stunned for instead of being fabricated with leather, the armor was forged with light steel. It was cold to touch, but warmed him with excitement.

"You can put it on," Malachius said with a hint of excitement.

Alexander quickly removed the armor that he was wearing and without stopping put on the breastplate and fastened the leather attachments. The new armor fit him perfectly. The front and back afforded him equal protection against sword, spear, and arrow. It included woven armor at the elbow and shoulder for increased movement and flexibility. The armor also afforded extra protection with the tassels that protected his legs. Alexander was excited because this armor rivaled Edward and the Kings armor in beauty and expense.

"This is incredible," he murmured as he looked down. "Why?"

"For years I have been your mentor. You've done everything I've asked. You've learned and studied. I would hold you to be one of the most superior minds in this kingdom. And yet, I fear that the future of this kingdom will one day be decided with cold steel, and not a philosopher's mind."

"Father, I think that your fears are misplaced. Edward will be an excellent king and I will do all I can to be loyal and keep those around him loyal. You can count on that." Alexander tapped the breastplate with his hand to add emphasis that his heart believed what he said.

"Alexander, I find your lack of ambition...refreshing. Nevertheless, we cannot change destiny. It comes at us like a flood. And this is why your armor...it was forged not only with steel, but with gryphon's blood."

Alexander looked at the priest, stifling a laugh. "Gryphon's blood? I thought they were myth and legend. Why do you poke fun at me?"

"This is no joke, Alexander," the Priest sighed. "There are many myths and legends that are born out of true events. Tell me, from your studies, what do you remember of gryphons?"

Alexander leaned back against the table and folded his arms. His mind raced to recall the parchments from which he once studied. "Gryphons are powerful and majestic creatures. They're a symbol of divine power and the main guardian of the divine. The myths tell us that they guard the entrance to heaven."

Father Malachius was impressed and patted him on the shoulder. "Exactly, Guardians of the divine. So, what else would protect you so absolutely thoroughly against all matter of darkness and evil than the blood of the gryphon?"

"What evil would that be?" Alexander had never heard the Priest talk about anything more evil than the persecution of the poor and the accumulation of wealth.

"Alexander," Malachius said as he leaned closer, "The church is responsible for protecting the people...not the kingdom...from spiritual darkness. There are times where our protecting comes into direct conflict with the machinations of Princes and Kings. Remember all of the lessons I have taught you. Your duty is to your people from the lowliest peasant to the richest noble. Your responsibility is to protect the less fortunate and not exploit them like so many of your father's predecessors have done. Doing the right thing, our royalty makes it seem so difficult. But you, there is so much destiny for you."

"Thank you Father," Alexander said humbly, "But I'm just the youngest Prince. I'm not important in the grand scheme of anything. I do not understand why anyone is making a big deal out of the bodyguard."

"You are so vital to this kingdom's success! Don't steal credit from yourself."

"Alexander the savior of Alveus?" Alexander said mockingly. "I'm nothing special, I was just born into this family. I am not part of it."

"Have you considered a name for your guard?" Father Malachius said as he quickly shifted the conversations topic. Alexander obliged happily.

"I had thoughts to name them dragons. I love the old legends about dragons, but father became irritated with me. Says they aren't real. Maybe I'll choose the falcons as a symbol."

"Why not gryphons," Malachius asked as he pointed at Alexander's armor.

"Because gryphons are mythological….," Alexander said deliberately. Why would he choose another mythological beast as an irritation to his father?

"Will you be at the Great Hall tonight for my banquet?" Alexander changed the subject matter quickly.

"I will indeed. If you leave your armor here I will deliver it to the castle tonight and have it placed in your room. God's blessings on you, give my regards to your mother and your sister." Father Malachius motioned his hands in the shape of the cross as a blessing towards Alexander.

"I will my Father." Alexander took great care and removed his armor one piece at a time. He was giddy with anticipation and wanted to wear the armor at the feast as he thought of the jealousy it would stir in Mattias and the attention that it would siphon away from Edward.

When he finished removing the armor, Alexander thanked Father Malachius again and returned up the stairwell. As he walked out of the chapel, Father Malachius' warnings of danger were all but forgotten amongst the long wooden benches.

Alexander's mind focused strictly on his wondrous new gift and the great feast in process of being prepared for his birthday.

CHAPTER VI

Alexander was extremely excited and nervous for the night's festivities. Tonight would be a night to remember for all of his father's nobles would be there to pay their respects, and perhaps, pay them with a trinket or two. Alexander hoped to receive a small bit of gold for himself, to perhaps set up a merchant's house that would deal primarily in trading over the seas. The more he thought about the future, the more he desired to sail away from Alveus and explore the horizon.

His thoughts were enough to keep him occupied as he walked through the citadel's courtyard. He was so engrossed that he almost missed noticing the shadowy figure lurking behind a pillar. The figure concealed in the shade and attempted to avoid sunlight at all costs.

Alexander was not fooled. "Calimus! Why do you hide in the shadows, brother?" he called.

The figure offered a halfhearted greeting and spoke very deliberately. "Alexander....happy birthday."

"Thank you," he grinned in reply. He reached the column by which Calimus hid behind. "Have you seen Sofia?"

"No. No wait, yes. She has been busy with her handmaidens for most of the day. You'd think this was her wedding day. I'll tell you what…wouldn't mind being busy with her handmaidens though, eh?" He let out a deep laugh.

Alexander shook his head and sighed. Here was the true black sheep in the family. Calimus had sullied his reputation over the years through his drinking, gambling, and penchant for loose women. He was often ignored by King Magnus and therefore rarely addressed in his behaviors.

"You'd think the last episode would have at least calmed your endeavors, or quieted them down. Why do you have to bring shame on us Calimus?" Alexander felt genuine sympathy towards his brother.

"There was no episode." Calimus was deeply offended and resented the accusation. "If women were less inclined to open their arms to me, I might be more inclined to take up a new hobby. Maybe, reading? You've spent enough time reading. Is it fun? The scholarly prince. That will do you a lot of good when you're king…oh wait…you're not going to be king. Sorry."

"You won't be king either." Alexander bristled. "You have one year more than I and if it came to wits, knowledge, or any basic skill, I would be superior. What can you claim other than a greater thirst?" Alexander felt the heat rise in his chest. He had already fought one brother that day; he did not want to fight this one. "I'm sorry Calimus, I'm not trying to make you angry with me."

"It does not matter if I am, does it? Nothing I do matters." Calimus sighed and his eyes drifted elsewhere.

Alexander understood Calimus's hopelessness, for while Mattias and Alexander were able to find passions to divest their energy, Calimus just simply rotted away with the stench of alcohol on his breath. Alexander pitied him and tried many times to wake an interest in him, but Calimus went his own way, and the family hoped for as little scandal as possible as he did what he pleased.

"You will attend tonight? Please?" Alexander put his hand out to Calimus in an effort to soothe his hurt feelings.

"They still have ale at feasts, yes?" Calimus ignored Alexander's outstretched hand.

"Yes, Calimus." Alexander withdrew his hand and placed his hands on his hips.

"Well," Calimus said with a bow and a flourish, "I will make it my highest level of importance amongst all the important things I have today....but first, I feel the need to assist young handmaidens and the easing of your sisters demands. My yoke is very light indeed."

Calimus departed with a wink and stumbled toward the castle's gardens. Other than the alehouse, the gardens seemed to be Calimus's preferred place of sleep. He often fell asleep in a drunken stupor only to be awakened by the chatter of servants as they bustled about. Still, it was usually peaceful there. When they were younger, Calimus, Sofia, and Alexander climbed the tall trees in the citadel and attached ropes to their branches. The three siblings swung foolhardily from tree to tree pretending to be adventurers or pirates. It was also at that point that Calimus and Alexander began to grow apart. Alexander wished to see beyond the city walls, but Calimus had no desire to lift a finger or effort into any endeavor except that which pleased his person to immense satisfaction. His desire of gambling, drinking, and the fairer sex grew until his appetite for them rivaled man's need for meat.

Alexander passed through the thick walls of the royal tower and nearly ran into Manfred the house steward.

"Young prince, my apologies," he quickly bowed in respect.

"It's alright, Manfred. No injury done."

Manfred had been house steward for years, which means that in all matters of the castle, he was the one not of noble blood that ensured the citadel ran smoothly. Long before Alexander remembered, there had always been Manfred. His long grey hair was always well kept, and he kept himself very clean. When the brothers and Sofia were younger, he shrieked at the children when they tracked in mud and dirt from playing in the gardens. He was a stickler for details, and everything in the citadel was very clean. He loathed Kiera and often followed her around quietly in vain attempts to discredit her and have her banished to the grounds. Past his obsession with Alexander's dog, he was very diligent and very faithful in his duties. No one entered the citadel without his knowledge, and no secrets left the royal apartments which at this time, was a necessity.

"Young sir, before you go, there is a small matter I need to discuss with you." Manfred bowed his head slightly, as if a deferential nod to Alexander's status, but not a true sign of respect.

"What is it?"

"Has the young Master decided on his tunic for this evening?" Manfred was quite keen on proper appearances and Alexander couldn't resist ruining his temperament.

"Tunic? Well yes...this one should be alright." Alexander looked down at his shirt and now he noticed a slight tear below his left shoulder. "Oh but if we could just sew this sleeve up, it should be very nice." He grinned at Manfred who quickly paled at the suggestion.

"Indeed, it is very becoming on you Master Alexander but perhaps we could consider something without a dark bodily fluid on it." Manfred reached his hand out to touch Alexander's tunic to which Alexander immediately took affront and swatted at his hand.

"Bodily what? What are you saying Manfred? Honestly, sometimes I don't understand-." Alexander stopped talking long enough to follow Manfred's gaze down the bottom of his shirt where several noticeable blood stains stood out from his tunic.

"Oh. I apologize for swatting at you Manfred. Whatever you recommend."

"Very good sir. I will send a page to your room with a tunic of the finest cloth. Maybe something in a blue perhaps, to match your sister's dress." Manfred responded with an amused air and Alexander was deeply irritated with Manfred's suggestion.

Should twins match colors for the feast, he asked himself. They were enough of a novelty. He loved his sister, she was a great companion and someone he devoted a great deal of trust in, but there were just sometimes that he wished he could be identified separately from her. Mattias's words from earlier that day had struck a chord within him. He was his own person and tonight was more than his ascent into manhood; tonight he wanted to display some independence and begin his own journey.

"I think, Manfred, that maybe something in a forest green...something different. Please." He didn't mean for his tone to sound like he begged, but it sounded like it anyway. He took his tunic off and shoved it in Manfred's chest. "You may want to burn that, it isn't clean." Alexander grinned slightly as Manfred held the tunic with his forefingers, and away from his body.

"The Queen preferred blue, but if you insist, I understand completely. I will let Her Majesty know." Manfred let out a grunt and shuffled off towards the royal sewing room.

Alexander let out a deep sigh. This was his mother's idea to match colors. He quietly tiptoed up the steps into the royal living area in order to avoid conversation with his family members. The steps led to a large common area where doorways led to each bedroom. Alexander was very close to his own room so he crept quietly across a beautiful burgundy tapestry rug. He was almost to his room when a voice startled him.

"Alexander!" The sharp voice of a woman froze him in his tracks.

"Yes mother?"

"Where have you been? It is two hours to nightfall. I'm hearing all sorts of troubling news. What is that?" She pointed at his shirtless torso.

"It's my chest."

"Do not speak to your mother with that tone. I know that it is your chest, I want to know why it lacks a shirt to cover it."

"I fell off my horse and ripped it," he lied. "I gave it to Manfred to dispose of it."

"Indeed?" she queried with her arms folded. Alexander loved his mother dearly and had no doubts that she already knew each part of the day's events. Of all of his immediate family he felt his mother, Queen Caroline of Alveus, was the most formidable of them all. Although of medium height and slender build, she commanded supreme authority and suffered no foolishness. She remained an advocate of traditional roles, took charge of hosting events and ensured the royal family maintained its place in society. She was also a political force to be reckoned with. Alexander noticed that ambassadors who had interacted with the royal family remarked frequently that the Queen's voice was always the last one heard and therefore her ears were the first ones sought.

It amazed Alexander that while the marriage between Caroline and Magnus had been arranged over thirty years ago, they still loved and respected each other.

"Alex, you would speak in a tone to your mother and then lie to her? Do you not think Edward would have told us straight away?"

"Mother, I-," she cut him off with a wave of the hand.

"Walk with me Alex." She walked back towards the stairs and went up through the winding stairs. Step by step, Alexander used the silence and reflected on the day's activities. He knew what his mother was going to say. He just needed an idea.

They finally reached the end of the stairs and Alexander and his mother stood on top of one of the citadel's towers that overlooked the eastern part of the kingdom. The sun had begun to set in the west and was disappearing behind the mountains. From their spot in the tower Alexander noticed the moon was closer to the land than normal and for the first time he noticed its dark shadows.

They observed the moon for a moment before Caroline spoke.

"Your father knows of your tussle with Mattias. He's enraged by it. How could you let your personal feelings with your brother spill out into an open conflict in front of the men? What if you rode out to battle tomorrow? Would their loyalties be divided? And you chose no bodyguards? None? Do you know the terrible position that you have put us in with the army? The generals are furious that their men were insulted. And to make matters worse....the townsfolk! Why Alexander, in God's name, would you be involved in a conflict in front of the peasantry!"

"I know mother, I'm sorry." Alexander tried to plead his case to his mother. He explained the insults, the derogatory remarks to Sofia, and reminded her that he didn't strike the first blow.

"Alexander, I am not saying the choice you made was wrong, but you must control your emotions. You know how much favor Mattias carries. Your father still holds him in high esteem for breaking the rebels in the east." His mother seemed less concerned with Mattias's behavior than with Alexander's.

"They were peasants."

"They were traitors!" Caroline was exasperated. "Regardless of whom they were in rank or stature they were traitors. They threatened the stability of the kingdom and our family and they were dealt with. Accept that.....Alexander, truth be told you would make a finer king than Mattias and a finer statue than Calimus, but Mattias has the experience of war under his belt. That is something I cannot do for you."

"Let me go then," Alexander pleaded. "Let me go my own way, and make my own way."

"I don't understand? You want to leave?" his mother asked. She was a little startled at the request. She took Alexander's face in her hands. "Alexander I love you, don't disappoint me like that. You belong here. This is your home."

"I'm nothing here. I'm disregarded by my own father. What is there for me? I don't want to become Calimus. At least talk to my father, let me travel the kingdom. What if I go to your people? Another court?" Alexander had long listened to stories that his mother told him in his youth of her people the Atreides. They were a kingdom of wayfarers who discovered and settled strange new worlds and that idea resonated strongly within Alexander.

"What about protection? You haven't a bodyguard."

"I'll find my own. Father Malachius can help with

training. Mother, please. Let me do something on my own."

"You're breaking my heart. All I've ever wanted was for you to grow up and be happy. I never knew you were so miserable." The queen's eyes moistened.

"I did not mean it that way. It's just for a short time. Two years at the most and I'll return, I swear, with a bodyguard and I'll apply myself to whatever duties my father or Edward will have me be a part of....perhaps I'll enter the abbey and apprentice under Father Malachius for induction into the order."

"I wish you would reconsider and just be content with what you have here." Caroline paused and looked into Alexander's sad blue eyes. Very well Alex, I will speak to your father on your behalf."

"Thank you so much. It means more to me than you will ever know." Alexander's heart beat rapidly for he had found a way to salvage his life.

CHAPTER VII

The final preparations for the Great Feast had been completed. Food and drink were brought in from the kitchen and placed on the tables in front of the guests. Alexander observed the colorful nobility as they approached the outer steps of the Great Hall from the perch of his small window. Several high ranking Army officers walked together with their wives, the clerics from the different parishes also arrived, and very finely dressed merchants from the richest merchant houses walked up the Palace steps along with their splendidly dressed wives and daughters. The seven barons and their retinue had a great procession through the city, while they were followed by several lesser lords and mayors.

Alexander enjoyed the spectacle from his window for the gathering of Alveus' finest stirred anxiousness within him as he paid special attention to several of the young ladies who had accompanied their parents to the feast. They were dressed in beautiful brightly colored robes and several of them had brightly colored flowers positioned carefully within their hair that matched their dresses.

Alexander heaved a sigh at the thought of having to marry one of them. As a member of the royal family every noble wanted to position their daughters to marry one of the four brothers. Edward was the obvious desire being heir to the throne but with a potential marriage with Lady Elsie in discussion, the focus turned to the remaining three brothers. Alexander's eye caught one, and he marveled at how similar she was to Angelica. His thoughts were suddenly consumed by the feelings he had for her; he had never before kissed a girl, and he yearned to learn what excitement it contained within Angelica regardless of her station.

His thoughts were interrupted by a knock at the door.

"In," Alexander responded absently.

Edward entered the room regally and Sofia dutifully followed. Sofia wore a beautiful blue dress that brought out the color in her eyes and her hair was pulled up with very fancy ribbons. Edward wore his finest tunic colored with a deep royal purple that signified his station.

"Well, you two look astonishing," Edward commented. He motioned towards Sofia. "Sofia may come away with a marriage proposal or three tonight. Look at this! Our own dear brother Alexander might actually steal away some of my attention!"

Alexander laughed. The thought of him stealing away any attention from the Great Prince Edward was an enjoyable one.

"It's not your night tonight Edward," Sofia reminded Edward gently as she straightened his collar.

"But I do agree with you Edward," Alexander chuckled. "Our sister looks decent enough when she decides to comb her hair."

"Yes and when I am the one dancing and you're not, you'll wish you combed that messy head of yours.

Honestly, it looks like snakes dancing." Sofia licked her palm and tried to straighten Alexander's unruly hair. He ducked and swatted her hands away from his head.

"I happen to like it messy!" Alexander sniffed the air that permeated from Sofia. "What is that smell? You smell like a field of flowers." Alexander tried to resist the urge to sneeze but lost control of his nose. He sneezed and exclaimed an objection to Sofia's perfume.

"This aroma is the latest in perfumes that Baron Iden brought for me in Brookehaven. You should thank me for wearing it for I assume you did not bathe before tonight did you?"

"I washed my face!" Alexander insisted hotly.

"Is your face the only place that dirties Alexander? What is that?" She pointed to his elbow which was smudged with dirt. Alexander stood for a moment and thought of a retort. He sneezed instead.

"Okay you two," Edward interjected. "Let's keep the banter to a minimum tonight. This is your ascent into adulthood."

"How can I ascend if my own sister plots treachery against my nose?" Alexander groaned and sneezed again. "He waved Sofia to move away from him and he stuck his head outside of the window for fresh air. He breathed in and out and smelled that which he truly loved; the scent of freedom.

"Oh Sofia," Edward continued, "I almost forgot. Mother is waiting for you. Don't worry; I'll see that Alex makes it down in one piece."

Sofia groaned because their mother would undoubtedly want to make sure everything was perfect. Once Sofia left the room, Edward turned to Alexander with a serious look on his face.

"The King wishes to speak with you."

Alexander sighed but kept his eyes on the horizon, for it was not a conversation he looked forward to having.

"Alexander, there were questions that I had to answer. When the Prince comes home with no bodyguard as is required by our customs, and you know as well as I do the general was the first one in line behind me….what do you expect me to say?"

"I know. I wasn't thinking of the consequences. It is my responsibility for having put you in this position." Alexander pulled his head back inside his room and looked at his brother who appeared genuinely sorry for having reported to their father.

The brothers walked down the stairs to the room behind the Great Dining Hall where they found their father as he conferred last minute instructions with Manfred. Manfred walked away nodding so that the King turned his full attention to Alexander.

When Alexander was much younger he always looked up at his father. He took a moment and assessed his father for an honest moment. Although at six foot four inches Alexander still physically looked up at him their strained relationship made Magnus a less imposing figure. The advanced years had taken its toll on his figure and he often hunched over.

His father's hair was no longer blonde but had whitened in color and his once proud frame now required support and he walked with a staff so that he straightened out the haunch his back had developed. Regardless of how his physical condition appeared, he was very much in control of his kingdom although he had turned over certain parts of the administration to Edward. It was only a matter of time before Edward was named Co-Regent at which time the King was expected to relinquish all administrative control of the kingdom. The Co-Regent had the voice of the

King, and enacted all domestic laws. Alexander embraced the future with a sigh of relief because he saw hope and progress with Edward as King.

And now here he stood in front of the battle hardened, highly respected and revered King of Kings, and he braced himself for his father's disappointment.

"There are many things I want to say to you, Alexander. Many things you need to hear from me. However the stings of my words have been softened because of what your brother has informed me. First and foremost, this contention between yourself and Mattias needs to be resolved."

"Yes, your Majesty," were the only words Alexander had on his lips.

Magnus closed his eyes and tipped his head back, as if he thought the words before he uttered them.

"I have long hoped that the academic pursuits and energy that you have dedicated yourself to would have brought you success by now. It is disappointing that you haven't committed to anything yet. I would be satisfied if you were to set yourself up to be a help to your brother. And I am deeply disappointed to hear of you wanting to join the clergy." King Magnus scoffed at his own words. "What a ridiculous notion that would be."

Alexander had been privy to several of his father's conflicts with the church during his long reign. Questions of immorality and corruption within his own progeny went unanswered and infuriated the Great King that someone dared cast suspicion on his family. His father often blustered that it was Divine Right that gave him his power, and that the church had no right to question him, for he was above such questioning. Alexander found himself in the middle of these conflicts for Father Malachius was compelled by the order to call into question any immorality that existed.

'Now your mother says that you want to leave? You want to put yourself at the mercy of thieves and barbarians?"

"No, your Majesty. My idea is to travel the kingdom and find good men that would be loyal and courageous. I believe that I can find men in fields better suited to be my bodyguard than the soldiers we have now." Alexander answered his father honestly and directly. He had no other way to answer him.

"This is utter nonsense. I can't believe what I'm hearing. You would rather be surrounded by peasants? Is this what your studies have taught you? Who would believe that a peasant could be trained to be a soldier? Impossible, Ridiculous notions."

"But father"

Magnus refused to let him answer. "Your mother has already come to me on the matter. I will give you some money for what you need. I will allow you provisions....but I will not afford you the protection of my realm. That means if you are captured and held for ransom by any band of thieves or barbarians I will not respond. You do this against my wishes.....Do we have an understanding?"

Alexander agreed. Being the King's youngest son presented more difficulties than anyone could ever know. You are bound to greatness, but never allowed to touch it.

Queen Caroline approached them with Manfred behind her. She beamed with excitement and Alexander quickly asked Manfred a question about the servants.

"Manfred," Alexander said curiously, "I couldn't help but notice but the maidservant Angelica did not deliver my tunic tonight. Is she in good health?"

"The young lady disappeared earlier today,"

Manfred responded. "I am quite upset, for there were many things left undone for the feast."

"What do you mean she left?" Alexander responded. His heart sank deep into chest.

"Gone, young sir," Manfred said flatly. "No longer in the castle's employ. Good riddance too, for she was melancholic all day with tears in her eyes."

Manfred moved on to join the conversation between the King and Queen and Alexander's heart continued to sink a little further. She left him, he thought. He faulted himself for her leaving; he should never have said anything about his feelings. Sofia noticed his frown and was about to question him, when Queen Caroline took command of the proceeding.

"Good, we are all here. For heaven's sake Sofia, stop fussing with your hair. Calimus, straighten up. Mattias, you will try to be cordial tonight won't you? Maybe a smile? Yes, that's something. My King, are you ready for your subjects?"

"Yes, my Queen," Magnus replied. He gave her a soft kiss on her cheek. "Once again, you have outdone yourself."

"My liege," Manfred interrupted. "The guests are ready for you. Shall I announce?"

"Yes Manfred."

Manfred bowed his grey head and exited through the small door to the Dining Hall. The noise of the Hall temporarily quieted.

"Ladies and gentlemen. Honored guests. May I present your hosts for this evening? Prince Alexander Wolfield, Princess Sofia Wolfield, Prince Calimus Wolfield."

At the sounds of their names the three siblings walked through the door. There was polite applause for each one of them as they bowed toward their guests and made their way to the royal table.

Alexander took the opportunity and glanced around the Great Hall. Large tapestries had been hung on the walls and each fabric told the story of a significant moment in Alvean history. There were nine of them and each one represented a story for one of the great Kings of Alveus.

Great oak tables were arranged in columns and joined together. Each table was filled with food and drink. Each guest stood at their place in honor of their hosts. Finally, Alexander's eyes fell upon the skin of four separate animals that had been placed in front of the royal table. A magnificent bearskin lay directly in front of his father's place at the table. A skinned mane-less lion lay directly in front of Edward's place and panther and boar lay in front of Mattias and Calimus. This strategic placement of these animals with jaws open was meant to reinforce the authority that the Alveun royalty assumed.

The royal table was also set with all manner of food and drink. Alexander hungrily looked over the meats and he slid his hand slyly towards a few grapes. He was ready to eat, ceremony be damned. One glance at Calimus told him that Calimus was fixated on a nearby tankard of ale. As the three siblings impatiently stood behind their chairs, Manfred continued with his formalities.

"Prince Mattias Wolfield." Alexander noticed several of the generals clapped with more effort for Mattias than their crusty old personalities would generally let them.

"Crown Prince Edward Theodosius Wolfield." A cheerful noise surged through the Great Hall. The people looked forward to a peaceful royal succession. This would be a rare occasion in a kingdom's history where no blood needed to be spilt over the King's successor and they enjoyed this fortunate moment in their history with a sigh of relief.

"Their royal Majesties. Queen Caroline du Plessis Wolfield and His Royal Highness, the King of all Kings, High King Magnus Wolfield the Ninth."

As tradition stated, when the king and queen were announced, everyone with hearing stood immediately to honor the rulers. Everyone in the hall, including the royal family stood and raised an outstretched hand.

"To the King," they toasted and cheered King Magnus while they drank the entire glass. King Magnus smiled and stood in front of his massive oak chair to address the Great Hall.

"I thank you, friends and countrymen, for being here tonight. A King is fortunate enough with loyal subjects but God," he paused here to nod at Father Malachius, "Has blessed me with a bountiful family. It is for that reason we celebrate. Many congratulations to Alexander and my beloved daughter Sofia for their passage from children to adulthood. Make merry my friends. Tonight the crown knows no expense."

The crowd generously cheered King Magnus as he sat down in his throne and soon everyone had been seated and began to eat. The Great Hall bustled with activity as servants ran from the Hall to the Kitchen, as they fetched wine and meat at a rapid pace. The clergy, notoriously somber at banquets, seemed to be smiling and enjoying themselves. At another table sat some high ranking army officers, and Alexander could make out the distinguished head of General Henri Valmont. Henri Valmont was a career army officer, having risen through the ranks since being a regular foot soldier.

Alexander loved the early stories about his father, and General Valmont was a frequent character in them. King Magnus and Henri fought together when they were younger and as it was said, were two of the finest horse soldiers in the land. He advanced well with age, but his position as General played more of a political role instead of a military one. There hadn't been a war other than a brief peasant's rebellion in over twenty five years so a title of General a ceremonial post, one that carried a great deal of weight with young ladies, but no one else seemed to care. None that is, except for Mattias. Mattias regularly held counsel and included the venerable General. Alexander would have easily disregarded this as a vain attempt to procure support should succession prove to be an issue, but with Mattias there was no trivial movement.

At another table was a group of oddly dressed nobleman. They wore long flowing robes and the older men at the table fashioned medium well-kept beards. It was easy to distinguish them as foreigners because very few people in the kingdom grew a beard.

The remainder of the guests included various rich merchants and nobles from the towns and villages within the king's borders. Alexander had no special liking for any of the nobles. Stories from the towns included allegations of corruption, waste, and vice. One noble in particular had a predominantly bad reputation of being his town's father. As the rumors went, he had sired more bastards than a single goat in a herd of lonely sheep. Father Malachius was always quick to point out that a peasant revolt rarely started because of their disdain for the King. It had to do with the nobles with whom they interact constantly.

Alexander decided to try to enjoy the feast, although the talk with his father had already ruined his night. He decided to attack the roasted chicken in front of him....and what was that? There was some jerky hidden under it. God bless you Sara, you are a fine woman, he thought to himself.

"Pssst." Sofia hissed. "Look! Mother arranged for minstrels and jugglers. Oh! I love jugglers. I wonder if they'll do the flaming swords bit. I wish I could do flaming swords."

Sofia rambled and talked incessantly about the entertainment. She tended to do that when she was excited.

"Sofia?" Alexander asked.

"Yes?"

"Those men with the robes. Where are they from?" Alexander observed the table intently.

"They're from the Kingdom of the Western Isles. That's Prince Youssef and his advisors. Why do you ask?" Her cheeks reddened slightly as one man returned her gaze.

"No reason." In truth, she had a reason. This Prince Youssef continually looked towards his side of the table, more than likely at his sister. He decided immediately that he did not like this foreigner.

The minstrels played skillfully, and the entire Hall focused on the entertainment of the evening. The jugglers and acrobats performed flawlessly, and elicited excited roars from the audience. At certain times between performances, an honored guest visited the Royal Table, and bestowed a gift upon Alexander and Sofia. With each present Sofia grew more and more excited to the point of being insufferable. Alexander was content with his suit of armor that was given to him earlier that day, and the thoughts of Angelica threatened to rob him of the expected gratefulness of receiving these gifts.

The barons of the seven great towns, the lords of the four fiefdoms, the generals, merchants, and other honored guests were treated lavishly, and intermingled with each other to discuss the events of the day. The events usually turned into a discussion on finances, as currency ruled Alveus, and an unexpected population growth was promising new farms and villages would spring up within a few years. The visiting dignitaries from other lands watched and listened, hoping to exploit what secrets the Alveuns had for their riches.

Alexander watched the foreigner Prince Youssef approach the table. The closer he approached the table the redder Sofia became. His swarthy looks provided an air of mystery about him. (All Western Isles men were sailors, and as such spent much time in the sun.) He had a beautiful pendant around his neck, with a fiery red ruby in its center. The beauty of the jewel distracted, but Alexander didn't think that Sofia noticed the jewel at all.

"Prince Alexander, Princess Sofia. I am Prince Youssef from the Kingdom of the Western Isles. I am the crown prince and heir to my father's throne. I salute you on this happy day and hope many blessings will rain down on you."

He spoke with a heavy yet understandable accent and Alexander read between the lines and took the initiative of conversation.

"Well, thank you, Prince Youssef," he said dismissively. "We will remember your kindness."

"And I have a gift for her young highness, the Princess." He removed the pendant from his neck and placed it in Sofia's hand. Her eyes widened. She was obviously smitten and desperate to say some words.

"My sister who is short of words on this day, thanks you for your gift, and will treasure it upon your return to your own house." Alexander hoped the Prince would understand the underlying meaning to his diplomatic entreats.

"Of course," Prince Youssef said. "Forgive me being forward. In my country we have a great dance in celebration of such an occasion. Is that a custom here?"

"Yes!" Sofia blurted. "I mean, after the feasting we do have a great dance."

"Would you do me the honor of a dance?"

Sofia hesitated before an answer as to avoid blurting out another sentence. Alexander seized the moment.

"I'm afraid she's committed to a dance with me." He waved his hand. "Birthdays." His tone was apologetic, but Alexander found it difficult to hide his disdain.

"Of course perhaps after?" He was persistent in his tone.

"No, see…we have to dance together eighteen times. One dance for every year."

"Oh," the prince was puzzled. "That is a strange custom."

"What can you do?" Alexander shrugged his shoulders in mock dismay. The prince bowed at Sofia and walked away with an injured air.

"What are you doing?" Sofia hissed. "I cannot believe that. How dare you. A prince asked me to dance. I have every right to answer the question myself."

"I didn't like him," Alexander remarked matter-of-factly.

"It's not for you to make that decision. Have you completely missed the reason for this feast? It is about us turning into adults so stop treating me as if I am a child! I will dance with whomever I please!" Sofia stood up for a moment if to leave but stopped as the minstrels simultaneously silenced their instruments and the jugglers stopped performing. Manfred stood next to the minstrels, held his hands up in the air, and signified he had an announcement to make.

"Ladies and Gentlemen, your King would have you hear his words." The entire audience shifted their gaze to the King who gingerly stood to address the Great Hall.

Sofia quickly sat down.

"My friends. I have ruled for thirty years but I am now starting to feel my age. My days are long, but my nights are becoming longer. The management of a large kingdom such as ours needs the strong hands of a young man. As you know, Edward has been my heir since he was eighteen years old. He has shown himself to be a virtuous prince and a respected leader. I would like to announce that Edward will be Prince Regent, having all powers of the King, effective immediately. From here on he will be known as Magnus the tenth."

The Great Hall burst into thunderous applause. Almost everyone stood and cheered at this announcement except for Alexander and Mattias. Mattias looked as though someone had snatched away his last meal, but Alexander cared little about Mattias's sour expression. Once again, his father had completely trivialized any special event that was associated with Alexander. Maybe it didn't matter; maybe it would just speed up his decision to leave. He had thought about going on his journey in a month, but maybe this would hasten his decision to leave. Tomorrow. That's it. He'll say his goodbyes and ride off. Alexander decided he was in need of fresh air. He got up to leave but felt his sister's hand on his shoulder.

"Don't go," she whispered.

"I can't be in here anymore. Again, on my birthday. OUR birthday," he hissed. His feelings were hurt and he was tired of being marginalized.

"No, I mean don't GO." It was clear that Sofia knew about his journey. "Or take me with you."

"Father would never forgive me if anything happened to you. I am riding out without his blessing or his protection."

"Don't do this Alex," she pleaded. "I couldn't bear

to hear of anything happening to you."

Alex chuckled sadly.

"That's the whole point isn't it? Nothing's going to happen because no one cares about me. I have to do this Sofia. I have to find my own way."

She gave him a soft hug.

"Please send me news from time to time to let me know you're in good health."

"I will. And promise me you'll stay away from the tall, dark, and handsome beast over there."

"I promise not to marry without you in attendance."

"Nag!" Alexander's responded playfully. He grinned while he said it.

"Child," she mocked in response and stuck her tongue out at him.

Alexander smiled and started across the great hall towards the door. Everyone was involved with the entertainment or surrounding Edward to express their loyalties. He moved through the crowd, unnoticed.

But behind a pillar, someone noticed him. A very young girl wearing a beautiful green dress stepped in front of him. Her hair was the color of autumn leaves and its length fell below her shoulders. Her slender frame made it easier for Alexander to move around her before he realized that she intentionally blocked him from carrying on.

"I'm sorry, my prince," she said breathlessly curtsying in front of him. "Please forgive your servant's clumsiness."

He took her hand and raised her to a standing level with him.

"You're forgiven," Alexander smiled politely and again attempted to move past her.

"My lord?" She walked with him and kept his pace. He stopped walking so he would not be perceived as rude.

"Yes?" he replied impatiently, "What do you need from me?"

"Begging your pardon Prince Alexander. I am Lady Emma from the house of King Jarius. My father is Count Gustav of the Northern Islands. I hoped that you might remember me. I knew you some years ago. You visited our ports several times."

Alexander scrutinized every freckle on her face. He remembered back to his apprenticeship with the merchants. He thought long and hard about every detail but no details of his journey included freckles. He felt uncomfortable as he began to formulate excuses of why he held no memory of her.

The awkward silence lasted longer than Alexander meant it to last. Emma also recognized the awkwardness and spoke quickly.

"My apologies Prince Alexander. How could you know me? We were never formally introduced. I used to sneak away to the docks when I learned of your visits. I hoped to meet you but my shyness prevented me." Her face grew redder with embarrassment. Even Alexander felt sympathetic towards her plight, no matter how disturbed this revelation made him.

"Well," he began as he searched for kind words, "I regret....us not being formally introduced. I welcome the opportunity to meet others who live on my father's kingdoms horizon. It was very nice to meet you. I hope you are enjoying our kingdom's hospitality." Alexander once again moved to walk around her, but Emma persisted and stayed in the prince's path.

"I chose to wear a dress of forest green as I heard that was your favorite color. I am happy to see that we are matched." Alexander's lack of response created an awkward moment between the two.

"Green is a great color; it is the color of life and sustenance. If I may say, you look like the fields of grass." He meant it as a compliment, but failed miserably.

"I look like grass?" Emma's face was twisted in confusion, but she continued on, undaunted, "I was hoping Prince, and if I am not being too bold....I would be honored if I may dance with the Prince tonight."

She is persistent, Alexander thought to himself. He felt badly, but he had no time for dancing. He could leave the castle within an hour if he hurried.

"Lady Emma," he said consolingly. "Your beauty is unsurpassed in this Hall. I regret to say that I am feeling ill this evening and I am retiring for the night. Perhaps another time if you would be so gracious?"

She looked crestfallen. Her eyes, so excited and full of life before, dimmed.

"I am sorry to hear that Prince Alexander. Please, forgive my persistence. Another time then?" With that she moved back to the crowd and to an older man who by all accounts looked to be her father. Once again, Alexander turned to leave, only to find himself face to face with Edward.

"Oh!" Alexander said, startled. Would he have to receive permission from everyone to leave including the peasantry?

"Alex....I'm sorry. I had no idea..." Edward stumbled through his words. He nervously ran his hands through his perfect hair. Alexander assumed his brother blamed himself for him leaving.

"It's not you Edward. I know it's not you. All my life I've been a prince with absolutely no importance. I refuse to turn out like Calimus and just waste away." They both looked back at Calimus who, cup in hand, looked absolutely miserable. "I need to find my own way.

Whatever fate or destiny has chosen for me is what I need. And if they have chosen me for absolutely nothing, than I swear upon the King that I will make something of myself."

Edward nodded his head. He heard the earnestness that was within Alexander.

"Alright, but do me one favor. If anything happens. If you're injured, or kidnapped, or starving, send word to me, and only me, and I will send help."

Alexander shook his head no.

"I can't do that Edward. This is my journey. If it's my end, then so be it."

"Take this then." Edward pressed a large sack of coins into his hand. "This is my gift to you on this day. I heard from mother that you were leaving. I figured you'd probably go tonight. Zeus is saddled and ready to go."

Alexander smiled for he was happy that Edward understood his plight and wasn't going to stand in his way.

"One last thing," Edward added. "There are several pouches of jerky in the saddle bags. I had Sara make them special for you. She wanted me to let you know that its deer jerky."

Alexander and Edward shared a brief hug and slapped each other's back twice. Edward placed his hand on his brother's shoulder, sighed, and walked away.

Alexander turned and continued to the door where he spied Father Malachius who seemed to be stationed there waiting for him.

"Are you going to stop me too, Father?" Alexander asked.

Father Malachius shook his head no.

"I think you've made an excellent decision Alexander." He reached forward and grabbed Alexander's hand. Alexander felt a small bag of coins being forced into his hands. Father Malachius raised his other hand. "A small token from the church for your years of patronage. And also, might I add two things. One, return to your room, there you will find your armor. Two, you might find what you're looking for in the northern forests. I would suggest reacquainting yourself with old friends. You may very well find what you're looking for."

"Isn't the Northern Forests also the hiding place of thieves and marauders?" Alexander was puzzled for this put him in the danger his father had ordered him to avoid.

"If you remember all of your training, you'll be more than up to the task. I have two more things for you," Father Malachius said and he produced a wafer of bread, and a small goblet. "Please kneel, Alexander, for the sacrament."

Alexander obeyed and knelt on the ground with his head bowed. Father Malachius spoke the Eucharist and gave Alexander the wafer. Alexander chewed it thoughtfully and wished to be absolved of all of his wrong doings.

"This cup is the blood of Christ," Malachius continued. "His blood will keep you from harm."

Alexander sipped from the goblet and the warm wine raced down his throat. He wished for something different to be in his path. He wanted more than anything to find what he was searching for. Father Malachius motioned the sign of the cross and Alexander stood up.

"Goodbye my son and Godspeed to you." Father Malachius smiled enigmatically and returned to the gaiety. The tables were being moved to make room for dancing and over the servants he watched as Sofia entered into a conversation with Prince Youssef. Alexander's eyes met Sofia's, and even at a distance he could tell that she had been crying. She gave him a brave smile and a slight wave. He nodded back to her and felt a brief twinge of guilt for not having taken her with him. His mother stood behind Sofia and she also gave a slight wave. Her face was torn with emotion, but ever the strong Queen, she was able to manage her emotions more effectively than Sofia.

His brothers were huddled in a corner. Mattias had an evil grin on his face. Doubtless he was happy to be rid of Alexander. Calimus looked morose and Alexander wondered if he should have invited Calimus along. No, it was difficult enough for himself to procure the Great King's approval. The King would never allow both of them to wander off. That further reinforced Alexander's feelings of unimportance. He felt a pair of eyes staring at him and he glanced to the right and caught Lady Emma looking his way. Her eyes widened as they made eye contact and she quickly looked away.

He took a deep breath, straightened up and turned his back on the Hall. He didn't know how long it would be before he saw his family again. He made his way to his room to quickly collect up the armor and whatever weapons he found. As he entered and collected his armor, he noticed a white flower had been placed on his bed. It was a lily, the flower he had given to Angelica. He wondered for a moment about her, why she fled the city, and why this flower had been left.

Had his father found out, and removed her? Or did she leave on her own free will? Where would she go? He asked himself. Alexander continued collecting weapons as he moved through the rooms. He took two swords, a longbow, a quiver of arrows, and a dagger that he placed in his belt. He exited the Palace through the back entry and made his way to the Royal Stables.

He found Zeus ready for the journey, so he mounted him and remembered he forgot someone important.

"Keira!" he shouted. Nothing happened, so he

whistled loudly.

Keira barked and ran towards him with her tongue hanging carelessly out of her mouth. Even with a faint torchlight burning he could make out her smile.

"Keira! Ready to explore the horizon?" She wagged her tail in agreement. "Come Keira!"

Alexander wheeled Zeus around and commanded him in the direction of the northern gate. Keira ran alongside the horse and barked excitedly. When he approached the gate he was halted by its guards.

"Halt! Who goes there?"

"It is I, Prince Alexander, requesting opening of the gate." His voice boomed with command and confidence surged through his veins. The challenge of finding himself lay in front of him.

The soldier swung a torch in his direction so that he could see his face clearly. Satisfied, the soldier walked to the gate.

"Open the gate for the Prince!"

"Aye Captain," shouted the men as they lifted the wooden bar from the gate.

The gate was now open and there was no turning back. Alexander didn't stop to think of anything behind him. He dug his spurs into the horse and galloped away from the city as quickly as possible with Keira in close pursuit.

CHAPTER VIII

It took Alexander two days to reach the northern towns. He took advantage of the solitude and reflected on Father Malachius's suggestion to enter the Northern Forests. The Northern Forests was the largest forest in Alveus for it spanned a minimum of thirty miles. It was here that the border of Alveus had been established by Alexander's father some thirty years ago. While the Northern Forests were still considered part of the Alveun kingdom, very few of the kingdom's inhabitants dared to venture into it, and even fewer went past it. The forest was located a mere ten miles from the walls of Edgebrooke, but the citizens of that fair city swore that the Forest was haunted by the evil and the dead. If any livestock strayed away from its herd and into the forest, its owner ceased trying to retrieve it, and returned home. Only the foolhardy ventured into the forest, and very few lived to tell about it.

Five miles west from the town Edgebrooke and closer to the forest was the village of Greystone. It was considerably smaller than Edgebrooke and instead of being protected by a stone wall, it was surrounded by a wooden palisade. This kept them safe for the most part from any unfortunate incidents that occurred. It was a rough mining community which produced many of the metals that were eventually transported to Middlebrooke and refined in their smiths.

Alexander picked the path to Greystone for he planned his travels to be accomplished in anonymity, and decided to avoid the major cities where he would be recognized. Not being recognized avoided delays, suspicion, and best of all, trouble. Perhaps, he thought, the villagers of Greystone would be more inclined to guide him through the Forest than the nobles in Middlebrooke.

The stories that came from these villages couldn't possibly be true. He had heard of a band of thieves who used all manner of tricks to strike fear into the northerners. They were the ones you had to watch out for. If Alexander had one unlucky encounter, he could end up shirtless and horseless in a haunted forest.

Alexander smiled at his new fortune. Any fate was better than the mundane life he faced behind the walls of Middlebrooke.

Alexander arrived at the village of Greystone on the evening of the second day of his travels. He briefly halted at the top of a hill outside of the small village. He observed from atop Zeus as several villagers loaded bags into a horse cart. Alexander thought nothing from the ordinary and that they loaded goods to take to Edgebrooke. Then something unexpected occurred. A woman stumbled and spilled the contents of a bag onto the ground. Alexander was too far away to see what she spilled, but its weight suggested some sort of heavy metals. The old peasant quickly knelt down and hurriedly picked the contents off of the ground and shoved them back into the bag. A pudgy armed man who stood nearby saw this and walked towards her. Without so much of a warning, he struck her in the head with his fist.

Alexander was mortified at this behavior. He had never seen this type of cruelty displayed. The peasant crumpled to the ground in agony, but continued to clean the mess that she had made and still managed to get it onto the cart.

Alexander was enraged at the treatment of this old peasant. He knew a cooler head needed to prevail and he did not want anyone to know his identity so he quickly swung a cloak over his shoulders and concealed the armor he wore by wrapping the cloak around his body. He slowly nudged Zeus in the direction of the village. Zeus whinnied and clopped in that direction.

His approach did not go unnoticed. The cruel taskmaster heard Zeus's whinny and addressed the Prince as he reached the entrance of the village.

"Here now. State your business," he ordered. He put his right hand down on his sword as if he dared Alexander to challenge him.

Alexander sorely wanted to pick up the challenge. By the way of his sloppy appearance, Alexander deduced he was nothing more than a common thug. More than likely, not part of a thieves' guild, but hired by someone to do his bidding. An uneasy silence passed but in the corner of his eye, Alexander saw something he did not see before. Five other armed men, dressed much like this one, advanced very slowly from beneath an awning.

Alexander smiled at the thug in an attempt to defuse the situation.

"Well, I'll tell you my business. I am tired!" he proclaimed excitedly. "I have been walking horse and dog through this beautiful country of yours. For five days I have slept on a blanket on the ground under the stars. I have eaten more dried meat than I care to remember. I am in need of a soft bed and some ale. And maybe something more, eh?" he winked at the guard. "Oh, but I am starving."

He pulled out a piece of jerky and bit into it. He looked at the guard whose dirty face was bewildered.

"Would you like a piece?" Alexander asked in mid chew.

"Aye." The thug took a piece and slowly chewed it. "So, where you from stranger? And what's with all those swords?" He eyed Alexander suspiciously.

Alexander noticed the suspicious tone and happily bantered on.

"I am from Count.....Gustav's lands in the northern islands. I was a sailor until two weeks ago when I quit. As for my swords....I have heard you have bandits in these lands and that your forests are haunted. I came to see myself."

"You want to go into the forests? Be our guest, friend. Stories are true. No one comes out from the forests, but do what you will then. Take in the scenery." He turned to a similarly dressed man with a very large belly. "Are we ready then? Alright let's be off." He turned back to Alexander. "Good night to you then, and safe travels."

Alexander nodded nonchalantly and watched cautiously to make sure all the men left the village. When they left his sight, he nudged Zeus onward in hopes of finding lodging. Alexander's impatience grew after he rode up and down paths for an hour without seeing any signs that denoted a haven of rest for him or his weary beast. He knew the villagers watched him down every path and felt as if he was being followed. They were obviously suspicious of strangers, so he needed to get inside quickly. He decided the best thing to do was force the issue, so he dismounted Zeus and walked over to the nearest villager. The villager was a young girl, and couldn't have been older than eight. She sat quietly and drew a circle in the dirt with a small pointed stick. Alexander thought that the easiest information could be drawn from the youngest.

"Good evening, little Princess. I am in need of lodging and food. Do you know where the tavern is? Or even a stable for my horse for the night?" Alexander smiled at the little girl for effect and hoped that his charm might win her approval.

The girl brushed the curls out of her face, looked up at him, and then resumed drawing in the dirt. She didn't say a word.

"Excuse me? Do you know," he paused for effect and widened his smile, "where the stable is?"

"I heard you the first time." She refused to look directly at him and looked to where a tall man stood and watched their conversation. "I'm not allowed to talk to strangers."

"A good idea, too," Alexander agreed as he followed her gaze. "Perhaps you could just point to it?" He tried to sound patient but felt as though he rushed his request.

"I could," she said and looked at him. "If I had something in my hand." She held her hand out to him expectantly.

"I see. Perhaps something shiny?"

"I think that will be fine."

"Very well, you are a sharp one aren't you?" He reached into a small moneybag that hung on his belt and produced a coin. He left Zeus's side and placed the gold coin firmly in her hand. "Does this help?"

"Yes." She began to draw an arrow that pointed behind Alexander. "That building's the tavern. The other one's the stable." The arrow pointed at two buildings directly across from Alexander.

Alexander sighed for he must have gone past the stables three times. How did he miss it?

"Thank you for your kindness to a stranger, little

lady." He whistled for Keira who whined loudly but followed him. She was exhausted from the long trip for she had never traveled this far before. Alexander wondered if maybe he should have left Keira with Sofia, but the need for a loyal friend in strange surroundings was desperate.

At the stables he left Zeus and lectured the stable boy explicit directions on how to take care of such a fine beast. The stable boy seemed uninterested in Alexander's requests, so Alexander provided food to his own horse and removed the saddle from Zeus's back. When he finished, he gave the stable boy an angry look and headed to the tavern with Keira. It was a surprisingly quiet place. Calimus had told stories that a tavern was a wild place with thieves and questionable characters and a place where fights were commonplace. The only question this tavern served was in its décor. Everything in this tavern was rough and liable to leave a scar. The benches were splintering, the tables were old and rotted, and there were lots of brown dirt. The dirt was everywhere, and there was nothing that didn't have a dirty and used appearance.

It took a moment before the tavern owner and his wife realized they had a guest. After a moment of conversation, Alexander realized that the only choice he had for food was stew, but for an added coin the innkeeper managed to procure some additional raw meat for Keira. She laid on the floor, unconcerned with its filth, and contentedly gnawed at her meal.

Before he sat down, Alexander brushed most of the dirt off a bench. With the stew that was served, he spotted meat and a few potatoes in his stew. He was overjoyed at the sight of a carrot, but upon further inspection determined it was better not to eat it. At least the pint of whatever the tavern owner gave him to drink was worth bringing home. It was deliciously light and frothy, and it left a warm feeling in his stomach. These feelings of satisfaction distracted him from the three men who entered the tavern and approached him.

Alexander ignored them until they sat down at the same table directly in front of him. He recognized the bigger one from the paths he continued to ride in the village. The stranger seemed to be on every other path and was the one who the little girl glanced at. The other two looked familiar, but he couldn't quite place them. With the reddishness of the hair, Alexander assumed the two men were brothers. The larger of the men addressed Alexander first.

"Where you from? You from Edgebrooke?" he demanded. Alexander looked up from his stew and briefly took in the man's countenance. He looked slightly older than Alexander and more about Mattias's age. He was not bald, but the lack of hair on his head distracted from the rest of his appearance. He wore a shirt stained with the lands soil while the dirt and cracks on his hand caused Alexander to believe that he and his red-haired friends were nothing more than miners, and could be disregarded easily.

"I am merely a stranger passing through your lands. I heard it was beautiful this time of year." He dipped a piece of bread into his stew and took a bite.

"You're LYING!" The stranger pounded his fist on the table. "That stallion of yours gives it away, friend. Anyone who rides a horse like that is either well off or has killed the man that rode it. Which one are you?"

Alexander took a small swig of his ale, placed his glass down and patiently looked at the three men who now sat directly in front of him. With the temperament that was being displayed and the cracked skin on his knuckles, Alexander figured the man to be a brawler. The twins seemed influenced to do whatever the talkative one told them to do. It also looked like they enjoyed a good fight and with matching black eyes, probably fought each other as much as they fought with others. They sat there for a brief moment and waited for an answer, but Alexander sopped up more stew with his bread, and then ate it.

"Well?" The talkative one became antsy.

"Well then," Alexander replied with irritation in his voice. "Let's say I'm well off. Is this a robbery? Should I hand you my one hundred gold coins now?"

"You don't have any coins. You're just a boy," he smirked at the last part.

"I'm a man," Alexander replied firmly. "I'll have a go at you if that's what you are looking for."

"I just want the truth." The man sat up straight and crossed his huge forearms in front of him.

"I told you the truth." Alexander mimicked his movement and crossed his arms as well and dared the man to challenge what he said.

"No. Let's talk why you look the spitting image of a boy that worked for me father some eight years ago. I don't know what you're doing here..."and he hushed his voice..."Prince. But whatever it is can't be good for this village. So why don't you keep riding at daybreak?"

A flood of memories washed away any of the haze the ale had left.

"Wait a minute," Alexander said. He went deep into his memories. He had been in this town before, of course, how did he miss that? The children that he played with once...one of them was named..."Jack?" He said with astonishment. "If you're Jack, then you two....Fergus? Chauncey? Is it really you?"

Jack smiled. "It is you, Alexander! I knew it! I told you Fergus!" He turned and slapped Fergus on the shoulder.

"Kevin! Rounds of your finest for our friend here!" Jack slammed a few coins down on the table. "What are you doing in Greystone? It's a long way from your palace 'Prince' Alexander?"

"If it's all the same to you, I'm disguising my identity for the time being. Please, just call me Alex."

Alex understood that he'd have to explain the entire story start to finish or these three would never let him leave. After four rounds of ale, he had sufficiently regaled them with the story of his father, brothers, and the minor quest he was on. All three agreed that Alex had lost all sense of reason for even talking about going into the forest. But after two more rounds of strong drink, Chauncey and Fergus offered to guide Alex into the forest. They both boasted how they often crept into the forest to appropriate "lost" livestock.

Jack in turn caught Alex up on the events of his family. After Alex left, more villagers turned to Edgebrooke for most of their smith-work. Jack's father eventually moved into Greystone with them, and although he still retained knowledge of smithing, he had worked in the mines for the last few years.

Jack became very emotional when he talked about his father's passing. They kept his shop open and from time to time still did some work there, but there was nothing to do except work in the mines. Chauncey and Fergus were still young enough to hold a dream of moving to the city and apprenticing themselves to one of the larger smiths in hope of one day opening a shop of their own.

Alexander remembered the events from earlier and was desperate to know more.

"Jack, who were those men with the wagon?"

"Those men? Hmph. Those men were the tax collectors." The three villagers had the bitterest expressions on their face.

"Tax collectors from whom? Who collects taxes in a wagon? What are they collecting?" Alexander fired questions at them rapidly.

"What do you mean from whom? They're from the crown. Everyone knows that. They go to all the villages in this area." Jack nervously shifted in his chair but caught Alexander's glare for his insinuation. "They're bad characters. If they don't work for the Crown then fine, they don't work for the Crown. They work for someone and the Crown isn't doing anything about it....all of our people are miserable. We've barely got anything to make ends meet. We hide our coins and hope their greed does not go any further."

"How long has this been happening?"

"It doesn't matter, it's not your fight," Jack said quietly and stood up. "Good night Alex."

Jack left the three men to contemplate his departure. Alexander turned his attention to Chauncey and Fergus. He knew they'd be more inclined to talk and he was right. Chauncey started talking as soon as Jack was no longer in sight.

"So, these men come to our town three years ago, claiming they were collecting taxes for the Crown. Well the town throws them out, see? So they come back with soldiers. Soldiers turn the town upside down, smashing stuff, burning a building here and there and hung....what was his name?"

"Donald," Fergus said as he snuck a piece of Alexander's bread into his mouth.

"Right. Hung the mayor in front of everyone and left him there for a month. That's a pretty bad sight when the birds get done with you, see? After that, everyone loads the wagon. And no disrespect to you Prince, but if anyone in this town thought you were one of them, you'd be dead before morning." Chauncey waved his hands passionately about.

Alexander was astonished. How dare these men, these soldiers of the crown defy the royal house and take matters into their own hands. Is this why Father Malachius sent him here? Who taxed these people and stole gold from the Royal Treasury?

"Listen to me, both of you. None of this money is coming back to my family, I swear it. I just came from Middlebrooke, and I have eyes and ears. Nothing reaches our family from this....Do they just take the gold, or is there more?

"They take anything they want. Some gold ore here, some iron ore there. Whatever extra coins we might have. The pigs."

"Aye, the bloody pigs," Chauncey added. This seemed to affect his mood more than the gold coins.

"Why would they take the pigs?" Alexander asked curiously.

"Maybe they liked sausage," Fergus joked but after he caught a dirty look from Chauncey, he whispered an explanation to Alexander.

"Chauncey loves to eat from the pig. The lack of pig has soured his disposition of late."

A moment of silence passed as the three of them looked at the bottom of their glasses. Alexander felt the exhaustion of his trip catching up with him. It had already caught up to Keira, and she snored loudly from her place on the floor. He stood up to make arrangements for his room.

"Chauncey. Fergus. I bid you goodnight and I will see you tomorrow for our trip. Remember...I'm not here." he winked badly, and it took a moment before the men caught on.

"Of course. Good night, Alex, the weary traveler," Chauncey joked.

Alexander quickly made arrangements for his room with the tavern keeper. He made it upstairs without incident of falling down from the ale and within minutes of entering his room, he fell asleep in his armor and remained in it all night.

CHAPTER IX

Morning came to Greystone with the subtlety of a maelstrom, and Alexander welcomed it less than today's days jaunt into the forest. He moved his head and buried it under a brick. No, that was straw inside of cloth, and it poked and pricked Alexander's head. The pillow discomforted him, as well as the amount of ale that contributed to his aversion to sunlight.

Alexander's eyes refused to open so he continued his thoughts. He thought about buying a tavern and making it a successful venture. That was it! He would become a successful tavern owner. That's what he wanted to be. He didn't know much about the preparation and serving of food, but he knew what good food was and was sure he could hire an experienced person to run it for him. He thought about the Royal Cook. He imagined the look on his family's face if he announced that he had taken the Royal Cook into his employ.

He had forgotten how he got to his room, so he glanced about the tiny room for his armor. The room was very small and held enough room for one cot and a fireplace. He was concerned that he saw only his sword and could not find the armor, even when he checked under the cot.

He was losing patience over the armor when a loud knock was heard at the door. Keira immediately sat up and stared at the door.

"Who's that?" Alex demanded.

"Your hired guides, good sir," the voice said from the other side of the wooden door.

Ah good. They were on time. At least he wouldn't have to hunt them down but maybe they could assist him and hunt down his armor.

"In!"

The trio from the previous night walked into his room and stood before him. Chauncey and Fergus looked and smelled as if they slept downstairs in the tavern. Jack was refreshed from a night's sleep and definitely in a better humor.

"Prince Alexander, did you really sleep in your armor?" Fergus queried. It was abnormal for men to sleep in their armor, for it was a very uncomfortable experience.

Alexander looked down at his body and rolled his eyes.

"Please remember, I am traveling in disguise," Alex corrected Fergus, "No one is to know my true identity. I am Alex, a visitor from the Northern Islands. I am exploring places I've never been. And yes, I slept in my armor and it's killing me."

"Perhaps it would be best, to take off the armor until we get to the stables and are out of town. That way we won't have as many questions," Jack suggested.

Alex was impressed with Jack's suggestion. It showed amazing cleverness from an unlikely source.

"Absolutely Jack, that's a great idea. Help me off with this armor then."

Together the three men were able to remove the armor from Alexander. His body heaved a huge sigh of relief to be rid of it for a little while. He had worn his armor for three days in case he should be ambushed by marauders.

He stretched and yawned happy to be free of the burden of wearing it. He grabbed the remainder of his personal effects and together they headed to the stables.

Once at the stables, Alex was relieved to see that the horses had already been prepared for their journey. Jack had fed and watered all the horses, and had food and drink prepared for the group as a quick breakfast. Alexander was again impressed for Jack was becoming increasingly useful.

"You've got a nice horse Alex. Where'd you get him?" Jack stroked Zeus' black hair in admiration.

"I've raised him since he was a foal. Between Zeus and Kiera, I've never been alone."

"What's his name?"

"His name is Zeus." Alex mounted his horse and stroked Zeus's neck. "I named him after the god of thunder. If you heard his hoof beats I'm sure you'd agree they sound like thunder."

"We've got a two mile ride to the forest. After that, its eyes and ears open. No telling what we'll find in there." Jack's countenance became very stoic and unemotional. If he was nervous, he did a fine job hiding it. "We're going in early in the morning. Evil likes to sleep during the day."

Chauncey and Fergus nodded their agreement. Together they guided their horses out of the village and headed north to the forest. As they got closer, the horizon held nothing but trees from one end to the other. The nearer they got to it, the more imposing it became. Huge thick trees, with large leaves to match, swayed gently in the breeze. Alexander couldn't see into the forest but past a few yards of trees due to their thickness. He could see no path entering the forest. He realized they would have to use their wits to guide their way through.

Alexander noticed a wooden sign that stood out of the ground. He read it quietly to himself. TURN BACK was inscribed sloppily as it must have been done very hastily as the person who left the sign there did not want to stay any longer than necessary. The remains of a rotted sheep's corpse lay near the sign and Alexander guessed that the sign had been written in its blood.

"That's a cheery thought, isn't it?' Fergus chuckled as he scoffed at the sign. His chuckle grew uneasy as no one appreciated his humor.

They all sat quietly on their horses and contemplated the forest. Alexander's thoughts vacillated between the navigation of the forest to the unseen dangers that lay hidden in wait for them. He knew that at some point his sword would need to be drawn. He quietly hoped the other three had remembered the lessons of swordsmanship that he had given to them in their youth. Finally, Alexander dismounted and removed the armor from Zeus's back. He fastened it on very quietly.

"So....Alex," Fergus said worriedly. "What exactly are we looking for in here?"

"Haven't a clue Fergus." Alexander remounted Zeus, satisfied that his armor was fastened tightly. He looked at Fergus' freckled face which looked even paler than usual. "I know Fergus. All I know is that I was sent here to find my purpose. I suppose I'll know it when I see it."

"Your purpose isn't to die young is it?" Chauncey asked nervously. Even Keira seemed a bit overwhelmed by the forest. Her tail and ears sat lower than normal and she let out a soft whimper.

"No, Chauncey. I have no desire to die today." He

remounted Zeus and sat confidently in the saddle. His eyes caught sight of the wooden sign again and its dire warning and his confidence wavered for just a moment.

"Buck up you two," Jack challenged. "Let's find what our young master is looking for. It's not that we've got anything better to do." Jack snapped the reins on his horse and immediately went towards the forest.

"HYAAAH!" Fergus, Chauncey, and Alexander followed Jack into the forest and were immediately swallowed up by the trees. After a brief whimper and pacing back and forth, Keira also followed her master into the dark forest.

For all the stories that Alexander had heard in his youth, he never heard anything but fear about the forest. Every story ended with death and there were always tiny little evil creatures ready to tear your heart out behind every rock and tree. His new companions did very little to lighten the situation, but instead were wary and tense as they pressed on.

At first glance it was easy to tell that this was an ancient forest, perhaps more ancient than even the Bete'szek that originally lived here. The forest ground was scarce with grass, except in a few patches, for the lack of sunlight. The trees bark were such a dark shade of brown that they could have been identified as black and rotted. At certain places in the forest, the trees were so close together that their canopies blotted out the sunlight.

The trees were old, he surmised, but they held no danger. There certainly were no spirits or creatures hiding in them. Alexander reflected on the stories of strange creatures and evil spirits that allegedly inhabited the forests. For years Father Malachius taught that there were no such things that existed on earth, and that the stories that were whispered at bedtime by the servants were nothing more than excrement from the ignorant. The young man found it ironic that this was the same man that had sent him into a haunted forest. Perhaps Alexander had been sent here to dispel the myth of the forest once and for all? The forest represented more than just the fear of the Alveun peasantry.

The Alveun nobility had wanted to expand the kingdom for generations. To the west was the ocean, and to the east was a small conglomerate of loosely ruled fiefdoms under the protection of the Atreides. The northern frontier was for all intents and purposes, wide open but both the church and the nobility could not convince the Alveun population into settling new villages beyond the forest. It was a shame too for untold riches lay beyond the trees.

Alexander brought his thoughts back to the present. A breeze rustled through the trees and a leaf left its brand and gently floated through the air. Satisfied that the wind dispatched the leaf and not a small goblin he rode on confidently, but still made sure he glanced at a few trees as they rode past them.

After an hour of riding, they arrived at a small stream. It seemed a likely spot to rest and water the horses. At this point Alexander wanted to get the bearings and head in whatever direction they needed to be free of the forest. No one felt the need to stay in the forest after dark. Although Alex felt no fear from the forest, he had the distinct feeling that someone or something had been watching them. Even Keira had stopped lapping up the water and sat very still. Her ears perked as she listened intently and scanned the trees.

Alexander was slightly shocked at the sight of lilies next to Keira. They were the exact same shape and size as the flowers that Sofia had purchased in Brookehaven and Alexander had given to Angelica.

"Jack," Alex whispered. He kept his voice down for

fear of being over heard. They were definitely being watched and by all accounts that feeling of being followed had been with them since they entered the forest.

"I feel it," Jack whispered back. "Someone's watching us." Chauncey and Fergus moved their heads slowly, and slowly moved their hands to their saddles in search of their weapons. They sought to draw their swords but were startled by an unseen voice.

"Hello, my friends, and welcome to the Northern Woods," the tough voice frayed their already nervous frame of mind. Their heads turned quickly to a large fallen tree where a hooded figure stood and leaned upon a staff for support.

Everyone's so friendly here; Alexander thought mockingly and remembered a teaching from Father Malachius. Beware the man who calls you friend. You will want none of him.

Alexander stepped forward two paces for a closer look at the cloaked figure. The man's curly grey hair fell out beneath the hood and gave the indication a man far older than Edward. The stranger did not seem to pose a threat by himself because the wooden staff he leaned on was for walking and not fighting.

"Good day to you stranger, I hope you are in good health," Alexander said diplomatically. Perhaps he could talk his way out of a conflict. The stranger was obviously trying to gather his opinions about the travelers, so if Alexander could avoid revealing his identity and yet keep this rogue feeling wary, he would do his best to manipulate the situation.

"Aye. I am in good health." The stranger carefully used his staff to step down from the log and limped towards Alex. "But you see my friends, it is not my health that concerns me today. It is the health of four strangers as they walk through the most dangerous forest in all of Alveus."

"Your concern is appreciated and from what I hear, warranted. We are but simple travelers who wish to pass these woods. We neither have gold or other coins to protect us, but merely our humble faith in God." Alexander smiled as he spoke these words. He hoped to provoke the stranger to foolish action or at least to reveal his hand.

The stranger shook his head sadly and frowned at the men.

"Alas, I still feel for your health young man. With no gold….no coins… I'm very sorry to disappoint you. Once you enter this forest, your God leaves you." He brought the hood down from his head. He fashioned a short beard, and it looked as if it had been some time since he had cleaned himself. His shoulder length grey hair and his scarred face revealed a man who was used to getting what he wanted through violence, and had been successful over the years. Although his hair was already grey, he couldn't have been much older than Edward. He held no sword, and Alexander was curious of how he was to lose any money this day.

"I fear for your health because you cannot pay for your life and the life of your companions, everyone who enters these woods must pay, or never see the light of day. So tell me again, my young friend, how you intend to pay us this day."

Before Alexander responded, thirty men stepped out from their hiding places in the trees and they slowly formed a circle around the four men. Alexander backed cautiously towards Zeus with a few short steps. The way they had come in was now blocked. Even if they mounted their horses it would be a very short fight, and would end with one of his companions wounded or dead.

Alexander was irritated with himself. He had been so consumed with this solitary figure that his mind never allowed himself to envision any other scenarios. He really should have realized there would be more.

"I see you have caught me at a disadvantage. I must either part with life or money. I have no money, and I am loath to part with my life."

Fergus's eyes widened and he whined quietly while Jack wiped his sweaty brow. Keira refused to cower and she stood and growled at the nearest villain. Her jaws clenched tightly and her lips rose which revealed her razor sharp teeth. The marauder nearest to her backed away from the dog. Alexander's mind raced quickly. What would Edward do? Would he fight or would he flee?

"Alex," Chauncey hissed. "I don't want to die. What do we do?"

Alexander felt an idea take hold and courage swelled inside his heart. The warmth of it spread through his body and into his hands and head. Boldness took over his thoughts and he felt strengthened. Alexander looked to his companions and smiled.

"Fear not," he whispered confidently. "This day does not bring my fate…or yours. Stay here with the horses." He walked directly to the cloaked stranger. The cloaked stranger backed up suspiciously of Alexander's bold movement while several of his group quickly joined him at his side with swords drawn. They were all decidedly unnerved by Alexander's boldness.

"That's far enough," a familiar woman's voice called from behind them. Alexander heard the tight draw of a bowstring. He didn't have to turn to know the arrow was aimed directly at his heart.

"Turn around," she said again. Alexander's heart lifted for the voice was soft and familiar yet a warning of dangerous events to come.

Alexander raised his hands up in the air very slowly

and showed that he would not grab any of his weapons. He turned sideways and caught a glance of the archer.

She had dark curly hair that fell just below her shoulders. Her face was clean, unlike the others, and she seemed to take great pride in standing apart from them. Alexander's heart skipped a beat when he looked into her dark green eyes. Although spotless in her appearance she was dressed much like the others and armed with more weapons. A sword rested in a scabbard tied to her back, and a dagger sheathed on her lower right leg.

"Angelica," he whispered. Her face flickered with recognition, but instead of relaxing the bowstring, she drew it tighter.

"Good day to you, friend," Alexander said as he bowed to her.

"I'm not your friend," was her curt reply. She relaxed her bow and walked towards him. Alexander kept his eyes on her, partly ready to pull out his sword in case of treachery and partly because he liked keeping his eyes on her. As she neared him she directed herself closer until she was less than a hair from him. He felt light headed as she drew closer. She leaned her mouth next to his ears as she smiled.

"But I could be your angel."

Her whispered breath caught Alexander's ear. The warmth of her breath caused an intense reaction within Alexander's head. He felt his knees briefly weaken and his mind became clouded.

"Angel of Death!" someone shouted. Alexander quickly regained control of his thoughts and strengthened his posture.

"YEAH!" the others shouted in agreement.

The lady smiled and kept eye contact with Alexander until she reached the cloaked man.

"So, we have a small problem, the stranger in our woods has no money," she said slowly, "and we owe him no favors. But doubtless, with his fancy armor, he's someone of great importance. Nobility, perhaps? He'd fetch a nice sack of gold coins."

"I'm afraid to disappoint you," Alexander responded. "I'm no nobleman. My name is Alex. I took this armor off of a man I killed. I'm fleeing, just like all of you. These men," he pointed back at the group, "Are my guides, showing me safely to the border."

He had never needed to lie before, and he quickly wondered if his story was believable enough. Angelica's face showed disappointment and the man's expression was unsympathetic.

"Very well, friend, then your life holds no value. No hard feelings?" The man sat down on the log and leaned against his staff. He looked towards his female companion.

"Angelica, will you show the man out? You know what to do...."

Angelica smiled and nodded her head at the rogue. She placed her right hand behind her head and with one smooth motion pulled out her sword and held it in front of her. Keira instantly reacted and walked towards her and snarled. Keira had no intention to let her master be killed while she stood.

"Call off your dog, or I'll have my men finish you where you stand." The bandits drew whatever weapon they held, while Jack, Chauncey, and Fergus drew their swords and waited for the next move.

"I am staring my death in the face...." Angelica's sword pointed directly at him. "Why would I call off my protector? Perhaps if we were to meet on even turns?" Alexander kept his hands up in the air. "If you strike at me unarmed, you'll be dead before my body hits the ground and I would be loath to see such a beautiful angel of the forest die before her time."

"Why?" He whispered, just loud enough for her to hear him.

Angelica's face flickered with her internal conflict.

"I'll meet your terms, now call off your dog," she said quietly.

Alexander whistled at Keira and walked back towards the horses. Jack, Fergus, and Chauncey anxiously met him.

"Fergus, get my gloves from Zeus." Fergus ran over to the horse, and quickly fetched his gloves.

"Jack, take Keira. If I should fall, then unleash her. Then get on your horses and flee. Understand?" Alexander pulled the gloves onto his hands. The gloves afforded some protection from cuts and also lessened the impact when their swords clashed. Jack agreed to Alexander's request with a hesitant nod.

"Good." He noticed Jack's frown and tried to encourage him. "Don't be worried. It's not my day to die."

He winked at them with confidence and strutted back to the waiting Angelica. He clapped his gloves together, checked the fastenings of his armor and slowly unsheathed his sword for effect. There was a brief moment as the two opponents looked each other over and assessed their opponent's weaknesses. Alexander had never seen a sword in Angelica's hands and confidently assessed that he would be able to defeat her easily without harming her.

He was immediately proved correct. Angelica leaped forward and immediately sliced at his head. Alexander easily blocked her swing and pushed her away. Angelica would not be so easily beaten and she feinted to his right. Alexander overreacted and blocked air. Angelica laughed and smiled confidently. Alexander was irritated by his reaction because although he had never fought an actual duel, he was well trained for one.

Angelica thrust her sword towards Alexander's chest. Alexander spun in time for the blade to narrowly miss his body. Angelica's momentum carried her head just passed his body. Alexander saw an opportunity and he spun with a half circle, used his left elbow, and slammed it into the back of her head which caused her to fall face first in the dirt.

He didn't press his advantage and she quickly jumped to her feet. She was visibly angry now and her once spotless face was now covered with dirt. Alexander knew he shouldn't mock his opponent, but he couldn't resist.

"Are you hurt, my angel?" He bowed slightly and touched his head and swept his arm out to her.

"Oh don't worry my love, I'm still the only one for you," she replied flirtatiously, and brushed her curly black hair away from her face.

She closed the small distance to Alexander and he held up his sword to meet her. She bent down momentarily and produced the dagger from her legs scabbard with her left hand. She held them both menacingly as she stalked Alexander.

Alexander was patient and waited for the attack. This visibly frustrated Angelica.

"I don't believe you've killed anyone to get that armor. You don't have it in you to kill. I can see it in your eyes," she hissed.

Alexander resisted the temptation to attack. He knew that one misstep would be his end. He ignored the thieves as they jeered and taunted him. They tightened their circle around the two combatants and ignored Jack, Chauncey, and Fergus as they pushed past them. Only one man stayed next to them to keep an eye on them.

"I'm going to cut out your tongue and eat it," Angelica boasted and the brigands cheered and taunted Alexander. She straightened up and looked him in the eyes. Her previously sultry green eyes blazed with rage.

Alexander felt a burning sensation on his back. The burning was so intense that it delivered a searing message to his brain. He closed his eyes in reaction to the pain, and beheld images that came from behind. Turn and block were the commands that whispered to him.

Alexander instinctively listened and swung his sword behind him. He blocked a sword that was crashing down on him. The thief clearly didn't expect his swing to be blocked and Alexander pinned the man's arm between his own arm and his chest and violently kicked the man backwards and held onto the man's sword. He brandished the two swords in one hand when he felt another sensation.

He closed his eyes and envisioned an attacker coming from behind him.

Alexander dropped to the ground in time and opened his eyes and saw a sword swing through where his head had just been. He spun and kicked the legs out from his opponent who fell to the earth with a thud.

Events became more precarious. Alexander realized that he would soon have to fight all thirty men if he did not act quickly to end this fight. He looked up and saw Angelica running towards him. He quickly rolled out of the way of her sword's downward swing but in the process of rolling away he dropped both swords. He sprang up just as Angelica was turning to try again. She raised her sword and he lunged into her body and dragged her to the ground. Her sword fell to the ground and she gathered all of her strength behind her left hand as she attempted to stab him with her dagger. He grabbed her hand and pushed it to the ground. With her right hand she struck his face with enough force to weaken his grip. She pushed herself on top of him and again tried to plunge the dagger into his heart. He grabbed on to her arms with both hands. The knife inched closer to his chest and both of their faces reddened from the strain of the fight. Alexander had a matter of seconds before the knife pierced his skin. He twisted his body and his elbow slammed into Angelica's face. Her attempt to plunge the dagger into his heart weakened and he quickly ripped the knife out of her hand. He wrapped his free arm around her neck and pointed the dagger directly into her neck.

She immediately stopped thrashing about and slowly brought her hands up. The thieves were angry and screamed obscenities at Alexander. They brandished their swords and inched closer to Alexander. The distracted focus afforded his companions an opportunity. Jack released Keira who leaped into the crowd to take a side next to her master. She immediately flashed her teeth at the marauders and growled intimidating.

"Enough," the cloaked thief yelled. "Stranger, give me one good reason why I should not have you and your friends killed this instant."

Alexander's mind raced and he examined the faces of the two leaders.

"Because..." he started. "I have...a knife...pointed at your sister's throat. And if you come near me I will plunge it in her neck and she will die a slow and painful death."

The figure scowled at him.

"And how do you know she's my sister and not just some common mercenary?"

"The family resemblance with the..." He pointed at the nose. "Face. You look the same." Alexander winced at his words.

"Put away your swords. He just paid for his life."

The hooded man's words were not readily accepted by the other men and some of them grumbled. They moved slowly so Alexander poked Angelica's neck which elicited a stern warning from Angelica to any man that failed to put their swords away.

"Excellent," Alexander exclaimed once the thieves put their swords down. He released the dagger from Angelica's neck and stood up. He reached down and offered her his hand. "And to think, you were about to be my guardian angel."

She took his hand, stood straight up, and looked him in the eye.

"There's always tomorrow. May I have my blade back?"

He handed the dagger, handle first to her. She reached for the hilt, but instead, touched his hand before taking the dagger from him. The soft touch weakened Alexander's knees again and he felt light headed.

The rogue limped over to them and stuck out his hand. "So strangers, as our contest of wills has taken us the better part of the day, my men and I will be returning to our home. You are more than welcome to stay in my forest. Perhaps you would share food with us?"

"I couldn't think of anything better. Perhaps you could help me out with my situation?" Alexander clasped his hand firmly and they eyed each other.

"Of course. Anything for a friend of the family." He smiled to reveal a few missing teeth, but it was a sincere smile so Alexander trusted it. Chauncey brought up the horses and without further entanglement, followed the thieves deeper into the forest.

After an hour of silence had passed, they came across what looked to be an unused wooden shack. There were boards missing from the sides, and it looked very near collapse.

The thieves' leader called back to them.

"Tie your horses up in the barn. Angelica, lead them to the cave from there."

"Yes, Duncan. I'll make sure they get up there in one piece." Angelica hovered towards Alexander and smiled. She had a beautifully deceitful smile. Alexander surmised that her lips were filled with secrets, more than she was willing to share. "Follow me, young sir. I'll find a place for your horse."

As she turned and walked towards the barn, Alexander noticed how confident her stride had become. Gone was the timid servant girl and in front of him was a girl used to leading men and not being questioned. Although Duncan seemed to give the orders, it was more than likely that Angelica carried them out.

"I am relieved to have found you," Alexander said. "When Manfred told me-"

She interrupted him quickly. "We are not in the palace," she said menacingly. "You are not in command here. It was foolish of you to follow me."

"I haven't followed you," he hissed. "God has brought me to you. Don't you see, I was told to come north to find my destiny, and that is the two of us."

Angelica turned her head and looked back at Alexander. He could tell there was a small smile with her lips but she shook her head and kept walking ahead.

"Perhaps your words are better suited for softer skin. Put your horses in here for the night. Don't worry, they'll be safe. We keep most of our livestock here."

That was a true statement indeed. The barn held several chickens and pigs that walked freely about. There were a few horses kept in stalls, but they looked matted and unkempt.

Alexander motioned for his men to tie up the horses because he wanted to try to pry information from Angelica again. He found her as she attended to feeding the pigs with a few rotten vegetables.

"This barn doesn't quite fit with my idea of a band of ruthless marauders. I expected to find Hell here. Instead I find the reason for my every waking, thirty men, and a barn. I'm not sure I quite understand. Why do all the tales of this forest foretell of doom and fear?"

"Alexander," she said softly, "You're not out of the woods yet."

This caused Alexander some discomfort. His hand must have brushed his sword enough for Angelica to notice.

"No," she said. "You have nothing to fear from me or from any of us, unless Duncan says otherwise. But I won't make you any promises Alex, because I never lie."

"A woman after my own heart," Alexander smiled slyly. "Or maybe I truly have found my guardian angel."

A tear started to form in Angelica's eye, but as quickly as Alexander noticed the tear, it disappeared just as fast.

"Stop your illusions, Alex," she said. "I am the Angel of Death. That's the life I've chosen, and there is no escaping it. Even if..." she began to walk towards Alex slowly, "I ever feel so much of a drop of any other emotion..." She placed her hand on his shoulder. "I can never be anything more than what I am. None of us can. We all borrowed time back from the Devil, and we have to pay his heavy price."

Alexander wanted to press further, but Jack had entered the barn to find him.

"Master...Alex. The horses are taken care of and are bolted in. There won't be a chance of escape."

"Very good." He turned back to Angelica whose blue eyes had now moistened. "Shall we join your brother?"

She motioned for them to follow her. They walked a short distance until they came to one edge of the forest, and arrived to the base of a small mountain. It was very rocky and would be impossible for a horse to climb successfully.

She led them up the mountain, and navigated a path that had been cleared. Although the path was cleared, that didn't make it any easier to walk up the mountain. At certain spots the dirt path would turn to broken stones, which caused great aggravation and slowed them down. Keira found her walk miserable for the jagged rocks jabbed at her sore feet. At certain rocky points the pain overwhelmed her so she lay down and whimpered. Only constant encouragement from Alexander helped her to keep following them.

They came to a flat surface and found one of the men sitting on a rock waiting for them. Once he spotted them and made sure they were all together, he walked over to a large bush and pushed up some branches to reveal the entrance to a cave. He yelled at them to hurry up and they quickened their pace. They ducked into the cave and as the branches covered the entrance again, they stopped to allow their eyes to adjust to the darkness. There were several lit torches ahead of them, and as they drew closer they were amazed at the length of the cave.

They had no time to be awed. Duncan walked forward to greet them.

"There you are. We were concerned that you were lost."

"No such concern needed. Your sister is an excellent guide," Alexander replied diplomatically. The grey haired Duncan reminded him of a silver fox. Although his physical condition limited him to continually lean upon a staff for support, Alexander didn't trust him for a moment. Angelica's delicate warning in the barn increased his vigilance. He hoped Jack, Chauncey and Fergus would be on guard as well. He began to feel apologetic that he had brought them into this situation, but not once had they complained.

Duncan invited them to sit down and partake in some stew that was cooked in an iron cauldron. Alexander decided that although Duncan was not to be trusted, he may have some particularly useful information. Duncan seemed to read Alexander's mind for he was quick to question him.

"Alex, you are a very impressive sword fighter. My sister does not lose very often, or ever, so it was good to see her learn humility. Where did you learn to handle a blade?"

Alex knew Duncan didn't believe his story either. The fox laid a trap for a chicken but Alexander had learned cleverness as well.

"I was on board a galley out of the port city of Brookehaven. We were running trade routes to the Northern and Western Isles. There was a lot of time to practice, and so I did, every day." Alexander wanted to move the conversation quickly. "So tell me, are the stories real? Is this forest haunted?"

Duncan chuckled softly and Alexander understood that this was an honest chuckle.

"This forest is haunted...by us. This is our forest."

"But why here? You have a barn, you grow vegetables. That is the work of farmer's, not thieves."

Duncan's face darkened. Alexander's words had obviously stirred emotion within him.

"What we are, we were not always. We are men, forced out of homes. They were stolen from us, along with anything that tied us to the King. Our families were forced into servitude, cottages burned. I watched my children cut down before me. So we fled to the forest, vowing revenge on the Kingdom. We will deliver this kingdom into the hands of an even greater evil, and watch it burn in flames."

Alexander felt genuinely sad for Duncan, but was alarmed at his traitorous words.

"I'm sorry. I can't see the King doing this-"

"It's the King. Every deed in this kingdom, good or bad, lies at the feet of the King. Where was the royal decree protecting in my family? Were those the royal soldiers butchering my family?" Duncan's breath quickened and his fury mounted. The pain on his face was indescribable.

"So, how will you avenge them?"

Duncan smiled and leaned towards Alexander.

"Across the mountains is the Bete'szek, the rightful inhabitants of this land. It wasn't long ago that they ruled before your people came. Eventually they were defeated in battle, and when their holy city of Edgebrooke fell, they escaped across the mountains. They are still there, gathering their forces for their return. They will spill the blood and I will have my revenge."

Alexander knew he was in danger if they knew who he was, for he would be cut down. His only hope lay in his companion's silence. One look at their faces told him that they too, felt uneasy with the conversation. Alexander knew the conversation was risky, but he just need a little more.

"But Duncan, you've told me that they're coming....what are you doing to avenge your family? Are you just killing people that wander into your forest?"

Duncan just smiled and took a bite of his stew. From across the cave, a sound was made that sounded like a boy whimpering. Duncan looked straight into Alexander's eyes.

"Five years ago I had nothing. I escaped from the King's men half dead into this very forest with a few men. We ran and we ran until we passed out from near exhaustion. When I came to, I saw..." He began to lower his voice. "I saw one of them. One of their priests. He promised to spare our lives if we swore our lives to him. We ALL swore a blood oath that we were one of them. And a blood oath to the devil is unbreakable. We harvest the fools that enter this forest and then we function as sort of a ferry between our world and theirs."

"What, then, is your cargo," Alexander mused.

"The soon to be departed," Duncan smiled. He raised his eyebrows, stood up with the help of his staff, and walked towards the source of the moaning. Alexander watched as Duncan raised his staff up and quickly struck the source. The whimpering stopped and silence commanded the cave. Alexander knew it was one of his own people but he had no way to help.

"Alex?" Jack whispered. "What do we do now?"

"We need to leave, before we become one of their victims."

Duncan noticed they had begun to whisper, and came back to where they sat. "Everything well, friends?" He asked.

"Perfect. My guides were curious about when they could guide me to the edge of the borders. They wanted to return to their families in the village before nightfall."

Duncan eyed him cautiously. He appeared to be growing suspicious of Alexander's motives.

"What you might not understand," Duncan explained slowly, "Is that they do not like outsiders, and they will kill you."

"Perhaps if I were to offer you ten gold coins to safely escort me past them?"

"And here I thought you were just a poor traveler," Duncan smiled greedily.

"There's no doubts that I'm poor, I just might be able to arrange that payment."

"Where are these ten gold coins? Do you have them now?"

"No, sadly. I have them hidden in a safe place. Just outside of Greystone. I can be back by tomorrow."

Duncan thought for a very brief moment. Alexander saw the greed in Duncan's face which made it difficult for him to reject the proposal.

"Very well, Alex. Bring me ten gold coins, and I will get you across the border." He extended his hand and Alexander immediately shook it. There was a brief uncomfortable moment as their hands gripped. Duncan squeezed his hand just a tiny bit harder than a normal handshake. Alexander matched the grip, and as the grip became firmer, neither Alexander nor Duncan broke eye contact. At last, both satisfied that neither man would relent, they released their grip.

"You have until nightfall tomorrow. If you aren't here, we will leave without you. And...," he said while looking at Jack, "it's ten gold coins per traveler."

Angelica weighed in on the agreement. "You're a foolish one," she said, shaking her head.

"It looks like you'll have to deal with my company a bit longer," Alexander smiled. Angelica walked away without another word and Duncan cocked his head in curiosity.

"It's just me. Tomorrow night then," Alexander affirmed. He motioned for his companions to follow him and together they left and started down the mountain. They kept their silence for a distance, and once they were at the bottom, Fergus started to speak. Alexander abruptly cut him off with a finger to the lips letting everyone know to keep quiet.

Once at the barn, they quickly saddled their horses and began riding back to Greystone. The journey back was much easier than their journey in. When they were finally outside the forest, Alexander felt as if a tremendous burden had been lifted off his shoulders and he breathed a sigh of relief. The forest atmosphere was oppressive and Alexander was glad to be rid of it.

When they arrived in Greystone, Alexander headed directly to the stable. As he entered the village, he paid no mind to the stares of the villagers. Time was short, evening had come.

"Fergus? Chauncey? Take care of the horses, please. Jack, come with me." Alexander dismounted Zeus and walked towards the tavern

"So what now?" Jack's voice was full of excitement. "Are you going to get your army and come back here to destroy their hideout?"

Alexander scoffed at the idea. He was pretty sure no one outside of the peasant class would believe him about any of the things he had seen in the forest; especially not the ties to the barbarians. Everyone believed them to be scattered and broken, and certainly nobody believed that there was any sort of Dark Magic.

"No, Jack, now I sleep, gather up ten coins, and ride back into the forest."

"We're going back? Why?" Jack was alarmed by this.

"Not you. Me. Just me. You've done enough for me and I thank you for that. Here…" Alexander pulled out three coins. "Give one to Chauncey and one to Fergus. I will also need you to do two favors for me."

Alexander produced a bag of gold coins containing

all of the coins that he had received on his birthday.

"I need you to look after this bag. Don't let anything happen to it. I should be back within a week or so. I also need you to take Keira. She's a good dog, but I need to let them feel safe in whatever it is they will try to do. Keira will only keep them on their constant guard."

Jack shook his head sadly. "You shouldn't be going alone. They're thieves, I don't trust them. If you go with them across the border, they'll probably kill you. You know where they hide and who they are. They won't take any chances."

"I know Jack. But I feel like…." his voice trailed off. "I feel that there's something across the border. Maybe it's my destiny. I have this burning inside of me that I'm on the right path."

"What if it's fate?" Jack argued. "What if it's fate that you die tomorrow if you go over that mountain? You have a choice here."

"I don't really feel like I do have a choice. I either go to it. Or it comes to me."

Alexander patted Jack on the shoulder.

"I'll be fine," he said, "just take care of this bag." Alexander handed Jack the bag of coins. He knelt down and put Keira's face in his hands.

"Keira, go with Jack."

Keira whimpered. She understood what Alexander was saying, and she was not going to leave easily.

"Keira…go with Jack."

"May destiny be your guide, Prince," Jack said and he turned and walked away. Keira followed Jack, with her tail between her legs. It made Alexander sad to watch Keira leave. They had been inseparable and this was the first time that he rode without her.

Alexander decided it would be best to turn in for the

night so he could get started early. He was very anxious, because he would be going alone, and he was quite sure that it was a trap. He remembered to remove his armor this night, offered up a quiet prayer for protection, and retired to his bed.

CHAPTER X

Alexander awoke early the next morning with even greater feelings of apprehension than those gripping him the night before. His stomach felt nauseous and every so often he broke into a cold sweat. Yesterday, he had a dog, three companions, and confidence. Today, he only had his sword and his wits.

Alexander quickly fitted in his armor, and headed towards the stable. He reached into one of his pouches and produced some jerky. Chewing on the jerky began to relieve him of some of the tensions he was feeling. He tried focusing clearly on what lay before him.

The task was simple, he thought as he mounted Zeus. Get over the border. Once that was accomplished he would sneak away from the thieves. After gathering the information he needed, he would cross back over the border. His only concerns lay on the unpredictability of the thieves' nature. Would they attempt to kill him? So far no one had recognized him other than Angelica and she had not revealed who he was so he felt safe in that regard. Jack also has the rest of his coins, so if a ransom was needed, Alexander still had one bluff left. If Duncan was talked into letting him leave the forest for ten gold coins, what would he do for one hundred?

As he rode Zeus towards the forest his nerves calmed down, but Alexander stopped at the same sign that had warned him the day before. He stopped a moment to ponder the danger he was truly facing. He was excited to continue this dangerous journey and maybe a bit nervous, but he could not shake an ever growing feeling of dread.

He heard voices whisper in the distance so he stood tall in his saddle and scanned the trees ahead of him. Satisfied that he could not pinpoint the whispers, he assumed it was merely the wind that blew on the trees.

"Or more so, my mind does play with me," he commented to Zeus who returned his master's nervous feeling by shifting his weight. Alexander nudged Zeus forward into the trees and to the direction of the whispers.

They eventually returned to the brook where they had met Duncan and briefly paused so Zeus could quench his thirst. As Zeus drank from the brook, Alexander gathered a lily when he noticed the shape of a figure that concealed herself behind a small tree.

"You're not that good at hiding Angelica." Alexander turned his attention back to Zeus and nudged him towards Angelica.

The dark haired maiden walked out from behind the tree and greeted him.

"Very good, Alexander. How did you know I was there?"

"Leaves and branches from the tree may move, but it's rare for a tree to sprout hair as dark as the night that moves with the breeze."

"I see," Angelica said. "My brother sent me to see if you were still coming."

"And here I am," Alexander chuckled and bowed

courteously from atop Zeus. He dismounted and stepped towards Angelica. "Why would he be concerned?"

"We thrive on secrecy and not being seen. If you hadn't come, we would have come for you." Angelica said it so matter-of-factly that Alexander believed he would die by her hand if he had not come back.

"Where is your dog?" Angelica glanced around and behind her. Her eyes left no detail untouched in the forest.

"I sold her," Alexander lied. He bit his lip and looked directly at Angelica.

"You're a poor liar, Alex," Angelica said and shook her head. "It doesn't become you."

"She isn't here," he insisted. "You may search the forest further if you like."

"Very well," she replied, "I will take you for your word. She is not here." Angelica turned in the direction of the thieves' hideout and Alexander took up position behind her. He noticed that her curly hair had been straightened and she smelt less like a forest and more like a field of flowers.

What now?" Alexander asked to break the silence.

"They should be ready for travel the moment we get there. From there we will be traveling through the mountain range until we come to a stone mound. That is where our journey ends."

"And so when do I leave?" Alexander asked. He gazed directly at Angelica but she refused to look at him.

"You could leave right now. Ride away Alexander." Her voice stopped being commanding and turned into a plaintive whine, as Sofia would do when she would not get her way/

"Where would I run?" He laughed. "You have said they would come looking for me, should I hide in a tree? In a rock? Perhaps in the King's cities?"

Angelica finally looked at him and tears formed in her eyes.

"This is not a game Alex. First, they'll go to the village looking for you. When they find that you're not there, they'll send spies through the kingdom. Our reach is vast Alexander, and we kill from the shadows. You would not be safe to return to the kingdom. Ride east from here. Go to another kingdom, and don't stop. Please Alex, you are in danger."

"Oh, so I should pick a cave?" Alexander grinned and slipped his hand into hers. He squeezed it playfully but she gave him no response. Although Angelica warned him of certain danger, Alexander felt braver for knowing. The feelings of apprehension had been replaced with confidence that he was close to discovering the machinations behind this forest. It also showed that there was some caring in her.

"I'll go if you come with me," he stopped her midstride and drew her closer to him. "Tell me where you would go and I will follow you there."

Angelica freed her hands from his hands and rubbed her eyes vigorously. "I have told you once already that I can't. Why won't you understand? I am sworn a slave to them? It's a bond that can only be broken with death."

He grabbed her hand again and pulled her into a tight embrace. Her beautiful blue eyes were soft and wet. She fought the emotion in her face, but couldn't hide her misery.

"I'll free you," Alexander promised. He leaned closer to her and their lips met. It was only for a moment, but for Alexander, it felt like an eternity. Their lips parted and Angelica smiled for the first time that day. She brought her hand to his face and gently rubbed his cheek.

"I have wanted to do that since the first moment I laid eyes on you," he proclaimed.

"Please understand I can't protect you Alex," she sniffed. "If you travel with us, you're on your own."

"I understand," Alexander said stiffly. He was disappointed. At that moment he would have left title and destiny for her. Here in the forest, being a prince meant nothing. It could be just the two of them.

They said nothing to each other for the remainder of their walk but continued in awkward silence. Once they reached the barn Alexander led Zeus inside and grabbed another piece of jerky from the pouch. He felt hungry but once it was satisfied the jerky's saltiness forced him to look for some water.

He closed the barn door and found Angelica holding a water pouch. She offered it to him and he took it and drank greedily. With his thirst sufficiently quenched he tossed the pouch back to Angelica.

"Thanks," he said. The whispers returned to him and Alexander looked around him for their source. Angelica stood with a baffled look on her face.

"Do you hear that?" he asked.

"Hear what?" She asked in return.

Alexander's sight started to blur so he began to squint in order to focus his vision. His head rocked back and forth slowly and he had a hard time steadying himself so he didn't keel over. The dizziness progressively worsened and Alexander backed up and steadied himself against the barn wall.

"I'm sorry," he heard Angelica say as Duncan and several thieves emerged from behind her. His stomach became nauseous and churned inside of him. Although he leaned back against the barn wall his upper body started to lean forward. He fought to regain control of his senses with all of his strength, but whatever poison he had been given overpowered his senses. He pushed himself back against the wall once more but his legs crumpled underneath him and he sat helplessly.

A shadow that he recognized as Duncan approached him, but Alexander lost focus on what was happening around him.

"Good work Angelica," Duncan said. "And now, we say good night, *Prince* Alexander."

Alexander's body fell onto the ground and for a moment he laid there. Finally, he convulsed and threw up what little he had eaten that day and then his mind surrendered to the poison.

CHAPTER XI

Alexander didn't know how long he had been unconscious, but he knew it had been long enough that he was no longer in the forest. His last clear memory was Angelica's tearful face, and Duncan's menacing look behind her. He had swung in and out of consciousness since that time and felt jostled, as if he had been pulled on a wagon of some sort.

As his thoughts started to come into focus, his ears became aware of a buzzing, but much like his sight, the sound was also not clearly identifiable to him. The buzzing slowly grew into a clearer sound and from there it developed into a rhythmic chant. The sounds of the chant grew louder and the anger behind it was unmistakable. Alexander focused on the chants and followed their sound to climb out of his minds darkness. At long last he opened his eyes, afraid of what he would find, and expected the bright light of the sun to blind him. Instead of the sun shining high above him, dark clouds blotted out the sky, and little sunlight was had.

Alexander tried to rub his eyes with his hands but realized they were bound behind him. He briefly struggled to loosen the cords, but they would not give help to his efforts. Alexander groggily turned his head to the right and saw that he had been laid on a stone platform; next to his head was an immense stone block that looked to be an altar. The altar was made of blood stained stone, and looked as if it had been created by the finest mason. It was decorated with grotesquely shaped figures and a language that Alexander couldn't identify. He turned his head in disgust and focused back on his surroundings. Alexander listened carefully past the chants and heard the sounds of a man struggling above him on the altar.

Alexander turned his head to his left. Three other men, not older than Alexander, sat with hands tied behind their back and feet bound together. The youngest one who sat closest to him cried and repeated the Lord's Prayer over and over. Alexander struggled to sit up and when he accomplished that, he was amazed at what he saw.

Before the altar, over one hundred barbarians had gathered at the bottom of this stone mound. He recognized them as the barbarians of legend because they painted their bodies and drove themselves into their pagan frenzy. Still, in the midst of this frenetic energy, Alexander noticed the crowd parted orderly to allow a figure to pass through. The figure strode regally through the partition and Alexander assumed he was the leader of this ceremony. The man walked with a wooden staff which was not used as a crutch but as if it served a purpose. It was beautifully made, and had a blood-red finish to it. It split into three wooden fingers at the top and within those three fingers it held a crystal that, although no sun shone down through the clouds, held its own powerful brilliance.

The man who carried the staff bore an unusual presence. His hair and beard matched the same length and both were white as snow. He was thin and gaunt, and looked as though he hadn't eaten for weeks. Alexander felt heaviness in his spirit that bore down on his chest and made it difficult to breathe as the figure drew nearer. The heaviness turned into apprehension and he felt panic set in. He closed his eyes and took a deep breath, and slowly exhaled to calm himself.

The figure was not alone as he approached the stone mound. As he began to walk up the stairs, Alexander recognized Duncan and Angelica behind him, with a barbarian chieftain behind them. The chieftain was a large man, as large as King Magnus, and walked forward with a giant battle axe strapped to his back. He was painted with the same markings as his people with only his hair covering what was on his shoulders and neck. Angelica looked Alexander's way and they shared a glance, but Angelica turned her eyes away immediately. He felt his heart sink and was at a loss of what to do. Events seemed hopeless. If he got free, he thought, he might be able to get down the back of the mound and make a run for it. Unfortunately, that would have been the wrong way and he was unsure of any terrain that was in that direction. He somehow had to get down from the stone mound, run through the barbarians and either back through the pass or over the mountain. Either path looked like certain death to him.

The mob quieted down as the figure stood up behind the altar. He chanted some words in a language that Alexander didn't recognize. The warriors understood him word for word and they howled loudly in response. Alexander looked up as the figure pulled out a ceremonial knife and brandished it before the mob. He held it up to the sky and chanted what sounded like an even different language. The mob stayed silent with their eyes fixated on the action behind the altar. A cold wind blew hard and chilled Alexander as white flashes briefly illuminated the darkness from the sky above. Alexander was terrified but awestruck. Alveus maintained a perfect climate year round, and it never experienced extreme weathers of any kind. The figure clutched the knife above his head and a lightning bolt shot down from the sky and struck the knife. The priest chanted faster with his heathen tongue. The barbarians, who had stayed silent once again howled at the spectacle.

Once the lightning retreated into the sky, the figure brought the knife down swiftly. There was a brief scream, but that was overshadowed by the barbarians cheer. In less than a moment, the deed was done. The screaming from on top of the altar ceased. Blood trickled down the back of the altar and made a large pool at the priest's feet. The priest ignored the blood that collected around his feet and lifted up the man's heart. Alexander was mortified and dry heaved immediately. He was thankful that he had thrown up the contents of his stomach earlier and had nothing left to expel. One of the boys next to Alexander buried his head into his knees, as his hands were tied and he was unable to bury them there.

The barbarian chief barked a command and two warriors ran to the top of the mound and quickly cut the cords that were used to tie the man to the altar. The two barbarians carried him down the steps and shuffled to the side of the mountain where Alexander noticed there was a giant opening to what appeared to be a cave.

Alexander was confused. Why would they murder someone, and then take the time to bury them in a cave?

Alexander looked around quickly for anything he could use to his advantage. Could he find a rock to tear into the cords? Was there a way out? His senses were now highly alerted; he sensed he was minutes from death. He looked around and his eyes fell upon a rock that sat undisturbed behind the throng. The rock was large, and besides the fact that two barbarians leaned against its front, this unusual rock had a black tail that was visible only to Alexander.

Alexander knew the black tail had to belong to Kiera. His relief changed to dread as the barbarians started their chant again. Alexander turned to the boy next to him who still sobbed into his knees.

"Hey…," he whispered.

The boy stopped crying for a moment and turned his head slowly to Alexander. He was filthy. His face was swollen and covered with bruises.

"Listen to me," Alexander said firmly. "Pass the word. When I go, we all go."

The boy looked at him blankly and perhaps dazed, said nothing.

"Wake up," Alexander said. "Wake up or die here."

"On your feet!"

A huge pair of hands grabbed his shoulders and clamped down with immense pressure. Alexander winced in pain as the fingers bore into his shoulders but stayed still obediently. One of the strong hands left his shoulder, and a dagger cut the cord that tied him to the boy.

"Up you go." He grabbed Alexander by the hair and forced him up. Alexander tried to get up quickly while he felt that his hair might be ripped from his head. Once on his feet, he was pushed forward to the priest who moved his finger slowly in a small crevice that had collected blood. When Alexander was but a hair away him, the priest turned to look at him. The man's eyes were closed and he mumbled in the language that Alexander identified as neither barbarian nor Alveun. The man placed his bloody hands in the air and moved them towards Alexander. Alexander yelped in surprise and tried to back away. There was nowhere to go, as the strong hands seized him again and pushed him forward. The priest kept his eyes closed and brought his fingertips to Alexander's temples. At the exact moment his fingers touched Alexander's head, Alexander felt the most excruciating pain inside of him.

"Prince Alexander, I am honored that you would join us." He spoke slowly and calculated, as if he were hearing the words from source and needed to repeat them. Alexander struggled against the pain and felt as if someone tried to move through every thought he held as flashes of his past rapidly sped past him.

"How do you know who I am?" Alexander struggled to speak.

"We have foreseen your arrival. This is your destiny." The priest smiled but did not let go of his hold on Alexander. Memories of each member of his family flashed before his eyes.

"You are ignored and unloved by your family. You constantly walk in the shadows of your brothers. Join us."

"Why would I do that?" Alexander struggled to break free but now the strong hands were replaced by a strong arm that wrapped around his throat. With his hands tied, it made it impossible to break free.

"Swear allegiance to us. Be free and be feared. Be awed. Be respected. Yes, that thing which you want most. Your place is here among us, we can give you everything you ask for and more." The priests head moved back and forth as if it were a puppet. "Join us with power, Prince...or...." his voice trailed off as his fingers let go their hold of Alexander.

"Or what?" Alexander demanded as his body appreciated the lack of pain coursing through it.

"Or DIE! Swear allegiance, or I'll take your heart and you'll be ours forever." The figure brandished the ceremonial knife at Alexander and held it to his neck.

Alexander looked towards Angelica and he finally understood the gravity of her situation. He had thoughts....his own thoughts of Edward, Sofia, and his mother. He thought about the people of the town of Greystone and the citizens of Alveus. He could join this group and forever be a murderer. Or he could make this his defining moment and die for something he believed in.

"I choose...," he began. The priest smiled expectantly. "I choose to kill you if I get a half a chance." Alexander gave the priest a defiant look and even tried to spit on him unsuccessfully.

The priests smile disappeared and turned into a deep frown.

"My apologies, Prince Alexander. Our hospitality only goes so far. I hope your next life is a more successful one." He opened his eyes and Alexander gasped in horror. The man's eyes had been cut out and yet he had moved about as freely as someone who had sight.

"No!" Alexander muttered in disbelief. "Let me go! If you harm me, this will be an act of war."

"Does anyone know where you are, oh son of Alveus?" The priest laughed and directed for the hands to continue their evil deeds.

The hands behind him temporarily loosened his cords and spun him around to finish tying them in front. Alexander came face to face with the hulking barbarian chief. He snarled at Alexander and with the assistance of two other men standing by him, the barbarian chief quickly tied Alexander to the altar.

Alexander's hands were bound together and tied to a hook above his head. Both of his feet were spread apart and tied to separate hooks. There was very little room to move. The priest chanted his words and the throng below the altar were again focused on his every word. Alexander watched the knife ascend above the priest's head as the clouds darkened and lightning flashed against the sky. Out of nowhere, Alexander heard the sound of an arrow slicing through the air. The priest heard it too and he stopped chanting and brought the knife down slowly. The barbarians were confused why the priest stopped. They looked at each and back to the priest.

"SWOOSH." Another arrow flew in Alexander's direction. The priest yelled some words and Alexander looked above him to see an arrow suspended above his chest, pointing towards the priest. The barbarian chief noticed it immediately and yelled to his warriors to move in the direction the arrow had come from. No sooner had he yelled out his command that two arrows found their marks in the two barbarians that stood beside him. Enraged, the chief brought forth his battle axe, jumped down off the mound and shouted commands to his warriors.

"Help!" Alexander shouted. He was quite aware someone was trying to rescue him, but he felt the need to yell anyway. It made him feel better. "HELP!"

The priest put the dagger to his throat. "I prefer for you to die nobly for your next life. Don't make me do this so quickly."

Another arrow flew directly at the priest. He put his hands up to stop the arrow with his charm which distracted him from his immediate danger. Angelica, who stood close by, had managed to sneak next to the Priest. When his hands went up to stop the arrow she grabbed his staff and pushed him off the steps. He fell back off of the stone platform with his staff onto the ground. Angelica dropped the staff, whipped out her dagger, and quickly cut his cords.

"Here," she said breathlessly. "Take my sword."

"Yes," Alexander agreed. "Free the boys quickly." He motioned to the boys that were now struggling to loosen their ropes.

He grabbed her and gave her a passionate kiss. "I made my choice, I am forever with you," Angelica whispered with a huge smile.

The sound of horses' hooves grabbed Alexander's attention. Chauncey and Fergus rode hard into the barbarian midst on horseback. They brought with them three extra horses and Zeus. Alexander glanced at the hidden archer on the mountain. It was Jack. Jack had left his hidden spot and was attempting to draw the barbarians up the mountain after him. He ran up the mountain and took a position on a small ridge. The barbarians couldn't run up the hill directly after him, so they approached him from the sides. This helped Jack cut down the Bete'szek warriors one by one with his arrows.

Keira emerged from behind the rock and furiously rushed to her master. One barbarian fell to the ground and had his throat immediately torn out by her relentless jaws. She would never stop as long as Alexander was in danger. Chauncey and Fergus easily plowed a path through the lightly armored barbarians as the enemy bounced off of the horses. The Bete'szek had not prepared for a fight, and many barbarians were cut down by their swords. As Chauncey and Fergus slashed their way through their midst, Keira finished off anyone who didn't survive their lethal cuts.

Alexander checked Angelica's progress as she freed the other prisoners. They were almost free. He spotted his armor at the end of the platform. Angelica was closer to it than he was.

"Boys! Get to the horses. Angelica, my armor!" He pointed to his armor that was behind her.

Angelica finished untying the last captive and turned to retrieve Alexander's armor.

"Alexander- behind you," she warned.

Alexander swung his sword and clashed steel with Duncan. For a moment they locked swords and pushed against each other, trying to gain an advantage.

"What have you done?" Duncan asked emptily.

Alexander pushed him off the mound and watched Duncan fall backwards. That was too easy, Alexander thought. Duncan allowed him to do that.

He turned as Angelica tossed the armor towards him. The boys that had been freed ran towards the horses. He retrieved the armor and quickly put it on, but noticed that the priest, staff in hand had gotten up and walked up the steps. He walked towards Angelica and appeared to be chanting a curse.

Alexander yelled and pointed to Angelica that she was in danger. He ran down the steps after the priest. He heard Angelica scream. The priest held his staff upwards and the power of the staff lifted Angelica into the air. The closer Alexander got to the priest, the angrier he sounded. Then, without a sound, the priest swung his staff towards the rocks. Angelica's body followed motion, and her body hurtled towards the rocks.

"No!" Alexander yelled. Before the priest could turn and face him, Alexander ran his blade through the priest's back and out his chest. The priest gasped for air. Alexander withdrew the blade and in one motion, swung his sword and separated the priests head from his body.

Alexander ran to where Angelica had fallen. Her body was limp, her back broken in two. Blood began trickling out of her mouth.

"Angelica, can you get up? Here let me carry you." He removed a few rocks that had fallen on her from her body's impact into the mountain.

"No, no." Her voice was pain to him. "I can't move.

Alex…"

"Please no. We can make it. I promised I'd free you."

"You kept your promise Alex. I am…forever free." She tried to smile but her injuries were too great, and she was in too much pain. She choked on her words and stopped breathing.   Hatred began to course through Alexander's veins.

A hand grabbed Alexander's shoulder and he whirled around and found Fergus out of breath and off of his horse.

"Prince Alex, we've got to be going!"

He didn't want to leave her body. He didn't want to leave her.

"Prince! We've got no time!" Fergus' tone carried a sense of urgency. The barbarians realized they were much easier targets than Jack and had turned back to them.

Alexander stood and took one last longing look at Angelica. His spirit was broken and he felt a burning desire for revenge. But that will come later, he thought. He hurried with Fergus to the horses while the other three captives followed and mounted the spare horses. Alexander ran his sword through a barbarian that tried to pull Chauncey off of his horse.

Alexander mounted Zeus and took the reins. "Where's Jack headed?" he demanded.

"Parting gift for the Bete'szek, sir." Chauncey pointed up the mountain. Jack had left his position on the cliff and had run further up the mountain where he reached a large boulder. He worked to leverage his body to loosen the boulder. "He'll meet up with us."

Together the riders continued to fight their way back to the mountain pass. The barbarians ran back and forth and were ineffective against the armed horsemen. Jack finally loosened the large rock. It rolled down the mountain and crashed through several warriors, killing them instantly. Satisfied with his handiwork, Jack continued his quick trek around the side of mountain. Disheartened and confused, the barbarians stopped following both the horsemen and Jack, and attended to their dead.

The six horsemen quickly galloped through the pass. Once outside of the pass, they reentered the forest where Fergus reared his horse to a halt.

"Why are we stopping?" Alexander demanded. He was done with barbarians and the forest. He wanted to get away as quickly as possible. He knew that the thieves would give chase to them as soon as they could.

"We're waiting for Jack. He should be here soon."

"Fine," Alex said. "Dismount and find something to hide behind." As he slid off Zeus, he turned to the boy that had been tied to him. The boy's face showed the same terrified expression. He was definitely panicked and looked to do something foolish. Alexander hoped that he wasn't about to do something that would get them killed.

"Boy, what's your name?"

"Jean."

"Jean, I am Prince Alexander Wolfield. Listen to me. Take the horses out of sight. Don't go too far. We need to stick together if we're going to survive. Do you understand me?"

Jean shook his head in understanding. Along with severe bruising, he was skinny and frail, and Alexander attributed his smallish stature from a lack of food. Duncan did not seem to offer much in the way of hospitality; however, he hoped the boy could complete this simple task. If he lost the horses, they would have to run out of the forest on foot. His fears were calmed when the boy managed to take the horses and disappeared quietly into the forest.

The other two boys had dismounted their horses, and to their credit, concealed themselves in the brush.

"Fergus?"

"Yes sir?"

"Can you get up that tree with your bow and keep a sharp eye out? If it's not Jack coming, then we need to go."

"Yes sir. I'll keep a weather eye out." Fergus jogged quickly to a tall thick tree that Chauncey stood near. Chauncey had a puzzled look on his face.

"We're keeping a weather eye out, are we Fergus? We've become sailors now?" Chauncey crouched behind the tree and scrunched his nose.

"I just meant that I'll keep my eyes open," Fergus hissed. "Sailors say it all the time."

"Exactly when have you sailed Fergus?" Fergus said nothing and ignored Chauncey. "Alright then Admiral, keep your weather eye out, maybe it'll rain." Fergus rolled his eyes at Chauncey and selected a different tree to climb, away from his brother. He climbed past three large branches and gingerly sat on the thickest one. Once settled, he brought an arrow out of his quiver, and sat very quietly.

Keira and Alexander crouched down behind a separate tree and settled in. Alexander placed his sword on the ground next to him, and finished fastening his armor. In all of the confusion, he had forgotten to tighten it. His thoughts started to drift back to Angelica and her broken body. He replayed the event over and over in his mind. He tried desperately to assure himself that there was nothing more he could have done.

He was jarred back to the present with the sound of an arrow next to his ear. The arrow found its mark, one hand space away from Alexander's head. Alexander looked up at Fergus who started to mouth an apology. Chauncey had also seen the arrow and gestured angrily at Fergus. Since Fergus had their attention, he flashed three fingers and pointed in the direction they had come.

Alexander heard the rapid pounding of hooves as their riders rode them past the breaking point. He motioned to Keira to stay hidden. She shuffled backwards and laid flat on her stomach. Alexander peered around his tree to get an idea of who was coming. Jack rode a chestnut mare, and he had three lengths on his pursuers. Three men that Alexander immediately recognized as part of the thieves guild pursued Jack and closed the distance rapidly.

Alexander had an idea. He quickly pulled himself up to where Chauncey sat.

"Chauncey?" he whispered, "don't use your bow. Just follow me."

Fergus looked down at him. Alexander made a quick hand gesture at the bow, and then shook his head no. Fergus shook his head as if he understood.

"So what are we doing?" Chauncey asked.

"We jump when they get close." Alexander said it so confidently that even he believed it was possible.

"We're going to jump off a branch onto a moving horse?" Chauncey's eyes widened.

"We'll be fine," Alexander lied. "I've done it before." Chauncey tossed his bow behind the tree and assumed a position to jump out of the tree.

The horsemen emerged closer to them. Jack passed underneath them, at full gallop. In an instant the lead thief passed under Alexander but Alexander decided he would wait for the next one. The other thief was nearing them and Alexander had to time it perfectly so he didn't use the ground to break his fall.

The moment was now. Alexander perfectly timed his jump from the branch and fell so that his right arm locked around the thief's throat. The thief began to fall backwards, and as he fell, pulled the horse's reigns backwards. The horse reared up and nearly fell backwards on them.

Alexander and the thief fell to the ground. The thief landed on his neck and the impact broke his bones so that he died instantly. The thief that followed them sprang off of his horse, pulled out his sword and rushed towards Alexander. Alexander looked around quickly for his sword that he dropped. As the thief closed in, Chauncey jumped down from the tree on top of him. The thief crumpled to the ground and lay motionless. Alexander was relieved that when he nudged the thief with his foot, the thief moaned in return. Alexander wanted a prisoner and he wanted answers to all of his questions.

The thief who had nearly caught Jack turned his head and was surprised to see his companions lying on the forest floor. He knew his situation was perilous, so he turned his horse around and charged back the way he came. As he charged past Alexander he took a swipe at him with his sword. Alexander ducked out of the swords way and fell to the ground. The thief kept riding past him and into the forest.

Alexander looked up at Fergus and motioned at the thief. Fergus raised his bow and shot his arrow. The men watched as the thief fell of his horse. Fergus' arrow had found its mark.

Alexander sat up and wiped his face which was wet with sweat. Jack rode his mare back to where Alexander sat.

"My prince," he said smiling. "Many thanks for waiting for me."

"It seems…." Alexander said as he stood up. "That I owe you my life. Thank you for disobeying my wish."

"I was just thinking about all the gold coins we could

save by rescuing you instead of ransoming." Jack smiled broadly.

"Not that I'm complaining, but that was incredibly foolish." Alexander clapped Jack on his back and looked about for the horses.

"Yeah well, when you've got a rogue prince roaming the countryside stirring up trouble, someone has to watch out for him." Jack contorted his face in mock concern and shook his head.

"Couldn't agree with you more," Alexander replied. "Shall we leave? JEAN!"

There was a brief period of silence before Jean emerged from the forest with the horses. Alexander was extremely relieved, and vowed silently to never entrust Jean with any tasks ever again.

"Okay, mount up, and let's get out to Greystone," Alexander ordered.

"What about him?" Chauncey asked. Kiera stood over the thief and uttered a low menacing growl.

"Bring him. I need answers. Chauncey, make sure he's good and tied. This thieving bastard knows this forest better than us. We can't afford losing him."

Alexander took a moment and considered their predicament. To the north and the west lay mountains and barbarians and to the south was Greystone. There was no doubt in Alexander's mind that traps would be set by the thieves in that direction. The only direction that they had not tried was east.

As he considered their options, Alexander watched the wind as it rustled through the trees, and he heard those same whispers from before. He wiped off what sweat was left on his face onto his sleeve and he decided upon the direction.

It was easy, like a coin had been flipped. Fate would

take them east. He finally found the sword he dropped and picked it up. He examined its handle and realized that this wasn't his sword....it was Angelica's. He felt a twinge of pain, but was happy that he had something of hers to remember her by. He figured that he honored her memory by wearing it and by killing those responsible for her death it would give him some satisfaction.

"Everyone, mount up. We're heading east." Alexander said firmly.

"East? I'm not going east. You can kill me right now." The thief's tone was defiant. Alexander ignored his tone and said nothing in response.

He motioned for the riders to follow him. Fergus grabbed the thief's reigns to prevent him from escaping and Chauncey followed close behind. Jack rode on the other side of the thief while the three boys followed Jack closely.

The thief would not be deterred from complaining. "There's something in these eastern woods. No one goes in there. Not even the Bete'szek will enter."

Alexander halted Zeus and rode Zeus backwards to the thief's horse. Zeus stepped perfectly in sync and without hesitation. Alexander placed the tip of Angelica's sword against the thief's throat.

"I've killed people today, for a cause I know nothing about. Everything I have seen does not exist in any corner of my father's kingdom. There are only myths, never proof. And yet, today, someone tried to cut my heart out. We are riding east, and when we get back to Middlebrooke, you are going to answer every question I have. Do I make myself clear?"

"Quite," the thief replied. Alexander watched the perspiration gather on his brow. Alexander looked at the other riders and ensured they wouldn't question him.

"Let's pick up the pace. I've no more stomach for

his kind."

To Alexander, the forest seemed endless. It was like a cruel maze that had no way to leave. It was impossible to track the sun's position, or the stars. The canopy of the trees made it difficult to tell if they were going in the right direction, or in circles. The thief happily remarked that many of the people that they found wandering in the forest were near death and were eager to exchange one fate for another.

Alexander felt extremely uneasy with his decision. Up until now, he had felt confident in each direction he had gone, but there was no end to this forest and all he had to navigate by was the sound of the voices that it seemed no one else heard. They rode over rough, hilly terrain, and at times the riders lost their focus on the surroundings as they tried to steer their horses.

He was frustrated to no end, and he was afraid that it would show. He was lost. Any hope of leaving the forest was rapidly disappearing. To make matters worse, it was starting to darken. They were all nervous now for no one, not even the thief, dared to speak.

Alexander rode to the top of a tall slope and he saw a small stone hut in the middle of a small clearing. The sun shone down into the clearing, and for the first time, they weren't riding through the dark. The hut was square and Alexander thought it was too small to house anyone. Alexander might have ridden past it, but as soon as he had seen the hut, the whispers had stopped. This intrigued him further, so he rode over the slope and into the clearing.

"What is it?" Jack asked.

"I don't know," Alexander said. "There's something...." He sighed. "I wish Father Malachius was here. He'd help me straighten this out."

Alexander decided the best thing to do was to go

inside and investigate. The hut held a purpose and Alexander wanted to know it.

"Did anyone bring a torch?" he asked, hopefully. Seeing no one had a torch, he dismounted Zeus and drew his sword. Alexander moved cautiously towards the opening while the others stayed on their horses.

The atmosphere was very quiet and very tense. Jack drew his sword, and Fergus and Chauncey followed his lead. All three men sat still in their saddles and looked around the clearing for any unseen enemy. The quietness was suddenly pierced by a shrill screech that reminded Alexander of a hawk. Alexander backed away from the entrance and looked towards the sky.

"What is it?" Chauncey asked as he too looked up.

"We've been in this forest twice. Both times, I haven't heard bird or beast." Alexander watched above him for a moment.

"I told you we shouldn't have come this way. Something's out there! It's going to kill us! We'll never see it coming." The thief was frantic. He babbled on and Alexander was tired of listening. He turned his focus back on the stone hut.

As soon as he reached the arch, he heard that screech again. This time it was louder and more piercing than before. It pierced at such a high pitch, that all of the riders and Alexander covered their ears. The horses bucked and whinnied as their hearing was also affected. Alexander fell to his knees and covered his ears to block out the sound. There was a massive thud as something hit the top of the stone hut. There were equally powerful but softer thuds to the sides of the men.

The screeching mercifully ended and Alexander uncovered his head, stood up, and looked up towards the top of the stone hut. He came face to face with the source of the screeching.

"My God, they're real," he whispered in disbelief.

CHAPTER XII

Alexander found himself in the presence of the strangest and most fearsome beast he had ever encountered. The gryphon was twice as long as Keira and a foot taller than the largest wardog. The gryphon had the head of a bird of prey, but the body of a lion. The gryphon's fierce yellow eyes were unlike anything he had ever seen. The gryphon peered angrily at him from the top of the stone hut and Alexander felt as if its gaze pierced through him. It crouched low as if it meant to pounce on him.

Alexander respectfully backed away from the gryphon. He looked slowly to the left and the right. Six gryphons had taken up places in a circle and surrounded the riders. The men kept their horses as still as they could to not provoke these fearsome creatures. Even fearless Keira retreated under Zeus and whimpered in their presence.

Alexander thought back to the abbey and his conversation with Father Malachius. He had laughed when the priest told him that gryphon's blood was mixed with his armor. Had Father Malachius known about this brood of gryphons?

"Alex, what should we do?" Jack whispered through

clenched teeth.

Alexander thought carefully. The gryphons were the guardians of the divine and the adversary of evil. They also hoarded treasure so Alexander deduced that perhaps this was a place of buried treasure.

"I think," he said in a guarded voice, "That we are okay. They seem to be unhappy that we are here. If we move very slowly away from this hut, I think they will let us go on with our journey. So I want everyone to not make eye contact, and slowly back away."

Alexander backed away in the direction of Zeus but the gryphon would not break eye contact and stared at him cautiously, following his every move.

The thief started to become agitated. "Maybe we need to get inside the stone hut to be safe. Maybe they're just looking for whoever's weakest." He glanced around wildly at the other animals, while his horse shifted hooves in agreement.

"Great," Alexander said, "that would mean you're first." The gryphon that held guard on the hut lifted its head, opened its beak, and screeched loudly. Again, everyone covered their ears. The gryphon leapt down from the roof he stood on, and walked menacingly towards Alexander. Although unsure of what was about to happen, Alexander grew more curious at the first good look he had of the entire body of the gryphon. Its head and neck were covered in feathers, like a falcon, and its beautiful white wings reminded him of an eagle. Its front feet were like a bird of prey, perfect for catching and flying away with its victim and it had the razor sharp beak to tear at its quarry's flesh. The creature's hind legs resembled a lions and had powerful muscles for running down its prey.

Alexander and the gryphon continued their cautious behavior towards each other. Alexander finally felt the breath of Zeus on his neck. He needed to get on Zeus if he could. He had gotten far enough away from the hut that he didn't feel the gryphon viewed him as a threat any longer.

Alexander looked at everyone to make sure they were holding still. The boys held still, even Jean, and so were Fergus, Jack, and Chauncey. The thief was overcome with fear and looked about wildly for an escape. Alexander began to say something that encouraged him to stay still, but it was too late. The thief dug his heels into his horse and began a quick gallop to the stone hut.

"No!" Alexander yelled.

The gryphon closest to Alexander turned its head and screeched. Immediately, two gryphons on opposite sides of the group flew towards the rider. The first gryphon reached the thief, pulled him off his horse and flung him into the air. The second gryphon sank its claws into the back of the horse, and like the first used its powerful talons to throw the horse into the air. The thief was the first to meet his death. As soon as his body hit the ground another gryphon immediately pounced and tore at his flesh with its beak.

The horse met the same fate. Once the horse hit the ground it tried valiantly to get up but it was no match for the gryphons. The horse's fate was sealed and its plaintive whinnies ended once all the gryphons except for the one in front of Alexander joined in and feasted on the victims.

It was now or never. Alexander was angry that he had lost the thief, for now his questions would go unanswered, but they had to leave now or suffer the same fate. Alexander slowly mounted Zeus and nodded towards his companions. They delicately began to ride to the opposite side of the clearing to go back into the woods.

Again, the same gryphon from the hut flew before them. This time however, none of the other gryphons joined it. Alexander watched as it sat before them, and quietly waited.

"What's it doing now?" Chauncey asked.

Alexander felt sure that this gryphon was trying to communicate with him. He dismounted off of his horse and walked towards it.

"Prince Alex, what are you doing?" Jack called.

"It's alright, I'm alright." Alexander walked directly to the gryphon without breaking eye contact. He stopped when he was right in front of the Gryphon.

"Your move," he said to the gryphon. The gryphon lowered its head, and examined the crest on his breastplate. Alexander could feel his armor beginning to burn. He felt this once before when he dueled with Angelica in the forest. Alexander heard the whispers on the wind and this time they were louder but he still could not make out what they said.

The nearer the gryphon approached, the hotter the armor became. The gryphon spread its wings and screeched and Alexander felt his flesh begin to burn. The other gryphons stopped their feeding and took positions to surround the travelers. Each one mimicked the lead gryphon and stretched out their wings and joined in the screeching. Alexander's body urged him to scream in agony. His flesh burned, and the voices drove him to the point of madness but he continued to resist the pain as best he could. He clawed at the armor but lacked the focus to unfasten it. Finally, he was overcome with pain and he closed his eyes and lips tightly. His whole torso was in agony and he opened his mouth to scream.

As quickly as the pain had built inside of him, it just as quickly dissipated. Alexander opened his eyes to an astonishing sight. He was no longer in the forest and he no longer stood. He now lay on his back and stared up into a blue sky. The trees had disappeared and so had the hut. Gone was any sign of his companions or the gryphons. Confused, he sat up and examined his surroundings.

In front of him lay the ocean and its waves quietly lapped against the sand. Alexander watched as water raced up the shoreline to where he sat. He waited as the water came to meet his legs, then after a brief greeting, the water raced back down the shore to the ocean. Alexander studied his pant legs. Although the water had just touched them, neither of his legs were wet. Intrigued, he stood up and walked toward the ocean. Another wave crashed down on the surf, and sent more water racing up to meet him. Alexander dropped to his knees and placed his hands in the water. He felt a cool sensation, but nothing more. The water retreated once more to the ocean as if everything was as it should be, but he touched his face in confusion. There was no feeling of wetness, no residual droplets of water. He was completely dry.

Alexander thought back to the forest. Am I dead, he wondered? He gazed out over the celestial sea and felt a wave of peace wash over him. I suppose this is as good a place of any to spend eternity, he thought.

Alexander turned to walk up the beach when he caught sight of a massive temple constructed just above the sand dunes. Alexander felt drawn towards this impressive building. He climbed the dunes and made his way to the temple. As he began to get closer, he was amazed at how massive the structure was for this building was as large as the tallest wall in Alveus. Eight marble columns stood outside the entrance of the temple holding up the archway into the opening.

Past the archway was one door. The door was made of solid oak and ordained with an etching of a gryphon. The gryphon looked exactly like the ones in the forest and was the entire length of the door. Alexander saw a brass ring, for opening the door, to the left. He pulled on it and swung the door open. As the door opened, light began to creep into the temple. He walked into the temple and was immediately awed by the wood carvings of seven gryphons; three gryphons per side, and one in the front. Each carving was set on a block of marble.

The walls inside of the temple were inlaid with gold. As the light touched the gold, a brilliant reflection was produced that was too intense for Alexander's eyes. He turned his eyes back to the statues and noticed that the eyes of the gryphons and changed. They were now open, with a yellowish glow. Alexander stood in front of the statues and was filled with awe. His first thought was to run but a voice shattered the silence and froze him.

"Who are you?"

Alexander looked around the room. There was no one there except for the statues. The yellow eyes of the gryphons began to have a reddish tinge.

"State your name."

Alexander at once knelt down on one knee and looked at the lone gryphon statue.

"I am Prince Alexander Wolfield, fourth son of His Majesty King Magnus, Ruler of Alveus."

"Why have you called us here?"

"I have not, I assure you. My friends and I are in need of safe passage through your forest. We mean you no harm, I swear it."

"Your armor," the gryphon replied softly, "That armor is familiar to us." Its eyes started losing the reddish tinge, and returned to its original fiery yellow look.

"Familiar," the other statues whispered.

"The priest who gave it to me said that it was mixed with gryphon blood."

"And yet," the gryphon stated, "All that remain of our kind here in this forest have gone undisturbed for generations."

"Until today," Alexander said, "I didn't believe such creatures existed. There are no stories of you, no reason to believe any of you exist. Do you have names?"

"I am TA'LON. These are my sons. We are the last gryphons living in this forest," he said sadly.

"Where are the rest of your kind?" Alexander asked.

"Gone away," Ta'lon said.

"Gone away," the others echoed in unison.

"Your kind hunts as down as if we were common livestock. We protected you for so long. Now we remove our protection. Let your fate be what is already written."

"I don't understand who hunts you down? None of my people enter the forest."

"The Magic hunts us in greater numbers. Although Magic cannot hurt us, the weapons of man can inflict our deaths. They have driven away those who survived. We cannot stay much longer."

"What can I do?" Alexander asked. "Let me help." Maybe there was some way to help these creatures. Maybe they could be important allies.

The gryphon thought for a moment and its response to him was slow and measured.

"I can sense your future young Prince. It is not a pleasant one. Pain will be your constant companion.....You have the mark of death upon you. Death will come after you ruthlessly and swiftly. It will cut you down. It will cut down your family like a flood. Your country will lie in ruin and make slaves of your people....I am sorry Prince Alexander Wolfield. Your end is much like ours. Your fate has been decided."

"It doesn't have to be like that," Alexander insisted,

as he quickly stood to plead his case. "Aren't you the protectors of the divine? The sacred? Aren't gryphons the beasts that guard the gates of heaven? You are said to be impervious to magic. You can help me end this before it's too late. It's them, the Bete'szek that are killing you, not my people. Please. Help me." He stretched his arms out and entreated the gryphons to be his people's allies.

"It is not our battle Prince. I can no longer be bold with the lives of my sons. I am sorry." Ta'lon sounded sincere in his apology, but sincerity didn't help Alexander.

"Fine," Alexander said, disappointed. "Then will you let my men and I leave the forest?"

"You may," Ta'lon agreed. "I am truly sorry Prince. I have seen the horror that is to come. And no one should bear that alone."

"What do you mean? What's going to happen?" Alexander demanded to know.

The sound of a rushing wind came from behind Ta'lon's statue. The yellow eyes of all the gryphons began to fade, leaving closed stone eyes. The wind was picking up in strength, but Alexander resisted it as best he could.

"Tell me!" he yelled. "Tell me!"

The wind's strength became too much for him. He became like a leaf that could not stand a breeze. The wind knocked him off of his feet and blew him out of the temple hurtling down towards the ocean from where he had come. Alexander turned to face the ocean on his descent. The water was calm as the waves no longer crashed on the beach. The closer he came to the water, he could see beneath the surface and he saw a reflection of himself. He was much older, and instead of fine fabric, he wore tattered rags. His hair was long and his general manner disheveled. His face showed no emotion and he leaned against a stone wall. His hands were chained to an iron ring. A feeling of hopelessness gripped Alexander for he felt that he had been shown his future.

He neared the water but he refused to feel hopeless.

"NO!" he defiantly yelled as he closed his eyes. He hit the water like a rock, but no splash was affected.

Alexander opened eyes and found himself back in the forest. Ta'lon sat down and the other gryphons flapped their wings and flew to the top of the trees that surrounded them. Ta'lon and Alexander's eyes met. Ta'lon stretched out his great white wing and pointed to a direction of the forest. When Alexander nodded his head as if he understood, Ta'lon flew to the top of the trees and out of sight. Alexander was amazed, the gryphons were a majestic sight to behold in flight, full of grace and power.

No one spoke as Alexander looked in the direction of the thief's body. He was dead and Alexander could not help but feel disappointed. All of the answers he needed, he would have to wait to get them. He picked Angelica's sword off the ground and swung himself on Zeus. His companion's eyes were fixated on him.

"Well," Alexander said, "I know the way out." He turned Zeus in the direction Ta'lon had pointed in, and began to ride in that direction. He was worried at what Ta'lon had told him, and he wondered how long it would be before his new enemies caught up to him.

It was several hours after nightfall when they finally arrived at Greystone. Alexander was beyond tired and teetering on exhaustion. He hadn't eaten in over a day and hadn't tasted a drop of water on his lips. He had also been having incredibly intense headaches since they left the forest. He surmised it was a leftover feeling from the potion that he had drunk that subsequently rendered him unconscious. His group was no worse for the wear but they needed food and drink as well.

Jack and Chauncey rode side by side, and kept each other awake with idle banter. Alexander appreciated the banter, although towards the end of the journey every word began to feel like hammer and his head was the iron. Fergus had been kind enough to carry Keira with him on his horse. She slept in the saddle but would readily open both eyes if need be. The three boys that they had rescued were a different story.

The three boys were extremely affected by their harrowing experience. They were pale and morose. They said very little and went about their business. Their clothes were torn and their clothes were covered with a mixture of blood and dirt. They were a sad sight to behold.

The one named Jean hid his face from the group most of the time. Alexander suspected he wept for most of the ride. From a quiet conversation Alexander learned that the other two, Devin and Shawn, were brothers. Their parents lived in a lone cottage just outside of Greystone. Ten days ago the thieves fell upon them, and took them and their parents into the forest. The thieves also slaughtered their livestock and burned their cottage. After that night, they never saw their parents again, and assumed them to be dead.

Jean felt the worst of it. His family had built a small farm near their home a year ago. A month before the thieves attacked Jean and Shawn's home, Jean and his family disappeared. It had been assumed that they left to another part of the kingdom, but now they knew that wasn't true. Jean had been imprisoned for almost a month before they finally took them to the altar. During that time, he rarely ate, and was frequently beaten by the thieves. They were delivered at the altar to find Jean's father was to be sacrificed first. That was the man Alexander whose screams terrified Jean.

Alexander felt pity for Jean. Through brief glances, Alexander would catch Jean whispering to himself and slowly rock back and forth. When Alexander engaged him in conversation Jean would leave the trance he was in and respond guardedly. When the conversation was over he would again lose himself in his thoughts and gently rock back and forth in his saddle.

When they finally reached the outskirts of Greystone, Alexander sent Fergus and Chauncey ahead to carefully observe and ensure no ambushers waited. When satisfied the village held no surprises, Fergus and Chauncey silently waved back to Alexander that all was well.

"Where to Prince?" Jack asked. Alexander had preferred to lose the title when he came here, but somehow the barbarians found who he was, and that he was coming. There was no point hiding his royalty anymore.

"We need sleep," Alexander said as he looked at Jean. "It would do us a lot of good."

"I'm too tired to sleep," Fergus yawned. "But I need sleep to look my best."

"Your best was never good to begin with," Jack laughed.

"Best give up looking for a wife," Chauncey chimed in. "Right now you'd have better luck attracting livestock."

The men laughed easily. It felt good to laugh and even better to smile.

"So much has gone on today," Alexander said. "I don't understand any of it. Never in my life could I have dreamed any of this."

They all muttered in agreement. Chauncey and Fergus volunteered to dress down the horses and put them in the stable. Alexander was grateful for it. He wanted to get back to his room and fall asleep. Fortunately for them, there was still a light on in the tavern.

Jack and Alexander entered the tavern first, followed by the three young ones.

"Good evening sir," he said very loudly to the portly man sweeping the floor. "We need four of your very best drink, lots of food, and…three milks."

The portly fellow bowed his head and smiled at the thought of making money. The tavern was just as dingy as when Alexander left it that morning, but he embraced it with all of his heart. Even the dirt did not bother him as much.

"Begging your pardon sirs, I will have your drinks right up. The food I will cook for you. I will wake my wife. You will enjoy her stew, I promise."

"Don't be miserly with the carrots this time," Alexander warned him.

The innkeeper left the room quickly to wake his wife. Very soon he returned with cups filled with drink for all, and two extra for Chauncey and Fergus who were still in the barn with the horses and Kiera.

"To our health," Alexander toasted with a hint of sarcasm.

"To our health," Jack toasted in agreement and the boys toasted with their milks.

The mead was delicious to his lips and turned him reflective to the last few days. The death of the priest disturbed him. The feeling of taking a man's life, and the way he did it, by chopping off his head…Alexander sighed.

It had been a busy week. He was taken prisoner, was very close to being ritually sacrificed, and saw an enchanted beast that existed only in the annals of mythology. And today….today he lost someone very close to his heart. He still wrestled with the blame over her death. Was it his fault? Was there anything else he could have done differently? He took a long drink to quench his thirst, stopping only when there was nothing more in the cup to consume. He scoffed.

"I'm out," he said to Jack, and turned his cup upside down.

"Prince Alexander, that's the strongest drink in the village. We tend to drink it slowly," Jack warned with a frown. A feeling of light-headedness quickly came over Alexander. He looked at Jack and noticed that Jack had a funny look on his face. It was the same look that Jack had given him since the encounter with the gryphons. It was a face full of questions that Alexander tried to ignore.

"Alright!" Alexander exclaimed. "What? You look like you are about to burst."

"I have questions," Jack said relieved.

"Ask them," Alexander retorted.

"Back in the forest....the gryphons. There was a moment when it seemed like time stood still. I can't explain it. I've never seen anything like it. What was this?"

Alexander's light-headedness started to dissipate. Try as he would, being drunk would not improve his situation, and would make him no better than his brother Calimus, who made it a regular habit of hiding at the bottom of beer steins. He leaned closer to the table so the men could hear him.

"The armor I wear," he started, "was a gift from the Priest of Middlebrooke. He claimed that it was forged with steel and gryphon's blood. I didn't believe him but the gryphons could sense it. And then when they all started screeching together, I couldn't stand it anymore so I closed my eyes, and there I was on a beach. And a temple where the gryphon's warned me..." he paused to catch his breath and to capture the gryphon's words clearly. "It said that death is coming for me and that my fate is assured."

There was a moment of silence at the table. Alexander grabbed Jack's unfinished drink and took a giant swig.

"It's God's irony, I suppose," Alexander continued, "That one week ago, I was celebrating my own birthday in the comfort and security of my family's castle and I could not be content in that. So now I've managed to nearly get killed, anger an entire people, ruin the thieves' guild, put a death mark on my head, and find that my death is coming. And let that be a lesson for you on your birthdays," he said pointing a finger at the wide eyed Sean. "I hate birthdays," he said matter-of-factly.

Fergus and Chauncey entered the tavern at the same time the innkeeper served a very watery stew. Alexander sniffed at it disappointedly.

"Innkeeper?" he asked. "Would you have any meat in this?"

"I'm sorry sir, but meat is rather scarce. But I can promise you all the vegetables are fresh." Alexander saw fear on his formerly jolly face and began to feel bad. He never imagined how bad a peasant's life was. The last two days had given him a firsthand account.

"No I apologize. Your food and care has been excellent over these last few days. I do however wish to make a complaint that my cup is empty," he said winking at the innkeeper.

"Oh right sir," he laughed. "I know just the right thing then." He quickly ran back to his casks and set about refilling all of their cups. They all set to eating and drinking except for Jean who sat and picked at his food.

"What will you do now?" Jean asked quietly.

Everyone lowered their forks and looked in amazement at Jean. Any unforced words from Jean were unexpected but he had asked the question that seemed to be on everyone's mind. Everyone at the table watched for a response from Alexander. Alexander felt their eyes, but after consuming his third glass, he felt very bold and less diplomatic.

"I….I am going to go….no. I am going to flee. I am going home to Middlebrooke, gather up my belongings, say goodbye to my family, and head for the ports. I will then embark upon a voyage, and discover a new land that has no barbarians or witchcraft and I shall raise potatoes contentedly. And own an inn." He lowered his voice to a whisper. "An inn that has meat stew. Not vegetable stew." He picked up his fork, and skewered a radish.

"You're running away?" Jean exclaimed. His face had lost all its color, and was again panic stricken.

"You heard my story. I am marked for death. If at the very least I am on a boat, then I doubt that any barbarian would be sailing like a fish under water. I would be safe, ergo outwitting a very stupid people who wish me ill." Alexander took another swig, and noticed the pain he associated with Angelica started to dissipate.

Maybe Calimus was on to himself by hiding in taverns, he mused.

"But you saved us," Jean persisted.

"No I didn't." Alexander insisted quickly. "If it wasn't for these three men, we'd be lying dead in a cold cave. I walked into a trap, that's all I did."

"Prince Alexander," Fergus started, "You've taken us down this path. It was your idea to explore the forest. You found the thieves and stood up to them. You found their hideout. You tricked them into taking you to the barbarians. You directed us back through the woods. You've been leading us this whole time."

"And you've had a vision with mythological beasts," Jack added. They all nodded in agreement. "Look, before you came here, we hated the nobility and everything that it's stood for. They steal from us; they kick us off our lands. The King cares more about his Treasury than us. We're nothing. It's different with you. We have a purpose. We believe in you."

"I'm not understanding what you're saying Jack." Alexander said, genuinely confused. What was the big deal with him leaving, he thought.

"You travel alone. It's not fitting a Prince," Chauncey said. Fergus nodded his agreement.

"Then I hereby renounce my Princely duties. It is not something that concerns me." Alexander felt very giddy. "I will send a letter to my father immediately."

"What does concern you?" Jean screeched. "You've killed a dark priest, they'll most likely come after you, and it's us who stand in their way. I won't die as my father did. I will die with a sword in my hand and take as many Bete'szek as I can."

"It's true. Better chance we stand with a sword in our hand than a pitchfork." Fergus nodded his red locks in agreement.

"What do you want from me?' Alexander said exasperated. "I'm the fourth son of the King. I'm ignored. Would you have me betray my father now? Should I now travel the road to treason and add that to my sins? I would never betray the crown."

"The crown doesn't matter to us. You do," Chauncey said firmly. "What we're trying to say is this…the skills we have…Jack with the bow, us with the sword, in our limited ability, we pledge to you. Where you go, we go."

"You're saying you want to serve me in my bodyguard? Have you not heard what I have said? I have a mark of death upon me. If you stand close to me, you will feel its effects. You will die." Alexander pleaded with the men to be sensible.

"Isn't that what we swear too?" Jack asked. "We swear to die for our Lord. You have our pledges," he said firmly, "and we will not take no for an answer. We've all seen what hell looks like today, we all know what our fates may be. We ignore it so that we may be free in going about our daily lives."

"The armor," Alexander objected. "How are we to fabricate the armor?"

"We are smiths! And if we do not forge the armor, we know who can!" Jack laughed. "And…if you'll allow me…" He reached into his belt and tossed out the bag of coins that Alexander had given him to hold, "I'd say we have more than enough gold to purchase what we need."

"There are only three of you," Alexander objected again.

"Five," Sean interjected. They had stayed quiet and listened all this time that Alexander forgot they were there. "We have no homes to return to, and we owe you our lives."

"Six," Jean said.

"We still need more," Alexander said. "If we are going to war we will need more men."

"I can find a few good men that I've known for a while," Fergus said. "They're a little rough around the edges, but they're honest and true."

Alexander sighed. This was a defining choice. Being alone and becoming a merchant, and owning a tavern had rapidly fallen out of his grasp. It was time to embrace his fate.

"Very well," Alexander agreed. "I will give you one week's time to gather six men. When that time comes we will journey to a monastery that I spent my younger days learning the art of combat. There the monks will train you in combat, just as I have been trained. It will not be easy and it will take a year. So whatever family you may have left, bid them farewell."

The group nodded their heads. Chauncey raised his cup.

"Long live Prince Alexander."

The group raised their cups in unison to toast Alexander.

"Long live Prince Alexander!"

After the toast, they retired to their separate rooms. Alexander felt relief knowing that he had at least three decent fighters who would stand with him through all times. They had proved their mettle and their loyalty. Time would tell if the other ones could do the same.

As he prepared to retire for the night, he took one last nervous look in the direction of the forest. In the far distance, he spotted a reddish tinge on the horizon. His first thought was of a fire. He thought about it another moment but concluded that it was not the section of the forest the gryphon's were in. If it was the eastern part of the forest the color red would be unmistakable. It was the thieves' part of the forest.

Alexander's thoughts wandered to Duncan. What part would he play in this vendetta? Would he send his thieves and assassins after him? He lay back in his bed and thought about Angelica. He pictured her in his mind and began to miss her beauty and her feistiness. He thought about the warmth and passion of the kiss and wondered if he would ever feel that way about anyone ever again.

He fell asleep quickly, and slept longingly through the night.

The week at Greystone moved quickly. Summer began its slow change into fall and the leaves began to change to their auburn hues. From his room at the tavern,

Alexander kept watch over the forest, waiting for riders or raiders to come for him. At times, he thought he saw what appeared to be the silhouette of a gryphon flying over the trees, but it never turned to be more than wishful thinking.

The leaves on the trees outside of his window began to turn brown and one by one, fell to the ground. Alexander watched each individual leaf fall to the ground, and then turned his attention back to the forest. Occasionally he left his room and made his way downstairs to eat. Only once did he venture outside of the tavern.

When he finally left his room, he walked around the village for he wanted to ensure no strangers entered Greystone while he had slept. During his walk, he spotted a familiar face.

"There you are sir," a young girl chirped from behind a barrel.

"I know you," Alexander said smiling. "You're my guide. Did you spend that coin already?"

"Not yet," she replied. "I hid it so I wouldn't lose it though. If my dad saw it he'd take it away and buy drink with it."

"I'm sorry," he said sympathetically.

"It doesn't matter. Someday I'm leaving this town and I'm going to go out on my own. That coin will help me."

"Where are you going to go?" This was a curious little girl, he thought.

"The city. Or somewhere. Just to have an adventure away from here. Have you ever wanted to have an adventure?"

"I did," he said slowly. "But now that I've had one, I'm not so sure I'd want another."

"Not me," was her firm response. "I'd have an adventure every day."

"You're an odd sort," he laughed. "What's your name?"

"Katrina."

"Katrina, my name is Alexander. Here…," he took another coin out of his small moneybag. "This is so you can have as big an adventure as you want….I'd suggest that you be on your way soon."

"Why?"

"No reason… I'm just someone that wanted to have adventures too. Here, I would advise you to go south." He pressed two gold coins in her small hand and watched her dark eyes light up with delight. She opened her mouth to thank him, but no words came out.

"It's okay," Alexander said softly. "These coins are enough to get you where you want to go. We'll see each other again, and I wish you happiness. It was a pleasure to have met you."

He left Katrina where she stood and heard her squeal with delight as he walked away. He couldn't explain his newfound generosity, but felt a kindred spirit for adventure with Katrina. He continued his mindless walk around the village until he ended up back at the tavern where he waited for his men to return.

Fergus and Jack had left to find the men they promised to deliver. Devin, Shawn, and Jean had left two days later and traveled to their burned homes, to gather whatever possessions they may still have had. Fergus had stayed behind to keep an eye on Alexander, and to make sure no harm fell on him. He was usually seated in the tavern and always faced the door. Keira typically took her place underneath Fergus' table. She had been worn out by all of the activity of the previous days, so she was contented to sleep at his feet.

Alexander's thoughts drifted home to his family. He

might be in Greystone which was as far off the path as one could get, but he would have assumed that some news of the royal family, some gossip, might have reached this town. But nothing ever did. The tavern was emptied most days, and at nights the constant vigil of Fergus and the great dog was enough to keep away even the most stalwart of drinkers.

It was evening of the twelfth day when everyone finally returned. Alexander was ecstatic to see his monotony relieved, and Fergus was relieved to be relieved of his duties! Devin, Jean, and Shawn also returned that same night. They found very little but some stores of grain and feed that they had sold in town for a decent change of clothes.

Jack and Fergus also returned and had done a passable job recruiting potential bodyguards. Each man was still in his early youth, and could therefore be trained to endure the harshest conditions. They looked strong, and Alexander guessed their backgrounds to be farmers or those that worked in the mines.

Jack confirmed that as he introduced Alexander to the new recruits.

"Men!" Jack shouted to gain their attention. "I promised you a more dangerous and thrilling life to leave the mines and the fields. I promised you sunlight and a chance for glory." Men murmured approval. "I give you his highness, Prince Alexander."

The room went silent and all of the men's eyes were upon him. Alexander guessed their thoughts. They're thinking about me, he thought. Am I worth their lives? Can't blame them.

The silence continued for an awkward moment until Chauncey spoke up.

"You were chatty on the way here about it and we

told you about what you were signing up for. If you're a coward let us know now so we can say goodbye and send you back."

"No one's a coward," a man in the back said. "We've been working in the mines since we were old enough to hold an axe. For his family. Why should we consider protecting him."

"Because he's the man to save the kingdom," Jean piped. "Our homes, our families. He's marked by God!"

Alexander disagreed with Jeans words, but he kept it to himself.

"We've seen horrors across the border," Jean continued. "And it's threatening to spill over into our lands and into our families. My family's already been murdered. How much longer should we live in fear of what's out there? I've seen what the Prince is capable of in battle. I'll follow him. I'll give my life for his."

Alexander was impressed. This was a lot of courage coming from young Jean, but the men deserved to know what they were getting themselves into. He would make a gambit with honesty and see if that paid off in their loyalty.

"I understand what you're thinking," he started. "I'm a noble, and since when did nobles pay attention to anything outside of their purse strings or outside of their own walls? I know that, I understand that. But past that, the fact remains that we are still men, with blood flowing in our veins. That blood is the same. There is no difference in the color that flows from peasant or noble. And when one of our countrymen's blood is spilled, we all mourn that loss."

"Jack has told me that you are trustworthy men, honest and decent. I need men like that in my service, but make no mistake. You come with me….you agree to serve me….you serve me with your life and at point of death. I don't say this because I am a reckless fool and I do not value your lives to be more than my whim. I say this, because in all honesty....I am marked for death. You ride with me at your own peril."

The men murmured their thoughts with each other. Alexander noticed Jack and Chauncey's face pale. This was not the strategy they employed to get these men to come to the tavern, but every man deserved honestly.

"I know," Alexander said, "That you weren't told that. But what is a mark of death? We are all marked for death. You can die in the mines, you can die of old age, or you can die fighting against an evil that threatens our lives, our families, and our grandchildren's future. Come with me. Swear your lives to me. I will put it to good use. Obey me. Fight when I say fight. Stand when I say stand. And together, you'll have a life worth living for."

Alexander looked each man in the eye. They were silent; captivated on every word he spoke. A few men nodded as if Alexander had touched the unconscious of their souls. His words resonated throughout the tavern.

"We're not warriors! We're farmers and miners!" yelled out one of the men.

"To the East there is a monastery where the monks are trained and learned in the art of war. They themselves are knights of the church. I have trained with them; their doors will be open to us. They can train you within two years to be an invincible warrior, and you will fight with the strength of ten men, and together we will be more powerful than one hundred barbarian axe men."

Alexander felt himself stirring inside. He began to believe his own words, and his confidence grew with each word. This was a brand new feeling, a confidence to lead men into battle and into greatness. If his fate was death, so be it. Better dead in battle than dead of apathy and despair.

His week of solitude had made him extremely agitated and he wanted desperately to bring this to an end so he could stop looking over his shoulder.

"Men!" he shouted as he stood on a table, "will you pledge your loyalty to me? Will you stand with me in the face of overwhelming odds, confident that you will prevail? Will you be free men and fight to protect your Prince and your people?"

All of the men shouted in agreement and roared with approval. They clapped each other on the back and cheered again as the tavern keeper brought drinks to them.

Fergus grabbed his cup and held it in the air. "To the Prince."

Instantly, all of the men straightened their postures and lifted their cups to Alexander.

"The Prince!"

Alexander raised his cup to join them.

"Men, tomorrow we ride to the east," he proclaimed.

As the men retired for the evening and went upstairs to their rooms, Alexander extended his hand to each man that passed by him. They smiled and clapped each other on the back as if they had suddenly amassed a large fortune. Alexander silently hoped each man would have the courage and fortitude to do what needed to be done no matter the stakes.

Jack was the last one to the stairs, and he paused briefly in front of Alexander. He smiled at Alexander and placed his fist on his chest.

"Wherever and whenever you choose to go into battle, you can count on each man drawing the sword and fighting until the last breath. No harm will ever come to you, I swear it."

Alexander smiled at Jack and clapped his hands on his shoulder.

"Jack, it's not me that we're fighting for. It's our kingdom and our people. Even if I fall, I would leave it to you and the men to carry on and fight for what's right in my place. You have been right there and seen the evil that lurked, but together we are going to eradicate it."

Jack nodded and made his way up the steps. A thought had just occurred to Alexander. Perhaps this fight with the barbarians would be no more than a private war between himself and Duncan and whoever else they held in esteem. Alexander was encouraged by this thought for he would soon command the elite warriors in the kingdom.

CHAPTER XIII

The men greeted the dawn with regret and each man stumbled out of his room and looked the worse for the wear. As they rubbed the sleep from their eyes and walked out of the door, they found themselves being waited on impatiently by Alexander. Alexander was anxious to travel, so he had awoke early and settled his debts with the tavern keeper. Jack had also woken early and roused the blacksmith. After a brief negotiation, Alexander procured an agreement for twelve new suits of armor, to be readied by the time their training was completed.

Chauncey bartered for a small wagon, and loaded what supplies they needed for the journey to the monastery. Keira decided she would make the journey in comfort, so she jumped inside the wagon, stretched her legs lazily, and rolled onto her back.

Fergus had completed saddling all of the horses so that the group was ready to ride once all of the riders were present and accounted for. Each man mounted his own horse while Chauncey tied his mount to the wagon. His responsibility was to ensure all supplies were cared for during the journey.

Their destination of the monastery was located a week to the south east of Greystone on top of one of the mountains in what was called the Western Range. The Western Range was a formidable barrier of mountains that prevented any city from being built along the western shoreline. Instead, many towns were hidden within the mountains and loosely allied themselves with the Alveuns. Because of their remoteness and inability to be anything more than a strategic defense, the Alveuns had built small watch forts overlooking the ocean, and the church had established a monastery. It had been years since Alexander had visited and trained there, but Alexander remembered the way and had no doubt that he would be remembered by the Monsignor.

The man known as the Monsignor once fought as a captain for Alexander's father, King Magnus. He was known as a resolute and stalwart warrior, whose strength was reflected in the weaponry he carried. His favorite sword was the two handed long sword, a sword so feared for it could cut a man in two regardless if he wore armor.

The Monsignor, whose real name was Francis Abernathy, fought in several battles in the early years of King Magnus' reign and distinguished himself for his courage and military skill that he was often whispered to succeed as a general one day. He would have too, if not for his constant quarrelling over the kings domestic policies. He had begun to see peasants as the backbone of the kingdom and often sought to place their voices ahead of the nobles.

This often caused animosity between Francis Abernathy and the nobles. Their petty bickering along with their constant politicking frustrated him, and he left military service when he felt that King Magnus had no interest in providing to the welfare of all the people.

He joined the Abbey under Father Malachius, took the Christian name of Jean Paul, and quickly advanced through the Order with his piety and zeal. It was always a strange sight to see this formerly terrifying warrior as he walked through the streets of Middlebrooke and blessed the poor. He ignored the odd looks and sarcastic comments from his previous comrades and set about to help the poor. He built their houses and tilled their fields with them. All the money that King Magnus had bestowed upon Jean Paul was given as charitable donations to widows and orphans, all in God's name.

Eventually, Father Malachius chose to move him to the monastery, and bestowed upon him the title of Monsignor. It was there that the Monsignor trained other young men who wished to serve the Church with more than just a cross.

It had always crossed Alexander's mind that this was an odd co-existence that a man who left the army to care for the poor trained others in the art of killing but there was no time to waste and Alexander had little stomach for philosophy. The monastery was a place with no distractions where his men could be trained quickly and easily and a place where they would be protected from anyone who might care to do them harm.

As they rode across the countryside, Alexander rediscovered the western side of the kingdom. It was terrain made of rolling hills for the first half of their journey, and it stretched for miles. It seemed to him that after every hill was a field of crops. Every few miles they came across a wooden palisade that oversaw the fields and the peasants that worked them.

The peasants paid them no mind, and continued on with their back breaking labor. The nobles eyed the travelers inquisitively as they rode through their lands, but did not attempt to question them.

As the journey progressed Alexander worked to learn more about each man and where they came from. He spent much time involved in lengthy conversations to learn their backgrounds.

Fergus and Chauncey, both brothers, were miners whom Alexander had known through his apprenticeships from his youth. They were part of a group of miners that roamed the countryside and set up small villages in areas that they felt would be rich in gold and silver. Once they discovered a vein of gold or silver, they mined the surface of that area which then became quite profitable for the kingdom. The Baron of Edgebrooke set apart several tracks of land to encourage their permanence, and that resulted in the town of Greystone. From this town, miners gathered their metals and transported it to Edgebrooke where the merchants bartered and eventually sailed the metals to Middlebrooke to the smithies.

For Alexander, this apprenticeship helped him ascertain knowledge of mining and metals, and the back-breaking work that was put into it. It also included a lot of digging, on a daily basis. It made him exhausted and during his apprenticeship as a miner he often lapsed into a quick slumber after his dinner.

On the other hand, Fergus and Chauncey were quite used to it, and after dinner they took part in their favorite activity of driving everyone mad. After one particularly hard day of work, Fergus and Chauncey decided they needed a day of rest. After everyone had retired for the night, they snuck out and loosened every wheel of every wagon so that as they were being driven out, the pins eventually fell out of the wheels, which caused great delay. Fergus and Chauncey surmised that this would be enough that they could run off and fish the Alveus. They were wrong. Their father, Fergus the Elder, made them put back together each and every wagon. As Alexander was the apprentice, he was made to help.

The red headed monsters didn't stop there. Horses disappeared and were found tied to a fence on the way to Edgebrooke. Their crowning achievement happened one night when they somehow managed to move every animal in the stable into their father's house. He was fit to be tied, and Angus, Fergus, and Alexander spent the rest of the day cleaning the house, and all the animal droppings that were left.

One night, the villagers called a town meeting, at which point they elected a night watchman. The night watchman had worked ever since. Chauncey and Fergus were clearly disappointed, but undaunted.

Jack, on the other hand, was not a miner. He was the son of a blacksmith, also named Jack, and was given the proper name of Jackson. He and his father had moved to Greystone once his mother died because of the opportunity to work with the miners. They shoed horses, repaired mining equipment, and often made and repaired weapons.

Jack was always quiet and seldom joined Fergus and Chauncey in their shenanigans. He was older by three years, and was looked on by his father to carry out many of the blacksmith's duties. It was Jack who taught Alexander the proper care and maintenance of horses, and how to use the forge in the making of a sword. Alexander had his uses at a young age as well, and if there was no work to be done for the day, he taught the three boys basic swordsmanship.

He fashioned swords from wood for each one of them, and they played together often as they pretended to be heroes and villains' and they battled for control of the land. Alexander had often wondered what his mother thought if she saw him playing with those under his station.

The palace was lonely, so Alexander enjoyed the time he spent in the countryside more than that of the castle walls.

When Alexander finally left Greystone, it was a sad day for him. The memories eventually faded over time, and it was now that his memories were being awakened. He wondered if their meeting was indeed chance, or was it fate that their lives were once again entwined.

Jack had managed to recruit two young apprentice smiths from Middlebrooke in the week that he was gone. The first, Brennan, was a loud and boisterous lad with huge fists. When Alexander shook his hand it felt as if it were being crushed by stone. By virtue of being the largest, he also had the biggest appetite. His appetite was so large, that Alexander had to caution the men to ration their food to ensure they had enough for their journey.

Brennan was good natured and jolly. His eyes would twinkle with any joke he told, and even better, laughed at his own girth. Fergus tested his humor by unbuckling his saddle one morning while he looked the other way. Once Brennan put his foot in the stirrup, the saddle shifted and fell off the horse, and caused Brennan to fall backwards into a puddle of mud. The men laughed, and even Brennan stood up and nodded that the joke was funny. Later that same day, Brennan offered to shake Fergus' hand to show no ill feelings existed. Fergus clasped his hand and was immediately pulled out of his saddle and completed a somersault over Brennan's horse and once he landed on the ground, began to roll down a grassy knoll. Brennan laughed so hard that Alexander thought he would join Fergus at the bottom of the knoll.

The other smith's name was Ferris. He was not as large as Brennan, but his stature was impressive. He carried a large war hammer with him and used it very dexterously. He had come from another country and hoped to start a new life as a blacksmith. He never talked about where he came from, but Jack recommended him because Brennan had worked with him for a long time.

There was one member of the group that made Alexander uncomfortable. He had the eyes of the devil and sent shivers down Alexander's spine with this one particular gaze he held. Alexander had seen it before, in the barbarians chief's eyes. His eyes held a cat-like glow to them, and they peered out from under his shoulder length dark hair. He was unshaven and dirty, as if he held an aversion to water. His name was Farkas. Jack said he was the best hunter in the area. The villagers told stories that Farkas could sneak up on Death and steal souls back before Death knew he was there.

Another man who seemed out of place was Gerard. Gerard was part of the town militia in Middlebrooke, and held himself to be a man of learning. He was very clean and dressed in finer linens then any of the other men were used to seeing. He often tried to ride next to Alexander and worked very hard to try and impress the Prince. Alexander was amused but often found Gerard's smug arrogance to be an annoyance. Gerard was trained with the spear, and held himself to be an expert. Unfortunately for Gerard, his mouth was better for talking than his talent was for spearing. When he boasted his skills to Brennan, Brennan simply grabbed Gerard, spear in hand, and held him over his head. Brennan didn't stop there. He spun around in circles until Gerard begged him to stop. Once back on the ground, Gerard's useless assessments of battle tactics ceased.

The final two additions were farmers from the fields they were passing through. Mayer and Linus were both sons of peasants and doomed to a very short life as they tilled the fields. They seemed to be the happiest of the twelve, and were eager to begin a new life.

Both of them were indistinguishable from any other peasant. They were dressed in rags, and they rode mules. The only difference between the two that Alexander could tell was Linus' yellow hair. Other than that, they seemed to be the same person. They also had a darker complexion than the others because they worked in the fields every day.

After two weeks of laughing and riding, the men had bonded into a good natured group of friends. Alexander was happy to see that happen. He felt that if the men were friends, they would fight harder for one another.

Once they reached the mountains, the group proceeded up the steep path with their mounts. When the monastery came into view, Alexander's mind flooded with memories. He spent an entire year under Monsignor Jean Paul's tutelage and hoped that the Monsignor would agree to help train his men. There was no finer military mind in the kingdom, King Magnus included. It was a shame that he left the army, but with only a peasant revolt in the last five years, he was best served helping the poor, which he found to be his primary mission.

As they approached, Alexander noticed several armed guards stationed at various points along the stone wall and two guards stationed at the entrance to the monastery. They also saw Alexander and walked forward to stop the strangers.

"Here now," the first guard said. He carried a short sword with his right hand and a shield in his left hand. His companion did the same. "What brings you men to the monastery of St. Pietro today?"

"I am seeking counsel with the Monsignor," Alexander answered.

"And why would he counsel with you?" the second guard asked as he eyed the men behind Alexander. Several more guards appeared on the wall, interested in the conversation that was going on.

"Very well," Alexander sighed impatiently. "I am Prince Alexander Wolfield. You will let me pass in the King's name, and you will go and tell the Monsignor I wish to speak with him or I can take you back to Middlebrooke where you can be properly punished for insulting the King's Son."

Alexander said this was such authority that a hint of fear appeared in the guards eyes. They looked at each other and quickly dropped to one knee.

"My apologies, Prince Alexander. We are following the orders of the Monsignor that no one is allowed entrance to the monastery. Perhaps if the Prince would allow himself to be escorted in while his men waited outside?"

"That is not acceptable, but I will respect the Monsignors wishes." Alexander turned to Jack and whispered. "Keep an eye on the men on the wall."

The second guard escorted Alexander into the monastery and Alexander took a quick look around the courtyard. Nothing had changed since he trained here, except that there were now armed guards. There were still men that trained in the courtyard; some trained with swords, some with axes, and a few clubs. There was something elusive that continuously nagged at Alexander but he could not pinpoint exactly what he felt.

Eventually, the large stature of the man that was Monsignor Jean Paul appeared from the chapel door. He was dressed in traditional friar's robes, and approached Alexander with hands clasped behind his back.

"Prince Alexander!" he exclaimed with surprise. "I haven't seen you in years. What brings you back to the monastery? More lessons?"

"Indeed," Alexander replied. "I'm in need of

desperate help. I have twelve good men who know their way around hammers and plows but not swords. I need your help to train them into the fiercest bodyguard in the kingdom."

The Monsignor furrowed his brow and his face darkened.

"Prince…I agreed to tutor you as a favor to Father Malachius. He sees great potential in you. This monastery is not for the training of the King's men. It is for God's men."

"Does God need an army, Monsignor?" Alexander wanted to pry about what was happening at the abbey because there seemed to be too many conflicting visuals.

"I see," Alexander continued and he turned around, "Guards on the wall and at the gate. I see men being trained. What would they be trained for Monsignor?" He glared at the Monsignor. Jean Paul was an intimidating figure, but Alexander was going to force him to help.

"These men are part of the church," Jean Paul insisted. "They train to protect the poor from whoever would oppress them. They protect the church hierarchy and any pilgrims that choose to visit our holy places."

"That may be true," Alexander countered, "But I need you to do this for me. If not for me, then for Father Malachius."

"What does Father Malachius have to do with your protection? How is this a matter for the Holy Church?"

"He sent me to find them," Alexander explained. "You want to protect the poor and that is a cause that unites us. There's an evil coming to our lands, I've seen it. Those twelve men outside of these walls have sworn their loyalty to stand with me to the death and that is something that very well may be coming, especially if we cannot be trained by the best mind in the kingdom. I know what this evil is and I might be able to stop it. If I cannot, then we are all doomed....Please. Train my men for two years like you did for me. When we're done, I will return to Father Malachius immediately and tell him of all the events I've seen."

Jean Paul did not appear dissuaded but he agreed.

"I will train you and your men," he said. "For two years. You will be my guest, and you will receive all of the amenities therein. Have your men stay in the monk's quarters. We have some rooms available."

"Thank you, sir," Alexander said in surprise. He did not expect Jean Paul to cave in so easily. He bowed slightly to the Monsignor and showed respect then quickly turned and walked out of the gate to where his men waited. He smiled excitedly and he felt a strong sense of happiness wash over him.

"Good news, sir?" Jack asked.

"Men!" Alexander called out. "Welcome to your new home for the next two years. Place all of your belongings in the monk's quarters, and let's start training. This time will pass quickly and we must be good stewards of our time."

The twelve men dismounted their horses and clapped each other on their backs in excitement. They chattered endlessly, grabbed the reins of their horses, and entered through the doors of the monastery. Alexander watched as they entered the monastery. He caught sight of Keira as she still lay in the back of the wagon. Her head was erect, and her eyes and ears were alert. Her mouth opened to pant, and she wagged her tail elatedly as the wagon jostled about.

That's right Keira, he thought, suddenly I mean something. I just wish I knew what it was.

CHAPTER XIV

Monsignor Jean Paul fulfilled his promise to train the men. For six days out of every week, Jean Paul and the monastery's friars put the men through the most comprehensive combat training that had been developed to that time. The friars started the agony every morning by having them run down the path to the bottom of the mountain, and then back to the monastery. To add insult, they added the additional weight of a sword and shield. If any man dropped either item, they would be punished by being made to run the sharp descent, then back up the mountain.

The mountain air, although fresh, taxed the lowlanders and for the first six months they gasped for air during every morning ritual. The men grabbed their sides in pain, but pressed on while they carried sword and shield for fear of failure. When they successfully completed their trek, the friars mercifully allowed them a short drink to quench their thirst.

From there, Jean Paul insisted that they attended the daily benediction held for the monks and friars in the monastery's chapel. To add to their hardships, during the benediction they were instructed to kneel rigidly on the cold wooden floor until the short service was over. Their knees ached in pain, and their bodies begged for rest, but each man pressed on and determined not to be the one to fail. They whispered words of encouragement to one another and drew courage from their unified struggles.

Once the service was completed, they were finally allowed to eat. The typical breakfast was a type of porridge, with some fresh bread to help sop it up. It was not what any of the men were accustomed too, especially Brennan. He loathed breakfast and mentioned it often. He begged any man within sight for meat and was refused daily. He took to eating any food that was leftover or being sent back to the kitchen. Mayer and Linus commented that breakfast was a blessing, for they had eaten far worse in their former lives as peasants.

After breakfast they assembled in the courtyard and trained in the different weapons of war. Each friar was an expert with a different weapon. They learned how to fight and defend with a variety of weapons which included the spear, bow, sword, war club, and battle axe.

It didn't stop there. They learned how to fight individually, how to fight in tandem, how to fight as one group, and how to fight on horseback. They learned and worked through the day until they thought their arms might fall off. The friars took no pity on them. The friars took to quoting Proverbs and condemned each thought of failure as sin and unnatural. Such was the friars own training, that they were frequently beaten when they began their training, and learned through pain how to manage their own suffering. As they were trained, so they transferred their knowledge to Alexander and his guard.

For dinner, those that desired to eat were required to make their way to the monastery's garden and harvest that which they wanted to eat. They initially protested, but Alexander understood the regimen, and humbled himself from his princely station to uproot the first vegetables. His men watched and slowly joined in, as each man picked his own dinner. From that first day, Alexander established himself as the leader, but continued to ignore the privileges that came with his title. His men responded in kind. Each man trained harder at the behest of their leader.

If a man struggled running up the mountain, Alexander barked encouragement. If one of his men struggled with a particular weapon, Alexander spent whatever moment was spared to them to ensure his man understood. He gained favor with his men as he continuously led by example. He never complained and he never spoke against the friars. He attempted each task first and neither complained nor hesitated.

He never hesitated to discipline if he didn't think a particular person listened fully or purposefully dragged his heels through any training. Fergus was the first to feel Alexander's wrath for not being properly prepared for spear combat. While the friar gave instruction, Alexander noticed Fergus began to look off towards the walls and missed what the friar had told them. Alexander was so enraged that he asked Fergus if he wanted to be beyond the walls and if he needed help getting there. Fergus apologized quickly but Alexander wasn't finished. He berated the entire group of men for not listening to their capacity and threatened to send them home if one of them lost focus. It never happened again.

Jean was another frequent target of Alexander's impatience. Although eager back in the tavern, he now showed signs of being hesitant on the battle field. He hesitated when he used a sword, and preferred to fight defensively, and never attacked his opponent. Alexander never understood the hesitation, and believed Jean would look for revenge and therefore careless in his approach, but Jean valued his personal safety too much during the combat sparring. Alexander noticed that spars with Jean slowed down as the men seemed reluctant to engage him because they too had picked up on his hesitance.

Alexander felt if Jean carried this hesitation into a life or death situation it could mean all of their deaths. He stopped the sparring and took Jean's wooden sword away from him. In its place he gave Jean a real sword. Alexander called out to Farkas to spar with Jean and challenged them with a simple message. Defeat your opponent or be carried off to the grave.

Farkas smiled wickedly and immediately swung his sword towards Jean's head. Jean reacted out of reflex and blocked Farkas' sword. Farkas wasn't finished. He swung wildly at Jean and Jean ably blocked the wild swings and managed to attempt some impressive parries at Farkas. After several close calls for injury, Alexander had seen enough. He stopped the spar, and instructed loudly that Jean was to spar with real weapons, as well as anyone who sparred with him. While it sounded cruel, he saw that Jean handled the sword well, and that since his life depended on it, Jean responded.

Once in a while, Alexander made his way up to the top of the wall and looked east, towards his home in Middlebrooke. The city was too far away to see, which made Alexander miss it even more. He missed his sister and his mother mostly, and even Edward strayed into his thoughts. The monastery was closed to outsiders so Alexander received no news of the kingdoms affairs. He thought about the health of his father and surmised that if something did happen to his father, even this remote monastery would have heard the news.

The one blessing that Alexander saw in this isolation was that he was protected. There were no outsiders allowed within the monastery so there could be no attempts upon his life. Anyone seeking to sneak into the monastery would be quickly spotted and dealt with.

And such was the routine, six days every week, for two years. Their time passed quickly and Alexander soon found himself on the eve of his twentieth birthday. He felt stronger and more confident than at any other time in his life. He felt fearless and found a growing sense of excitement within him. He wanted to return home and show his father the finished results of his training. He wanted to prove to his father that he was worthy to be called son. He was ready for anything, and his men were too.

During the last six months, Alexander became more comfortable with his armor. The gryphon's blood that it was forged with seemed to make it come to life in sparring, and communicated with him as he fought. It saw behind him when he did not. It recognized the immediate threat, when he did not. With the armor, he relied upon his reflexes and quickness and responded to each command. The armor made him a formidable opponent and unbeatable. His confidence knew no limit with his armor.

One starry night, he wanted to attempt something even more dangerous. He called his men together at the practice ground and issued a challenge.

"Men," Alexander explained, "I am going to blindfold myself. I want four of you to pick up a wooden weapon and once we begin, I want you to attack me one at a time."

"Isn't that dangerous?" Gerard asked. "We might hurt you."

"You won't be able to touch me," Alexander said confidently. He strapped the armor about his torso and immediately picked up on the now familiar voices. Alexander still hadn't figured out where they came from, but seeing as how no harm had come to him, he felt protected whenever he put the armor on. He attributed the voices to nerves and that this was his minds way of focusing on the present.

Gerard, Brennan, Fergus, and Devon picked up wooden swords and maneuvered into positions around him. Alexander took a small scarf and wrapped it around his head which completely blocked his vision. He drew his sword and steadied it above his head with two hands. He cleared his mind of all thoughts and focused on the silence.

"Now!" he ordered.

He heard nothing except the whoosh of a weapon. A wooden sword crashed into his armor and sent Alexander backwards. As he stumbled he heard sounds of wood being splintered. He fell back onto the ground and gasped for air. He ripped off his blindfold in pain and looked up to see all of his men with their mouths opened in shock. Even Alexander had to admit he was confused.

"Why didn't the armor warn me," he wondered.

Jack quickly made his way to Alexander and put out his hand to lift him up. Alexander grabbed his hand and was lifted onto his feet.

"My lord, I am so sorry for hitting you!" Jack was breathless and his face was completely pale.

"No," Alexander replied and rubbed his stomach woefully. "Not your fault."

"Why did you have us do that?" Jack asked.

Alexander thought about the wooden swords for a moment.

"It's the wooden swords," Alexander said as he ignored Jack's question. Alexander guessed that he was never in any danger with a wooden sword about to hit him.

"Perhaps, we need real weapons."

"I don't think that we want your highness in danger," Jack cautioned. His face was deeply disturbed with Alexander's display of recklessness.

Alexander insisted upon his royal prerogative and the four men picked up their weapons, but this time Jack insisted and replaced Fergus as the first attacker. Alexander turned in a complete circle and observed every detail of the practice field around him. An empty wooden wagon stood just outside their practice area and untended bags of flour were piled on either side. Their practice area was close to the monastery's wall and two unoccupied stone benches were just feet away. Alexander shut his eyes and placed the blindfold back over his eyes. He concentrated intently on his surroundings and felt the presence of the weapons that were near him. He held his sword above his head and readied himself for the attackers.

"Now!" Jack shouted and the practice began.

Alexander felt Jack's sword approaching his midsection. It was slow and half-hearted and Alexander blocked it easily.

"Faster, Jack!" He shouted angrily. "It is not women I have recruited to fight nor tentative snails. Attack me as if your life depended on it."

Alexander heard the "swoosh" of a sword and although blindfolded, he saw it all with his eyes closed. Alexander blocked it quickly and spun around to block the next attack. His mind communicated to his body and he seamlessly moved his sword from one clash to the next. Alexander felt completely confident and moved into an attack. He blocked a sword, and swung his fist back towards the man's face. He connected with a thump and the man staggered backward with a grunt. He wheeled around and took five steps towards another combatant. He swung his sword down on the man, who was blocked but Alexander carried his body's momentum into the man and kicked at his midsection. The man's breath exhaled from his body and he dropped his sword. Alexander felt the presence of the remaining two men as they chased him down from behind. Alexander pushed past the man he had just kicked and visualized the two benches next to the wall. He sprang to the benches and jumped on one. As he jumped, Alexander felt the breeze of the swords cut beneath his feet. He then ran along the bench as the men followed and jumped towards the wall; his feet still moved as if he tried to run up the wall. The presence of the weapons stopped as if the men stared in amazement. Alexander pushed off the wall with both of his feet and flipped his body over the men. He swung his sword quickly at the dumbfounded men and together they parried several moves against each other.

Alexander felt the presence of swords behind him and he immediately ran to the side and where the wagons were. He slowed briefly and engaged the four men in a quick clash of swords. One man over estimated his balance and Alexander sent him sprawling along the floor. Another one made the mistake of allowing Alexander a free hand which Alexander gladly buried into his nose. As he freed himself from the entanglement Alexander leapt over the sacks of flour and used them as a barrier between himself and his men.

Finally, Alexander tired and yelled for the attacks to cease. He took off his blindfold and opened his eyes. All four of his men sweated profusely and moaned of aches and pains, while Gerard and Devon nursed bloody noses. Alexander smiled broadly and clapped Jack on his back.

"How did you do that my lord?" Devon wondered aloud.

"I have never seen a man fight like that," Jack added.

"Were you peeking through the blindfold?" Fergus moaned.

"No," Alexander laughed. He tossed the blindfold to Fergus who placed it on his face to test it.

"I am the greatest swordsman in Alveus," Alexander boasted. The armor protected him against danger in the forest, and it would continue to do its work. He was now a formidable opponent for any man or barbarian army.

As his men stored their weapons and finished nursing their wounds, Alexander went inside the monastery's dining hall and sat down on the wooden bench to rest. In just a few weeks, he thought, they'd be on their way home. Outside of the hall a ruckus had started and it continued into the dining hall. Brennan carried a large keg on his shoulder and had a large grin on his face. Fergus and Jack carried a cauldron and they set it down right next to the table. After they placed the cauldron on the floor, Jack stood up and spoke.

"My Lord, your men would wish you a Happy Birthday. Now we realize that if you were in your castle, you would be fed fresh fruits, vegetables, and lots of meat. You'd also receive a fair share of ale!" All the men nodded upon hearing the word ale.

"We have however, made a hearty stew out of rabbit, potatoes, and the carrots that the rabbit was trying to eat. Fergus here also managed to barter a keg of ale from the monks. Being how they're God-fearing, it's probably water."

All the men laughed. Alexander was touched by their generosity and made sure he thanked each one of them. Brennan opened up the keg and ensured that everyone's flagon was filled. When they were filled, each man toasted Alexander's health. Throughout dinner they laughed and told tales of their former lives and even haughty Gerard joined in. At long last the subject was broached, what would come after training was finally completed.

"I have some ideas," Alexander said. "We need to pick up armor and weapons from the smiths in Edgebrooke. After that, to head back to Middlebrooke and swap all of your nags for some fine steeds. With apologies to Linus and Mayer, no one wants to ride to war with men on mules. When this crisis is passed, we can all go back to a better life."

Linus and Mayer laughed, and were visibly happy with their good fortune. The men chatted merrily about armor and weapons, and what they fashioned as their favorite. Alexander felt that each one of them had completed their training successfully, and he was eager to leave the monastery, even if that meant leaving a few weeks early.

Early the next morning, Alexander arose and went to see Monsignor Jean Paul. Alexander found him in his study amidst parchments and scrolls reading vigorously.

"Monsignor, may I speak with you for a moment?" Alexander asked. For such a great man, Alexander noticed that his study had very few items of comfort. The desk was as plain as one could have, and what the chairs lacked in cushions they made up with plenty of splinters. A picture of the Holy Father was the only decoration that hung from the walls, save for a map of Alveus and the world surrounding it. Alexander studied it for a moment as he waited for Jean Paul to finish his parchment work. Alexander noted that the maps of Alveus ended with the forests, and the word "Terra Incognita" was scribbled beyond them. It was curious that in three hundred years, not one explorer had ventured north. There was a west, a south, and an east, but truly, north did not exist to the Alveuns.

"Yes, Prince Alexander?" Jean Paul finally responded.

"I know our commitment was for two years, but I would like to release you from that commitment and leave a few weeks early. My men and I are eager for home."

"I see no problem with that," Jean Paul said. "Several of the monks have complained that Brennan's appetite will cause a famine within our monastery walls." He chuckled at the thought but then his face turned serious. "I watched you....last night. With the blindfold. Very impressive. How do you do that?"

Alexander explained to Jean Paul the mysteries of the armor, and relayed what Father Malachius had told him about the gryphon's blood.

"Gryphon's blood?" Jean Paul asked surprisingly. "Very interesting." He leaned forward and looked directly into Alexander's eyes. "Listen to me. This is not a child's game. Regardless if Father Malachius entertains your fancies, if you continue to be reckless with your life you will pay dearly for it. There is only one armor like yours. It doesn't take a scholar to understand its uniqueness. Men have murdered over that armor. The way you've behaved....you might as well set up a tent in the market and have people pay to come touch it."

"I'm sorry...." Alexander was at a loss for words. "That was not my intent at all."

"I know," Jean Paul nodded in agreement. "I know you trust your men. But in the end, they are men, and men are ruled by desire. Keep that in mind, and you'll do well....But for a happier occasion. The monastery wishes the Prince a blessed birthday. We will outfit you with enough supplies to take you as far as Edgebrooke. Will that be sufficient?"

"Yes. Thank you Monsignor, for everything. I pray that we meet again, and for you to stay in good health. In return, I will give you two mules, to help you with your planting." Alexander imagined a brief period of sorrow for the farmers he commanded, but what they lost in stubbornness with mules they would gain in regality with true war horses.

"You are most generous, Prince Alexander." Jean Paul smiled and offered his hand in friendship. Alexander grabbed it and shook it. "Until we meet again....Godspeed."

Alexander left the Monsignor's study and felt properly chastised. He should have been more responsible, but he wanted to test the armor's limits.

I am tired of being given every man's opinions, he thought. Everyone commands me, and yet I am a Prince. At what time will I make my own way?

He met with his men shortly after meeting with the Monsignor and explained to them that they would be leaving that same day. He instructed them to gather all of their personal belongings and ready their horses. He explained to Linus and Mayer that they would be riding in the wagon, for their mules were being donated to the monastery. The men were excited and went about their preparations with vigor. After two years of blood and sweat, they were going home.

CHAPTER XV

It took the men most of the morning to be properly prepared for their journey home. The Monsignor stayed true to his word and the wagon was loaded with supplies. They left the monastery and started down the winding road. With spirits riding high, the men sang folk songs and told jokes to one another. Once down the mountain, Alexander decided it was time for them to function as a military unit. Although deep in Alveun territory, the assassins could easily find a place to hide and send a shower of arrows their way. This was their lot in life, and it was time to be tested. He sent scouts out, two at a time to ensure that they were not being followed and that they would not be ambushed.

A few days into the journey, Mayer and Linus approached Alexander and requested that they be allowed to visit the homes of their parents. Alexander understood how proud they were with their training and how they wanted to make their parents proud, so he dismissed them and ordered them to meet at Middlebrooke in two weeks' time. They borrowed Angus' horse and Angus was relieved to care for the wagon.

He then sent Jack, Girard, and Brennan with Angus

and the wagon to Edgebrooke to procure the armor that had been ordered two years ago. Once procured, they would be able to visit their families and make it to Middlebrooke within the same timeframe.

This left Alexander with seven men so he decided to stop by the village of Greystone. The others were happy with the news, as most of them hailed from near that village. Alexander's curiosity nagged at him about his first night there, and still desired to know more about the men that extorted a large amount of precious metals from that village on a regular basis. He hoped to catch the brigands unawares and be able to pull information from them.

From information provided by Fergus, Alexander learned that the men came at the beginning of each month except during the winter, and always claimed to be acting in the name of the Crown. If any villager argued with these men, they were murdered and served as a warning to the other villagers.

There was a new moon in the sky, so Alexander hoped to be fortunate enough to run into them. It angered Alexander to think that someone masqueraded in the King's name and built resentment amongst the peasants and miners. It was as Father Malachius told him, the peasant rebelled against the nobles more often than the crown. The resentment that each one of his men carried with them only reinforced Alexander's passion to unmask these thieves. Alexander wanted to take some important information back to the castle, and be thanked for his efforts. That's all he ever wanted.

He quickly drew up a plan that enabled them to sneak into the town. Chauncey, Farkas, and Fergus were commanded to ride ahead and infiltrate the town before they arrived. They observed the brigands from inside the village and ensured that every man was accounted for.

Sean, Ferris, Devin, and Jean accompanied Alexander as he approached the village and Keira followed them.

After he waited a few hours for his three men to infiltrate the village, Alexander and the remaining five rode towards Greystone. Just as before, a wagon was being loaded by villagers with five brigands looking nearby. They were large men, and each man was armed with a sword and shield. They wore very light armor, and looked more bandit than soldier. Light armor protected these men from the peasants, but would not be effective against the King's soldiers.

Alexander rode at a steady pace, and his men followed on their mounts. They rode in a tight formation, and postured aggressively. They kept the same pace and did not slow down even when the brigands noticed them. They drew their swords but stayed near their wagon until Alexander closed the distance.

"That's far enough," the closest one yelled. "Hold your horse and stay where you are. This be the King's business."

Alexander bade his men to hold position. From his saddle he watched Chauncey as his men crept silently behind the ruffians. Alexander smiled at the one who had spoken.

"Well good sir," Alexander said sarcastically. "I would have you tell me the King's business as I am the King's son." The brigand exchanged quick nervous glances. "I am Prince Alexander, fourth son of His Majesty King Magnus the ninth. You say that this is the King's business. As the son of his Majesty I will say that you are a liar. I demand that you tell me for whom you work."

"It is what we say," the ruffian said. His face was a monument to the rough aspect of his trade. A crooked nose and a toothy smile showed that for this brigand, deterrents rarely stayed that way.

"We are told to take payment," he waved his arm towards the village, and noticed the armed men behind him. "We wouldn't stop what we're doing your Highness. We have our orders. And we won't be telling you from whom."

"Give me your name," Alexander demanded.

"Jacob. And that's all you'll ever need to know."

Each one of Jacob's men had their swords drawn, as did the men on horseback behind Alexander. Alexander wished to avoid an armed confrontation, although his men were well trained, he had no doubt these thugs would be as well. To compound matters, none of his men wore armor since they had not met Jack and received the armor from Edgebrooke. He didn't want any of his men injured when it was obvious that this was a determined group. He nodded at Fergus who stood unnoticed behind the wagon. Fergus tossed the torch he held into the back of the wagon. Flames enveloped the wagon as the wood quickly caught fire and spread. The ruffian's leader turned his head back to Alexander with severe annoyance on his face.

"You shouldn't a done that," he said.

"There are lots of things I shouldn't a do," Alexander retorted. "One is to let my people be oppressed. The other is to make you walk back." He pointed his finger towards their horses.

"Ride out now, or be carried out."

Jacob snapped his fingers and his men slowly mounted their horses. He also walked quickly to his. Alexander saw the temptation in his face to cross swords. Jacob smartly resisted it as his eyes darted towards the giant dog that sat behind Alexander's horse. Jacob mounted his horse with the rest of his men and stood out as a lone figure against the brilliant glow of the fire. The light flickered and revealed the anger on his face.

"Very well, you've had your laugh. My employer might not be so happy."

"You can tell your employer that he can find me at any time. I will be more than happy to have words with him."

"I have a feeling you'll hear from him soon enough." Jacob glared at Alexander before he and his men rode out of the village. Dusk had begun so Alexander decided it would be best if they stayed in the village overnight.

"Fergus!" he called out. Fergus walked over to his horse. "Let's stay here for the night. Go down to the tavern and get us some rooms."

Fergus looked worried. As he opened his mouth to speak, a huge clap of thunder shook the ground. Zeus neighed loudly and fidgeted nervously.

"Whoa, boy. Easy!" exclaimed Alexander while he patted the horse's neck. He looked up towards the darkening sky. The moonlight became obscured by the dark storm clouds that had gathered.

Storms were an oddity in the kingdom. That's not to say that it never rained, but clouds never gathered in and released strength and fury upon the land. It rained lightly, and passed through quickly, enough that crops were watered and that brooks and streams kept flowing. This storm looked different and it gathered in anger and strength. A streak of lightning flashed across the sky and the horses fidgeted under their riders. The only time Alexander had seen lightning was across the border and he felt an evil force gathered in the distance.

"Fergus!" he exclaimed. Fergus looked around fearfully and looked back towards Alexander.

"Highness, I don't think it's a good idea to be here."

"Why not?" Alexander growled impatiently.

"There are men here that I've not seen before. They

don't look like our kingdom's people. I have a very bad feeling. It's not right here."

Raindrops began to fall. A few glanced off of Alexander's eyes and he swatted at them irritatingly. He had to make his decision quickly.

"Are you sure, Fergus?" The other men stood and waited.

"I'm sure Sir."

"Good enough then. Get to your mounts and let's go. Hurry!" Fergus nodded and ran towards his mount, as Farkas and Chauncey followed him. The raindrops quickened into a furious pace, as each second passed the rainfall became harder. Each raindrop was both cold and filled with anger, this rain meant to suck them in. Thunder crashed and lightning streaked across the sky and the rain formed a liquid wall that bogged the horses down. Alexander managed to bark out an order once his men had mounted their horses. They struggled in the rain but eventually managed to ride away from the village.

Once they were a mile away from the village, they were finally able to push ahead of the storm. Each man was soaked wet, and water ran down their horses and created little pools of water underneath them. Based on the feeling that Fergus had, Alexander decided against stopping and insisted that they quicken their pace and ride directly to the castle at Middlebrooke.

When morning finally came, the sun peaked from behind the clouds and began to dry the clothes of the soaked riders. Alexander allowed them time to dismount and make camp and made each man take turns to stand guard to ensure no one had followed them from the village. They had been fortunate, as none of the men reported anyone following them.

Alexander woke past noon and didn't feel refreshed.

He wished for a soft bed and feathers for a pillow instead of a saddle. He felt unrecognizable. He hadn't shaved in months and except for the rain, hadn't had a bath either. With all of the training they had done at the Abbey, personal hygiene had been neglected. They were only six days away from Middlebrooke but Alexander decided to move slowly to the castle. He wanted to ensure that all of his men made it without incident. He was especially concerned with the armor. It was expensive and if it were lost he did not have the funds to have them replaced.

They traveled slowly over the next two days. Alexander allowed Keira to run unimpeded, and she hunted rabbits at her leisure. She killed a fair few and triumphantly trotted back to their camp with her quarry. After a brief interlude of play, she lay down and voraciously tore into them.

On the third day, they spotted the remainder of their group with wagon that held the armor in tow. They had met along the road outside of Edgebrooke and traveled together. Jack reported no issues when he received the armor. No one had questioned him or paid him any mind. Each man excitedly crowded around the wagon and began to put on their armor. The armor was much like Alexander's in design. The armor was flexible and lightweight, yet protective and covered their torso and back. They each crowed that they were more than horsemen, they were knights. As a finishing touch, each breastplate had the engravings of the gryphon. Alexander had decided that regardless of his father's opinions, gryphons were decidedly real and they would be the standard that his men followed. His men would rise above their opponents in battle and fight with superior strength. He became flush with excitement and wanted to make haste to home so that he may be welcomed into the family with the respect due a

Prince.

Once their fitting was finished, each man excitedly mounted his horse. Alexander led the way and each man and his horse fell in line behind Alexander.

Within two days' time, they stood in front of the castle's impressive stone wall. Alexander had forgotten its size, and felt a little intimidated by it as he approached the gate. The gate guards stood ready to meet him and six swordsmen walked towards them.

"Halt!" the first guard called to them. Alexander recognized him as the guard that allowed him passage the night he left. "Who are you and what's your business in Middlebrooke?"

"I am Prince Alexander," Alexander responded.

"Prince Alexander eh? He's been gone for almost two years. How do we know? You aren't very clean for a prince. And who are these others with you? You look like a revolutionary."

"Well spotted," Alexander said sarcastically. "My twelve men and I were going to siege the city, but we found your doors open and accommodating. We have therefore come to kill your king, love your women, and otherwise subvert the populace. Now may we have passage?"

The guard studied them for a moment. He waved off the other men behind him to lift up their poleaxes and bowed stiffly to Alexander.

Alexander nodded his head at the guard and began to ride through the gates while his men followed him. Alexander overheard Fergus' conversation to Chauncey.

"How'd they know he was a prince?" Fergus asked.

"He uses a lot of big words and to a better effect. You see Fergus, if you read more you could be a learned scholar instead of a soldier. You might even make it into the merchant class one day. Of course you'll need to learn how to count."

"I can count!" was the reply.

"Oh right, what number comes after twenty nine then?" Fergus mocked.

"That's a trick question then," Chauncey retorted. "There's no such number as twenty nine."

Alexander burst out laughing although he felt he shouldn't have. He felt bad for Chauncey but the joke was funny and that's what mattered. When they reached the Royal Palace Alexander felt like a stranger as he dismounted.

There were no guards guarding the Royal Palace, but that didn't surprise Alexander. Years of peace had caused complacency. It amazed Alexander that he hadn't noticed before. It was a sleepy kingdom that completely ignored the dangers that threatened to walk across the border and swallow it whole. Perhaps this would change once Alexander reported his observations to his father.

The thirteen men walked through the doors of the Royal Palace and one lone guard stood sentry in the entranceway. He looked directly at Alexander and failed to recognize him. He drew his sword quickly and yelled the alarm. Alexander tried to calm the situation, but it was too late as the room filled quickly with armed palace guards and Edward's bodyguard.

Well, Alexander thought, at least they're awake.

Alexander's men responded and drew out their weapons, ready for a fight. The room was filled with noise as the men taunted each other. Alexander observed the madness for his efforts to quiet the room had gone unfulfilled. This wasn't exactly what he had planned for his return.

From the top of the stairs into the entranceway a voice yelled a command to cease. The room quieted down as a regal feature walked down the steps. It was Edward who was flanked with the remainder of his heavily armed guards. They were armed with huge broadswords and carried round bronze shields with the Lions emblem on them, which signified that they were Edwards's men. On Edward's head sat a small crown, not his father's crown, but a crown none the less. Sofia was aside Edward and wore a plain blue dress, but she also carried a sword in one hand, ready to defend her home.

Edward walked to the bottom of the stairs and stood in front of his guards. He looked directly at Alexander but failed to recognize him. Alexander attributed it to his unshaven appearance and the lack of bathing over the last few weeks. As Alexander glanced down at his general appearance, he was dismayed to find that his entire body was covered with grass and dirt.

"Who are you to dare step inside the Royal Palace?" Edward demanded. His hand firmly planted on his sword within its sheathe. "What is your business here?"

Alexander smiled and decided the opportunity to toy with his brother was too good to pass up. He deepened his voice as he spoke.

"The guards at the gate were accommodating enough to let us pass as we said we wanted to pay homage to your majesty. Our business is quite simple. My twelve men and I wish to sack your city and carry off the finest treasures in the world. We would also love your women and take some fine wenches as house slaves. I'd also like a bath if I could get one."

"How dare you," Edward yelled with an infuriated tone and he drew his sword. "You dare insult my sister's honor in my presence?"

"What?" Alexander said, confused. "Oh...no! No! No! Not meaning her royal highness...no...disgusting."

Sofia marched down the stairs, sword still in hand.

"Am I to understand," she started, "that you find me disgusting? I should strike you down for that. Why would you say such a thing?"

Edward glanced at her with a confused look on his face. Alexander knew his exact thoughts. He was confused by her madness over repulsion. It's easy, Alexander thought to himself. Vanity! Edward looked back at the intruder, Alexander looked at Sofia, and Sofia looked at Edward.

"Edward, he insulted my honor," Sofia pouted. "Run him through!"

Edward's countenance was confused but he felt compelled to question the intruders.

"Very well, scoundrel, explain why you find my sister repulsive," was his half-hearted command.

"I don't find her repulsive. If I found her repulsive I'd find myself repulsive. I merely find the thought of loving her as the farthest thing from my mind. So I'll thank you very much to not infer that upon me." Alexander felt a little uneasy about this conversation, and desperately felt like fleeing the castle.

"Pardon me your highnesses," boomed a proper voice behind Alexander. The voice surprised everyone in the room and they turned to see Manfred standing with hands clasped behind his back. "Perhaps Prince Alexander would enjoy the luxury of a bath before dinner? And maybe a fresh tunic and if I may burn the ones you currently have on. If I may be so bold young prince?"

"Everybody hold your tongue," Sofia commanded. She handed Edward her sword and walked closer to Alexander. She made eye contact with him and shook her head. With a quick strike she slapped his cheek playfully.

"You're an absolute scoundrel Alexander. How dare

you!" She was so overjoyed she was going to hug him but stopped. "Why do you come back smelling like a field?"

"Alexander?" Edward gasped with recognition. Alexander grinned at his brother and was happy to be reunited with him.

"Come here, you scoundrel." Edward turned his nose from the smell but embraced Alexander tightly.

"You are returned?" he asked.

"I am returned."

Edward dispatched two of his men to find the King and Queen and let them know their prodigal son had returned. He ordered another man to bring fresh food and drink for all of the weary travelers. Within minutes the rest of the royal family had joined them. Queen Caroline was ecstatic to see him home.

"Oh son," she smiled. "You smell like the earth, but I have missed you."

Even King Magnus smiled upon his return.

"Look at you!" he exclaimed. "You're more of a prince then when you left. Why you look like me when I was your age. I was always dirty," he whispered. "Are these your men?"

"Yes father. All trained. All completely loyal."

"Good," King Magnus said proudly as he nodded towards the men. "Tonight we will have a family celebration that our prodigal son has returned. Everyone put your swords up and go about your business. Someone seek out Calimus and Mattias. Let them know their presence is required tonight." King Magnus looked towards Alexander's knights.

"It will be required for the lot of you to bathe," King Magnus added. "Manfred! See that these men are properly cleaned."

"At once sire. The preparations are in place."

Manfred's efficiency was commendable for he always seemed to know more than the royal family and always anticipated their every whim. Alexander turned his attention back to King Magnus.

"Father? Might I be granted two requests?"

"Speak, my son," Magnus replied.

"First, my men are in need of proper mounts. May I pick from the Royal Stables? Second, I would like audience with your Majesty to discuss matters of great importance that I have seen in my travels."

King Magnus nodded in agreement and turned to leave. He walked away slowly with Edward's assistance and left the room. Queen Caroline was still very happy and took Alexander's hands.

"Even with your dirty appearance, you still look like my son," she beamed. "There were nights I thought I might not see you again."

You have no idea, Alexander thought. A tear fell from her eyes and ran down her cheek.

"I'm sorry. I'm just happy to see you. You'll tell me everything? Good. I will go and make sure the feast is taken care of...and you're bath...I'll make sure it's ready very soon. It's so good to see you home." Caroline wiped her eyes and walked towards the kitchen.

Sofia was the only one that remained and she grinned from ear to ear. Her blue eyes sparkled with mischief.

"So," she started. "What have you been doing for the last two years?"

"You look like a cat that caught the mouse Sofia, I have a feeling that you know."

Who me?" Sofia clucked. "Maybe I know for the last two years you've been training in the Western Mountains with Monsignor Jean Paul, much to father's chagrin."

"How is father?" Alexander avoided the reason for his training.

"He's well enough but I fear for his health. He's become more reliant upon Edward for the daily administration of the kingdom."

Alexander and Sofia walked past the busy servants as they rushed to prepare for the night's feast. Off to the side of the kitchen was a private room with an iron tub. The tub was filled with hot water, as hot stones had been removed off of the fire and dumped into the water, which created an ecstatic experience. Alexander realized Sofia had followed him so he turned around and looked at her with a blank expression on his face.

She smiled but then realized what his look meant. She immediately found a chair and sat behind a curtain that partitioned the room. As soon as she sat behind the partition he took off his armor and sank into the tub. He sighed contentedly as the hot water relieved him of his tension and dirt. The water smelled distinctly of lavender.

"Alex?" Sofia asked. "What's it like out there?"

"Dangerous," he replied without a pause. "It's no place for you sister. It's best you stay in the city. There are monsters out there that you can scarcely imagine....but enough about me. What about you? How many suitors have you had in the last two years?" He joked but he was also serious. He was very committed to ensuring that a suitor be good enough for her.

"There have been some," came her vague reply.

"What's some? Two? Three?"

"I believe that's a few."

"You're splitting hairs. How many is some."

"Well, maybe just a few then."

"ARGH!" he groaned with mock exasperation. "What are their names? Are they nice men? Or are they the backend of a mule? Are they deserving of your affections?" He splashed the hot water onto his face and was surprised at how cloudy the clear water had become.

"There's an excellent one. He sends me letters every month."

Alexander was very intrigued and he started running through the men that he knew from around the kingdom.

"Who is it!" he demanded, as he splashed water over the partition.

"Alex!" yelled Sofia. "You've gotten me wet. Fine. If you must know, Prince Youssef, a man of fine quality writes me many letters. And I write back."

"Sofia!" Alexander was enraged. "Of all the men in our noble houses, how can you come up with a suitor like him?"

"Alexander, I will not have you talk about him like that, especially when you left me to go traipsing around the country like a peasant. He's a good man, and he's in love with me."

"In love with you? He makes dishonorable advances? Does Father or Mother know? Does Edward even know?"

"Yes, they all know. Father thinks it would bring a great benefit to our two kingdoms. It would mean a smart trading alliance and bring our country wealth."

There was a brief silence as Alexander soaked in the water. He scooped up some warm water and splashed his face. He reached to the small table nearby and picked up a shaving knife. He hoped to ignore the conversation with an awkward silence. Maybe she'll leave, he thought. There was no such luck, and she stayed right where she was.

"Very well," Alexander finally stated and broke the silence. "If mother and father are in approval then who am I to stand in the way of your happiness."

"I'm so happy to hear you say that," Sofia said cheerfully. "Maybe you could do me a small favor?"

"What would that be?"

"In a weeks' time you could sail me to the grand ball that will be celebrated in His Royal Highness' honor. Our royal family has been invited but unfortunately no one can make the journey. Father's health will keep Mother and Edward home, and I'll be damned if I sail with Calimus or Mattias. With you back-" Alexander interrupted her.

"With me back, you thought I'd have nothing important to do, because what I do is not important right? That's great Sofia. That's exactly why I left in the first place." Alexander was irritated at his sister. He knew she didn't mean to be dense. Her thoughts were on this prince. He rolled his eyes and continued to shave.

"I just thought you might like to go," she offered. "There will be a large group of the noble houses from all across the seas. Lady Emma will be there…"

"I don't care if His Holiness is there. Doesn't make me want to take my boat and sail to Youssef's palace to see him make advances upon my sister!" Alexander knew that he was being manipulated. It didn't mean he'd make it easy. Besides, he didn't know who anyone was anymore anyway.

"Alex!" Sofia exclaimed in frustration. "Listen. Lady Emma from the Northern Isles will be there."

Alex was amused. He didn't know why she repeated herself.

"I give up. Who is Lady Emma? Is she a dowager? Does she hold the secrets to time and nature? Is she a learned scholar from the highest levels of learning our world has to offer? Oh no…wasn't she our governess? The fat one? Good lord, wouldn't want to meet up with her again." Alexander shuddered at the thought. The governess he remembered was a tyrant. She watched the children in their earlier years, and always favored Mattias over him.

"Lady Emma from our eighteenth birthday. She asked you for a dance.....red hair?"

Alexander thought hard. Oh....the red hair. He remembered why he didn't like red heads.

"Oh? Her? A bit young. Isn't she twelve? Very bold. Ummm....no thank you but I'm very appreciative." He shook off that suggestion quicker than an armed barbarian warrior.

"Emma isn't twelve. She's eighteen now. She was very taken with you and she was very hurt that you made up an excuse not to dance with her. She even came out for a visit and stayed with us this summer hoping to get an opportunity to get to know you. We put her up in your room and mother rolled out every bit of hospitality for her. Spared no expense."

Alexander was absolutely horrified. They put her up in his bed? Alexander's mouth opened in disgust. He wanted to protest, but figured it would be of no use. Sofia had turned into a woman, there was no doubt. He took one last splash on the face, and felt the smoothness of his cheeks. It felt good to be clean again. He finally chased Sofia out of the room so he could be alone and finished getting ready. A new change of clothes hung off the back of a chair. It was good to be pampered again and he hoped his men felt the same way.

CHAPTER XVI

Alexander felt like a visitor in the castle. He sat in the dining hall and watched the servants run to and fro as they prepared the great hall. After two years of fending for himself, Alexander felt uncomfortable to sit quietly and alone. Edward took notice of this and joined him. Alexander had noticed a change in his brother even greater than the regent's crown for now he seemed reserved and slightly unhappy. The crown will do that for you, mused Alexander, but this wasn't enough to prevent Alexander from teasing Edward.

"That's a nice crown Edward. Father couldn't part with his?" Alexander grinned and waited for Edward's response.

"Alex, you're not still sore over your birthday are you?"

"I was never sore at you Edward. I've learned so much since I have been away. Birthdays can be better celebrated in the arms of friends than in front of a nation. I'm happy for you. I don't want the crown. I want a tavern. You know, a tavern would do well here."

"They've already got one," Edward chided. The

tavern he referred to was seedy and populated by the criminal element.

"No, I mean a proper tavern, somewhere where you can get a decent meal and drink. Good surroundings and most importantly, clean. Being clean is an enjoyable feeling. You have no idea until you've had to smell your own sweat and the sweat of others around you for months at a time. You get used to it, so you have no idea how bad you stink, until it's removed from you."

"Well brother, I'm glad you found what you were looking for," Edward smiled.

"You have no idea what I found out there," Alexander snarled back. For a moment he hated Edward. Edward the King with his crown, for what did Edward know about the dangers in the kingdom or outside of it? What was he doing about it behind his walls? Resentment started to well up inside of Alexander and he felt a twinge of remorse, he had never felt this way before.

"I'm sorry Edward, I don't know what got into me."

Edward forgave him and poured a drink into two flagons. He handed one to Alexander.

"Alexander," Edward said slowly, "I drink to your health, and to an offer I have for you. You are my favorite brother, and you are the most competent out of all my father's advisors. You know so much more than I about everything in this kingdom. I need you with me."

"What are you saying?" Alexander asked curiously.

"I want you to be my right hand when I am King. I want you to be Chancellor. You have knowledge of domestic affairs that I will never have. Think about it. With me as King, and you as Chancellor we can reform this kingdom. The military is far too powerful with its generals and its continual siphoning of our treasury. But, with you and me together, we can curb their power, and help our people and be even more prosperous. It's prosperity for all, not just nobles, royals, and merchants."

Alexander was amazed. He had never heard Edward passionate about the people. Perhaps being Regent had opened his eyes towards the plight of his countrymen.

"Why me? Why not my older brothers?" Alexander asked with earnestness.

"No," Edward said sadly shaking his head. "Mattias and Calimus are disreputable. Mattias is constantly scheming, and I fear giving Calimus the purse strings would ruin our country….That leaves you Alexander. Will you join me? And bring a new age of prosperity to Alveus, Just think…." Edward raised his flagon to a plain tapestry that hung against a wall. "Just think, a tapestry recognizing the Golden Age of Alveus and the achievements of Edward and Alexander."

Alexander thought long and hard as he stared at the flagon in Edwards' hands. Chancellor! It all seemed so easy, all so perfect. Edward would rule and Alexander would stand behind him. Prosperity for everyone! Removal of the corrupt and ushering in a new era! Alexander was positively giddy over the thought. Edward had indeed come to be the savior of their kingdom.

"To our kingdom's prosperity," Alexander responded and he clanked his flagon to Edward's. After he took a few gulps, Alexander noticed Mattias and Calimus approached the bench where he and Edward sat. Mattias's face was easily read; his contempt for Alexander's return was only too evident. He strutted self-importantly which forced Calimus to accept his superiority.

"So," Mattias said in a mocked tone. "The prodigal son returns. With tales of heroism no doubt? How many peasants did you save, brother? Enough to save your soul and gain passage to heaven."

"Worry about your own soul," Alexander warned. Years of training at the monastery stirred his spirit and he wanted to beg Mattias to pick up a sword. Alexander stood up and faced Mattias confidently.

Calimus immediately stepped between them and hugged Alexander. It was a distinct act of contempt directed to Mattias. Mattias just sneered at them.

"Good to see you brother," Calimus whispered. Alexander rejoiced to hear those words, even with the stench of wine on Calimus's breath.

Perhaps his disposition has improved, Alexander thought.

Mattias smiled at Alexander and quietly stated, "There will come a day. Mark my words." and he continued to glare directly at Alexander. "This might just be the last time we're gathered together."

Alexander smiled as behind him the doors of the hall swung open and his men entered and chatted amicably, each one shaven and refreshed. For Alexander, it felt like he was seeing each one of them for the first time. Their cleanliness carried with it a sense of confidence and importance.

"Mattias, have you met my bodyguard?" Alexander grinned as he waved towards the new attendees that approached the hall.

Mattias looked back and saw the twelve tough looking men as they strolled into the hall. He turned his attention back to Alexander and smiled.

"Touché," he said. "Welcome home brother." With that, he turned and beckoned Calimus to follow him towards the place at the table. An idea woke inside of Alexander, what if the thugs at Greystone were in league with the Bete'szek. Stealing our gold would be the beginning. They could purchase weapons and mercenaries, or even broker alliances with other kingdoms.

He pulled Edward to him and spoke in a soft voice.

"Edward, you have to make sure I speak with our father tonight. Nothing must stop it."

"Alright," Edward said with his voice hushed, "But first," he said loudly, "introduce me to those worthy to be chosen to guard and serve my brother as knights."

The men cheered loudly for they recognized Edward with his crown and realized he was the heir to the throne. This was the closest any of the men had been to the throne and they acted like excited children. Fergus and Chauncey talked excitedly and each one of them tried to gain Edwards attention. Soon their excitement erupted into brotherly conflict and they started to jostle. Jack was nearby and separated them quickly before they embarrassed themselves further.

"Gentlemen." a voice called from the royal table. It was Manfred, and while he stood there looking as dour as ever, everyone heard a genuine inflection in his voice.

"Gentlemen..." he said again. "I present to you Princess Sofia. And I present to you Queen Caroline and your King, King Magnus the ninth. Come now and kneel before your King."

As soon as the words left his mouth, Manfred immediately knelt on one knee. Every man in the room followed suit and knelt down.

"Rise my family. Rise honored guests," Magnus said graciously. "I welcome you as warriors for the crown. Eat and drink. My hall is your hall."

The men cheered loudly and banged the tables with their fists in approval. Servants brought forth plates mounted with meat while other servants brought bowls of fruits and vegetables. They were joined by the royal stewards who brought them goblets of wine and flagons of mead. The sight of the food impressed all of the men, and Brennan looked as if he were overcome with happiness. He had his plate filled and emptied faster than anyone else.

Laughter and merriment filled the hall. Even King Magnus dignified himself to laugh at some jokes and told a few of his own. When everyone had eaten their fill, and the evening had quieted down, Alexander bade his men good night as they retired to the royal barracks. He cast a knowing look toward Edward and Edward nodded as if he understood that Alexander desired a private audience with his father. With the room emptied of all souls, except for the King, Queen, Edward, and Alexander; Edward broached the topic of conversation.

"Father, Alexander desires an audience with you."

"Come forward and speak son, you have honored my halls with noble warriors this evening. I could not help but notice the armor. It is very unique armor."

"Yes father," Alexander said as he followed them into the small room behind the throne. A servant lit several torches in the room for light. "I had the armor forged specially from our smiths in Edgebrooke. I used only my money and not the kingdoms," he mentioned proudly.

"And the emblem on that armor?" Magnus asked curiously.

"They are gryphons. They are mentioned throughout the manuscripts of our kingdom's history."

"More legends and nonsense," the king muttered to himself. "What is it that you would have me know?" Magnus sat down and proceeded to pick at a plate of grapes in front of him.

"I wish to speak about the events that I have seen in my travels over the last two years."

"Then proceed," King Magnus responded with a hint of irritation in his voice. Queen Caroline stood behind

Magnus' chair and placed a hand upon his shoulder. He looked up at his the Queen with a kind hearted expression and took her hand in his. It was one of the very rare moments that Alexander saw his parents show affection to one another. He felt steadied with his mother's presence and spoke up.

"Two years ago, I left this castle without a desire to return. My travels took me north toward the village of Greystone. What I saw there troubled me. A band of ruffians was stealing newly mined gold and silver and carrying it off in a wagon."

"Stealing from us?" King Magnus asked as he stroked his white beard. "It is prone to happen. I would think that maybe we should have a small garrison there."

"We have a garrison in Edgebrooke that's responsible to look after the villages in that area," Edward answered quickly.

"Very well," Magnus said annoyingly. "Have them dispatched to investigate the matter. Let the local authorities handle it and do not waste the Crown's time with such a small matter." He waved his hand with disregard and his attention wavered.

"They claim to work for the crown!" Alexander exclaimed. "They claim to work for the King and they steal it from our very noses. How do we know that it is not the garrison from Edgebrooke?" Alexander wanted them to hear the urgency in his voice.

"So what would you have me do? Chase every band of thieves that masquerades behind the throne? The people know it's not us."

"Father, the people hate us. They think of us as lazy dogs that care only for gold and silver. The nobles chase them and hound them and tax them to death. Two of my men were peasants. They came to me in rags, half starved, living off whatever fell off their baron's tables. What does that say about us if we choose not to act?"

"Alexander, the King is concerned for his people's well-being. I am sure His Majesty would agree to send out a small band of soldiers from Middlebrooke so that the people can see how he is their benefactor." Edward was being skillfully diplomatic as he maneuvered between Alexander and King Magnus. Alexander understood Edward's maneuvering but felt contempt and irritation for it.

"If I send out a small band of soldiers every time a peasant loses a meal, I would be poor. Would you have me send the army to the Northern Forests and clear out the Thieves Guild? Should my men wander about on a wild goose chase looking for the gryphons as well?" King Magnus scoffed.

"What about the attack on the river?" Alexander insisted. "Did we forget that happened as well? We have evil men slipping into our kingdom under our very noses. I have no doubt the Thieves Guild was behind the attack, and if the Thieves are in league with the Bete'szek, they could be plotting to overthrow you-". Alexander stopped mid-sentence. He was never supposed to be there and he was not supposed to know what he knew. His father's face furrowed in puzzlement.

"Wait…." the King breathed raspily. "The forests. Greystone. What have you done?"

"I crossed the border." Alexander admitted it with regret, thinking that it would have been better to stay silent on the matter.

"You did what?" Magnus shrieked. He stood up out of his chair quickly. He limped around the table and grabbed Alexander's shirt. The Queen quickly came between them, and worked to release his grip.

"I've been across the border. I've seen the people that live there. I've seen what they can do. We are in danger Father."

"Alexander, you are too bold with your speech," Caroline scolded. "Remember who it is you are addressing."

Magnus released Alexander's shirt and looked to sit down. He placed his head in his hands and let out a mournful sigh.

"Thirty years ago, your grandfather, your uncle, and I took an army north to wipe them out. We killed every one of them we could find until our arms could no longer carry our swords. They were wiped from the annals of history. Should they be awakened, their bloodlust knows no satisfying. But you....you cross the border and awaken the last of them." He slumped in his chair. "My own son, a constant disappointment...has brought death upon his father's house."

Alexander was infuriated. Was his father so quick to judgment? Did he not understand the horrors that he had seen?

"Maybe I'm a disappointment to you, but I rescued three men while they tried to take my heart. Has that been you? Did they try to take your heart thirty years ago? I'll bet you stood with your mighty army in front of you and to the sides. I faced their horde with four men. And I killed their chief, and I killed their priest. And I ran back to my home thinking that my father would embrace me. But no, my father chooses to sit in his gilded tower and watch it fall down around him. Well father, I went and I faced that evil. And whether it brings death, we shall wait and see, but I will not hide behind these walls."

King Magnus' face was crimson with rage. No one in their life ever spoke to the King with the words that

Alexander spoke freely. He rose up from his chair and moved towards Alexander. Alexander thought his father capable of striking him and moved backwards away from the table.

"You would call your King a coward? You are a boy! I release you from your loyalties to me right now. Accept and be gone!"

"No father," Alexander said. "I am one of the last to show you undying loyalty. And someday, I will prove that to you."

"Get....out." The King walked out of the room and muttered angrily as he left. Edward and Queen Caroline looked at Alexander. Alexander again felt his world crashed down around him. There was no hope of ever bridging the gap between father and son.

"Alex," Edward said softly. "You've got to be more diplomatic with him. I'll get him to change his mind by tomorrow, but in the meantime stay away from him." Alexander nodded his agreement and Edward too left the room.

"I'm sorry mother," Alexander said softly.

"Alex," she whispered. She put his face in her hands and forced him to look at her face. Her eyes were filled with concern and yet he could almost sense a certain pride for himself.

"You were magnificent. You stood for your convictions against a great King. Although you and your father have never seen eye to eye, he does respect you."

"But he also hates me," he murmured.

"You stay true to who you are. Your destiny will work itself around you." The Queen gave her son a quizzical look. "Alex, why do you look at me so?"

He grinned playfully.

"There's just a wrinkle on your face that I've never

seen before." He meant to say it playfully but the resounding thud of her hand connecting to the back of his head made him feel otherwise. She gave him a strong hug anyway.

"I've missed you. It's good to have you home." She left Alexander alone in the throne room with his thoughts.

Alexander's first thought was to run away again. He had at first enjoyed the castle, but the conflicts with Mattias and his father drained him of all energy. He missed the life beyond the walls. Even if he was being hunted by some unseen enemy, at least his heart was beating free.

His second thought was dire concern for his mother. When he left the castle, he had no knowledge of death. His grandparents died before he was born, and he had never buried a friend or family member. Yet here it was, two years after his eighteenth birthday, he had realized his own mortality in a very real way. And what of his father? What of his mother? What would he do if his mother died? She had been his confidante and besides his sister, a very loyal and caring person in his life.

He realized that his thoughts had carried him into the royal garden where he wasn't alone. A lone robed figure stood silhouetted against the torchlight and the church robes were easily distinguishable.

"Father Malachius! I expected you at dinner."

"Alexander, my son! Welcome home!" He clasped Alexander's hands and shook them vigorously.

"I'm glad you're home my son. I was afraid your mother's daily visits to the abbey to pray for your safe return would never end." His words trailed off and he studied Alexander's expression.

"Your father won't understand. He's been in this castle for far too long. Tell me though, I am dying to hear. Tell me everything."

Alexander could tell him a hundred things but one stood out to him.

"They're real. I saw them," he whispered.

Alexander told Father Malachius everything. He started with the extortion at the village of Greystone, he explained his adventure with the Thieves Guild, and how they tied into the barbarians. The barbarians as it turned out were sacrificing human victims and cut out their hearts. He went into detail about the stone hut and the gryphons. Then he explained how he chose his twelve men, and their two years at the monastery. His story ended with his last visit to Greystone and the strange weather that occurred. At the end of the story, Alexander waited for Father Malachius's comments. Father Malachius stayed quiet and rubbed his face with his hands.

"What does it mean," Alexander asked impatiently.

"Much more than I realized," Malachius responded. "Come with me. We need answers."

Alexander and Malachius hurried down the dark streets. Very few people walked at night except for the guards and night watchmen. Being with a cleric had its advantages, for no one liked to be accused of marauding the clerics. That and having assaulted a member of the royal family were two easy ways to have your life cut short.

Eventually they arrived at the abbey. Father Malachius led Alexander to a small apartment within the clerical rooms. Father Malachius knocked on a small door. At first there was no noise, so Malachius knocked again. A small scuffling noise started than stopped. A latch clicked and the door slowly opened to reveal the small frame of an elderly man.

The man that stood before them was older than Alexander's father by at least twenty years. He had a slight hunch and trembled as he spoke.

"Yes Bishop? You wanted to see me?"

"Yes," Malachius responded. "We have much to read. Let us hurry downstairs and not awaken anyone."

The small monk led them in the direction of the secret room and Alexander had a question that needed to be asked and satisfy a sudden curiosity.

"Did he address you as Bishop?"

"Yes."

"When did that happen?" Alexander was shocked that no one had mentioned that during training.

"Six months ago."

"Everything seemed to happen six months ago," Alexander muttered ruefully.

"His Holiness saw fit to grant me the office of Bishop. There was a ceremony. You didn't miss anything. It's more of a celebratory office anyway. Ah, here we are." Bishop Malachius pulled the doorway open and revealed the secret passage.

Alexander felt offended that there had been no mention of it at the monastery. It was very curious, but Alexander felt no reason to be suspicious.

The three men quietly snuck through the secret passageway and down the last flight of stairs. Once there, the frail monk began to light several torches around the room. The room lit up to reveal several cases of parchments and scrolls and here were also some huge volumes of paper bound together with leather on a large wooden table.

"Father Peter, The History and Mythology of Gryphons, if you please."

The old man nodded to the request of the bishop, and after he poked around a few shelves, produced a book for them. He opened it to the pages that contained stories about gryphons, and produced a copy of the history of Alveus for reference.

"Here it is," the Bishop stated as he peered over the books pages. "Gryphons are extremely protective of secrets and treasures. There was something in that white hut they don't want anyone to see."

"What could that be," Alexander asked?

"Anything," Father Peter said. "It could be a nest. It could be treasure. It could be a passageway to God."

"Do you really believe that?" asked Alexander. He was awed at the thought that a passage to God existed in the hut.

"No," was Father Peter's short reply. "It's got to be treasure. That's all they concern themselves with. Maybe a nest of pure gold?"

"It can't be that," Alexander said. "All the gryphons that live in that forest are male."

"Perhaps if we were to ask the prophet," Father Peter said hesitantly. Bishop Malachius's face darkened.

"He's left our employ. No one knows where he is now. For all we know, he could be in league with the Bete'szek."

"Who's the prophet?" Alexander asked. He seemed to be someone worth knowing.

"A question better not asked, or answered. A man whose allegiance knows no masters," Malachius said irritatingly. "Alexander, do you know where the hut is? Can you get to it?" His voice reflected his desperation.

"All I remember is that it's in a certain section of the forest. But Malachius, what would we want with treasure? We mine enough gold and silver in our lands, why would we want more."

"There might be gold in it. This may be true, but there has to be more. Why would it be in a stone hut? Why would you have a vision? Why would they not kill all of you if it was indeed a nest? There are so many unanswered questions…" Father Malachius moved to the other book that Father Peter had brought him.

"Please, tell me everything you know," Alexander begged. "I am nothing more than slow to learn and five steps behind my enemies."

"Very well," Malachius sighed. "Let me remind you of the history of the Kingdom of Alveus and the fisherman that changed the course of this land. He lived in a small village and fished day after lonely day. At times the sea smiled on him and bestowed him with fine fish. He traded some of the fish with other people in the village for vegetables and kept the remainder for his family. Most times he failed and watched his family go hungry. He often wished to try something else, but all he knew was fishing."

"During one particularly unfortunate week in which he caught only the smallest fish, he tearfully listened to his children cry from their hunger pangs. He was so heartbroken that he failed to provide food for his wife and sons, that he could no longer bear the shame of being an unsuccessful fisherman. Being poor was his station in life, but his frustration with being unable to provide for his family increased. His wife and children wasted away from their lack of food. His wife begged daily in the tiny market for cheap vegetables or a small coin to help feed their family. This humiliation of his wife became too much for him to bear."

"No one reached their hands out to the poor fisherman. At that time the custom of the village was to care for the widows and orphans, not those who had a man that failed to provide. To have his family saved, he decided that he would make them fatherless. He thought it best to disappear, forever."

"One night he crafted a tiny sail for his fishing boat and snuck it aboard his boat before anyone awoke. He quietly pushed the boat out from its mooring and jumped in. He unfurled the sail and began to sail west. He chose that direction because no one from his country had sailed that way and so no one would think to look for him there."

"Fortunately, the wind provided a strong breeze and quickly pushed his tiny boat out to sea. The wind blew for three days but then on the fourth it stopped completely. The fisherman could do nothing so he sat there in his boat in the middle of the sea and waited."

"He fell asleep exhausted and blistered from the sun. He tried to escape its light and huddled under a small blanket. Soon, he fell into unconsciousness. Unbeknownst to him, the wind blew again, and carried his little vessel westward to land."

"When he finally regained consciousness, he found his boat had beached at the mouth of a river. He knew that this was not his land. His country's coastline had very few hospitable areas. This land was luscious and green, a near paradise. He immediately jumped into the river, and drank to his heart's content. He found wild game nearby, and feasted to his hearts content."

"He was sure to be considered dead to his family now and he was sure they would be cared for by the village so he chose to explore this new land. Feeling refreshed from the food and water, he hid his boat in an area of tall grass and followed the river north."

"He observed that he was not alone on this strange land. There were many tribal villages dotted along the landscape. He took this opportunity and observed the native life in the villages he passed. They were a primitive folk, to him anyway, and seemed to be simple unobtrusive people. He might have seen fit to be welcomed into their midst had he not seen the most gruesome rituals take place before his eyes. Holy men of the village brought forth villagers to be sacrificed on altars while they still lived."

"He was terrified out of his wits by this barbarism, but still desired to know more about the land. After days of travel, he came to a region of hills. It was at the hills that he found the very items that would change the landscape over the next few hundred years. He found gold. Gold was in the top level of the soil. He didn't grasp what the implications were, but he knew what gold was, and so stuffed his pants full of the precious ore."

"One night he sat and pondered his future. He traveled the land without detection. It was possible to find a place to live, out of the way of the native population who held the name of Bete'szek. Or, he could return home to his family that he missed so deeply. He now possessed gold, and that solved all of his family's woes. His children could eat forever, and his wife could be a woman of prominence in the village. He made up his mind that night that he'd return to his land and his family."

"The next week he traveled back to his boat. While he walked he carried a flat piece of wood to use as an oar. He found his boat exactly where he hid it; gathered food and fresh water, and set sail to the east. It took him five days to return to his shores, and when he sailed into sight of the village, the people were amazed. The fisherman had disappeared a few months ago, and returned with gold. After a joyous reunion with his wife and children, the elders demanded he tell them where he had been."

"He eagerly told them about the land, so prosperous and rich that every villager strained to set sail. The elders quickly sent him to the King. The King listened to his tale in amazement. The King immediately commissioned a fleet of twenty ships be built and an army be conscripted to conquer this new land. Villagers from across the realm eagerly volunteered for this opportunity and gathered their families in hopes to settle this land."

"Within a year's time, the ships and army were prepared. Soldiers boarded the ships, and horses were loaded for the cavalry. Another ship carried a few families, to immediately claim their land through settlement. The King named the fisherman his general, since he had explored the terrain and knew where the indigenous people lived. The fisherman was overwhelmed by the King's generosity and swore allegiance of this new land to the King. He loaded his wife and sons into the largest galley with him, and sailed for the new land."

"When the fleet arrived, they unloaded and immediately built themselves a walled fortification at the same location the fisherman initially landed. The fisher-general commanded diplomats to all corners of the new land to acquire the land through peace and not conquest. When the religious leaders rebuffed these overtures they launched a series of attacks to wipe out the intruders."

"The fisher-general realized that subjugation of the Bete'szek, would prove difficult, and launched an all-out war against the population. Where some villagers joined them to ease their burdens of these Holy Men, those loyal to the priests were driven far north, past the mountains and the wild frontiers."

"The Bete'szeks army struck many times, but the war machine of the intruders proved to be too much. New, stronger weapons, armor, and horses proved to be the natives undoing. Eventually, a peace was signed; a boundary given that gave the conquerors much of the lush green land and all those who fell in it became subjugated."

"The King was grateful, and gave the fisher-general the title of Duke. And he reigned for his King over the land of Alveus, as Duke Magnus the first. He is your ancestor."

Bishop Malachius stopped his lesson to ensure

Alexander was still listening. Alexander understood the dilemma that was upon them. They held lands that the Bete'szek had originally inhabited. His family was the conqueror and the Bete'szek were the subjugated masses that refused to stand down.

"So if it's land they want, and we've defeated them, why do they still try? What special powers can they hold that would strike fear in the heart of the church and the nobility?"

"It is not a question of fear. It is a question of compatibility. Here, the nobles fear a loss of power. The Bete'szek focus on human sacrifice and the dark magic as a means to control through fear. The Holy Church cannot abide with that and so the Bete'szek are interested in a complete removal of the house of Wolfield from power and an eradication of the Holy Church. It is a return to paganism or animism if you prefer. Even with all of the evil and corruption that exists within the houses we have brought progress and order to these lands. These people had nothing more than huts and disease."

"It was even said they could raise the dead," Father Peter muttered.

"Impossible," Malachius scoffed. "Only God holds the key to life and death. It's simply heretical to suggest such a thing."

Father Peter bowed his head in shame. When Malachius finished his admonishment of Father Peter he turned another page in the book. "See here. It says that the priest is identified by the staff he carries. Each priest has a staff, but the staff the high priest carries, burns with a never ending flame."

"I've seen a staff like that one," Alexander said as he remembered the priest's staff. "But it wasn't like that. It wasn't the high priest."

"The high priest is impossible to identify. He's shrouded in secrecy and cunning. Any agent we send out to find more information is either killed or returns empty handed. That guard you employ, Jean. His parents were agents for us.....tragic what happened to them." Malachius grew quiet and sat down at the table. His face grew distant as he looked into the torch's flames.

"So if they're all powerful, how do we live in this land and not them?" Alexander asked.

"When your ancestors sailed to this land, they found a people willing to rebel. The human sacrifice was distasteful to many in the south and west. They embraced the invaders and offered their lives to throw off their masters. There was one crucial element that the eastern villagers brought with them; gryphons. The gryphons were plentiful in number and assisted in the war against the Bete'szek. It was then that your armor was forged. That armor you wear is over one thousand years old and has been worn by several Kings of Alveus."

"Prince Alexander, you were born in a most unfortunate time. It's a war of good and evil and there is no clarity between the two. Each side commits horrible atrocities against the other. It is a wonder that God allows any of us to live in this place. And you Alexander, have the unenviable task of holding this kingdom together and stopping it from fracturing." Malachius's eyes never left the torchlight. His countenance was trancelike yet he was fully coherent in acknowledging Alexander's questions.

"How does my father figure into this," Alexander asked. He sat across from Malachius. If Malachius would not make eye contact, then Alexander decided he'd devote his full energies and attention into the responses.

"Your grandfather broke a centuries old peace treaty and in one act damned us. He took Edgebrooke from the barbarians and slaughtered the inhabitants, and didn't stop there. He took his army to the Shadowlands, to finish them off once and for all. There was a great battle, few survived, and even fewer are still alive. It was there that your grandfather and uncle were cut down. For this total shedding of blood, as the story goes from Jean Paul, who was there, a priest had cursed Magnus' house and said that your father will live to see its ruin. That was the last time anyone saw one of their priests. Your father had that one impaled upon a pole so the birds could pick at his flesh."

"What is this?" Alexander pointed at a silver orb on the parchment.

"There is a myth," Father Peter interjected, "That says the orb is the source of their power. Any man outside of their unholy practices that touches it will die in the most serious agony."

"Alexander…." Bishop Malachius said quietly. His eyes finally left the torchlight and he rubbed his forehead with his hands. "Our land is marked for turmoil. If what you have told me is true, then they are not wiped out. They have come back and they are gathering their forces. It is inevitable that an attack will come."

Alexander paused briefly to think about Bishop Malachius's words.

"Alexander," he pressed, "We need to know if there's anything valuable in that hut. And by valuable I mean information."

"No," Alexander said firmly as he shook his head. "I've spent the last two years sleeping on hard beds and training every day. I come home after two years and my father tells me I'm a disappointment. My brother is still an untrustworthy snake and my life is in danger because these characters from a parchment want to murder me. It's been made quite clear to me that all of this is not my concern."

Alexander paused and saw the dismay in the Bishop's eyes.

"I'm sorry, and besides it would take at least two weeks. I've promised Sofia that I would sail with her to the Kingdom of the Western Isles for their grand ball." Alexander knew he lied, but he wanted to leave and that was the best opportunity.

I promise you, when I come back, I will go back into the forest. I promise…I will find out what's hidden there." Alexander reckoned that he disappointed Malachius, but there was a lot of disappointment tonight from others.

"Very well," Malachius said in understanding. "You will do what you must. I will see you upon your return. But before you go…I have one more thing for you."

Bishop Malachius nodded to Father Peter. The tiny monk hobbled over to a small chest and carefully removed the ornate top. He reached inside and brought out a strange goblet. As he hobbled back, Alexander distinguished that the goblet was a claw, with a silver inlay to ensure its liquid would not spill. Bishop Malachius smiled at Alexander.

"This is a gryphon's claw, fashioned into a goblet. The claw is an expert in letting you know when someone is trying to murder you."

"How does it work?" Alexander asked genuinely intrigued.

"It's quite simple," the Bishop explained as he examined the cup. "If any drink is poisonous, and its contents are poured into this goblet, the goblet will change colors, therefore warning you of that poison."

"Fascinating," Alexander said as he picked up the goblet. It felt extremely cold. "So you've actually tried it?"

"Uh…no," Father Peter said. "But the book says it will work." He pointed at the gryphon mythology parchment.

Alexander rolled his eyes. It had gotten late, so he

thanked both men for the information and the goblet and made his way up the stairs. He left the abbey with conflicted feelings. He knew he should go back to that stone hut but he resisted any sort of strong feeling he had towards it. He hated the forest. It felt as if evil lived there. All of the blood that was spilled, and what was it for? Jean's parents were dead; Angelica was dead, would the forests claim his life as well?

As Alexander walked down the deserted street, he had the distinct feeling that he was being followed. He looked over his shoulder and saw nothing there. He continued walking and trying to decipher if it the danger was real or imagined. He had no sword and no armor, so he refrained from issuing a challenge to the darkness. There was no telling what would be called out from the shadows. He looked up into the sky where the moonlight shone down upon him and lit his way, but it did little to remove the shadows.

He convinced himself this was all in his mind and that no one followed him. It was then that Alexander noticed a large black dog sat nearby and watched him. At first Alexander assumed it was Keira, and he called to it. The dog did not attempt to move nor did it respond with a wag or a bark. Alexander turned back again in the direction of the castle and quickened his pace. He looked back over his shoulder and saw the dog walked very slowly behind him. It walked slow enough to keep an eye on him, but not fast enough to overtake him.

Once inside the palace gates, Alexander bid the guards to be extra vigilant that night. Don't let anyone pass through these gates without alerting me, he ordered.

Alexander looked back once more in the direction of the strange animals. The dog had been joined by two other dogs. They sat quietly and had stopped following him.

Satisfied that he was no longer in danger and they would not be able to enter the gates, Alexander went inside the palace and decided to look in on his sister to ensure her safety.

He peeked in quietly and saw that a candle was still lit in her room. She sat quietly at a table next to the candlelight and wrote hurriedly on a parchment. Alexander guessed she was writing to Prince Youssef.

"Didn't I ever tell you men don't like women scholars?" he said in jest.

Sofia shrieked and spun around to face him. She knocked over the candle and spilled wax onto the paper.

"Alexander! Really! Oh, look what you've made me do!" She quickly picked up the candle but it was too late. She held up the parchment to him.

"It's ruined! Now he'll never know about my unrequited love."

"I'm sorry Sofia. I guess your love will just have to stay requited. It's not proper how you carry about. It will embarrass us." He tossed himself onto her bed and lay upon the soft bearskin blanket.

"From what I hear, the family doesn't need to worry about me embarrassing anyone. I'm sorry. That was unkind of me." She placed the candle back on the desk and its flame flickered. Alexander said nothing in response.

"I heard everything Father said, Alex. I'm so sorry. I really am." The concerned tones of her voice only caused Alexander further pain.

"Do you really feel bad for me?" he asked mockingly.

"Of course I do. You're my brother, and I love you. What hurts you hurts me. I would defend you the same way that you would defend me. You know this is true."

"Then do me one small favor," he said as he sat up.

"Anything."

"Take me to that ball."

Sofia's mouth curled from a small grin to an astonished fit of laughter. She clasped her hands together and jumped up and down in excitement.

"Do you mean it? You'll really take me? Oh I knew you would, I knew it!" She ran about the room in fluttered excitement. "I knew it...I bought you something too. Where is it? It's of the finest traders. I bought it from the market in Brookhaven...I have a purchaser there. You'll look dashing....You'll pinch her heart for sure. Maybe we could have a dual wedding."

Sofia stopped when she at last found what she looked for. It was a beautiful silken green tunic, with gold leaf embroidery, which matched his armor perfectly.

"That's very nice. A bit much though?"

"A bit much?" Sofia said with bewilderment in her voice. "You're a prince. You deserve a bit much. You're so different Alexander. You're so serious. It's like you're pining...wait. Alex! You've fallen in love?!"

"I haven't fallen in love," Alexander answered reassuringly. "Can you make preparations for us to sail? We'll need provisions for my men and whatever handmaidens will be accompanying us."

"I've already taken care of it," Sofia said smugly. "I started the moment you arrived." She stuck her tongue out playfully at Alexander.

"Women! They can only be Queen, but they make such magnificent Kings."

"Queen's always rule better," Sofia retorted. "We don't need men's silly wars."

Alexander kissed his sister on the forehead firmly and bid her good night. He made his way to his room and saw that his armor and sword and been stored neatly. Keira slept quietly curled in a ball in the corner and Alexander decided this was an excellent idea. He stretched out on his magnificently comfortable bed and fell fast asleep.

Not long after, Alexander was awakened to the palace guard's alarms. He sprang from his bed and roused Keira. He grabbed his sword and ran down the stairs towards the noise while Keira rushed ahead of him. He ran into Edward and Sofia, both armed as well, in the royal hall.

"What is it?" Alexander demanded.

"We'll soon see." Edward answered.

In moments they had arrived at the palace gate. The royal barracks emptied and every man's bodyguard ran as if his master's life depended on it. All of the soldiers arrived at the gate together and halted in unison. Several men paled and turned their heads away quickly as their body relieved them of their horrified sensation.

The palace guards that Alexander had bid to lock the doors lay dead on the ground with their throats torn. Their swords lay undisturbed in their place of rest as if their attackers had fallen upon them in such a quick fury. Alexander stood silent for a moment and wondered how such a thing could happen.

No one, he thought. There was no human way for this to have happened.

Keira trotted towards the gate itself and silently crouched down. She sensed there was something out there. Alexander looked past the gate and into the moonlight. The three black dogs that had followed him earlier that evening sat in the same spot that he last saw them, and quietly watched the palace gate.

"What happened here," King Magnus demanded from behind them. He arrived with Mattias and Calimus at his side with their swords drawn. "What is it? Edward?"

"Their throats are cut right out of them," Edward remarked. He knelt down to get a closer look at the men. "They were good lads. Both had families. This was a brutal way to die."

Alexander tried to make his way through the throng to his men, but ended up facing his father. His father looked at him briefly. For a brief moment, Alexander thought that he saw sadness in his father's eyes.

"You've brought death to our door my son," he said quietly.

"Whatever blood I bring, is because I am your son…father. Have no fear, Sofia and I will leave shortly to the Western Isles by boat. There will be no need for them to trouble you here in your silver tower." Alexander tried to pass him.

"No. I directly forbid it. You will not put my daughter into danger." King Magnus raised his voice, which caused every warrior to back away very slowly.

"So I should stay here and endanger you all? Just tonight you wanted me to leave. What would be safer than a country that we have to cross water to visit? Do they have boats? Do they now have wings? If you want Sofia to be safe, let her go with me." Alexander paused and waited. He returned his father's fiery gaze and refused to look away.

King Magnus broke the stare first. He mumbled to Edward to ensure that the dead men were taken care of and to double the guard. He returned to the Palace and leaned on Mattias for support.

Alexander made his way to Jack for it was imperative that he had his own protection in place. If his enemies could pass through a closed gate, they could surely enter the castle undetected.

"Jack, I want you to post two men, every hour tonight. I fear our friends are back. Oh, and let the men know that we are traveling to Brookhaven tomorrow. We are accompanying my sister to the Kingdom of the Western Isles."

"Yes sir. Should we post outside your room?"

"No. I've got my personal guard. But post two outside my sister's room. No man enters her chambers. If anyone should try, then run them through." Alexander whistled to Kiera and together they went back to his room. He hoped that they were safe enough until they could leave port the next day.

CHAPTER XVII

Alexander was excited to return to Brookhaven for he missed the bustling of activities. Brookhaven was inhabited by a great mixture of people. Since the kingdom was so prosperous, merchants from many different kingdoms called Brookhaven home, and hoped to generate wealth for themselves and their liege. This cosmopolitan atmosphere increased the cities international prestige and favor with the royal court. The royal family made it their prerogative to frequent Brookhaven and it was also Calimus's preferred city of choice. The loose atmosphere helped his indiscretions blend into the background.

Going downstream to Brookhaven was a serene experience. Alexander and Sofia sat in cushioned chairs in the shade of an awning while the rest of their accompaniment sat on wooden benches on the side of the barge and laughed and joked as they splashed water at each other.

Altogether, they brought eighteen people with them. All twelve of Alexander's bodyguard were present for the journey, and Sofia brought six handmaidens to take care of her needs while traveling. Alexander chuckled to himself as his bodyguard was trying to be overly impressive and showed off to the handmaidens. Even Fergus tried to impress one of Sofia's pretty young handmaidens, a young dark haired beauty named Lauren.

"Do you happen to know what kind of strange animals live in this river?' he asked. She shook her head no.

"Legend has it that there are mermaids in the river. If you stay on the banks long enough and sit quietly, they'll show themselves." Fergus spoke very convincingly on the topic.

"I didn't know that mermaids lived in our river," she countered. "I thought merpeople lived in the ocean."

"A lot of learned people will tell you a lot of nonsense. But there are mermaids here, I'd stake my life on it."

Alexander shook his head. He'd been on the ocean, and he had never seen anyone resembling half a fish and half a man. Chauncey didn't believe it either.

"There aren't any such thing," Chauncey challenged.

"Is so," Fergus argued.

"Is not. It's local superstition. They say a young girl lost her sweet heart, and being so devastated, she drowned herself in the river. The local priest went and raised her from the dead. Only she drowned so she was stuck in the river." He stopped and chuckled at the story. Then he produced a rod with a string on it, tied a morsel of bread to it, and then tossed it in the river.

"So as I was saying before I was interrupted-" Fergus turned his attention back to Lauren but was again victim to his brother's teasing.

"Oh. Interrupted. There's a large word. Does it have more than twenty nine letters?" Chauncey let out a small laugh. He leaned back against a barrel and closed his eyes.

He wiggled his fishing stick a little.

"Pay him no mind, Lauren. He's got a scholar's mind, but nothing to show for it. Not even a fish."

Suddenly, Chauncey yelped. A fish pulled on his string. He quickly pulled it out and laughed triumphantly.

Alexander turned his attention back to Brookhaven. This was by far, the city he loved the most. Every time you turned down a different alley, it was a different adventure that waited to happen.

"So," he said to Sofia. "Everything is ready?"

"Yes," she said excitedly. "Oh Alex! I'm so excited. We're going on a boat to a different country entirely. I owe you so many favors! The first thing I am going to do is find Emma and introduce you properly. You'll love her...."

Sofia continued talking about her newest friend. Alexander was getting used to it, but his thoughts always moved to Angelica. Whenever he closed his eyes, he saw her face. It was always the last memory he had of her and it still caused him great affliction. His hand touched his sword, which had been hers, and he offered a silent prayer for her soul.

"Alex, are you even listening to me?" Sofia pouted and crossed her arms. "You're not listening to me."

"Of course I listened, I was just thinking what an excellent tunic you've made me and how I cannot wait to wear it."

She smiled and squeezed his arm. They were almost upon Brookhaven now and Alexander saw the landings with a path that fed into the city. Several other merchant barges were tied to stakes on the other side of the river. They were much larger than the royal barge as they transported heavier goods. The two men that piloted the barge tied it to the dock. Alexander's men graciously attended to the ladies and helped each one of them out of the barge. When the guards finished their attendant duties, the party made their way towards two waiting wagons. The women climbed into one, and the men loaded weapons into the second. When their task was completed, they made their way to the docks inside the city.

They didn't go far into the city before they were recognized. People came out to the streets and cheered festively and tossed flowers at Princess Sofia. She smiled and bravely waved back to the people on both sides of the street. Alexander walked behind the procession and found himself amused by the people's enraptured attention. Sofia was enamored with the extra attention that had been placed on her, and she handled it as gracefully as she could.

Although he tried to remain inconspicuous and wanted to blend in with his men, the people could not be fooled. Since Brookhaven was home to many merchants that traveled back and forth between the royal city and their own, they recognized Prince Alexander. It could also be attributed to the fact that regardless of his short, cropped hair, he was Sofia's twin brother.

Unlike his last visit, when he was an afterthought next to Edward, women thronged to be next to him while they blew kisses and grabbed whatever roses they could find to toss the petals at him. For him it seemed ridiculous and felt as if the mob of women wanted to tear him to pieces. His bodyguard sprang into action and happily protected him from being mauled to death by the young maidens. With this newfound space he jumped onto the back of the wagon and waved at all of his father's subjects.

"This is all for me and I welcome its embrace!" Alexander allowed his ego to accept the attention and he felt a newfound sense of confidence and self-awareness. He became lost in the moment and soaked it all in. He was quite fond of the, 'Long Live Prince Alexander', chants so much that he didn't realize that they had arrived at the docks. He heaved a contented sigh and jumped down to ensure all the barrels were loaded.

Fortunately, his ship was loaded quickly. Alexander walked on board and barked sailing orders to his men. They knew nothing about sailing, but his ship was so dynamic it didn't need expert sailors.

Alexander's ship was a fusta, one of the rarest of its kind. While other kingdoms including Alveus operated galleys with inefficiency, he added one piece that made his ship the fastest on water. He added a triangular sail that increased his speed, and could navigate the winds with ease.

His ship, The Resolute, was light and fast. If he so desired, he could sail to any of the nearby kingdoms. The ship moved swiftly up river, something other galleys could not do. During his youth he had sailed around the Western Isles, the Northern Islands, and made it as far east as the Atreides. Near the Atreides were powerful city-states which had their own laws, and were generally looked down upon as inferior. Alexander had met a few of the Atreides' merchants and while they were rough characters, they were noble in their dealings with one another. With foreigners, it was an entirely different situation. Each merchant had questionable ethics, according to traders. The honest merchants were no better than pirates and thieves, which many of them were. Stories abounded of trinkets being shipped to other nations, only to be found in markets across their kingdom weeks later.

King Magnus' father, Magnus II, had commissioned a fleet of twenty galleys that protected the merchant vessels from these marauders. Relations between the Alveans and Atreides had worsened over the years, as Alveus eyed expansions into their colonies. The Alveuns, although former vassals of the Atreides, were keen for conquest of their new rivals, something that Mattias brought up frequently. If Alexander sailed without a watchful eye, the sightseers might end up as galley slaves on a pirate ship, or purposefully ransomed back to Alveus.

Alexander noticed that two other galleys were prepared to escort his ship. Sofia had prepared everything within a moment's notice. How impressive she was in her organization, he thought. He would try not out run these slow warships for as long as he only needed protection as far as the Western shoreline. From there it was a short passage through the straits before they reached the Kingdom of the Western Isles.

"Jean!" he called to the young man that lashed the last trunks of Sofia's clothing.

"Yes Prince?" he called back.

"Prepare to cast off lines…Jack. Lend a hand." Alexander studied every item that was in the boat quickly and assumed everything was in its proper place. He stood up on the bow and addressed his men with a confident tone.

"Knights! Before we leave I ask that you take off your armor and place it below decks." Alexander pointed to the stern as they entry.

"But sir, what if we come across pirates? We'll need to defend ourselves," Sean said with earnest concern.

"Sean my lad, have you ever tried to float iron?"

"You can't float iron," Ferris said, confused.

"My point. If you fall overboard in armor, we will say a prayer for you in your watery grave, for there is no rescuing. So put the armor below, and let's set sail."

The men quickly took off their armor and Alexander made one final going over of his vessel.

"Everyone's armor below? Excellent. Keira? Good. Push off please, dock master." Alexander barked specific instructions to his men in order for his ship to leave the dock. He had no sailors among them, so he would have to teach them the finer parts of sailing over the next few days.

And teach he did. He went about the ship, teaching the men each part of the ship, its name, and its function. The handmaidens listened eagerly, and seemed to pay more attention to the nautical lessons then the men. Alexander kept his patience as best he could. Sofia encouraged him to be patient, as the men were still young and had undoubtedly never seen ladies like these. Their soft skin and radiant hair was a novelty compared to the dirty unwashed peasant women whose company they normally enjoyed.

They did learn though at a much slower pace than Alexander wished for. The most apt pupils were Jean and Devon. They followed Alexander around the ship and hung upon every word he said. Alexander quickly established Jean as the first mate, and allowed him free run of the ship. This allowed Alexander to free his hands and enjoy the beauty of the ocean.

Alexander loved sailing past the western coastline. There was a very sparse sandy beach, and it quickly turned into rocks. The rocks covered the rest of the open shore until it met a thick forest. The forest sloped upwards until it came to the edge of the Western Mountains. The palisades were incredibly steep, and only the most experienced guide could navigate up them. Occasionally Alexander would see deer make their way through the shoreline, and climbing up the mountain skillfully with their brilliant hooves.

The ocean itself was calm and peaceful and crystal blue. It had a calming effect on him, while his cares began to float listlessly away on the ocean with each tiny whitecap. He rarely noticed his men chattering away, or his sister's excitement that seemed to spill forth with every hour that passed. But as always, a voice stole away his calm.

"Prince Alexander!" Fergus yelled from the other end of the ship. Alexander looked his way and Fergus stood there with a dumbfounded look on his face, with the maiden Lauren by him.

"Sir? You've traveled these oceans...where do the mermaids hide? Are they in the little causeways in the rocks?"

"How many times do we have to go over this? There aren't any mermaids. They're a myth!" Chauncey interjected.

"Lot of things are myths," Jean said. "I think we've seen some of them."

All of the men nodded in agreement. Then they heard what sounded like a breath coming through the water. The passengers glanced at each other, unsure from where the sound came.

"Over there! Port side!" Farkus yelled. All the passengers ran to the opposite side that Farkus was on. From where he stood, Farkus was on the port side.

"You're on the port side," Alexander offered. Farkas sheepishly walked over to the starboard side with the rest of the group.

"That's the starboard side," Alexander offered.

"What did you see?" Mayer asked. Before Farkus could answer there was a grey mound that rose in the water and shot water into the air. Everyone except Alexander gasped. Several of the men quickly ran below and grabbed spears for protection.

"What is it?" they yelled.

Alexander laughed. "Those are your mermaids. They are gentle creatures that mean us no harm. Just don't sail next to them or we'll be swimming to shore."

The men and women watched these beautiful giants while they moved up and down in rhythm and sprayed water at the boat causing everyone to point and laugh at one another. Soon the gentle giants went their separate ways as Alexander turned the boat through the straights to the western isles.

CHAPTER XVIII

Alexander caught sight of the Western Isles which were so named because they were made up of five islands. The central island was the largest and it was on this land mass that their king lived along with most of the population. The other islands flanked the large island and each one of them held fortresses at their highest points to keep an eye on intruders.

Alexander held his course through the first two islands and ensured that he was still followed by his two galleys. He observed the hills on both islands were dark green but were covered with purple flowers so plentiful they were visible from miles offshore. Around the front of both islands were jagged rocks that could wreck Alexander's ship if he wasn't careful.

Once Alexander's ship passed through the two islands the main island came into view. Their capital was located near the water and small canals had been dug that stretched from the ocean into the city. From the port a visitor was able to take a barge down any of the canals to their destination. Although the city held several canals it remained well fortified for they constructed huge towers that looked over the oceanic entrance to the city with large ballistas placed on them. The city's walls were high enough and took up most of the island which ensured an attacker wouldn't be able to find a safe place to land an army. At the center of the city was a well-protected castle keep where the royal family lived.

Nightfall had come but Alexander had already safely navigated the currents and docked his ship at the port while the other two galleys followed suit. A finely dressed man waited at the dock and addressed Alexander and Sofia as they made their way to him.

"Good evening honored guests," he said as he stiffly bowed towards them. "I am Yanis, chief interpreter to the royal family. I trust you did have a fine journey to our kingdom. Please, a barge has been waiting here for you. If you and your party could board, I will take you to the royal apartments where you will be our guests."

Alexander and Sofia bowed warmly towards Yanis and stepped into the barge. Once everyone had seated, Yanis instructed the barge men to set sail. Alexander noticed that their barge had been filled with rose petals, a sign of love among the classes, but none of the other barges shared the same treatment. Several children gathered along the wall of the canal and walked alongside of the barge; they held candles in front of them and sang a haunting song in the Kingdom's native tongue.

"This is so beautiful," Sofia exclaimed. She was awestruck by the moment, and her handmaidens prattled excitedly.

Alexander felt annoyed for it didn't take a cleric or a scholar to understand Youssef's wooing. Rose petals, children singing, and lanterns streamed across the canal before them, as if they lighted the way to Sofia's heart. Alexander now felt nauseous for he might have to punch someone in the nose, and he began to feel very strongly about the morality of that action.

"Oh Alex! Isn't this beautiful! Is it for me? Oh do you think it's for me? Isn't this beautiful?"

A lump started rising in Alex's throat. He hoped it was seasickness or canal sickness. He loved Sofia dearly, and the thought of a foreigner wooing his sister was out of the question. She needed to marry an Alveun noble.

"Just think. We could be married sometime, and I could be a queen, just like mother. And I'd have servants and my own castle...oh listen to me....I'm sorry..."

That's better, Alex thought.

"I'm sorry...." she continued. "And you will meet Emma and you'll dance and fall in love...and there will be little Alexander's running around, and they will call me Aunt Sofia." She sighed. "This is the most perfect night of my life."

Alexander's face was contorted in a mixture of pain, sickness, and fury. He politely excused himself from Sofia's side and delicately walked over to Jack.

"Jack," he whispered.

"Yes, your highness?"

"Did you load the weapons?"

"Yes sir."

"Good. Get the swords. I'm going to have to cut down some people. Very soon." Alexander spoke very matter-of-factly.

"I don't understand," Jack said horrified. "Wouldn't that be wrong?"

"FINE." Alexander whispered with emphasis. "Give me a dagger so that I may kill myself. Or a pointed stick, Jack. Do we have any pointed sticks?? Or may I poke a dagger in the heart of the Prince that makes advances to my sister. That dirty unwashed foreigner, I will cut him down with my blade...." he stopped talking and looked beside him. Yanis the interpreter stood near to him.

"Is everything to your liking Prince Alexander? Do you not enjoy the folk songs of our country?" Alexander noticed the subtle undercurrent of mocking in Yanis' tone.

"No," Alexander said through clenched teeth. "I love your children. It's just that we are exhausted from our voyage over the sea, and hoped to refresh ourselves tonight."

Yanis smiled and was about to respond but Sofia interrupted.

"But Alex! This is the first night of the feast! Let us attend." She was firm in her response. When Sofia made up her mind, there was no changing it.

"I too would enjoy the feast dear sister, but I think for you and I to be more presentable may…make it more pleasing to our gracious….host." Alexander made a motion towards his hair and nodded to Sofia. He hoped she'd understand. It took several tries, and several attempts of suggested unseemliness until Sofia understood.

"Oh," she sniffed, "Perhaps we could do with freshening up and my hair needs a good brush."

"Oh your hair is beautiful your highness," one handmaiden expressed as she pulled out a brush.

Alexander's face darkened. She'd have to be eliminated also. Fortunately for Alexander, Sofia's vanity won over common sense as she agreed that they should arrive at the royal apartments. Alexander bid Keira farewell when they arrived at the Royal Apartments as she was required to be placed in the kennels. Keira whined and moaned, but one of the attendants produced a large bone that finally enticed her into the kennels.

Sofia's apartment was lavishly furnished, Alexander's was not. Alexander understood that Youssef was not going to be friendly, so there was no use in diplomacy. At this point, war could have started and Alexander wouldn't have felt sorry for it, for he now felt the sting of Youssef's insult.

Exhausted from the voyage and the hard benches, Alexander and his men slept soundly the first night. He did feel quite contented away from his home land, mostly because he felt he was in no danger, and that he could sleep without being awoken to all manner of hell.

When they finally awoke, Alexander readied himself for the Ball and took the traditional bath while his men unpacked his personal effects and arranged his tunics and pants. It was a social affair, so armor and weapons were not welcome and had to be left behind. At the bottom of his trunk was the gryphon goblet. The men were at first confused by the goblet, for it was shaped in the form of an animal's leg, but Alexander explained to what purpose it served. He decided to take it to the ball with him, regardless of the looks he'd receive from others.

The first person to question him was Sofia upon her arrival with her maidens to his apartment. He explained dutifully, but she rolled her eyes in frustration. He tied it to his belt, where his sword might have been so as not to embarrass his sister. Alexander bade his men farewell and tossed them a small purse for exploring the town with Sofia's handmaidens on their arms. The men cheered and extolled Alexander's virtues to every bystander they met. He took Sofia's arm and crossed the courtyard, and was quickly joined by several of Prince Youssef's bodyguard. They wore heavy chain mail and carried curved swords and marched behind them without expression.

Once they arrived, Yanis greeted them at the door to the Hall. His sly smile caused Alexander to mark him as untrustworthy but there was no reason to have him suspected of being disreputable. From the door, he escorted Alex and Sofia into the Great Hall, and much like Manfred, called attention to the visitors.

After saying Princess Sofia's name, the crowd gasped and stretched their necks to get a better look at her. There were whispers of her beauty on the lips of everyone in the room. Prince Youssef quickly made his way through the crowd and stood before her. He took the hand she offered him and kissed it delicately.

Alexander wanted to hit his head with the goblet, but he stayed still out of respect for his sister.

"Princess Sofia," Youssef began, "You are a star traveled from heaven, so beautiful and radiant."

Sofia blushed. It was an uncomfortable moment for Alexander, so he spoke up.

"Prince Youssef," he said with an arrogant air. "It's good to meet you again. I was hoping that you could give me a tour of your beautiful city."

"Perhaps another time," Youssef smiled diplomatically. "First I would have the honor of dancing with your sister."

"I'm sorry Prince Youssef, I thought the custom in my country was the brother reserves the right for the first dance." Alexander challenged him immediately.

"That may be true Prince Alexander, but we are in my country. And in my country, the suitor takes first dance."

Alexander wanted to run him through. How dare he be so bold and impugn his sister's honor as he called himself a suitor.

"Perhaps," Sofia said. "We might miss the first dance. Prince Youssef, I was wondering if you might check your guest list for an honored friend of mine."

"Of course Sofia, and who would that be?"

"Lady Emma, a noble of Northern Islands."

Youssef's face darkened.

"I am sorry," he said. "Two weeks ago the pirates laid great desolation upon them. They carried off many women into slavery. Several of the noble houses were completely wiped out."

Alexander grabbed a glass of ale from a passing servant and had only half heard the conversation.

"I'm so sorry Alex, I don't know what's happened to her. That's so sad." She patted him lovingly on the shoulders.

Alexander was confused and didn't know what she was sad about but she quickly disappeared onto the dance floor as Youssef whisked her away. Alexander went to drink the glass of ale, but then remembered his cup. He untied it from his belt and carefully poured the ale into the glass. It did not change color, so he proceeded to drink from it.

He moved about the room and looked for an open bench but before he sat down, a familiar voice greeted him.

"Hello, Alex."

Alexander turned around and found Mattias smirking behind him.

"What are you doing here? Sofia said you couldn't bother to be disturbed." Alexander's countenance sank quickly.

"I came in on one of the galley's following you." Mattias laughed at his cleverness.

"Clever fellow. You tricked me. Good one. Never suspected that for a minute." Alexander turned away but Mattias had a few more words for him.

"I came hoping to get a good look at the danger you're in. I love a good fight, and after all if my kingdom is in danger," Mattias let the last few words dangle in the air.

"It isn't your kingdom," Alexander whispered menacingly. "Don't think I missed those words. Now, if you'll excuse me, I would like to eat." Alexander walked towards a bench that held a vantage point of the entire room. He sat down and began to eat a roasted chicken leg.

Alexander sat for most of the evening. He kept one eye on Youssef and Sofia who flitted between eating, drinking, and dancing. He was disgusted by the amount of laughter that went on between the two. He kept his other eye on Mattias. He was surprised that Mattias laughed and charmed his way with several women. He never saw that side to Mattias in Middlebrooke.

The ale began to have a profound effect upon Alexander, and he felt his mood lifted. As he watched Youssef and Sofia, he mimicked their conversation and laughed at his cleverness.

"Darling Youssef," he began in quiet falsetto. "Yes, my sweet rose petal. Ha. I like rose petals. I know- I tried to bury you. You didn't bury me. I know. You're right here. I am right here? Where is here?"

Alexander immediately felt someone's presence behind him. He bent his head back slightly, and noticed a shapely dress. The dress passed in front of Alexander and it sat down next to him. He was a little stupefied from the ale, but he managed to open his eyes enough to make out her face.

At first glance, he thought he saw Angelica. His heart leaped. As he focused on her, he was disappointed that it was not her and immediately felt sad.

"Prince Alexander?" the dress asked.

"Yes?"

"Oh I knew it was you. Please forgive me for being so bold. I know we have not been formally introduced...I am Lady Isadora. I am the daughter of the Baron of

Middlebrooke, your father's faithful servant."

"It's nice to have met your acquaintance," he stated flatly.

"I had no idea you were going to be here. I've heard so much about you. Is it true that you crossed the border and fought a sorcerer?"

"I am unsure of what you are saying. Perhaps?" He was put off guard by questions about an event he was not aware had been whispered outside of the castle. A servant approached the table and poured ale into Alexander's goblet. As the ale sloshed about in the goblet, Alexander observed the faintest change of color. He looked up at the servant. The servant avoided eye contact with him, and sweat collected on his brow.

"Tell me servant," Alexander said methodically. "Who makes this ale?"

"I don't know Your Highness. I am merely your servant." The servant continued to avoid eye contact with Alexander.

"If you don't like the ale my Prince, perhaps you would consider my private stock of wine. It comes from my father's vineyards and is extremely well made." Isadora smiled at Alexander but he ignored her and kept his eyes squarely on the servant.

A small hint of recognition flickered in Alexander's eyes. He grabbed the servant's arm and pulled it to the table.

"When was the last time you were in the forest," he said to the servant with murder in his eyes.

The servant dropped the jug to the ground with a clatter that gained the attention of all in the room. Alexander noticed this and released the man's arm who then turned and walked hastily out of the room. Alexander turned to Lady Isadora and for a moment her black hair and blue eyes offered a haunting to his heart. He grabbed his goblet and poured its contents under the table then tucked it into his belt.

"I beg your leave, milady. I have urgent business to attend too."

Alexander stood up hastily and started moving after the servant. The incompetent assassin had a head start and had already entered the kitchen. Alexander followed with calm haste. Once he reached the entranceway he ran after the stranger but the would-be killer had an insurmountable lead. Alexander ignored this and ran as fast as his legs could carry him. At first they matched stride for stride as they raced down the nearby canal. Alexander struggled to keep pace with the would-be assassin as the food and ale he had consumed bogged him down. He stopped running and staggered to a bench that faced the canal to catch his breath.

His breath returned to him and he decided to try to pick up the trail. He wished he had Keira with him so that she could be unleashed. Once he stood up he went in the direction he last saw the assassin, but he caught a glimpse of a different man rushing him from his side. Alexander's reaction was slowed, and he was unable to grab the man. The man hit him with such force that Alexander fell backwards into the canal.

He pushed himself back towards the surface, and once his head was above water he looked in all directions for his attacker. The thief was nowhere to be found so Alexander swam to the closest boat dock on the canal. Once there he unsuccessfully tried to hoist himself onto the step but lost his grip and fell back into the water. He tried to hoist himself again, but this time a wooden staff was placed in front of him to grab. He gripped it and leveraged himself back onto the dock. He stood up and wiped the salt water out of his eyes then took stock of the man who held the staff.

The keeper of the staff was dressed in unfashionable clothing for any culture Alexander had contact with. He wore a long flowing robe and instead of a smoothed face, he fashioned a long grey beard. Alexander remembered the better part of his manners.

"I thank you for your help," Alexander mumbled. He spit the remaining seawater from his mouth and looked about the canal.

"I was sitting up there," the man pointed towards a small building. "I saw what happened; I thought you might need a hand." The voice was slow and thoughtful, as if he tried to sort through the scene he had just witnessed.

"Well, thank you again kind sir. I appreciate the hand. If you'll excuse me, I am late for an event. Godspeed." Alexander tried to move past him.

"My name is Abiyram. And you are....Prince Alexander of the Wolfield house, are you not?"

Alexander stopped. He wondered if this man were connected to Youssef's house, or was this a beggar looking for compensation?

"I am Prince Alexander. That's correct."

Abiyram smiled and revealed a mouth that missed its fair share of teeth. He chuckled and slapped Alexander's shoulders.

"I should have known immediately. Always running after something. It is the story of your life. Never satisfied with who you are, seeking to be someone else."

"I apologize sir, but I do not believe that I have made your acquaintance." Alexander eyed the old man carefully.

"Not in person." Abiyram started to walk alongside the canal. "But I know you Alexander, and you know me."

"I don't know you. We've never been introduced," Alexander said firmly. He followed the stranger for a moment, and he looked about to see if there was an ambush coming to him.

"Very well. Then I shall make you an introduction. I am Abiyram the High Priest of the Bete'szek. Now do you know who I am, Alexander?"

Alexander felt fear rise in every bone, and each bone buckled under the weight of Abiyram's words. Alexander felt his face pale, but quickly recovered so his fear would not show.

"I know you," he nodded. "And you have me at quite the disadvantage. No sword. No armor. What is it I can do for you?"

"It's what I can offer you, Alexander," he smiled, "To offer you the throne to a united kingdom."

"Throne to barbarians? I didn't know there was one."

"Not just the throne to the Bete'szek, Alexander, but the entire kingdom. Imagine…one king….bringing the north and the south together…the east and the west….you could be the most powerful Alveun king. More powerful than your father."

"I thought you had many kings," Alexander said suspiciously.

"We have chiefs, too many if you ask me. We need one king, someone young and courageous that people will follow…someone with charm and charisma. And it is because of that, that we have selected you."

"You flatter me Abiyram, but Edward will rule Alveus. Why not make him that offer? Why not submit to his authority while there is time?"

"Is your brother not Defender of the Faith?" Abiyram chuckled. "Should we submit to him so that your monks can take away our sacred beliefs and wipe us away from this land? This is our land and they are no longer welcome here."

"What makes you think I'd do anything differently?" Alexander felt very tempted at the prospect of power, but reminded himself...this was a lie that he was being led to believe.

"You are....the fourth son of a dying dynasty, and the only son that holds so much promise. But your family ignores you...they demean and devalue you. You're always on the outside looking in. They are...jealous...of you. Your nobles are fat and corrupt, they offer rebellious thoughts, and my people will soon fill your fields with blood. I offer you the chance that I know you want...the chance to be King. You can rule both kingdoms, it's what you're destined for. I can see the ambition in your eyes."

"You're wrong," Alexander said flatly. "I have no ambitions for the throne."

"Events will happen that are going to change the course of destiny. Join us Alexander. Let me show you your true path."

Abiyram slowly raised his hand to Alexander's head. He jutted out his thumb and pressed it between Alexander's eyes. Suddenly, Alexander was ushered into a vision. At first, he saw nothing but black smoke. He focused his mind on the blurred figures before him. He could hear the whispered voice of Abiyram as he concentrated on them.

He saw himself sitting on his father's throne with the crown. He was surrounded by his subjects who knelt in devoted admiration. The next vision showed limitless wealth.

"This could all be yours," whispered Abiyram. "Power....wealth...glory. Everything at your fingertips. The power to rule. Yield to me."

The vision dissipated and Alexander opened his eyes and watched Abiyram withdraw his hand. He thought about the visions. *"Why shouldn't I be king?"* he thought. *"I am more loved than any of my brothers. I deserve it."*

He studied Abiyram's face for a moment. Abiyram's smile showed nothing but deceit. A voice of reason rang out in Alexander's mind. Absolute power, it said, cannot be shared.

"No," Alexander said as he regained his focus. "The throne is not for me. I have no interest in being any party to this."

"I can teach you the secrets to my powers. You can unlock the power of the skies. Command men to do your bidding! Rule with no boundaries to the powers that you can acquire." Abiyram raised his staff into the air and a blue flame appeared at the top of it. It suspended in the air and clouds joined together in the sky.

"I must decline your offer. All that you offer me, you implicate me in a plot to murder my family and remove the beliefs of my people. I will not betray my ideals for your ambitions. I will offer a united kingdom....yes...submit to my bother. He is a good man and will treat you fairly. Believe in him." Alexander's earnestness showed no impact on Abiyram.

"I have no interests in continuing the rule of foreigners. You are different, which is why I have come to you, to ease the transition of power for the Alveun citizens. You decline my offer, very well, the next time we meet Prince, you will not be so fortunate." Abiyram's eyes flashed yellow at Alexander. Alexander backed away from Abiyram and stood next to the canal.

"Why not kill me now?"

"There's nothing that can be gained in killing you now. There would be no satisfaction. You see Alexander...the priest you killed, was my brother. One who kills a priest must take his place. I should kill you, but you show such ability. This will be the only time I will offer this to you. The choice will pass to another."

"I won't betray my family," Alexander said definitively. He felt braver and moved closer to Abiyram. "I don't need your power. I've seen what your people do. You're murderers and assassins. You had your chance to rule, and now your time is done. My brother will be king, and I will see you dead if you ever step into his kingdom regardless of the powers you bring with you."

"Alexander...." Abiyram said sadly. "We had such hope for you. I'm curious, tell me...how did you know the wine was poison?"

"I guess I am just blessed." Alexander smiled smugly.

"No. No one is that blessed. No one escapes death by my hand. Goodbye Alexander. May your next life be more productive."

Abiyram and Alexander faced each other for a moment. With lightning speed the priest threw out his hand to touch Alexander's chest. Alexander was too late to stop it from striking him. A blinding light flashed from the priests hand and connected with his chest. The impact felt as if a boulder had crashed into him. He fell back into the canal and with the brief moments he quickly took a breath while his body plunged through the water.

He struggled to return to the surface but found himself paralyzed and unable to move. His body continued to sink towards the bottom of the canal, his last breath slowly exhaling. Above him, another body splashed into the water, and then another. Alexander realized that it was not bodies that fell into water, rather someone had dove in after him. He recognized the larger silhouette as Jack and the other body that dove in after him was Jean.

Jack and Jean each grabbed an arm and pulled him

back to the surface. Alexander gasped for air as they lifted him back onto the dock.

"Prince Alexander! Are you alright? Can you hear me?" Jack shouted.

Alexander nodded but quickly turned his body to the side. He coughed and expulsed water that had been trapped in his lungs. He coughed some more as he caught his breath.

"Yes. I am fine. Thanks to you two. What are you doing out here anyway?"

"Well," Jack answered. "We figured you'd need us so we've been following you."

"Where did that man I was talking to go? Which way?"

"We didn't see. He moved too quickly for us." Jean replied.

They helped Alexander regain his footing as he regained control of his body.

"Help me back to the apartments," he mumbled. "I need a dry change of clothes and my armor. I will never be unarmed again."

The three of them walked back to the apartments or in Alexander's case, stumbled and coughed violently. When they finally arrived they found the Ball had ended and many of the nobles still milled about the courtyard.

The onlookers gawked and strained their necks to get a glimpse of this wet interloper. When Alexander came into view the onlookers turned and whispered to one another. Yet another grand entrance for the youngest son, he thought amusingly to himself. He was used to showing up disheveled.

A brief cry came from the crowd as Sofia rushed towards Alexander. Youssef followed her and motioned for two guards to follow.

"Prince Alexander!" Youssef exclaimed. "What's happened?"

"It's nothing," he said, wishing not to draw attention to himself. "I fell into the canal. I just need to change out of these wet clothes."

"You're lying," Sofia said. "Tell us the truth."

"If there was anything I needed to tell you, I would have already. Please don't worry yourself on my account. A warm bath and a stiff drink will do me good. Have you seen Mattias?"

Sofia shook her head no. Perhaps that was a good thing. Maybe he too fell into the canal and drowned. That news would make Alexander feel better. He hurried past the on-lookers with Jack and Jean. This situation had begun to escalate and it wouldn't be much longer before an open conflict erupted.

CHAPTER XIX

"You are the most handsome of your brothers," she sweetly crooned into his ear. Isadora's voice interrupted Alexander's thoughts and embarrassed him slightly. It had been two days since his meeting with Abiyram, yet he could not rid the conversation from his mind and yet here stood one of the fairer ladies of Alveus and she had not stayed in his thoughts. Isadora stood over him where he sat and flashed him a coy smile.

"I thank you for the kind words; however it is well known that Edward is the handsomest of us." Alexander's face reddened as he tried to dismiss her compliment.

"Perhaps that is the conventional thought," Isadora replied, "Yet I find myself always being drawn to look at you."

Alexander burned with embarrassment and sweat collected on his brow. He tried to keep his eyes focused on Isadora but felt himself tempted to inspect her physical appearance. As her eyes drifted towards the rest of the Meeting Hall, Alexander quickly assessed her appearance. Her long dark hair and blue eyes were mere compliments to her healthy physique. She was shorter than he, but stood with confidence, and had an aura about her that immediately put Alexander under her spell. He didn't mind it, for she was absolutely beautiful.

"Perhaps," she said, looking back at him, "When your brother selects an appropriate candidate for his wife, it would give us an opportunity to get to know each other better. Would you like some wine, my Prince? It's my father's private stock."

"It sounds delicious." Alexander took the goblet from her hand and sipped it. His mouth was awash with flavor and it warmed him even further as it went down his throat. His mind became more aware of Isadora's beauty and he became single minded in his thoughts towards her.

She reached out a hand towards his shoulder and gently ran it down his chest. He took another drink to steady his heart as it raced wildly.

"I'm sorry," Isadora said softly. "It's inappropriate of me to touch you without your permission." She moved her hand back to her own goblet and smiled seductively at him. "I hope to see more of you at the feast your highness." She smiled and curtsied at him as he stood there mindlessly and managed a ridiculous nod. As she moved away he quickly drank the rest of the wine and grabbed some ale. He poured the ale in his goblet and satisfied that it was not poisoned, he drank it quickly to steady his nerves.

The Grand Ball continued for a few more days. Alexander kept to himself and stayed within the confines of the Royal Palace. He dutifully escorted Sofia to the ball each night, and stayed within earshot to ensure that Youssef behaved like a complete gentleman and did not make unwelcome advances upon his sister.

Mattias was conspicuously absent from much of the frivolity. He always appeared at the beginning but disappeared from sight frequently. He showed up at the end of each evening and acted if he had always been there. Alexander thought to keep as much distance as possible from Mattias to avoid any unfortunate occurrences.

Lady Isadora and her wondrous wine elixir frequented his side and kept him in good spirits. She acted very proper, and reveled in her station in life and carried herself with an air of authority. At times she seemed an insurable snob as she ordered the servants around, but her beauty compensated for her irksome mannerisms. She coaxed several dances from him which helped lighten his mood and as they talked the nights away, he became distracted from all of his concerns. He even allowed his sister to encourage a friendly dialogue between Prince Youssef and himself.

On the fifth day of their stay, Mattias brought news to Alexander and Sofia that a messenger from King Magnus requested them to return home immediately. Edward's marriage had been announced, and was slated to occur within the next month. This was huge news for when the Crown Prince took a bride not only did this solidify his claim to the throne, but also opened up the possibility for the other sons to take brides.

Alexander and his men prepared for the voyage back to Alveus. Youssef was very generous and showered Sofia with many fine gifts which took some time to be loaded. Alexander's men complained very little as they were excited to get back to their own country. Alexander invited Isadora to return with them, since her family was invited to the wedding, as a noble family within the kingdom and she readily accepted.

Alexander watched as Sofia said her farewell to Youssef and she accepted a kiss from him. Alexander was amused as he watched the foreign prince clumsily take Sofia's hand and bring it close to his face. Sofia boldly moved closer as if she wanted to force the intimate encounter. Youssef trembled nervously at their closeness, it didn't matter that the last few evenings they had spent more than enough time dancing in each other's arms. Youssef was visibly affected by the number of eyes that watched his interaction with Sofia. Like a snake, his head quickly moved to Sofia's cheeks, and did not stop until his lips met her cheek. The lovers grew red faced and Sofia's smile was the biggest that Alexander had ever seen from his sister. Youssef quickly remembered that everyone stared at them, and he quickly withdrew from the closeness. He bowed stiffly to Sofia, whispered something to her, and then turned to Alexander and smirked and nodded his head.

Alexander rolled his eyes but resisted the urge to make a scene about its inappropriateness. He might have done the same to Isadora but was unsure there would be reciprocation. Sofia slowly boarded the vessel and she kept one eye on the plank, and another on the handsome Prince Youssef. She avoided any eye contact with Alexander, and Alexander thought it best not to ruin his sister's happiness. At long last, the ship was finally provisioned and the travelers were ready. Jean cast off the lines and they sailed away from the Western Isles.

The journey home was as calm as Alexander could have hoped. They sailed under beautiful clear blue skies and an easterly wind provided more than enough assistance to expedite their journey. Alexander's sleek ship easily outdistanced the two galleys that had escorted them with Mattias on board. Alexander enjoyed the thought that his ship was far superior, and couldn't resist taking satisfaction in it.

Sofia kept to her handmaidens for the majority of the voyage; they giggled back and forth and annoyed Alexander so much that he stayed on the opposite side of the ship for their entire voyage. Even Isadora's presence on board his ship did little to elevate his mood. He loved Sofia, and didn't like to think of her being married and away from him. He realized his thoughts were selfish, but he preferred her marrying a noble from their kingdom and not someone across the seas.

The rhythm of the sea eventually elevated his mood and made for a better journey. He ceased being so concerned with the details and positions of everyone on board his ship. He was contented to stand apart from everyone else, and he stood near the rudder and steered the ship. He lost his thoughts frequently and stared into the water at his reflection, and past that to the fish that swam undisturbed beneath them.

"You're in a fine mood, Sir," Jack interrupted. Alexander looked down from the rudder and saw Jack looking up at him grinning. "I am no sea farer but perhaps if we changed course a bit we could avoid the shoreline?"

Startled at his sudden loss of focus, Alexander swung the rudder hard to port causing several of the men to nearly fall over the side. Everyone looked at Alexander in astonishment and Alexander returned with their astonishment with an apologetic wave.

"Thank you Jack. That would never have done. Drowning us when we're so close to home." He turned to Jack and mocked sarcastically, "Imagine my father's disappointment-." Alexander cut himself short. He hadn't meant to say anything ever regarding the King. It was inappropriate to discuss such manners in front of those who were not part of the family.

"The nation would mourn Sir," Jack said empathetically. "It would be a terrible and irreplaceable loss."

"Thank you for your kindness," Alexander said

politely. "But I will have to disagree with you. I am merely a tool of fate. I exist for a sole purpose and am destined to drift into obscurity once my purpose is completed." He heaved a great sigh.

"What is your purpose Prince Alexander?"

Alexander looked out towards the waters and the horizon. There was something about the horizon that begged him towards it, as if it offered life over death. It gnawed at his soul so frequently now.

"My purpose," he began and shook his head, "Is to see Edward rule. My purpose is death for I am the Harbinger; the herald of destruction and I was made for such a time as this, correct?" He laughed at his words. "I am a sword in the hand of my kingdom and I will defend it with my life."

"And when that happens? What then?"

"Well Jack," he said smiling. "If we survive this I will run to that horizon." He pointed out in front of the boat. "And once I get to the horizon, I will go to the next one, and then the next one after that. Out there is where my future and happiness lie, and God willing I live, I will find and embrace it."

Jack stayed quiet for a moment and Alexander closed his eyes and allowed the winds to tussle his hair. He loved the seas and always found it a more religious experience than when he attended Mass.

"Well sir," Jack replied as he turned to rejoin the merriment below, "I don't know if chasing that horizon and always looking beyond it would ever make me happy. All I know is today, and I am happy just to be alive. Everything that's happened...I don't know...it seems like a dream come true to be alive."

Jack smiled at Alexander and the look on his face seemed so content and relaxed. Alexander never noticed how much Jack smiled, even when he berated them at the monastery. He thought about Jacks words and about finding joy in who he was and what he did. But Alexander found no joy in his life. He was honor bound to his brother, duty bound to his kingdom, and trapped in a war that began well before the world had met Alexander Wolfield. If fate forced him to be their tool, then he would be a hammer unto all that opposed Alveus.

A sharp pain in Alexander's forehead caused him to sit down quickly and he buried his head in his hands.

"My Prince! What is the matter?" Jack asked alarmed.

The pain crippled Alexander and he closed his eyes tightly. He felt Jack's hand on his shoulder. As quickly as the pain had come, it left just as suddenly. He sat up and opened his eyes. His hands trembled a bit and he looked at Jack. Jack stood there alarmed and unsure of what to do.

"I'm okay Jack, just a headache," he said quietly. "Take the till please." Jack grabbed the till and sat dutifully as Alexander recovered his wits.

The headaches continued throughout the short voyage but they eventually subsided and stopped coming back to him. Once they drew nearer to Brookhaven Alexander lost all memories of the headaches and instead he wished he could refit his ship and sail on to the horizon, but Edward's marriage was just one more step towards the realization of a new and better Alveus. Perhaps his father would abdicate the throne and live out his days in peace and comfort. If King Magnus chose this route, Edward would become Magnus X and the corruption and intrigue that surrounded the throne would meet its finality. Alexander would be named Chancellor and Mattias and his ambition would be shut out. Alexander allowed the momentum of exhilaration to build in his chest.

The other travelers laughed and joked pleasantly as they unloaded the ship and prepared to go through the town and take the river barge back to Middlebrooke. Alexander was also very cheery until he recognized Zeus and his men's horses tied to poles. A feeling of dread overwhelmed him for there was something very wrong and out of place. A young page who stood by Zeus ran to him as soon as they caught sight of each other.

"Prince Alexander...Sir!" the young page said breathlessly. "I bring news from your brother, Crown Prince Edward."

"What is it?" Alexander demanded. He feared the worst that his father had died, before either of them had been able to patch their relationship. As much as he had started to hate his father, he would hate himself if they were never able to build any sort of bond between the two of them.

"There's been barbarian activity on the frontier. Your brother believes there to be a war coming to Edgebrooke."

Alexander stopped all of his thoughts regarding his father and he thought back to his meeting with Abiyram. The pieces were being put into play. An assault on a fortified town seemed out of character for a nation whose only defined strategies to date were ambushes and fighting in places where the terrains restricted use of the cavalry.

Alexander looked back at his men to instruct them to mount their horses but his men already armed themselves. Jack handed Alexander's armor to him and continued to fasten his own.

"I have all of the horses sir," the page said proudly. He was young and couldn't have been more than thirteen, but he was extremely eager. "Your horse and your men's horses are saddled and ready to ride. The Crown Prince's orders are to meet him on the road to Edgebrooke. Bishop Malachius and the Monsignor are there waiting for you."

"Thank you young sir. You've done well. Ride ahead," Alexander spoke, "And let them know we will follow quickly."

The page smiled proudly at Alexander's praise and he nodded and mounted his horse. Alexander turned and encouraged his men.

"Men, this is what we've trained for," he said confidently. "I'm taking eight men with me. Linus, Mayer, Ferris, Sean…you four are to escort my sister and Isadora back to Middlebrooke and follow her everywhere."

"Yes your highness," they responded.

"Wait!" Sofia commanded. "What is this activity? What's going on?"

"Sofia, it would take too long to explain. But I need you to trust me. The safest place for you is in the Palace. I'll tell you everything when I get back." He attempted to hug her goodbye but she raised her arms and prevented him from embracing her.

"Are you saying that because I am a woman that I need to cower in my room while the fate of my father's city is imperiled?" She glared at Alexander so fiercely that he felt an intense burning inside of him.

"Sofia," he said sympathetically, "I am not saying that. With everything that has happened to this point, I do not want to put you in harm's way."

"I can handle a sword and a bow," she argued. "One might argue better than you."

Alexander ignored the implied insult. "Yes, you can, and you can handle it brilliantly. But this…..this is not an enemy to take lightly. They deal in treachery. You are not ready for this kind of an enemy. I am sorry Sofia. Your safety concerns me more than anyone else. I will not be effective to Edward if I have to watch out for you too." He paused and hoped that his earnestness would be received.

"You need not be concerned," Sofia said in frustration. There were tears in her eyes. "I just don't want you going without me…but I will…take your counsel."

"Isadora, can you make your way with Sofia?" Alexander asked loudly as he looked around for Isadora but she was nowhere in sight. There was no time to look for her so Alexander and his men finished their preparations. Besides the traditional sword and shield, they each armed themselves with a dagger, a longbow, and filled each quiver full of arrows. They also carried a spear with them and attached it to their saddles.

When Sofia was finished with her protesting she took her seat on the Royal Barge with her handmaidens, and Alexander and his men quickly rode out of Brookehaven. They had gone no further than a mile outside of the city when they spotted a rider on a brown horse coming closer to them. Although the rider dressed like a man the jet black hair that flew in the wind behind her and the shapeliness of a woman told Alexander that Isadora had joined them. Her defiance and disappearance irritated him.

"Why are you not going to Middlebrooke?" Alexander demanded with irritation in his voice. Regardless of her charm and her beauty she had defied a Prince, an offense punishable with death.

"If the frontier is in danger, then my city is in danger. I will not abandon my father or my city!" Her face carried a defiant expression, and there was no need to argue details. He could arrest her now, but that would make an uncomfortable situation when they arrived in Edgebrooke. Isadora was well armed, so Alexander felt somewhat comfortable in allowing her to continue in their journey. He hoped she would prove to be less of a nuisance.

The warriors rode as quickly as their horses would carry them. They followed the river north for guidance, and briefly stopped in Middlebrooke to replenish supplies. Alexander sent Farkas ahead of their group to ensure there were no ambushes. He fashioned a theory that the Bete'szek would try to ambush him on the road to Edgebrooke, anything to draw out the nobility and thin them out. Before he left Middlebrooke he dispatched a small compliment of men from the garrison down the river to ensure Sofia arrived safely.

Eventually, the encampment flags of the Crown Prince came into view. Alexander rode into the camp and realized this was the first time he had ever been in the midst of the army. Soldiers busied themselves and sharpened their weapons and practiced with one another. They paid little attention to Alexander and his guard as they rode through. When they reached Edwards tent he greeted them enthusiastically.

"Alex! I am glad to see you!" Edward exclaimed. Alexander dismounted Zeus and handed the reins to a young page that stood nearby. They embraced warmly and Edward mussed Alexander's hair playfully.

"This is a strange place for a wedding Edward," Alexander chuckled.

"It's no laughing matter," Edward said gravely. "I had to postpone the wedding until we get this sorted. We've had spies watching the frontier...there's a lot of activity. We think they'll be coming after Edgebrooke."

"What do we know about their strength? How many men?"

"They number the sands of the shore," a familiar voice said. Alexander turned and spotted Bishop Malachius dressed in battle armor. This was a rare sight indeed for Alexander for he had always seen the bishop in church robes. Alexander had no idea he knew how to carry a sword. Monsignor Jean Paul stood close by also.

"So they outnumber the army then? That's fine, I've fought them. One of your men is worth ten of theirs and one of my guards is worth thirty of theirs. If we can get them on the battlefield, we will do well." Alexander felt supremely confident in a pitched battle. Their professional army was more than a match for berserkers.

"This enemy has no desire for a tactical encounter," Jean-Paul groused. "They'll neutralize our strengths and try to draw us into the forests, where they can ambush us."

Edward considered their plight for a moment while he contemplated a map of the kingdom.

"Bishop, how much trust do you place in your spies?"

"I trust them implicitly."

"Perfect," Edward said. "Send out your spies and I will send out the army's scouts. It's almost nightfall, so when they report back, that will influence where the army marches. Agreed?"

Malachius and Jean-Paul agreed and turned away towards their men. Alexander watched them leave with curiosity.

"What are they doing here?" he asked quietly.

"Bishop Malachius says the Church has a definite interest. He calls it a struggle against evil." Edward rubbed his hands together and blew into them. The air had begun to grow colder.

"But," Alexander said and pointed at the men. "Where did these cloaked warriors come from? These are not peasants or monks with swords; these are well trained and well supplied men. Since when did the church have an army?"

"Jean-Paul's been training them. Or didn't you know

that already? I would have thought you knew since you were at the monastery not long ago."

"So they are monks? I don't understand." Alexander had the understanding that the monastery took in the poor to teach them how to survive…not to function as their own separate army. Alexander focused his attention on the clerics closest to them. Their piety was on display as they knelt in a circle in prayer. Alexander felt such a deep misgiving, but these men were doubtlessly more than capable of fighting in close quarters. They could be what they needed to ensure victory.

"Where's Mattias? I'm in need of his regiments as well." Edward's voice brought Alexander back to the present. Alexander realized that he hadn't see Mattias since they left the docks of the Western Isles.

"He's at least a few days behind us. We arrived ahead of our expectations," Alexander said proudly. Anything to lower Mattias, he thought.

"There are an extra three hundred men that I could sorely use as reserve and my brother takes his precious time in arriving. One would think that the opportunity to distinguish himself would be enough cause for him to be punctual." He sat for a moment, lost in his thoughts, until he saw Alexander's uninvited companion.

"Isadora?" Edward said when he saw her on horseback. "Milady, what brings you to our camp?"

"I heard that Edgebrooke may be in danger so I have come to fight with you and protect my home. I'm afraid I've been a nuisance to your brother." She smiled slyly at Alexander. "I'm in fear that your brother may arrest me and I would not have a chance to show my courage and loyalty to the house of Wolfield."

"You are more than welcome; the Crown extends its courtesy to such a loyal servant. I hope my brother has behaved himself!" Edward grinned as he offered his hand to allow Isadora to slide off of her mount. She took his hand and gracefully slid off the horse.

The charms of a beautiful woman sway even the most stalwart of men, Alexander mused as his eyes refused look elsewhere.

"He's a perfect gentleman. You should be proud of him." She smiled at Alexander. Her smile was so radiant he felt the radiance piercing his soul and he quickly forgot any ill feelings he harbored. He began to feel embarrassed from the compliment and his face grew hot. He dropped his sword intentionally and fell to his knees quickly to retrieve it. He wished for no one to see his reddened face.

"I am always proud of him. Please take advantage of our hospitality and rest yourself. Tomorrow we're breaking camp and moving north. Sleep light."

Alexander felt a nagging in his spirit. There had been an oddity in Greystone and they had ignored it. What was there now? Could they find information in Greystone?

"Farkas," he whispered.

"Yes sir," Farkas asked. Farkas ran his fingers through his hair and brushed it out of his eyes.

"I want you and Chauncey to scout the area. Head north. I have a nagging feeling. Look near the forest, and look near Greystone. If you see anything...anything that looks out of the ordinary head back immediately. Understand? And Farkas, don't be seen."

Farkas nodded in understanding and whispered the plan to Chauncey. They mounted their horses and rode out of camp together. Night had fallen so Alexander bade his men to sleep early and rest up for the following day. He made that suggestion to Isadora, but Isadora ignored it, and instead joined Edward as he walked around the camp. Alexander watched intently as she laughed at his brother's words. His brother smiled back at her and as it seemed to Alexander, encouraged the behavior. He grew tired of their interaction and went inside his tent and started to sulk. All of the attentiveness that she had given to him for the last week dissipated and was now focused on his brother. His feelings made it difficult to sleep so he lay awake, staring at the tent until his eyelids grew heavy and he fell asleep.

He awoke the next morning with an eagerness for battle. His men acted with a level of anticipation too for while they ate their breakfast they remained quiet and were not their usual jovial selves. They kept to themselves with a grim resign. After breakfast, Alexander sought Edward out and found him as he sat with Bishop Malachius while they both ate fruit and peered over the kingdom's map.

"Good morning your highness," Malachius said. "We were just discussing where the army should deploy. Where did you say that you made contact with them?"

Alexander looked over the map, and moved an iron figurine to the place where they had tried to kill him.

"Right here," Alexander said determinedly. "After the forest there's the mountain range. There's a road that cuts directly between the mountains. That should be the path that leads you to them. It's difficult terrain, and an excellent spot to be ambushed. You'll need every scout on the mountains themselves. There are many caves there as well, perfect for hiding small groups of men. Have any of the scouts returned?"

"Most of them have come back," Edward said as Bishop Malachius nodded. "There's been no sign of our enemy. I am afraid this is no better than if we were blind."

"Doubtless," Malachius said, "That they are hidden in the forests. Your best hope of engagement lies there."

"Your highness," Jack entered the tent with a hasty

bow to Edward. "The Prince's scouts have come back."

The riders drove their horses hard and past their breaking limit, and for a moment it seemed that the beasts would die within a few yards of arriving at camp. Alexander rushed out to meet them with his brother and the Bishop following closely. Farkas' face was clouded with fear. Chauncey's face was grey and ashen.

"What is it?" Alexander asked. "What did you find?"

"Whole town of Greystone. Gone. There's no one there," Farkas said as he dismounted the tired beast. Chauncey wiped his eyes and looked at his brother.

"Fergus," he said quietly. "Whole town's gone."

"How does a town of three hundred men and women disappear?" Edward asked in puzzlement.

"There are some bodies. Mutilated and hung on a spear. But not enough to fill a town. The rest have simply vanished," Farkas explained. "I looked for tracks everywhere. There's nothing. But I know where they went…The forest. Look towards it now."

Alexander lifted his eyes towards the direction of the forests. Dark clouds gathered and lightning flashed in the distance. In Alexander's mind there was no doubt that it was Abiyram. He had finally massed together his forces and whipped them into a blood frenzy across the frontier.

"Alexander," Edward said slowly and with concern. "Do you know what is happening here?"

Alexander had never seen his brother with a confused look on his face. He was master and commander of his and his men's fate always and forever. Men were sworn to follow him to glory, and yet here he stood, unsure and without control.

"There's a storm brewing Edward." Alexander chose his words carefully to prepare his brother of the horrors to come. "Know this, when we find them and join battle, our horses will be useless. We will be fighting men and the elements. If we are going to war it will be against all hell."

A commotion occurred behind them which grabbed their attention. Fergus and Chauncey had mounted horses and prepared to ride away from the camp

"Ferguson!" Alexander bellowed. "Where are you going?"

"My home! Our family! I have to see for myself!" Fergus was near tears.

Alexander grabbed the horse's reins away from Fergus. He looked up sympathetically to Fergus who did all he could to keep in his emotions. Alexander felt the pain and fear the brothers were keeping within them.

"Be patient. Give me one hour. We will take our men and go with you. If you go alone you are only putting yourself in their hands." Alexander put his hand on Fergus' shoulder. "One hour?"

Fergus nodded. He was barely coherent to any of Alexander's words but he sat quietly on a bench and gripped his horse's reigns. Alexander ordered his guard to prepare to leave camp. Malachius and Jean-Paul ordered their men to marshal and follow Alexander. Edward ordered his warriors to break down camp, and prepare to move northward to the forests. Together they would meet outside of Greystone.

The knights moved from camp and hurried to Greystone while Keira ran behind them. Once they arrived, it was exactly how Farkas described it. The repulsive sight of men impaled on spears greeted them when they reached the entrance to the village. Alexander recognized the innkeeper as one of them. The spear had been thrust through his back and out his chest, and then lifted and placed in the ground. Alexander wondered how anyone could be so grotesque and cruel. Was this repayment for his father's crimes, he asked himself. Or was this the old standard of how the two armies had conducted themselves over the last three hundred years? Cruelty after cruelty, death, murder, hatred, and as always, the peasants paid with their lives. Alexander wiped his eyes and looked past the bodies into the village. Buildings smoldered from previously being set ablaze. The tavern was gone, burnt to the ground. The only movement came from a lone chicken that wandered aimlessly across the dirt road in the center of the town.

The sun was blotted out by clouds, and a cold wind blew that sent chills down Alexander's spine. All of the men stayed alert and began to move about the town. Several men dismounted and drew their swords. They entered each building that still stood and searched for survivors. They didn't find anything except for a few more scattered chickens.

Alexander allowed a moment for Chauncey and Fergus to grieve over the loss of their families and ordered the other men to remove those that had been impaled in order to be buried. No one caught sight of a short cloaked figure that moved towards the horses. Alexander caught sight of a horse fleeing in the direction of the forest with the cloaked figure on its back. Alexander quickly mounted Zeus and galloped after the horse and rider. He did it so quickly he neglected to inform his men what he was doing. Keira noticed her master leaving and instantly ran after them in full pursuit.

The figure moved closer and closer towards the eastern part of the forest. Alexander felt sure it was a spy. He urged Zeus on, and Zeus' powerful shoulders strained as they closed in on the cloaked figure. Alexander momentarily worried that this was a trap, one that lured him inside the forest, but even that would not deter him.

He had almost caught up with the figure when he realized they had gone deep inside the forest. The figure cut their way through the forest around gigantic trees and over rotting fallen ones. Zeus matched the other horses pace and Alexander closed in on his quarry. Once Zeus ran alongside of the horse Alexander jumped from his saddle and knocked the other rider off of the horse. Together the two fell to the forest floor. Alexander braced himself for the impact and rolled along the floor. He sprang up, sword outstretched towards the fugitive. He ripped the hood off of the other riders head and revealed curly brown hair and the widening eyes of a frightened girl.

"Katrina?" Alexander said in shock. He was at once relieved to find her alive.

The girl said nothing in return and just stared frightened at the sword. Alexander realized his sword still pointed at her throat so he gingerly lowered his sword. Just then, a rain drop struck Alexander's check and caught his attention. He glanced upwards but could not see past the canopies of the trees. He knew that clouds were gathering and very soon the Bete'szek would be upon them. He knelt down next to Katrina and took her hand.

"I'm not here to hurt you. You need to trust me because we have to get out of this forest now. Do you understand?" His voice was firm but calm as he wanted to avoid scaring her any further. He reached for Zeus' reigns and offered Katrina his hand.

"We have to get out of here. Hurry, Take my hand." As Alexander helped her up off the ground he glanced around for his dog. Keira was still out there lost. Another dog arrived and sat quietly on top of a small embankment behind him. Its yellow eyes were focused directly on Alexander's movement and its lips parted and revealed razor sharp teeth. The two other dogs arrived on either side of the lead dog, and shadowed its behavior.

"Katrina?" Alexander whispered, "Do you trust me?"

The young girl heard the dogs growl and looked behind her. She nodded yes very quickly to Alexander and grabbed his hand. He lifted her quickly onto Zeus and handed her the reigns. He slapped Zeus and yelled for the horse to run fast and Zeus quickly responded by breaking into a gallop. Alexander looked back at the dogs that quickly stood up and began to advance towards him. The rain steadied and created thick mud under his feet. He ran in Zeus' direction but the mud slowed his progress. The dogs now chased him quickly but he continued to run as fast as he could.

Alexander also found it difficult to run as the darkness made it difficult to see in front of him. Branches scratched his face and he stumbled over objects on the forest floor. Lightning flashed which enabled him to see for a moment before it went completely black. The dogs were almost on him and one of them snipped at his heel as he came to the top of a small hill. He tripped over a root and tumbled down the hill. He came to a stop in a small clearing at the bottom of the hill. He quickly grabbed for his sword but it was not in its sheathe. He used the little light that was in the clearing and looked desperately for his sword.

The dogs realized their advantage circled around him and prepared to strike at him. Alexander found his sword and crawled to it quickly to pick it up. As soon as his hand grasped the hilt one of the dogs leapt forward and tried to clamp down on the back of his neck. Alexander managed to turn onto his back and blocked the dog with his sword. The dog pressed against the sword and snarled and bit at him. Alexander felt the hot breath of the dog on his face but strained to hold the sword between himself and the dog. With each snap, the dog's teeth came closer.

There was a roar and the dog stopped snapping and looked behind Alexander. Another dog jumped over Alexander and collided with the black dog. The dog stumbled backwards and yelped as it sprawled on the forest floor. The new combatant stood guard by Alexander and flashed her intimidating teeth. It was Kiera.

Oh you magnificent dog, Alexander thought.

Alexander jumped up and waved his sword at the dogs that still circled them. He glanced around and saw the stone hut. Relief came over him, there were no gryphons nearby and it looked to be their best chance of survival.

He whistled a command to Kiera and ran towards the hut. Kiera ran alongside him as the three dogs chased them. Man and beast entered the stone hut and a loud thud shook the hut. Alexander turned quickly with his sword drawn, ready for the hell to come; instead a loud shriek filled the air and he fell to the ground in agony. The shriek had stopped the menacing dogs in their tracks and they retreated hastily to the trees. Once satisfied they were safe from the gryphons, the dogs contented themselves by taking up their positions and watching the movement within stone hut.

Satisfied he was safe for the moment, Alexander took note of the inside of the structure. It had looked like a very small hut from the outside but Alexander found a lone torch that flickered light here and there. When Alexander took the torch and waved it around, the hut appeared to be an amazing chamber of riches. Gold trinkets covered the floor from end to end and in the center of the room was an immense gold nest. Alexander had never seen so much gold. There was more gold in this hut than the royal treasury held!

He soon realized he wasn't alone. A very old man sat below the nest and stirred as Alexander focused on his face.

"A-ha!" he said suddenly. "Prince Alexander is it?"

"Yes," was all Alexander could think of to say.

"It's very nice to meet you. Come. Sit down. We have a lot to talk about it, and little time to do it in." The priest extended the blanket he sat on and motioned for Alexander to take the spot by him. Alexander declined and remained standing.

"Who are you?" Alexander demanded.

"I am Brendan. A prophet by trade, although, prophets don't make any money. And there aren't many of us. So maybe I'm just a crazy old fool with no trade and no money! But no one likes to hear 'Hello, I'm Brendan, the poor crazy bastard. I guess you'll be forming your own thoughts."

An awkward moment of silence followed for Alexander had no idea what he should say.

"I'm sorry," Brendan said. "I should get to the point. It's not me who's important. You are feeling conflicted. You are confused. You doubt everything you believe. Am I right?"

"That's a fair assessment."

"Well then, enjoy how you feel now. Because in three days, everything you know to be real is gone. The fairy tale is over."

"So I'm going to die?" he asked bluntly. Alexander felt a twinge of remorse. He was no longer interested in his own life, he just sought finality. In any case, Alexander found the question to be a moot point. He wished he could take back the question.

"Is that what you think?" Brendan stood up and walked towards a small pool of water. He sat down beside it and looked at his reflection. He poked at a few of his many wrinkles and began to mash his face and hid his wrinkles. Alexander sat beside him and was amazed at Brendan's reflection. He looked to be forty years younger.

"I don't know what I think. I have a mark of death. There's a tribe of people that are trying to kill me. I'm in this forest with wild dogs chasing me…Every time I turn a corner, I see death."

"Well then!" Brendan exclaimed. "You're a lucky man. Think of all of those people that never see their death coming. It's all a surprise to go to sleep and never wake up. We're all going to die at some point. And what is the worst death? Is it quick and over in a moment? Or is it the slow degrading of our life? Is it feeling pain every day and never feeling quite whole?"

"I'd rather feel that way than always looking over my shoulder," Alexander remarked.

"Hmm. You might wish you hadn't ever said that." Brendan cupped his hand and dipped it in the tiny pool of water. He lifted his hand to his mouth and slurped loudly.

"Why?" Alexander waited for a response from Brendan. Brendan mumbled something incoherent and then got on his knees, hands raised. His eyelids opened and revealed nothing but the whites of his eyes. Alexander gasped in surprise and stood up when he heard a noise from the entrance. The massive gryphon Ta'lon entered the hut.

"Alexander, son of Magnus," Brendan said rhythmically. "You have a loyal heart. You do not desire the crown and yet the crown will be your undoing. The hour has come so they might live. Be vigilant. The enemy is in your walls. In three days, peace as you know it will end." Brendan stood up and walked towards Alexander, hands outstretched. When he stood directly in front of him, Brendan whispered.

"Allow me to open...your...eyes."

Alexander felt the rush of a mighty wind and closed his eyes. It felt as if he would blow away. Visions quickly flashed through his mind. He saw a green field covered with the bodies of the dead; blades of grass covered with blood. In the distance Middlebrooke burned while swarms of barbarians ran through the main gate and slaughtered everyone in their way. He saw the tomb of his father consumed with flames. Towards the coast he saw ships that unloaded fierce men and siege towers that provided them entrance into Brookhaven. Death and desolation were everywhere.

All action in the vision slowed to a crawl. Alexander recognized a figure that stood on a hill that overlooked the destruction. Alexander recognized it as Abiyram with his staff raised in the air. On either side of him there stood a cloaked figure. Alexander made his way through the battlefield to where they stood. He crept closer to the taller hooded figure and tried to remove its hood. The battle that surrounded him began to move at a normal pace. Out of the corner of his eye he saw Abiyram's staff had been swung at his head. It was too late to duck and avoid the impact. He closed his eyes and waited for the impact.

Nothing happened so Alexander opened his eyes. At the exact moment where staff should have met body, Alexander found himself standing in the gryphon temple where he had stood before Ta'lon and his sons. There were fewer columns than before as Alexander only counted four that remained.

"Prince Alexander," Ta'lon's voice thundered and echoed in through the Hall.

"Ta'lon, my friend," Alexander bowed in respect. "Why do I only count four of you in this room?"

"We're all that are left," the gryphon said sadly.

Tears streamed from the statue's yellow eyes.

"I grieve for your loss, noble Ta'lon. Come back with me to Middlebrooke. We can protect you."

"Our time in this land has ended," Ta'lon responded emptily. "We are no longer allowed to be in this land. We must move on if we wish to carry on in this life."

"Why have you not left?" Alexander asked. Surely they didn't stay for the gold, he thought.

"My last son has not yet hatched. We have waited a hundred years, protecting our nest. But we have run out of time. Evil draws closer. They want the gold. They can have it. But they cannot have my son. You Prince Alexander, you must take the egg and move it somewhere it can be hatched."

"Why can't you take it?" he asked.

"It needs to hatch to be allowed where we go. Please. In return I shall bestow upon you a great gift. It is something that will serve you well in the conflict ahead. Brendan will give it you. Now go, time is short for all of us."

"But wait-"

The cold wind swept Alexander out of the temple. He shut his eyes and allowed the wind to carry him back to the stone hut. At long last he opened his eyes. Brendan had stood patiently and waited for his vision to end. When the prophet saw that Alexander regained consciousness, he stood up and offered Alexander a large sack.

"What is in the sack?'

"The last gryphon egg in this world. Let's hope it's a female for their sake. Am I right?" Brendan handed it over to Alexander.

"Ta'lon spoke of a gift."

This gift," Brendan continued, "Is next to the wall." He pointed toward a sword that lay on the floor of the hut.

"Legend has it that angels once used it to guard this land but that sword was left behind when they left. Don't know why because it's quite incredible." Brendan walked towards Ta'lon and the gryphon crouched and allowed Brendan to mount it.

Alexander picked up the sword and handled it. It carried the same weight as his sword and seemed to hold no special quality about it. He fastened the sword to his back and looked back at Brendan and the gryphon.

"Where are you going?"

"This place is no longer safe for me either. Ta'lon will take me to a safe place. Goodbye Alexander. I am sorry that I can give you no answers that you want to hear." Brennan looked sympathetically at Alexander. "You are the harbinger of the war that is coming. Pain and suffering is your destiny. You will carry a heavier burden in your lifetime than any mortal can bear. But if there is a happy ending to be found, I wish for you to find it, for your sake and the sake of your people."

Brendan clasped Alexander's arm in an attempt to show friendship, and gave Alexander one last instruction. "My lord, as soon as Ta'lon and I walk out of this hut, it will begin to crumble. The treasures hidden here cannot fall so easily into their hands. You will need to leave at once or risk this to be your tomb."

"But the tempest outside?" Alexander looked towards the storm that raged outside of the hut. Every blade of grass was flattened and a large pool of water began to collect outside of the door.

"Are you not a mighty warrior?" Brendan chided him. "Warriors live for a day like today!" Ta'lon screeched impressively and stretched out his wings. Ta'lon lightly jogged towards the entrance, with his wings in perfect rhythm. Alexander ran to the door in time to see Ta'lon,

Brendan, and the other three gryphons brave the elements and fly eastward. Alexander retreated back into the hut and retrieved the sack that held the gryphon's egg and his swords. Several chunks of rock fell down from the ceiling, and water began to pour in through the cracks. He swung the sack over his shoulder, gripped his sword and grinned at Keira.

"Well girl," he said laughing, "If we die here, then let us make it interesting."

Keira barked at him and wagged her tail. He ran outside into the pouring rain and instantly felt its stinging wrath on his face. He hugged the egg tightly to his chest to keep it dry. He looked around for the dogs and was relieved to see that they were nowhere to be seen. Behind them the building imploded and made a large crashing sound that distracted him to look back at it.

There's only one way to run now, he thought, and the egg will just slow me down.

He whistled for Zeus. Was his stallion still there, or did he race back to Greystone? He heard a whinny and made his way towards the sound. He whistled again, and again received the whinny.

"Zeus!" he shouted. "Katrina?"

"She's here!" a raspy voice replied.

Alexander moved closer to where he heard a whinny and he caught sight of Zeus standing alone in the rain. He squinted through the rainfall and saw Katrina being held captive. The captor fashioned a blade across Katrina's neck and held it there tightly.

"Let her go!" an enraged Alexander yelled. "She's just a girl. She has no stake in our quarrel."

"Give me the egg!" The stranger yelled. "I promise to let her go."

"Why would I believe you?" Alexander asked.

"Have I ever lied to you Alex?"

Alexander had kept his distance from the stranger. He recognized the voice to be a woman's, but it seemed to have a guttural tone like a man's. It was not the soft and dulcet tones he was accustomed to hearing. He felt safer that it was a woman but the water began to make it difficult to determine who addressed him. He moved within two arm's length of the hostile.

"Who are you?" Alexander questioned for a moment, was this a witch?

"I'm sad Alex," was the reply. "I'm sad that you've forgotten me. I feel your heart is with other women Alex. Did you truly love me?"

Alexander was horrified at the possibility of who it was. He stared silently in disbelief and wiped the water from his eyes.

"It can't be." He gasped. "Angelica, is that you?"

The hand the held Katrina swept back the hood that covered her captor's face. Angelica's face was revealed but Alexander was immediately repulsed and he stumbled backwards. Gone was the beautiful dark hair, it was now matted and patchy. Her face was extremely dirty and bits of her skin were missing. Her eyes held no emotion, and she looked like a corpse.

"Angelica, what have they done to you?"

"They've given me a new life Alexander. Free from pain and sorrow. Come with me. There's still time."

Alexander was horrified. He shook his head no while riveted by her gaze. Angelica's blade began to dig into Katrina's neck.

"WAIT!" he shouted. "Angelica, this isn't what you want. Killing a little girl. I have the egg. Kill me, if you can, and take the egg. Then all of your problems....you and your people...die with me. You'll have very little left to oppose you."

Angelica appeared to think about this offer. Alexander prayed silently. Oh God, if you are merciful and just, allow me one chance to save a life.

"Search your heart, Angelica. This isn't right," he said softly.

"Oh haven't you heard Alexander," she scoffed, "I don't have a heart." She pulled down the top of her dress and exposed a crater in the place where her heart had been. When she released her grasp Katrina quickly broke free of her grip and ran to Alexander. He grabbed Katrina before she could run past him.

"Listen to me Katrina," he whispered, "I need you to stay right here and hold onto this sack, and don't leave the dog's side. Don't run. Don't do anything until I tell you. Keira…guard." Alexander motioned his hand to the ground. Keira willingly sat down beside Katrina and kept her eyes fixated on Angelica.

Angelica drew her sword and pointed the tip at Alexander. Even without a heart, even without emotion, he could tell her eyes now blazed with hatred. She wore no armor, and carried no other weapons except the sword she now pointed at him. He had an advantage for he carried the sword that Brendan had given him in the hut and his own broadsword. He also wore his armor and that afforded him protection to block glancing blows even though he carried no shield. The rain shower began to slow, and the ferocity of the raindrops decreased.

Angelica approached Alexander and thrusted towards him. He blocked it easily, and they continued to circle each other.

"Alex, this is fate," she said soothingly.

"Why's that?"

"I always knew I was to be your angel. Come with

me, for we can still be together."

For a moment, the thought entered his mind. He wanted Angelica to be alive and to be with her but this was impossible now. She was undead and there was no way of undoing her curse. One of them had to die.

She raised her sword and swung wildly at his head. He dropped to one knee below the swords cut, and thrust his sword at her unprotected stomach. He watched the cold blade slice into her rotted flesh. Sadly, he looked up and expected to find whatever life she had to be gone. Her eyes met his and her lips curled into an evil grin. She gave no yelp of pain, and no cry of surprise. There was no blood that oozed from the wound.

"What were you expecting?" she asked. "I'm already dead, or haven't you been listening?"

She pulled herself closer to Alexander and with her sword in hand; she delivered a brutal punch to Alexander's head. The force of the punch caught Alexander by surprise, the power of it felt as if being struck with an anvil. He fell back face first into a puddle of water. The water splashed into his nostrils and he coughed loudly and noticed blood started to collect in the puddle. He turned over quickly and got to his feet. Angelica stabbed her sword into the ground and grabbed the hilt of Alexander's sword. She pulled it slowly from her stomach and examined it when she was through.

"I know this sword," she said quietly.

"It's yours," Alexander admitted. "I took it that day as a constant reminder."

"How sweet," she replied in her empty voice.

"Angelica," Alexander pleaded, "Let us go. This isn't who you are."

Angelica tossed her sword at Alexander's feet.

"Pick it up Alexander," she commanded. "Pick it up

and die like a man for you, Alexander Wolfield, are going to die today.

She lunged towards him. Her sword flashed and he managed to block a swing. The swords clashed several times as Angelica tried to inflict a mortal wound on Alexander. The rain increased its furor again and turned into small hail. The hailstones caused distraction for Alexander as it pelted his face and eyes. The hailstones elicited no response from Angelica. She kept lunging and slashing.

Alexander knew he couldn't last much longer in the weather or against an opponent that was already dead. He swung his sword overhead and down at Angelica. At the point where she blocked it, he pressed down with all of his might. He maneuvered himself into a position where he was able to twist the sword out of her hand. Together both swords flew out of their hands and into the grass. Alexander and Angelica both ran after the swords, but Alexander still had his other sword in its sheath. He drew it out before him and noticed that it had a reddish glow to it. Angelica picked up her sword and faced Alexander. The three large dogs reappeared and took positions behind her.

His attention shifted to the dogs and he directed his anger towards them. He blamed Angelica's condition on them; they had stolen her away and they had murdered her. They forced his hand into fighting her and it was all so unforgivable.

The anger grew within him to such a great extent that his fury caused him to tremble. He gripped the sword tightly and focused his gaze intently on the dog that walked towards him. Its teeth bared, and its ears lowered as if it meant to attack. He was angered to a point that he focused so much on the dog that his vision became locked in a tunnel of blackness.

"Come on!!!" Alexander yelled. "What are you waiting for? You cowards!" He looked above Angelica and the dogs and into trees.

"Come and fight me!!!" Alexander roared. His voice echoed through the forest.

"You send these dogs to me? You insult me. I will send them back to hell. FIGHT ME!" Alexander reiterated his challenge and swung his sword at the lead dog and narrowly missed as the dog retreated quickly. Angelica stood quietly with her sword drawn and watched the dogs circle Alexander.

"I defy you Abiyram! I defy you. I will find you and I will kill you. I will destroy you. I will make you a mockery. Your women will cry tears about how they go to bury you but cannot tell your bones from your men because the ravens have picked you clean. I am death come for you!!!"

Alexander felt the swords hilt as it burned in his hand. He ignored the pain and lifted the sword above his head and held it in both hands. With one quick motion he drove it into the earth with all of his might. A spark flashed from the sword and a wall of fire sprang forth and blocked the dog's approach to Alexander. The wall of fire raged and ignored the rain and burned intensely. The black dogs whimpered and retreated from the heat of the flames. The heat did not faze Alexander. He marveled in amazement at the fire. He stood there stupefied at the spectacle for what seemed a lifetime.

He understood this fire was his chance to escape. He stuck his hand in the flame and grabbed the handle. The sword left the dirt easily, but the flame continued to burn. The flame had caused the rain to lessen in severity, so Alexander quickly yelled for Katrina to join him and together they quickly mounted Zeus. With Keira close behind they began their flight from the forest. Alexander didn't look behind him, but fortunately the light from the fire lighted their path back through the forest. At the moment the light finally disappeared, Alexander departed the forest into the sunlight where he immediately spotted Farkas and Jack as they rode towards him.

"Prince Alexander!" Jack yelled angrily. "As your bodyguard we cannot protect you if you don't let us know where you are." Jack was very angry and glared at Alexander but suddenly remembered who he addressed and he bowed his head in shame, "I'm sorry milord that was not right of me. Please forgive me."

"You are right my friend," Alexander said. "I do apologize sincerely but there wasn't time. I found our survivor." Alexander pointed at Katrina.

"Katrina!" Jack shouted happily. "I'm so glad to see you survived!"

With their brief discussion finished, the three horsemen hurried to Greystone to join the Monsignor and the rest of Alexander's men.

The Monsignor loathed Alexander's departure and again scolded Alexander for being reckless and foolish with his life. He would have continued for days until Alexander introduced him to Katrina as the lone surviving inhabitant of Greystone. Jean-Paul immediately addressed the frightened girl as a general addresses a soldier.

"What happened here? Tell me, please. We need to know." Jean-Paul's voice and demeanor seemed to instill more fright within her, so Alexander intervened and took Katrina's hand.

"Katrina…you remember me, right?" Katrina shook her head yes. "Good. Don't be afraid. You're safe with us. We won't let anything happen to you. I've kept you safe so far right? Are you hungry? Would you like something to eat?"

Katrina shook her head yes. Simon handed some bread and a cup of water to her. They left her alone for a little while as she regained her strength. Alexander stood near her to ensure she didn't run away again.

"They were here all the time," she said softly as tears streamed down her face.

"Who was here? When?" Alexander asked. He slowly sat down next as not to alarm her.

"Those men." They talked and spoke like kingdom folk. Just like you and I. They stayed at the tavern. Said they were hunting wild game. They came and went for two years. The village trusted them. And then everything changed."

"What changed?"

"You came back....they were waiting for you. And you were here. You never got close enough so they punished us. They had strange men who could do magic with them. They killed the village leaders in the worst ways before our eyes. Then they tied everyone together and forced them into wagons. I hid amongst the ruins. My father bid me to stay hidden and I watched them take him away."

She burst into tears. Alexander's heart was moved and he felt horrible for this. He wondered if she blamed him for her villages' demise. He couldn't help but wonder that if he had stayed and fought these men, that this village and its people would have been saved.

"Well," Jean Paul asked. "Who did this?" His concern sounded genuine so Alexander shared with him what Katrina had told him.

"Kingdom folk?" Jean Paul spat on the ground. "Mercenaries? This is going to get uglier before it gets any better. Lot of innocent people will die...have already died…traitors. God have mercy on their soul when I find them."

Alexander had an idea who perpetrated this horror. "It's about time for the Church and the kingdom to acknowledge that there is a common enemy and he is more powerful than you could possibly imagine."

Jean-Paul sneered. "They bleed don't they?"

The thieves have had their revenge. When I find Duncan, he will die a swift death, Alexander swore silently. He placed a hand on Katrina's hand and knelt in front of her and brought them to eye level with one another.

"Katrina, I swear the men who did this will not live to see another year. I swear your family will be avenged." Katrina stayed silent head buried into her hands.

"Prince Alexander!" Chauncey called out. "The Crown Prince and his army have come to meet us."

The impressive army marched in perfect formation. Edwards own heavily armed knights flanked him while they were followed by a hundred horsemen, and then several hundred heavily armed foot soldiers. Behind the foot soldiers were several supply wagons pulled by large horses. Behind them marched the rear guard of Edward's army and further behind were mercenaries from other kingdoms that the royals had kept in their employ. Once the entire army had reached the walls of Greystone, Edward bade his men to rest from their march and he galloped inside the burned village to find his brother.

"What's happened here?" Edward asked as he surveyed the burned out buildings. He sighed as his eyes fell upon the remainder of the bodies that were being buried.

"Entire village was carried off," Alexander reported. "We found one survivor and a few dead bodies, but mostly all inhabitants were carried off. The survivor says they were in the village, waiting, when they least expected it."

Edward waived his hand towards two pages that drove the royal wagon. They jumped off the wagon and disappeared behind it. One grabbed a table, the other a map, and they ran and set the map for Prince Edward. He dismounted and conferred over it with Alexander and Jean-Paul.

"Can you show me how I can get to the barbarians stronghold?" Edward asked.

"I don't know where their stronghold is, all I know is where we were. Your army will have to pass through the forest," Alexander answered. "If you move west, you will come to the thieves caves dug into the mountain that you can see from here. If you follow the river, you will come to a pass between two mountains. It's best to send scouts over the mountain to ensure no ambushes."

"Hmm." Edward sighed and nodded. "You say that this village already had these monsters waiting inside? Then we've got to do something bold. You've done well Alexander, and I will take it from here. You will take your men and some of my foot soldiers and travel to Edgebrooke to reinforce and prepare the garrison there. Should I be defeated, they will move directly against the city and with no one to defend it. That would be a slaughter."

"You want me to leave the battlefield and reinforce Edgebrooke? I know these barbarians! You need me." Alexander yearned for a face to face encounter in battle. "Let Jean-Paul reinforce that garrison."

"My soldiers are better in hand to hand combat in close quarters. Where else better than in this forest?" Jean-Paul snarled at the suggestion.

"Now's not the time to argue! You will do as I say or ride back in disgrace. Is that understood?" The raised voice of the Crown Prince quieted all men within the village's walls. Alexander felt the piercing eyes of the men as they waited to see how he responded. He quietly nodded his head in agreement with Edward.

"I'm sorry Your Majesty, my sword is at your command." Alexander stung at the tongue lashing he received from Edward. His lip quivered a bit but he quickly managed to control it.

"I know it is, brother," Edward said softly. "Jean Paul, I want you to hand pick your best men to accompany Alexander to Edgebrooke."

"Very well your majesty." Jean-Paul cast a disparaging look at Alexander and walked back to his warriors and picked the men to return with Alexander. Edward turned his attention to Alexander and placed a hand on his shoulder.

"Alexander, don't ever argue with me, you can disagree with me, but don't ever stand there and pout like a woman…especially in front of the men I command. This is war, not some impetuous teenage errand. You will take my orders. You have no experience in battle. You would have your men killed with your recklessness. And don't think that I have not heard of your willingness to go on your own. You have responsibilities, the fate of your men rest upon you being able to lead them cohesively and communicate clearly. You are no longer a lone child playing army with a wooden sword. Am I made clear to you?"

"Yes, you have my apologies milord." Alexander looked down to the ground. His brother's words stung him more than his father's. He looked back up to Edward's eyes and nodded his head to show that he was fine.

"Thank you….I am sending you to Edgebrooke because we need a member of the royal family there, and since Mattias has fallen increasingly behind, you are the only one fit for this task. The Baron is a schemer. I wouldn't put it past him to negotiate with those barbarians for that town. Jean Paul has no ability to persuade the Baron but you might and you are a better commander than anyone in that town. Regardless of what happens, the city cannot fall. Bishop Malachius will join you there and ensure your words are heard."

"Yes sir," Alexander said soberly. "I won't let you down. Will Isadora also be there?"

"She will indeed," Edward smiled. "But I fear for you in that regard?"

"Why?"

"Because," he grinned. "She will eat you alive." He clapped Alexander's back in great humor and laughed.

"Hardly!" Alexander scoffed.

"That woman has teeth. And with her upbringing, she bears all the characteristics of a serpent. Be careful that you don't fall under that family's influence like father has."

"Edward," Alexander teased, "Don't you know I have grown some sharp teeth as well?"

"Alexander," Edward chuckled, "You are quite a catch for any woman wanting to improve her social standing."

"And you're not?" Alexander retorted. "We could build a statue to your great looks and chiseled features and there would still be a line of women desperate to marry it."

"As opposed to any woman wanting you is just desperate," Edward chided.

They shared a momentary fraternal laugh over their banter, and Alexander reminisced to their childhood and easier times. Edward bade Alexander to break camp and ride for Edgebrooke so he gathered his own men with two detachments of swordsmen from Edward and Jean-Paul, and moved quickly to reinforce Edgebrooke. He also decided to take Katrina with him, as she would fare better in a city than in the countryside.

CHAPTER XX

Alexander and his men marched quickly to Edgebrooke. In all, his men consisted of thirteen horsemen, eighty swordsmen, and forty axe men. The heavily armored swordsmen slowed their procession down, and they wouldn't reach Edgebrooke until evening. Alexander hoped a large garrison within the city would already be in place to defend the walls and he felt confident that the extra reinforcement would easily protect Edgebrooke.

Katrina rode with them and kept quiet. Alexander could tell that she was still uncomfortable with the men, so he gave her a small task. He gave her the satchel that held the gryphon egg, and bade her not to look inside the satchel, and not to lose it. Since it was such a valuable commodity, he continued to keep an eye on her and the satchel as the day progressed.

None of his men had eaten that day, and Brennan started to agonize over the lack of food. Alexander rebuffed his pleadings to forage for a rabbit or even a duck. He also lamented the loss of the opportunity to have eaten the chickens in Greystone. Alexander sympathized through his

CHRISTOPHER HUNTINGFORD ≈

own hunger pangs, but made it clear that time was not on their side. If they stopped they endangered the kingdom. Privately, he doubted the barbarians understood assaulting a walled city in a grand scale. They were an army that specialized in terror. A pitched battle would spell their doom.

This realization was only strengthened as Edgebrooke sat upon their horizon. Conquered thirty years ago, King Magnus had bestowed the title of Baron to Brutus, one of his generals that participated in the siege. It was Brutus that broke the wooden palisade that surrounded the village, and captured the enemy priest. King Magnus VIII was so impressed with his skill that he was awarded the title of Baron after the battle. The Baron also shared the thirst for blood that his liege showed and happily carried out the King's execution order. The Baron continued to follow the King into the Shadowlands and to Alexander's surprise, came back.

The Baron was not a talentless monster and instead showed much skill as a builder. He razed the wooden palisade, constructed the stone wall, and oversaw the growth and development of Edgebrook into the raw materials epicenter of the kingdom. He recruited expert miners from all countries to mine the wealth that lay beneath the soil. Rumor held that he extorted a fee from these miners from their production before it was shipped down the river to Middlebrooke. No one doubted that the Baron had a soft spot for gold. But for whatever reason, any complaint or charge against the Baron was found to lack evidence.

The King loved him like a brother, and would not hear complaints against him so the Baron was allowed his continued pursuit of considerable wealth. His lust for money was only equaled by an insatiable lust for those around him. His power caused great trouble for many merchants and nobles in his court. The price of doing business in Edgebrooke was steep, you might have to shake hands with the devil and then find he owned your soul.

He was married to a beautiful woman who, as the story went, had mysterious origins. With his newfound control and influence, the Baron found himself incapable of loving this one woman. As the story ended, she climbed to the top of the keep, and walked off it, to be free of the shame she lived with.

His daughter, Isadora, mystified Alexander. She was a beautiful daughter, so well cultured and mannered. How did she turn out right, wondered Alexander, when all about her, corruption and debauchery were at every turn?

As they finally arrived at Edgebrooke's gates, Alexander was aghast at what he saw. The gate guards barely stood for his passing. They held food in their mouths and chewed listlessly as the men marched by. None of the men dared speak a challenge and only a few spit out their food and wiped their mouth when they recognized Alexander.

Alexander hoped that the rest of the city's inspection fared better upon his arrival. His pessimism won out and he chose to send a gate guard ahead to the Baron's table to ensure his arrival was noticed. The guard raced off on horseback to the middle of the city, where the Baron held court.

Alexander and his escort marched to the center of the town. As they passed through houses and markets, the citizens eyed them with suspicion. Alexander suspected they tried to decide whether they needed to hide their gold or not. Edgebrooke was the home to feckless merchants and traders, thieves and every other speck of dirt in the kingdom.

As they approached the court, Alexander became more and more irritated with the lack of soldiers that came to give him respect, and at the top of the stone stairs stood the Baron with very loose fitted robes and surrounded by very young boys. His robes appeared to be clothes that one wore for bed, and not the typical robes of the day. But the Baron had become so fat that perhaps there was not a tailor who could make clothes for him. Alexander scoffed at this rotund figure and the lackeys that surrounded him.

Caution is needed, he thought. Any word I say that offends will be reported back to my father. I need the Baron's support to ensure this town is defended.

"Prince Alexander! It's wonderful to see you? I must ask you, why do you come here so heavily armed?" The Baron eyed the foot soldiers suspiciously.

"I assure you, Baron, my business comes straight from the Crown Prince. If I may divulge a moment of your time?"

"Of course Prince Alexander, Edgebrooke welcomes you with open arms." His reply was less than sincere but he played pleasantries better than anyone.

Alexander dismounted, gave his reins to Jean, and made his way up the steps to confer with the Baron. The lackeys that surrounded the Baron took up their own positions on the steps.

"I'm afraid, Baron," he started, "That we worry that Edgebrooke will be soon attacked by the very same people you evicted from this village."

"Impossible," the Baron scoffed. "They could never breach these walls. I built them myself to keep them out. No barbarian shall step foot here. I do though thank the Crown for their show of concern. Please tell you Father that his General is on guard at all times." He extended his hands to Alexander, which Alexander ignored.

"I regret to inform you, that my orders come directly from the Crown Prince, his Majesty Prince Edward. My orders stand. I am to take over the garrison until my brother returns with the army and he feels the border is secure."

"Take over my garrison? I have commanded this garrison for thirty years. And I am told to hand over defense of my city to an untested Prince? The King shall hear of this!"

"I appreciate your concerns, Baron, if you prefer to address your concerns with the King I suggest you send someone on horseback now? We're bound to see a few barbarians at your gates, so send them sooner rather than later." Alexander tired quickly of pleasantries with the Baron. The Baron baited him into an argument and Alexander's frustration would doubtless play into the Baron's plan to embarrass him.

"I shall go myself," the Baron hissed.

This fat swine dares insult me, thought Alexander. Enough of this insult!

"Baron, before I-!" he stopped midsentence. He caught a glimpse of Isadora as she walked out of the court. The Baron followed his gaze to Isadora and grinned slightly.

"Isadora, my dear, have you met Prince Alexander?"

"Yes father, at the court of Prince Youssef. How are you my lord?" She curtsied before him. He bowed back and felt his face warm. She had changed her appearance and seemed to share Alexander's appraisal of the situation. Her long black hair was braided and she wore well fitted armor.

"I am well. I am sorry we missed the pleasure of your company in Greystone."

"You are too kind, but I had pressing matters to deal with here."

"Isadora," the Baron wheedled, "Crown Prince

Edward has suggested that I hand over command of the garrison to Prince Alexander. What are your thoughts? Should your father lead the troops to glory once more?"

"Father, I think you should listen to the crown." She kissed her father on the cheek. "Prince Alexander is a very capable commander. I have heard very encouraging things about him. Now if you'll excuse me? Perhaps Prince Alexander, I can have food and strong drink brought to your men?"

"I would be honored, milady. Only, please nothing stronger than water. We need our heads clear."

Isadora nodded and bowed as Alexander felt his cheeks burn again. The compliment she had paid him gave him goose bumps, and he tried desperately to contain his feelings. The Baron's face was clouded with anger. It seemed that Isadora had the means of influencing her father's decisions. Alexander wanted to kiss her for it.

"Well, Prince Alexander, it seems as though my men are at your command." His voice was flat but he managed a flicker of a smile.

"Very good Baron. I am happy to hear that. How many men do you have right now as part of your town's militia?"

"Well, I would venture to guess a standing garrison of one hundred and fifty men."

"I'm sorry," Alexander said, shocked. "Did you say that in a town of three thousand people you have one hundred and fifty that carry a weapon? One hundred and fifty?" Alexander repeated the words and was still baffled!

"That's our standing garrison. We have more that participate in monthly drills."

"One hundred and fifty!" Alex exclaimed again. "I have one hundred and thirty men! How am I supposed to defend a city with less than three hundred men?"

"Your Highness, let me assure you that the walls are sufficient. Fifty of those men are archers and they would be able to rain death upon the heathens. Should they reach the wall, we have enough traps to severely reduce any force. And the door is impregnable. There is no way any barbarian can breach this gate."

"What if they are already here?" Alexander asked. "What if they burn down your home with you in it while you sleep? In that chaos, who would defend the wall? This will not do. I need every person that has practiced with a weapon gathered in two days' time."

The Baron protested but was humbled by the conversation. It reflected poorly upon the Baron that he had neglected the garrison, an unforgivable offense before the King. Brutus had no response for Alexander but promised more men as soon as they could be found.

As Alexander took leave of the Baron and mounted Zeus, he sought out Girard to discuss his frustrations and unhappiness.

"Girard. It would have been nice to have received advice on what I would encounter."

"I'm sorry Prince Alexander. I guess I have forgotten what it's like to be one of them since I've been in your employ. This whole city fills me disgust."

"Nevertheless, our orders are to stand guard. Take Fergus and collect the militia. We're losing daylight, so make it fast. Meet us by the main gate."

Girard nodded and galloped towards the barracks with Fergus. Alexander made his way to the wall and began measuring the fortifications. On each side of the gate, there was a tower. At the bottom of the tower, next to the gate, were wooden doors. These doors opened to stairwells that led to the towers above the gate. The wood of the door seemed thick enough to hold against a light assault, it would take a battering ram or a catapult to destroy it. Alexander guessed that if they launched an assault it would come with ladders and try to swarm the walls.

As Alexander contemplated the defense of the city, servants brought the men food and water to replenish themselves. The knights tore into their food furiously and even Prince Alexander neglected to stand on proper ceremony. He made sure he ate his fill, and that Katrina ate some food as well.

A visitor passed through the gate, and Alexander was happy that a familiar figure approached them. "Bishop Malachius! Very happy to see that you made it safely."

"You as well milord. I've heard whispers of your encounter with the Baron."

Alexander laughed at the Bishops understatement. Politics of the court frustrated him and he realized that this was a game he needed to play but preferred not to nevertheless.

"What's that cloth you carry?" Alexander noticed the Bishop had a beautiful banner that he held under his arms.

"Another gift for the Prince," the Bishop said. "With the gryphon armor that you fashion I thought perhaps a standard for battle was in order."

Bishop Malachius unfurled the standard. It was very much like the other hidden objects in the secret room under the abbey. It was beautiful and ornate and a sense of inspiration and power resonated from it.

Alexander handed the standard to Fergus and sent him to the top of the battlement to ensure it was hoisted over the city. The gryphons guarded this city now. Alexander felt a sense of pride swell in his chest and noticed the same impact on his other men as the standard fluttered in the wind.

"Bishop, would you care to examine the defense of the wall?" Alexander needed to speak to him privately, away from prying ears. Together they walked up the stairs to the wall and overlooked the open field in front of the walls.

"I have been in the stone hut." Alexander whispered almost inaudibly but with a measure of excitement.

"Really?" Malachius's eyes widened. "Tell me, what did you find?"

"A lot. I saw the prophet. He gave me a vision."

"What did you see?"

"Death and desolation everywhere. Our whole kingdom burned. But that's not the important part. I have the last gryphon egg."

"You have a gryphon egg? Where?" Malachius's eyes widened.

"With Katrina. It's in her satchel."

"We need to hide that egg. The monastery?"

"I agree, Bishop. Jean-Paul is still with my brother, so can we hide it in the chapel here? If we were to allow you to leave with it, I fear the dangers on our frontier would seek to do it harm."

"That's a fair idea; no one in this town visits the chapel." Malachius shook his head in dismay.

"And I saw them raise the dead." Alexander felt the best approach was a blunt one.

Bishop Malachius was shocked. "That's heresy Alexander. Heresy!"

"So how would you explain it then? I fought one of them. My sword sliced her through her stomach," Alexander pointed to where his sword had sliced Angelica. "There was no blood. No cry of pain. You can call it heresy but nothing will dissuade me from what I've seen in the forest."

Bishop Malachius started to say something, but even he realized the gravity of the situation. Alexander was not one for stories.

"Alexander, what about the gryphons?"

"They left and took the prophet with them. I don't believe they will be coming back." Alexander shook his head sadly. "I think that's the last we will ever see of them."

"This is tremendous Alexander. You have seen things that we thought were just myths. I need to get back to my abbey as soon as possible. There's got to be more information in those books. When can I leave?"

"Once Edward returns for I have to secure Edgebrooke." Alexander looked out across the open fields before the gate. In the near distance, another smaller forest separated the towns influence from the open frontier. It was big enough to hide a small army, but there was absolute silence all around him.

"Bishop?"

"Yes my son?"

"In this vision, I saw Abiyram with two cloaked figures beside him. I tried to lift the hoods, but couldn't. What do you think that means?"

"I think that we can be sure that there are two chess pieces that we do not yet know about. Be careful the company you keep. I've warned you of that before. Why don't I take Katrina and the egg to the chapel now? It might do her some good to sleep in a bed."

"Agreed," Alexander nodded. "Rest would do her well and I don't want anyone else with the egg." He looked towards the inside of the city and saw a very pompously armored group of men strutting towards the gate. "Looks like the town militia is finally here. Can peacocks fight?" he wondered aloud. He was also distracted by a group of six riders that rode furiously towards the city.

"Sir!" Fergus yelled. "It's her highness Princess Sofia!"

Alexander was indeed surprised by the news. *"What was she thinking?"* he thought angrily. He took his leave of Bishop Malachius and ran down to the gate. He reached them in time to find Sofia and the rest of his men dismounting from their horses.

"Sofia?" he demanded. "What are you doing here? Why is she here and why did you not follow my orders?" He glared at his men who immediately knelt on one knee.

"Don't be mad at them Alexander," Sofia tried to say soothingly, "They followed your orders and are protecting me."

"But why are you here? Does mother know about this?"

"No, mother does not know about this." Sofia sighed and lifted her bow and quiver from her saddle. "If you must know, I am here to fight."

"I'd say that was obvious dear sister, but what I want to know is why. Calimus should be here and so should Mattias, not my sister." She ignored his objections and started walking towards the stairs that led to the top of the wall.

"Calimus is indisposed and Mattias is purposely moving slowly. Edward leads the army, so Mattias feels slighted. Be happy I am here." Sofia picked a spot for her quiver and set it down.

"I cannot protect you in battle Sofia. I will be too busy leading the defense of the city. You need to go home now." He picked up the quiver and handed it back to Sofia. Sofia took an arrow from the quiver and set into her bow.

"Do you see that chicken, Alexander?"

Alexander looked in the direction she pointed. Sixty

paces away a lone chicken clucked and pecked at the ground.

"I see the chicken," Alexander said irritated. "What does a chicken have to-"

Sofia interrupted him by releasing her bow string. The arrow cut through the air at a rapid speed and flew towards the chicken. There was a loud squawk and a few feathers flew into the air. Alexander stared the dead chicken in shock. Brennan quickly ran out from behind a building, grabbed the chicken, and disappeared back behind the building.

"As you were saying, my brother, you need an excellent archer. You need someone to command the city's archers and to ensure that the walls are protected. It would be even better if that defense was led by someone who has saved your life with an arrow! Is that not what you were thinking?" Sofia placed the bow next to the walls and folded her arms. Alexander quietly placed the quiver next to the bow and looked back to where the chicken had died.

"Alright," he said quietly, "This will be your part to command. If you are overpowered, you are to retreat back into the city. You will not engage anyone with a sword. Are we understood?"

"Perfectly," she said smugly.

"You could not persuade Calimus to leave the walls of Middlebrooke?" Calimus again disappointed Alexander.

"No Alexander, he is not coming. Mattias will be along presently. His regiments have finally gathered and they are ready to march."

Alexander was encouraged that Mattias ceased his delay and now made a concerted effort to bring his regiments. If Mattias was able to reach Edgebrooke they might be able to strike a decisive counterattack and eliminate the enemy army….should they assault the city.

"All right Sofia, I need to go address the militia, perhaps you should find that chicken and have some of it. You've earned it." He hugged her in uncharacteristic fashion and felt her arms as they slowly closed around him. He was glad he was no longer alone for he could draw strength from her. He released his sister from his embrace and looked at her widened eyes. Her blue eyes twinkled with mischief and she opened her mouth to speak.

"I forbid you to ever speak of it," Alexander said. "I am happy that you are here and if you ever tell anyone what I said, I will deny it."

Alexander flashed a grin at Sofia and continued downstairs to greet his men. He released Katrina into Malachius's care, and allowed Fergus and Girard an opportunity to eat and turned his attention to the town militia that the Baron had released into his command. They were a motley group of individuals but decently armed as this was their main source of income. The soldier's breastplates were painted black and had a gleaming yellow etching of a boar on their breastplate and their shield. Their helmets reflected the traditions of the kingdom and protected their head but the Baron had seen to it that large feathers stood out from their helmets and created a beautiful plumage. While Alexander found their armor quite impressive in pageantry he noticed their swords hung sloppily from their sword belts and their grip on their spears was at best casual.

They were an uninspired lot, and looked as if roused out of bed at this late hour. The moon was not quite above them, so Alexander decided to draw up his limited defense strategy. He had less than three hundred men at his disposal, but perhaps more the next day if the Baron was useful.

He called the leaders of each group of men to him as

he outlined his plan in the dirt with a staff he found. A light guard would be posted at the gate which would be barred and shut and no one would be allowed in or out without authorization from himself. The fifty archers would divide into three groups, and each group would sleep the night on the north wall's towers. Alexander figured any attack would come from the forests, as the barbarians could get closer under the cover of the trees. With archers in place, they could pepper the barbarians and inflict many casualties.

To repel any ladder assault, Alexander ordered the town militia to hold the wall on either side of the gate house. The cleric's soldiers would take positions as the second line behind them. One group of clerical swordsman was left to guard the gate. Their heavy armor and skill in hand to hand combat would prove useful. Alexander positioned Fergus and Sofia on the tower to command their respective soldiers while Girard was placed with the archers and over the guard gate. Should the enemy rush the gate, Girard had rocks and oil that he could pour down on the enemy.

The rest of Alexander's guard kept the horses nearby. Should the need arise they could mount their horses and quickly ride to any part of the city that they felt was in danger.

Alexander felt comfortable with the night's plan, so he allowed his men to sleep at their stations, and kept a light guard to alert them to any barbarian activity. Alexander observed the watchmen pace back and forth on top of the towers. He and his men commandeered a nearby house and laid out their weapons.

Alexander noticed that Jean looked uneasy, and he constantly rearranged his weapons while the others settled in to sleep.

"Jean."

"Yes Prince Alexander?" He trembled as he spoke.

"You seem a little tense. How are you?"

"I'm okay sir. Just a little nervous I guess."

"I understand what you're feeling, Jean." Alexander rolled his head to the side and made eye contact with Jean. "I feel nervous too."

"Really? You?"

"You are sixteen, isn't that right? Well I am twenty and this is my first war and in that war I have three hundred men to defend a city of three thousand against an enemy that multiplied from who knows where. My brother expects me to conjure a miracle." He quieted his voice and sighed. Thoughts of misgiving and dread rushed into his already cluttered mind.

"If they come, we're going to die aren't we? This is it for us." Jean tucked his knees into his chest and buried his head in his arms.

Not now Jean, thought Alexander. This is no time to go to pieces.

"Jean," Alexander said firmly, "This is not it for us. We are mightier than their entire army. They will come with their great numbers and they will hurl their bodies at the walls. We will stand as men. Their army is nothing to fear, what I fear is elsewhere….it's an evil. An evil that will come against this kingdom like a flood and for that evil, we are mere driftwood."

"Why do you stay in its path then? Why did you choose to lead us? You could have left that night in the tavern but you stayed. I couldn't believe that." Jean relaxed his legs and looked back up at Alexander.

"Because Jean, sometimes there has to be that person that makes that stand for what's right. Besides, nothing frustrates a wave more than a piece of driftwood. No matter what the wave does to it, it just floats. Eventually the waves will cease and the driftwood will float on." Alexander chuckled to himself. Truly he was a thorn in everyone's side these days.

"You miss your family don't you, Jean?"

"Yes sir, I miss them terribly. After going to Greystone...I don't know if I'll ever sleep. I miss them a great deal."

"I know you do. I mourn them with you. But do their memory honor. Fight harder against your enemies. Please get some sleep. We have no idea what's in store for us, but I'll tell you this Jean, if it is the end then it will be a glorious end and we will die and our names will be written in song for all of our people. Stand with courage." Alexander reached out his hand to the young lad. He had come far from the quivering child that he rescued two years ago.

"Yes sir. To the end." Jean reached out and grabbed Alexander's hand and grasped it firmly.

"Good lad. Now....get some sleep. That's my order to you."

Jean smiled and laid back onto some hay that he had gathered for a pillow. Alexander stood up and found a piece of parchment and a pen. Jean's worries were his own and more than likely every man under his command was consumed by fear. He would not allow himself to fear. He sat at a table near a torch and sat under its light. He wrote a letter to his mother and regarded how much she worried about him now. He would send a letter that expressed his boldness and his courage, for regardless of what was to come, his parents last memories of him would bring him respect and honor.

Soon after he finished the letter, he folded it and tied it to his belt. He was extremely tired from his journey and his body yearned for rest. He placed his head on the small table and quickly fell asleep. Soon dawn crept into the little house where Alexander and his men slept when he was finally awakened by one of the town's soldiers.

"Sir?" Devon asked.

"What is it?" Alexander stirred slightly and tried to wake himself up.

"Bishop Malachius wishes all men to be present outside."

Alexander sat up and rubbed the sleep out of his eyes. There was very little sunlight and Alexander was unhappy that he had not been allowed to sleep longer. He and his men stumbled listlessly out of the small house and found every soldier knelt on one knee and faced Bishop Malachius.

"Prince Alexander!" Malachius called out. "Will you join us and kneel in reverence to the Almighty?"

Alexander knelt to one knee and bowed his head and his men followed suit. Together they listened to Bishop Malachius as he exhorted them to bravery and that they fought not just for the kingdom, that this was now a fight against evil. The clerical warriors faces showed no emotion as Alexander assumed their zeal to do their duty needed no extra encouragements. Sofia was not in the midst of the small gathering and Alexander glanced around but did not see her amongst the men, but her voice overpowered the Bishops soliloquy.

"Alex!" She shouted from her battlement. "You need to see this. Hurry!" Her tone was urgent but not panicked and Alexander responded quickly and rose and ran to the stairs. The other men stayed still and even Bishop Malachius ceased talking. He followed the stairs to the top of the tower and to the battlement that looked over the battlefield. There stood Sofia as she looked across the plain. Her focus was completely on the activities away from the forest.

Alexander immediately saw what caused the urgency in Sofia's voice. He looked towards the forest and groaned as he watched barbarian axe men pour out of the forest. Some of them carried siege ladders for attacking the wall while others pulled on two giant siege towers, and worst of all, a shielded battering ram was wheeled forward for a direct assault on the gate. Alexander easily estimated the barbarian strength to be at eight hundred axe men. If correctly deployed, and they assaulted different points, Edgebrooke's garrison would be overwhelmed quickly.

Sofia looked directly at Alexander, her eyes widened in surprise.

"I didn't expect so many of them," she said quietly. Alexander saw the misgivings in her eyes.

"Sofia, I needed you and you are here. You will have fifteen archers with you. Make them pay with their lives for their treachery. I'll see what I can do to find you some pitch. If you use it on your arrows then concentrate the flames on the ram and the siege towers." Sofia nodded absently. "Sofia!" He said again. "We were made for this. Believe it!" He waited until she nodded in agreement and ran back down the stairs.

All of the men stood up as soon as he reached the ground and walked towards them.

"Bishop Malachius! I am afraid that our war will not wait. The time has come." The townsmen panicked and whispered amongst each other. Alexander knew they wanted to flee and he jumped on the back of a cart that stood undisturbed nearby.

"Listen to me men for I will tell you the truth about today. There sits our enemy and they would try to overwhelm us this day. They are relentless and they will not stop for they have little regard for their own lives. They wish to murder us and enslave your children. Those that would surrender will suffer a fate worse than death. If they want a war then here is where it begins. We must stand on this day. We must be relentless. We will not retreat, we will not surrender. I will fight to my last breath, I defy their army. They outnumber us, but we are better trained and better equipped. As long as we work together and stand side by side, we will defeat this foe. Will you fight to the death? Will you fight for the king?!"

All of the men except for the clerics lifted their swords into the air and shouted, "For the King!"

"I asked if you will fight and die for the King?!" Alexander roared this challenge at the men.

Every man, including the clerics, lifted their weapon into the air and roared back in unison.

"For the king!!"

"Archers to your battlements," Alexander commanded. "Stand fast in your positions. Every man to their stations." The throng broke quickly and each soldier ran to their station as if their life depended upon it Alexander's men stood by him and waited to receive their orders.

"I grieve deeply," he said, "For a lot of those men are going to die today. Fergus and Chauncey....you must keep watch over the siege towers and ladders. Move your men and ensure the barbarians have no safe place in which to deploy. Girard...you are responsible for the gate. Concentrate all of your arrows on the towers. See if you can find some pitch for flaming arrows. If we can burn it down, we can hold them off the walls. Jack, go and rouse the Baron. Let him know the city is under attack and that every man with a weapon needs to make their way to the gate. The rest of you mount your horses and prepare to ride down any of them that might get past the wall. Am I understood? Good. Do your part, and we live to see tomorrow. Go."

His men moved to their positions and Jack mounted his horse when a cry came down from the battlement.

"Alex!" Sofia's voice was filled with urgency. "They want to speak with you."

Good, thought Alexander. This will give me an opportunity to view what we are up against.

"Jack! Ride out with me." Alexander commanded.

"Alex hurry!" Sofia yelled. "The Baron has ridden out to talk to them."

Alexander felt immediate alarm. The treacherous bastard is trying to save his neck, he thought. He must have gone unnoticed from the southern gate and ridden around the city.

Alexander jumped on Zeus and quickly rode out of the city and Jack followed close behind. They got to the meeting between the Baron and the barbarian leader just in time. The large barbarian eyed them suspiciously but stayed very still. He rested his head on top of his long sword's hilt. He wore light armor, but it was heavier than the rest of his warriors. Alexander recognized him immediately.

"I know you," Alexander said. "I thought I killed you."

"No little Prince, you are not man enough to kill me. I was pushed down a flight of stairs. That's not a noble death for a chieftain." The barbarian flashed a toothless grin at him. "The Baron and I were discussing the terms of your surrender."

"I am sorry to have wasted your time…the Baron…," Alexander nodded in his direction, "and Edgebrooke is under army control at this time and I am in command of the army. Any negotiating will go through me."

"Very well," the chieftain snarled. "Leave Edgebrooke now or be slaughtered."

Alexander laughed sarcastically at the large warrior. "And who will be doing the slaughtering? This pack of dogs I see before me? I will put a sword through any man who dares enter the King's city. Here are my terms. Return to your borders and I grant you your life."

The chieftain stopped relaxing on the sword's hilt and lifted the large sword with two hands.

"Perhaps the Prince would partake in an ancient duel with me." The words baited Alexander and he understood the treachery behind them.

"Some other time when only our lives are at stake. If you'll forgive me we'll take our leave now. Baron, if you please?"

"Before you leave, perhaps one final gift?" The barbarian raised his hand quickly and dropped it. Flaming arrows flew over Alexander's head and headed towards Edgebrooke. Alexander wheeled Zeus and faced Edgebrooke. Several arrows stuck the gate and flames quickly spread across the gate. Alexander turned back to the chieftain in shock.

"Unfortunately, young prince, not everyone is so loyal to the king. Now, it will be much easier to walk through your gate. We can save our strength for your slaughter," the chieftain smiled. "I will see you very soon." He turned and walked back to the rest of his army who taunted Alexander. Alexander bade Jack and the Baron follow him and together they quickly rode towards the gate.

"Chauncey!" he yelled to the top of the wall.

"Yes sir?"

"Put as much water as you can inside of the gate."

Alexander hoped that some of the gate would remain. "Do you have a rope?"

"Yes!"

"Throw it down, and I'll climb up!" He turned to Jack. "Jack, ensure the Baron returns by the southern gate. And Baron, if I see any more treachery I will not hesitate to kill you on the spot. Do we understand each other?"

"We do," the Baron stated flatly.

"You will reinforce my men at this gate with every man that can carry a weapon within the hour." Alexander handed Zeus' reigns to Jack and watched them ride away.

He pulled Brendan's fire sword from the sheathe on his back. Perhaps, he thought, the fire wall could save them again. He closed his eyes and blocked out the screams of the approaching enemy. He focused on his anger at them. They sought to destroy his people and he would not let that happen.

With a decisive action he brought the sword up with both hands and with a shout he jammed the sword into the soft earth….and nothing happened. Alexander stared at the sword. Did he do it wrong he wondered.

"Your highness?!" Chauncey yelled urgently. Alexander looked up at Chauncey's confused face. He pulled the sword out of the ground, placed it back in its sheathe and grabbed onto the rope. Chauncey and the militia pulled him quickly up the wall. Alexander hung on tightly and looked across to the barbarian army. Their commander waved his battle axe and signaled his men to advance quickly. With a great cry the horde grabbed their siege ladders and hurried to the walls while other warriors pushed the battering forward. A few of their warriors stayed behind and fired a weak volley of arrows in Alexander's direction. He easily avoided them and shouted at Fergus and Simon who stood by.

"Chauncey! Pull faster! Fergus! Fire!"

"You heard the Prince!" Fergus shouted urgently. "Arrows! Loose!"

A deadly stream of arrows flew from the towns walls in the barbarian's direction. Although Alexander had mocked their appearances, the archers were deadly, and man after man fell, never to rise again. They continued their torrent until Alexander arrived safely on top of the wall. Alexander looked out, the barbarians had just reached the wall and ladders started to go up. His archers continued to fire freely into the throng and the swordsman that protected the archers readied themselves for the barbarian assault. Alexander caught sight of the battering ram, and decided it was not quite a threat to them. The fire that had burned had subsided and had not destroyed the gate but severely weakened it. Alexander worried that the barbarians would quickly overwhelm them once they broke through the gate.

"Prince Alexander!" Chauncey yelled from his position on the wall. "Take a look!" He pointed to a lone figure creeping across the wall. Alexander could make out the figure to be that of a young girl carrying a bow and a quiver of arrows. She looked familiar.

"Katrina?" Alexander hollered. The figure stopped. "What are you doing here? This is no place for you."

"I've come to fight. I won't hide like the people of this town and wait for them to come and get me. I'm good with a bow. Father always took me out hunting with him."

"This isn't a place for you!"

Katrina quickly fitted an arrow into her bow and pointed behind Alexander. She let it fly cleanly out of her hand and Alexander turned quickly and saw a barbarian fall from the ladder.

"Fine get to the top of the tower with my sister," he

pointed to the top of the tower where Sofia and her archers peppered the barbarians that pushed the ram forward. "Simon, ensure Katrina is clear of any hand to hand combat."

"Aye sir!"

Alexander turned his attention back to the ladders. Eight ladders had been laid against the wall, and huge axe men swung their weapons dangerously at the swordsman that were there to meet them. The Bete'szek warriors immediately began to make headway against the town militia to Alexander's right.

"Jean! Brennan!" He yelled to his to men who had just cleared one ladder and pushed it back into the throng below. "Follow me, hurry!" The three quickly ran along the edge of the wall past the hand to hand fighting that ensued. Once in the gate tower Alexander felt a strong vibration that caused him to stumble briefly.

"What was that?" asked Brennan.

"They're trying to break down the gate," Alexander replied sadly. He didn't have enough men to keep them at bay. Once the barbarians broke down the gate, they would swarm the walls and kill them all.

Several enemy warriors suddenly entered the stairwell and almost ran into Alexander. Swords flashed quickly and Alexander grabbed the arm of the closest warrior and prevented him from swinging his sword. Brennan quickly ran him through and he fell down the stairs. Jean threw a dagger at the other warrior and hit him in the shoulder. The pain caused him to lower his sword and Alexander stabbed him quickly. The last warrior turned around and ran back out of the stairwell and back into the fracas on the right side of the wall.

Alexander and his two men were quickly on his footsteps and Brennan pushed him off the wall before he warned his comrades. The three men fell upon the twenty warriors that had engaged the town militia and pushed them back. Brennan raised his massive axe and buried it into one man's back. Blood splattered and caught the attention of the warriors in front of him. Panic set in amongst the Bete'szek and the warriors floundered between Alexander and the militia.

Jean and Alexander worked in tandem and sliced through the barbarians while Brennan's raw power overwhelmed the lightly armored trespassers. After reestablishing control of the wall, Alexander turned his attention to the gate. He motioned for Jean to stay with him and he took Brennan and Farkas back down to the ground with him. Once on the ground he surveyed the damage the door had taken. It was severe; the fire had made it very easy for the ram to begin poking out various parts of the gate. It would not be long before the gate was torn down, and the wall overrun. He needed a miracle.

"Sir!" Jean said excitedly. "Jack's brought help!" Alexander allowed himself a smile as Jack ran quickly followed by Isadora and a flock of peacocks. Alexander didn't care, he would have worn a peacock feather himself, he was so happy.

"Change of plans," he called out. "Farkas, keep the archers on the wall, and have them pelt that battering ram! I want thirty clerics down to the gate immediately. Jean and Brennan, with me!"

"Sorry I'm late, your highness," Jack said breathlessly. "I've got one hundred men and it's all due to Lady Isadora."

"I couldn't let his Highness continue to fight our battles on his own." She smiled at him and for a brief moment it distracted him from the raging battle. The crack of the battering ram brought him back to the moment.

"I could never thank you enough Isadora." He fired commands in rapid succession. "Jack, take command of the right side of the wall. Isadora, the left side." He looked over the formation of peacocks that stood before him. Each one of them carried a sword and spear, with a small sword that hung from their belts.

"Brennan, take fifty men and position them on the left side of the gate. Farkas, fifty on the left side. Once they get through the gate, we'll have them on all sides. Also...." Alexander spied some wagons and barrels near the house they had slept in. "Put those wagons and barrels in front of the door. That will slow their advance."

Each man nodded and quickly ran about his business and ensured Alexander's orders were carried out.

Once Jean and the clerics made it to the ground Alexander arranged his men into three sections. Fifty men from the militia created a human wall on the left side, and the other forty took position on the opposite side. The clerics would then link the two groups together. Alexander created a funnel that could attack the intruders on three sides. The barrels and wagons were placed after the gate so the barbarians could not use their massive numbers to push his men back. If any gap was created in Alexander's lines, they would be engulfed and quickly killed.

Alexander checked the fortifications once more, and ensured his men were placed correctly. He surveyed the wall and heard Fergus and Chauncey barking orders to the archers. Sofia and her tower were untouched and they freely unleashed their arrows.

The ram again slammed into the gate. It shook mightily but held. The ram slammed into the gate again. The gate held, but the violence of the collisions combined with the weakening of the gate sent several pieces of burnt wood to the ground. Alexander's palms sweated and he found it difficult to grip his sword so he quickly wiped his hands on his pants to dry them off. He stood behind the men, but decided something different was in order. He moved in front of them.

He ordered Brennan and Farkas to join him in front. Jean was to stay behind them and act as the runner. The runner was to run back and forth with his orders to ensure they met any danger immediately. Alexander placed the helmet on his head, and held his shield ready. He would fight on the left side. Brennan eschewed the sword and shield and carried a huge two handed axe. This heavy weapon assured anyone who carried it an easy cut through most armor or its victim's body. His immense presence would hold the middle.

Farkas preferred a smaller double axe and shield and he would hold the right side. Together, the three would work in tandem to slow the barbarian onslaught and take pressure off of the militia.

Alexander turned his attention to the men behind him. The clerics armor were already covered in blood, and they seemed to appreciate the brief respite they had been given. The militia's faces showed fear, and several men in the front row had to be propped up by their comrades in arms so they did not faint.

"Men," Alexander said calmly. "Hell is coming. They will show you no mercy, so show them none....for any man that flees..." Alexander looked at one man in particular, "any man that flees will meet the same fate as his brothers, but without a sword in his hand...and perhaps even a worse fate." He sighed as he turned around. "And for the love of the Holy Church, take those damn feathers off your head. You look like a flock of peacocks."

Brennan and Farkas laughed uproariously at the militia as they slowly tore the feathers off of their helmets.

"Now that you look like men, you can fight like men," Brennan added mirthfully and together Alexander and his men smiled as they watched the final collapse that kept the hounds of hell at bay. Alexander looked at Keira who had awakened from her sleep and wandered next to him. She yawned at him and looked at the gate. She stood up and stretched and uttered a low growl towards the Bete'szek. She stood by her master and Alexander felt even more confident.

One final violent collision finished the demise of the gate. The gate swung open and revealed the battering ram. Several painted barbarians pushed it out of the path of the gate while several fell from the continual firestorm of arrows.

"For the King!" Alexander yelled as he raised his sword in the air.

"The King!" his men echoed and raised their weapons.

Alexander closed his eyes and listened to the whispers inside of his mind. With his eyes closed he saw the images of all the enemies that surrounded them. He breathed in deeply, and pushed all thoughts of fear and frailty from his mind. He opened his eyes and stared at the hell that awaited him.

The first few barbarians pushed through the gate, leaped over the carts, and were easily cut down by Farkas' sword. The other barbarians noticed this and did what they could to push the carts and barrels to the side. They rushed through the gate and into the funnel that Alexander had created. Brennan raised his giant double axe and sent it crashing down into a hapless barbarians shield. It broke it in two, and severed the man's arm. The man screamed in pain and fell while blood streamed from the wound.

The other barbarians ignored their cries and pressed

through. A swordsman swung his sword down on Alexander. Alexander anticipated the attack and ran his sword into the man's chest without so much of a drop of sweat. The life flickered from the axe man's eyes as Alexander pulled the sword from him. The other barbarians worked to avoid Brennan's swinging axe, which placed them next to Alexander and Farkas who made quick work of them. Any barbarian that stumbled and fell had their existence ended painfully by Keira who seized and tore their throats.

The barbarians were too many in number and many of them rushed past Alexander unscathed and reached the militia. The militia held with Jean's encouragement and fought bravely. They held ranks and refused to bend or back away. This stand created a killing zone in which the barbarians were trapped. The Bete'szek gamble to overpower the city with larger number had been met with failure. Alexander continued to hack his way through the barbarians but began to tire. The gryphon armor continued to communicate to him. He concentrated as best he could but his reflexes slowed.

There was imminent danger. The armor communicated to him that he needed to raise his shield but the battle had tired him and he responded slowly. An arrow pierced his shoulder while a second arrow immediately whizzed by his head and struck a barbarian that tried to take advantage of Alexander's pain. The barbarian died instantly as the arrow pierced his heart. Alexander clutched his shoulder and he could no longer raise his shield with the arrow embedded. Brennan and Farkas realized this immediately and fought through the throng to get to his side. They cleared a path through the barbarians and ensured Alexander could be moved out of harm's way.

Alexander resisted, but felt a pair of hands drag him

through the militia's line. Jean brought him to a place a few feet from the battle and attended to the wound. Alexander looked up to the wall and in the direction that the arrow had come from. The battle still raged although not as fierce as it had been. He scanned the wall for an archer but his eyes fell upon Katrina who he had ordered to join Sofia in the tower. She had found a spot away from the walls fray and was using her ability to fire into the maelstrom at the gate.

"Was this you?" he yelled in agony as Jean pulled the arrow from his shoulder. "Whose side are you on?"

Katrina aimed her bow at him and shot an arrow his way. It sailed high and Alexander followed the arrow's course. It landed in a barbarian who had broken through the line. Several more had followed him and tried to get to Alexander. Alexander and Jean quickly picked up their swords but another figure had come from behind and cut them down before they did any damage.

"Milady!" Alexander grinned. "I've missed you so." Her dark eyes flashed concern on Alexander's wound and she inspected its severity. Isadora smiled at him and brushed her dark hair back. She tore the bloody sleeve off of Alexander's shirt and quickly bandaged his shoulder to stop the bleeding. Alexander noticed the militia's line began to bend and were being pushed back. Now was the time to unleash his surprise.

"Jean! Go to Girard. Tell him it's time. Hurry!" Alexander stood up and ran up to the line with Isadora behind him. He picked up an axe from one of the dead warriors since his wound prevented him from carrying his shield. He shouted encouragement to his troops but militia began to fray apart with mounting losses. There were less than thirty men left on either side. The clerics held firm, but they would be easily overwhelmed if the militia fell.

Rocks rained down from the gatehouse above the

barbarians. Jean delivered the orders to Girard! The barbarians cried out in anger and put their shields above their heads to protect them. Girard and his men then poured several buckets of oil down upon the barbarians. This caused the ground to become slippery and they had trouble staying upright which reduced some of the pressure off of the militia. Finally, Girard unleashed the last surprise. Three lit torches fell down from the gatehouse and ignited the oil that had been poured down to the ground. Men screamed in pain as the fire caught on to every drop of oil on skin and clothing. The barbarians panicked as the middle of their assault was now enflamed. The men in front of the fire could not retreat and were cut down immediately by Alexander's men. The men that caught fire tried to run through their own lines outside of the town. Other barbarians ran away from them for fear of them meeting their end in the same way.

The men cheered as the barbarians began to run away from the city. Alexander tried to maneuver his way through the cheering militia so he could also see what happened. Just then, Jean issued a cry to his men to follow the barbarians out of the city. Jean and many of the militia ran after the retreating warriors. Alexander felt the surge of the left side wanted to run after Jean, but he worried of impending disaster. They had won the day if they stayed behind their walls.

"No! No! Jean!" he yelled. He yelled at the militia closest to him. "Stay here. Do not move." He fought through the ranks of the militia and grabbed any man that moved forward. He pulled each man back and together he, Farkas, and Brennan reached the outside of the gate.

Alexander feared the worst, and it came true immediately. Jean and the thirty men that followed him had been quickly surrounded by an angry enemy. The enemy saw a chance to deal a decisive blow to the defenders and hacked at the men and cut them down quickly.

Alexander looked up to his sister Sofia who, with her archers, stood ready.

"Sofia!" He yelled and pointed at the maelstrom in front of him. She waved back and within moments a stream of arrows began to pour into the enemy ahead of Alexander. He then yelled for Fergus to bring his men off the wall and seal the gap the militia's charge had created. With a nod to his two men he ran towards the enemy. He had to save Jean's life, time was precious.

As enemy axe men fell in front of him from Sofia's deadly aim. Alexander watched as Jean and his few remaining men tried desperately to get back to the safety of the wall.

Brennan lead the way with his giant sword and brought it down with such ferocity that several barbarians lost whole limbs before being finished off by Keira as they fell. If Brennan missed, Farkas finished them.

Alexander threw his mace at one barbarian and he crumpled immediately as it crushed his skull. With his sword Alexander whirled through the barbarians and sliced through them and worked quickly to save Jean. They moved closer.

"Hold on Jean!" Brennan yelled. His heavy frame sweated and he tired but he too refused to allow his body's mortality to slow him down.

Prince Alexander paused briefly in the midst of the struggle and surveyed the carnage before him. On the ground, hundreds of bodies lay silent, and the grass, once so brilliantly green, held onto every drop of blood. In the air, ravens circled and readied to gorge themselves on the flesh of the dead. The carnage momentarily unnerved him. It was his first battle, and the pressure of thousands of his people steeled his resolve to ensure this enemy would never step foot in his city. The glory and romanticism he expected in battle dissipated with every slash of his sword and every cut of his blade. The screams of the wounded seared his mind with fear and strengthened his resolve to fight harder despite his body's yearning for rest. Alexander could never rest again and he resigned himself to this fate.

He was made for such a time as this. Every step, every crossroads, every simple decision had led him to this place, here and now. And he called upon every memory of every training he had ever received.

Be decisive, he had told his men. Make the decision. We'll count and sort the bodies later. He was the harbinger of death. He would bring about the destruction of his people's enemies. This is what he was raised to do. The reality of his situation brought a long sought after clarity to his mind.

He briefly looked down to his appearance. The blood of his enemies stained his armor and his body. He was covered in their blood and yet he cared little for his appearance. If he made it through the day there would be plenty of time to wash the blood away.

He raised his sword and readied himself for the three barbarian axe men that ran towards him. He slashed one man and ran his sword through another. He counted with each cut. Sixteen. Seventeen. The last warrior swung and missed. Alexander ran his sword through his stomach. EIGHT...teen.

After he ran his sword through the enemy warrior, he immediately disengaged from the man's eyes. The hardest part for the Prince was watching the acknowledgement of death and the flicker of life as it left their eyes, he felt as if he needed to beg for their forgiveness for having taken their life away. It made it easier if he just slashed and moved to his next victim. To be distracted was an offering of your body to their axes. There were hundreds of them trying to make their way into the city to murder his people. He would not fail for it was his time. He swung his sword into his opponent's neck which quickly finished him.

I was born for such a time as this, Alexander thought. I am death, and I want all to marvel at my handiwork.

The last of Jean's men fell, and Alexander could no longer see Jean. Once Jean disappeared the barbarians turned their full attention on the three men. One barbarian raised his axe and swung at Alexander as he blocked another's sword. An arrow passed his nose by less than an inch and struck the warrior before the axe closed in upon him. Alexander stabbed the other barbarian with his second sword and looked towards the wall.

"Katrina!" he yelled. "Too close!"

The three of them retreated quickly towards the gate as a horn sounded from the western side of the city. Horsemen charged the barbarians and immediately began moving through their ranks.

"God bless you, Edward," Alexander breathed in relief. The horsemen carried Edward's banner and the Lions led the way. The barbarians saw the horseman and stopped their pursuit of Alexander and quickly dispersed and ran back towards the forest.

Edward's horsemen followed them and cut many of them down until they reached the border of the forest where they stopped and regrouped near the city. Alexander quickly moved through the dead bodies and searched for Jean. He found Jean lying on the ground with blood pouring from his side. He breathed slowly and painfully and had tears in his eyes.

"Prince?" His breath was labored and he shuddered

as he spoke.

"I'm right here Jean, don't speak. We'll get someone to look after your wound."

"It's too late sir. I'm so sorry. I heard you....I'm sorry. I failed you." The tears reflected Jean's knowledge of his fate. Alexander knelt down and removed Jean's helmet.

"Don't apologize Jean. You were magnificent today. A noble warrior."

"I didn't listen to you...I saw them running, I thought we had them...I'm sorry."

"Jean, we won the battle. You had so much to do with that."

Blood trickled out of Jean's mouth. He coughed violently and more blood seeped through his wound.

"My body feels like it's on fire," he whispered through clenched teeth. "I'm going to die," he said with a panicked voice.

"Just rest, we'll get you help." Jean's agony was too much to bear. Keira laid down beside Jean and whimpered.

"It's too late." he said with finality. "But Prince... I'll see my family again." Another tear streamed down Jean's cheek and then stopped. His head slowly rolled off to the side, and he breathed no more. Alexander quickly rubbed the tear out of his eyes. Farkas and Brennan also knelt beside Alexander with their heads bowed. Jack, who had run out behind them, also knelt beside them and grieved over the loss of their comrade.

"Take him inside the city," Alexander said quietly. "We will give him an honored burial."

Edward walked to where Alexander sat and noticed his bandaged shoulder.

"Alex! Thank God you're okay. That was incredible. You defended this city against these warriors? Amazing! I will tell father of this."

"How did you know?" Alexander asked emptily.

"We saw smoke. I don't see anything burning. That was fortunate then?"

Alexander sat there quietly and looked out across the field. Bodies of men lay everywhere and scavenger birds had already started to pick the flesh off of the dead while the stench of burnt flesh lingered in the air. The glory and romanticism of war would be buried with the bodies. A lot of good men had died that day; they would be hard pressed to replace them.

Another horseman rode towards them with an aggressive demeanor. The eye patch on the rider meant that Mattias and his regiment had finally arrived.

"Well Edward, you have certainly delivered a blow to our father's enemies today," Mattias said as he surveyed the dead. "My congratulations."

"The congratulations should go to our brother," Edward said as he pointed to Alexander who still knelt on the ground. "He's the savior of our kingdom today."

"Him?" Mattias asked incredulously. "He defended this city? He is responsible for this victory? Or was it Sofia again who should gain the credit?"

"No," Alexander said thoughtfully as he stood up. He looked back towards the town and Sofia who walked towards them. "These people....they're the heroes. My sister. My guard. I take no share of this victory."

Sofia finally reached him and together they shared a relieved embrace. Alexander wanted to weep, he grieved Jean's loss, and wished he had prevented it somehow.

"You're no warrior," Mattias said sardonically. "You would avoid the prestige from a great victory like this. The bodies of our enemy lay strewn across a field. Our banners still rise from this city. Look at you. Look at the blood.

Love every drop of it for it is not your blood."

Alexander looked back at Mattias with an expressionless face.

"I find no pleasure in ripping the life from someone," he said slowly. "But you're right. Our banners still wave. The bodies of our enemies lay across the field. And nothing has changed. They will kill us and we will kill them. I find no glory in this; this is not the life I want. Edward, I leave the city in your hands."

"Where are you going now?" Mattias demanded.

"Home. And then wherever I want." Alexander smiled as he turned to follow his men who carried Jean's body. They walked back towards what used to be the city's gate.

At once, the remaining militia grouped together and followed Alexander. Townspeople had gathered on the walls and had ventured outside of the city and surveyed the battlefield for themselves.

"Edgebrooke!" Girard shouted from the castle wall. "All hail Alexander, protector of Edgebrooke!"

The townspeople quieted for a moment and all eyes were upon Alexander. The awkward silence was broken as the militia who had followed him to the city gate began to beat their shields with their swords.

"Alexander! Protector!" They shouted. The townspeople joined in and they threw down flower petals from the walls to honor him. The petals floated in the breeze and covered him and his men. Sofia grabbed Alexander and hugged him tightly.

"You were absolutely brilliant today," she whispered. "You deserve this."

Alexander raised his sword in a salute to the villagers that he had bled for. They cheered even louder and chanted his name in reverence. Edward made his way through the militia and the petals and interrupted Alexander's acknowledgment.

"Alexander, I need you and your men to mount up and follow me. We have a chance to smash these barbarians and we need to do that quickly while they are in disarray."

Did Edward not hear him, Alexander thought.

"Your Majesty," he said, slowly choosing his words, "I appreciate your confidence. My men are exhausted and tired. Perhaps Mattias would be of greater use."

"Yes," Mattias agreed quickly. He had followed Edward and his voice was tinged with irritation. "Let me ride with you. My men are fresh. Edward?"

Edward looked at Mattias with a sour expression. His grey eyes darkened with anger.

"Your brother defended Edgebrooke, and now you can garrison it. Perhaps the next time I call for your assistance you will show some urgency and join the battle."

Mattias looked chastised and his face clouded with anger. Perhaps if Edward was a lesser man, Mattias would have drawn his sword. He remembered who addressed him and quickly responded.

"As your Majesty chooses," he said with a slight tick of the neck. He motioned to his regiment of swordsmen to make their way into the city and followed them.

"Alright," Alexander said softly. Perhaps it was the forcefulness of how Edward had chastised Mattias or maybe it was the inspiration that he drew from standing in Edward's presence. If Edward walked into darkness Alexander rode by his side.

He walked through the gate where the rest of the men waited. The people continued to cheer with so much force as Alexander walked into the city that he expected the walls to fall. The archers lifted their bows from their position on the wall. The clerics that survived bowed to him. They were all eager to thank him for they admired him. He had delivered them from death.

Alexander and his men prepared to follow Edward immediately. Although tired, they followed his orders without question and rode out of the gate without a second thought. The barbarians had failed today; Edgebrooke remained in the King's hands.

CHAPTER XXI

Alexander and Edward rode hastily after the barbarians. They had to move quickly so they took the horses while the other men were left under Mattias's command in the city. Alexander charged Farkas with being responsible to track the barbarians. They cut through the brush and looked for any trace to continue the pursuit.

As superb and thorough at tracking as Farkas was, he failed at finding anything more than just footprints which seemed if the Bete'szek vanished completely. The men continued to ride alertly and Alexander and his men kept tight watch on the trees and changed their direction of riding to confuse any would be ambushers.

They arrived at a stream and Edward decided the horses should be watered. The men dismounted the horses and allowed their horses to drink. Alexander and his men were especially parched and at the point of exhaustion. They had fought since sun up, and they desperately needed water.

"We need to fill our water pouches," Alexander said to Edward.

"You look tired," Edward said. "Why don't you and

your men return to Edgebrooke and rest? We'll continue to look for them. Perhaps they'll lead us to a camp."

"No," Alexander said and he shook his head. "That's just what they want. They'll overwhelm you. At least we have enough numbers in case we're surprised. By any rate, without swordsman or axe men, we should be out of this forest by sundown. And we're nearly there."

"That's good advice Alexander. We won't tarry much longer. Long enough for you to rest up and go. What happened to your shoulder?"

Alexander had forgotten his wound. He looked at the bandage which was now reddened with his blood.

"Arrow."

"I don't seem to remember any archers with them."

"It was one of ours. The little girl from Greystone."

"You should have known better than to put her in battle. What were you thinking?" Edward chided him as a father chided his son.

"She saved my life twice. I can handle a flesh wound but not death. I'll help her improve her aim. She might turn out to be a decent archer...for a girl. But don't worry. We'll rest when we're safely behind the walls. Not until then." Farkas called to Alexander and he and Edward walked over to him, and were shown a clearing that had only tree stumps.

"These are fresh sir. Looks like they were cut down recently," Farkas said as he examined the stumps. The other men began to enter the clearing with their horses and looked around curiously.

"What do you think Alex?" Edward asked.

"They had siege towers, a battering ram, and ladders. They cut down the wood here and constructed it elsewhere." Alexander was unconcerned with the trees but it did make them easy targets. He walked amongst the stumps with Zeus' reigns in his hands.

"Edward," he started to say. He bent down and snapped up a flower that grew from the ground.

"What is it?" Edward asked.

"A white lily," Alexander responded, studying it intently.

The men heard a loud crash and instantly drew their swords and looked around as if they expected men to rush from the trees. They waited another moment and held their breaths. Nothing happened and then Jack looked up in the air.

"Catapult!" he yelled. A large stone crashed into the earth sending dirt and rocks flying. It missed injuring any of them, but the shock knocked a few men down and sent the horses into a panic. As the men scrambled and tried to calm their horses two more stones crashed into the earth. The horses were in mutiny and strained against the will of the men to flee.

"Hold on to your mounts!" Alexander yelled. If they lost any of their mounts, those men would be as good as dead. Alexander handed Jack his horse's reigns and helped another man regain control of his beast and mount it.

"Alex!" Edward yelled from his horse. "What do you think? A noble charge to those catapults?"

"I'm disappointed in you," Alexander laughed. "They obviously want us to charge. It's a nice little trap, let's get you back home."

"No Alexander, let's go get them. I feel good about it." Edward smiled excitedly. This was what he loved, the thrill of the battle.

"I don't," Alexander said. "You're the Crown Prince, it's foolhardy and reckless. If we had the entire army, then yes. You're too important to this kingdom to throw your life away on a hunch."

"Alright mother," Edward scoffed. "Get on your horse and let us ride out of this forest."

Alexander nodded and slapped Edward's horse. He ran through the confusion to Zeus. He heard another stone falling to the earth. He glanced upwards to check the trajectory. Satisfied it wasn't heading for him, he slowed his run. As he reached Zeus he watched the stone fall to the earth several feet away from him. The stone impacted a large tree stump and ripped through it. A heavy piece of bark flew from the crater towards Alexander's head. Instinctively, he lifted his left arm, where his shield was usually held, to block the projectile. His wound limited his motion terribly, and he didn't get it up in time.

The bark glanced off his head and he fell backwards, as if hit by rock. He laid there dazed and felt blood gushing from his forehead. His vision blurred and the images danced mockingly around his head as he tried to regain control of the images. He refused to lay down and instantly tried to get back to his feet although he had lost all coordination.

This is the end, thought Alexander. I'm going to die in the damn forest. At least I can take solace that no man killed me. It was fate.

He saw Jack and Edward jump down from their horses and rush to his aid. They lifted him upon their shoulders.

"Can you hear me?" Edward yelled.

Alexander shook his head yes as they helped him onto his horse. His body refused to help them and he began to topple from his saddle. Jack leaned him forward into Zeus so that he was balanced perfectly. Together the men rapidly retreated through the forest. Arrows flew towards the men but missed badly.

They were ambushed, just as Alexander had

supposed. His head started to clear, but it throbbed intensely. He heard a war cry nearby and enemy soldiers ran through the trees alongside of them. His men had pulled their bows and used them to shoot arrows from horseback.

Alexander lost all sight. His head slumped forward and as Zeus jumped over a large tree root, Alexander lost grip of the reins and fell backwards. He lost consciousness momentarily, but regained it as his body hit the forest floor. He struggled to stand, but the head wound and loss of blood had drained all that remained of his energy. He heard excited shouts and again felt sure he was going to die.

Just then a bevy of horses surrounded Alexander and he heard the clashes of swords. The heavy hands of Brennan grabbed him and again swung him onto his horse. Several heavily armored men on horseback also attacked the fleeing men as they worked desperately to ensure Alexander stayed on his horse. The cries of dying men were close to him, and Alexander saw them being pulled from their horses as they met their end.

Edward was surrounded by vicious fighting. His men had been isolated, and although putting up a furious fight, fell one by one. Alexander's men began to fight their way through to Edward but Alexander felt himself being carried away quickly from the battle. Fergus had taken Zeus' reins and was quickly riding towards the edge of the small forest and ensuring Alexander's safety.

They finally arrived outside of the forest and Alexander commanded Fergus to stop.

"Where's my brother?" he demanded.

"He's coming. Everyone else is back with them. We've got to get you inside the city."

Alexander remembered riding to Edgebrooke but nothing else. He lay in a bed for days and paid no mind to any visitors or caregivers. The loss of blood from both his shoulder and head wound made him extremely weak. He could do nothing but sleep as his body worked to heal itself.

On the third day, Alexander finally opened his eyes. He looked around slowly and guessed that he was still in Edgebrooke. Sofia sat in a chair nearby and her eyes were closed. Probably asleep, he thought. He was very thirsty and saw a pitcher of water on a stool. Gingerly, he rose out of bed and tried to walk over to it. His head felt better, but he was weak from hunger. It had been four days since he ate. He poured water into the goblet and drank it furiously. The water was cold; it felt incredible to be refreshed from his thirst.

Sofia stirred in her chair and looked at him.

"Good morning sister," he said, smiling.

She shrieked with joy and jumped up. She gave him a hug and started to cry.

"Hey….there's no need to cry. I seem to be indestructible," he smiled mischievously. "They'll have to do better than that if they want to kill me. Although they do seem to be learning."

"Alex, you shouldn't be up. It's also time we dressed that wound with a fresh bandage." Sofia called in two handmaidens with fresh bandages and water. Together they carefully unwrapped the bandage around his head. A washcloth was dipped into a bowl of water and gently wiped against his head, and removed the dried blood. His shoulder wound had nearly healed, so they washed it and let it alone. His head was rewrapped with a bandage.

"It looks a lot better," Sofia said as she examined both wounds. "I'm so happy your awake, Alex. I was so worried."

"I'll bet Edward had a big laugh about it. Having to pull my body from the fire. Right? Where is he now? Is he leading the grand conquest?"

"Ask him yourself," she said grinning as Edward entered the room. He looked no worse for the wear, with a slight wound on his arm that matched Alexander's.

"Edward! You're alive!" Alexander exclaimed enthusiastically.

"Thanks to you."

"No, it seems as I am alive thanks to you," Alexander said dismissively as he lay back down. The injury and loss of blood robbed him of his energy. "What happened?"

"You were right," Edward sighed. "It was a trap. They came after us. Just getting out of that forest was hell. I lost a lot of men. A lot of horsemen went down in the forest and half of my bodyguard." He sat down next to Sofia and sighed.

"I shouldn't have followed them," he continued. "So reckless, Alex, I should have listened to you."

Alexander was shocked. Edward had never spoken regretfully about the work that had to be done. "I really thought that was the right thing to do. I'm so glad you were there, I might not have made it out of there."

"I didn't do anything though," Alexander said and pointed at his head's bandage.

"But your men did. Your men…fought like immortals. Once you were safely away they hacked through the enemy and they would not stop until they reached me. Alexander……I have to say that your men are the most courageous men I have ever seen. I am honored to be in their company and I am duly impressed with you. You have done a fantastic job with your guard."

"Thank you Edward," Alexander was overwhelmed and cast a glance at Sofia who smiled back proudly.

"Don't leave Alexander. You are so important to me

and my plans. The way you have handled everything has been brilliant. Swear to me that you will stand by my side. Don't worry....I will be your intermediary between Father and Mattias."

Alexander's facial expression changed. He frowned and his brow furrowed. He loved his brother and his brother's request showed the depth of respect that Edward had for him. He could not let Edward down, and felt such a duty to him and the kingdom.

"Alright," Alexander said. "You win. I'll stay."

Edward rose from his chair and walked to Alexander's bed. He stood over Alexander and clasped his hand.

"You will not regret it," Edward said happily. "I am proud of you."

Alexander felt a warmth creep over him as Edward walked out the door. Those words meant so much to him. Sofia came and sat by him and took his hand. She had changed from her warrior princess' appearance and wore a beautiful gown.

"My brother, the hero," she said jokingly. "Oh no, whatever will we do with you? Your head will become so large it will require its own room."

Alexander ignored the comment and tried to kick her unsuccessfully.

"Ow!" he shouldn't have moved.

"You need your rest," she said soothingly. "The Baron has planned a great feast and I am required to attend. In the meantime you need to sleep. We hope to return to Middlebrooke soon. I am sure Mattias will want to leave garrison duty as soon as possible."

"I am sure," Alexander said gleefully but curtailed his emotion as Sofia frowned at him.

"I worry," Sofia continued, "I worry that with your

success, Mattias's jealousy will only grow. It was not a pleasant sight after you and Edward rode off."

Alexander folded his hands behind his head and closed his eyes.

"Sister," he said gleefully, "The time for worrying about Mattias has ended. The time for an Alveun Golden Age is upon us." He reopened his eyes and smiled at Sofia. "Do not fear Sofia, Edward will be a great King and I will ensure Mattias swears fealty to him." He closed his eyes and began to drift off to sleep, quite pleased with the certainty of Mattias's fall from grace.

CHAPTER XXII

It soon became a listless night's sleep for Alexander. The town of Edgebrooke continued to be merry and festive and they had every reason to be. Their lives were saved and they return back to their normal contented lives. Music filled the air while the drunken revelry and escapades of the populace made it difficult for Alexander to sleep. Alexander's thoughts continued to allow him humorous whims of Mattias's fate. He imagined that instead of joining the frivolity Mattias had been assigned garrison duty himself or perhaps been forced to oversee the burial of the enemy dead. Eventually the city quieted down and Alexander was able to enjoy the silence and drifted off to sleep.

It was well past midnight when Alexander stirred from his sleep. He had grown nervous over the last hour for reasons unknown to him. He opened his eyes and let them adjust to the darkness. He listened intently for any noise that might give him an idea of why he felt so uneasy. His sword and his armor had been placed on a nearby chair and he began to reach for it when a voice froze him.

"That's far enough Prince." Alexander felt the sharp

cold tip of a sword press against his neck. Alexander thought about yelling for help, but his attacker had the advantage and would doubtless kill him before he uttered a sound.

"Alright," Alexander said, "You have me at your mercy. What do you want?"

"I want revenge," it said simply.

"I know your voice," Alexander replied. "You've come to finish me off in my bloody state. Finally doing your own unpleasant work are we.....Duncan?"

"Yes Alexander," Duncan answered as he pressed the tip even further into the side of Alexanders neck. Alexander felt his flesh tear slightly and a drop of blood ran down the side of his neck.

"Alright, do you worst. Kill me. It won't bring Angelica back."

"No!" Duncan exclaimed. "You don't say her name. You don't ever say her name."

"I loved her Duncan-"

"No!" Duncan yelled again. The tip of the sword left Alexander's neck and in its place a fist crashed down and slammed into the back of Alexander's head. Alexander cried out in pain as his wound robbed his head of any peace that was left. Alexander fell off the bed onto the floor and Duncan pounced on his weakened condition. Blow after blow, Duncan's powerful fists slammed into Alexander's head. Alexander tried to block the blows but he was in too much pain. Blood poured through his wound again.

The room lightened, someone else walked in.

"Duncan!" the torch holder commanded. "That's enough."

Duncan struck Alexander once more and then grabbed him and threw him on the bed. Alexander yelped in pain and gasped as he rolled onto his back. His eyes focused through the blood as he tried to guess the torch holders identity.

"You," Alexander coughed up blood as he spoke.

"I told you I'd be seeing you again, 'Prince'," Jacob said condescendingly. "My master sends his warmest regards."

"So this is it then? The young noble…finding his life ended by two jackals? I won't even dignify you by challenging you. You're both cowards….you're little more than rats beneath my family's feet…." Alexander laughed deliriously. He wanted to provoke them into a mistake.

"Beg for mercy," he demanded. Duncan stood between Alexander and his sword.

"Not yet Duncan, we still have one piece to move." Jacob moved to the door and looked outside. He motioned for someone to come in. Two armed men entered the room and they pulled a hooded captive with them. Their captive struggled uselessly against the rope that tied his hands behind his back. Alexander feared the worst now and when Jacob removed the hood, Alexander's fears were realized. It was Edward.

"No….," Alexander said as he shook his head. "You cannot touch him. He is the Crown Prince. How dare you. Let him go! Guards!"

Jacob brought the sword to Edward's throat. Alexander stopped talking immediately. Duncan loosened and removed the gag from Edward's mouth.

"It's okay Alex," Edward said soothingly.

"You all are kingdom men," Alexander challenged. "You are wearing our armor. Your allegiances are to the King and his house. Even you Duncan…you fight against the very house that raised you. Let him go before your life is forfeit."

"My life is forfeit. This is revenge."

"Alright then kill me. I'm responsible for your sister's death. Let my brother go." He looked at Edward and knew the hopelessness of the situation. Edward's bonds were too tight.

"So what now?" Edward asked. "Is it gold you want? Will you be kidnapping to ransom me?"

Jacob smiled and forced Edward to his knees.

"My brother's right," Edward continued. "You wear the armor. Is that how you snuck past all of the guards?"

"There's nothing like confusion in battle and the celebration that follows." Jacob laughed, obviously pleased with himself. "I would like to thank you for allowing the guards to attend to their wounds. Otherwise we might have had a struggle."

"And the other guards?" Edward demanded.

"I'm sorry Prince," Duncan said. "I'm really good at killing. Which brings us back to why we're here." Duncan stood behind Edward with his sword still drawn. Duncan took up a position that flanked Alexander across from one of the men who had brought Edward into the room. The last man stood nearby the door's entrance when he suddenly rushed outside and for a moment all the men were distracted by the commotion outside. There was a muffled cry as the man carried in a young girl.

"Katrina," Alexander moaned. This was getting worse.

"How long have you been outside," Duncan demanded.

"Long enough," Katrina retorted. She nervously looked about the room.

"Have you told anyone?"

"Lots. The whole army," she said sarcastically.

"Move it up," Jacob said. "We need to go now."

Just then, Katrina bit down on the man's hand that

held her. He yelped in surprise and she wiggled free from his grasp. She ran to the door.

"Get her!" Jacob shouted. Duncan attempted to stop her but missed her. Alexander summoned any strength he had and sprang up from the bed. He barreled into the guard that stood by him and knocked him down. Alexander grabbed his sword and ran his sword through the man's chest.

Jacob and Duncan both recovered quickly from attempting to catch Katrina and Duncan ordered the other guard to subdue Alexander.

Katrina's screams for help echoed through the building and the courtyard. The alarm rose quickly.

"Put your weapons down," Edward commanded. "I order you as-"

Jacob lifted his sword above his head and brought the blade down towards Edward's shoulders.

"NO!" Alexander shouted. He threw his sword at Jacob. Jacob's momentum slowed and he tried to jump out of the way but instead stumbled backwards. The sword bounced harmlessly off of the wall. Edward sprang to his feet and stumbled across the room to Alexander. Alexander picked up the dead intruders sword and faced Duncan. Duncan had drawn his bow and pointed his arrow at Alexander's heart.

"Do it," Alexander whispered. He braced himself for the arrows impact. He prayed that death would be swift.

Duncan let the arrow fly and at the moment where the arrow would have hit him, Edward moved in front of Alex.

"What have you done?" Alexander exclaimed in shock. Edward moaned slightly and exhaled in pain. His eyes which held so much life before the battle began to dim. Edward's weight shifted onto Alexander and he propped Edward up as he tried to reach the arrow.

"I'm saving the kingdom, brother," Edward sighed as he slumped towards the floor.

"An eye for an eye, Prince!" Duncan shouted. He and Jacob quickly ran out of the room. The other guard tried to follow but Alexander flew at him and grabbed onto his shoulder. They struggled for a brief moment. Alexander forgot all of the pain and exhaustion. He used his rage and adrenaline to gain the upper hand as he pushed the guard towards the window in his room. With a yell he threw the guard out of the window. The guard screamed for his life until his body met the ground.....then silence.

Alexander heard the footsteps of an army as they clattered up the stairs. He slumped down and dragged himself to Edward. He ignored the blood on the floor and quickly untied Edward's bonds.

"Edward," he whispered. "Edward!"

Edward opened his eyes and looked at Alexander. Edward's blue eyes were incredibly poignant and tears ran down his cheeks. Jack rushed into the room and stood over them both.

"Your highness?" He gasped.

Alexander looked up at Jack.

"Duncan. He's here and so is the thug from Greystone. Find them, and bring them to me. Find my sister and my brother. Now!!"

"At once!" Jack ran out of the room and shouted orders to the men that waited outside. Alexander looked back down at Edward.

"I'm sorry....Alex...," Edward tried to talk but his strength failed him.

"No," Alexander said firmly. "No! You cannot leave me. You are the next king of Alveus. You can't die."

Edward laughed and then stopped. His breaths

became quicker and more intense.

"You are destined for greatness Alexander. It is you who must carry on," Edward's breathing became longer as he struggled for air.

"No, I-I can't."

Sofia rushed in the room and knelt down by Edward.

"Edward?" Alex....Alex what's happened?" Alexander couldn't hear her speak. His focus lay dying in front of him.

"Alex, the Crown must pass to you. Swear you will tell father my last words." Edward lifted his bloody hand to Alexander.

"I swear it, brother." Alexander said as he grasped Edwards's hand.

"I am so proud of you Alex. You are a better man than any of us could hope to be. Sofia, look after him and protect him from his enemies." His grasp weakened as life slipped away from him. His hand fell from Alexander's grasp and lay quietly on the ground. The life that had always blazed in his eyes turned hollow and empty.

Time stopped for Alexander. He heard voices but they echoed like a dream. Sofia began to cry softly and she embraced her two brothers.

Mattias raced into the room and uttered a cry of shock when he saw Edward's lifeless body.

"What happened?" Mattias asked breathlessly.

"Edward's been murdered," Sofia said mournfully. "Alexander? Alexander talk to me."

"No...." Alexander felt the walls close in on him. He was in an ever shrinking room. "Edward?" The realization crept in on him. Edward was dead and all of his hope died with him.

Alexander stood up dazed and stumbled out of the room. The wound aggravated his senses and he could barely stand but he needed to get out of the building. Sofia got up and followed closely.

"Alexander," she said cautiously. "Where are you going? Please come back." She tried to take his hand to steady him.

"Don't touch me!" He shouted as he finally stumbled outside into the atrium. He looked down at his bloody hands.

"No...," he whimpered. "God...No!!!" He placed his face in his hands and rubbed his hands through his hair. He grabbed onto the sides of his head and yelled in pain. The action in the courtyard slowed as the men realized what Alexander's screams meant.

Alexander couldn't control his rage. He leaned forward and placed one hand on the ground to steady himself. The feelings overwhelmed him, he couldn't keep anything in. He hadn't eaten in two days but his body forced him to expel whatever there was left inside of him.

Blackness engulfed him and again he succumbed to his mind's void.

He awoke some hours later in a different room. Sofia dutifully sat near him, as did Jack. The entire bodyguard stood outside and guarded him with vigilance.

"Where's my brother's body?" Alexander remembered every detail and wanted control of the situation.

"They've taken Edward back to be buried near Middlebrooke," Sofia said softly.

"And Jean's body?"

"We took his body to his parent's home and buried him. Bishop Malachius came with us and said a prayer." Jack sat somberly.

"Am I to assume the Bishop returned to Middlebrooke? Mattias too?"

Jack nodded yes.

"The murderers?"

"They got away," Jack said grimly. "They wore our armor, it was impossible to tell the difference."

"Where are my things? My swords? My armor?"

"You're not going to Middlebrooke are you?" Sofia was concerned that the strain might cause the fatigue to overwhelm him.

"I'm not staying here while my brother is buried. He saved my life. I will honor his memory."

"We have all your equipment. We can have the horses ready in an hour." Jack spoke confidently. It seemed that he anticipated Alexander's wishes brilliantly.

"Make sure you bring Keira along. And find my sister a horse too. I want to be ready to go within half an hour." Jack and Fergus bowed their heads and left to attend to their duties.

"I'm sorry Sofia. Send your handmaidens via the barge. We should be there for his funeral. And if you could have them produce a scrap of food, I'd be eternally grateful."

"When will you tell father?" She asked once Jack left the room.

"There is nothing to tell him," Alexander denied flatly.

"Edward named you heir, what do you mean there is nothing to tell him? This is your time!" Sofia tried to tussle Alexander's hair but he gently slapped her hand away.

"You will never breathe a word of this to anyone, and if you do, I will deny it. Do you understand me?" Alexander was grim in his resolve. There would be no mention of this, ever.

"I do not understand. Help me understand."

"No, and you do not need to understand. This is my

decision and I do what I believe is the right thing."

"I cannot believe you are saying these things. There will be nothing good that comes from this decision." She added emphatically. "This is your destiny."

"Just last week my fate was death," Alexander said. "This week my destiny is to be a King. Now I have lost a brother, a mentor, and a friend." He shook his head. "No, please just attend to me with some soup for I am famished."

Sofia left the room with tears in her eyes, and Alexander felt a sense of dread wash over him. Should word of this get out it could mean civil war in the kingdom or worse. He was convinced only the King held the power to appoint his heir.

Alexander voraciously ate the food that Sofia had provided and felt his strength return. Every part of his body ached in pain; his guts churned from the bitter taste of frustration. Why Duncan could not have killed me and ended this once and for all, he asked himself. Now, he would have his vengeance even if he had to track Duncan to the gates of hell.

Soon after eating, Alexander and his bodyguard along with Sofia and Keira rode out of Middlebrooke towards Edgebrooke. Alexander expected Edward's death would tear his family apart. He imagined the anger of his father and the grief of his mother would overrule any rational feelings they needed in this matter. The future of the kingdom was now at stake.

CHAPTER XXIII

Once they arrived at Middlebrooke, Alexander immediately headed for the abbey. The church bells tolled, and the entire populace converged upon the church.

Alexander and Sofia fought through the streets and the crowds to make it in time to the service. His men tried to delicately move people out of the sibling's way. For the most part the people accommodated but there were certain areas where the people needed a gentle reminder to respect royalty.

They finally reached the closed doors of the abbey. Several guards tried to dissuade Alexander from entering, as the eulogy had begun, but Alexander and Sofia were in no mood to be trifled with.

Alexander grabbed the handle to the solid door and swung it open. The sudden burst of sunlight and noise into the solemnity caused a stir amongst the nobles. Alexander caught eye of his brothers, several high ranking army officers, the Baron and Isadora, and other nobles from across the kingdom. His mother sat in front with his father. She wore a black gown and her cheeks were stained with tears.

The guards sought to close the doors immediately, but Alexander had different plans.

"Keep these doors open," he commanded. "My brother was a man for the people. The people loved him and they should be able to say their goodbyes. We will all honor him, from every house regardless of status."

Sofia pushed the other door open as well. The abbey's empty seats were quickly filled by grieving townspeople. Many of them carried a single flower in their hand.

Alexander continued to the rectory where Bishop Malachius presided over the funeral. He took a seat beside his brothers. Neither Mattias nor his father looked at him or sought to make any eye contact.

I don't care, Alexander thought. *This is where it all ends.* Edward was the glue that held the family together, but now there would be open conflict between the King's Sons, and quite possibly conflict between Alexander and King Magnus.

Bishop Malachius had prepared a beautiful oratory. He read it as the congregation wept. Stoically, the royal family made no such noise, but behind them, the people wailed in their grief. When Bishop Malachius was finished, Mattias, Alexander, and Calimus all approached his casket. Together, they each took a shoulder. King Magnus was far too weak to hold a corner, and Sofia rose to take his place. Suddenly, a peasant rushed to the front and bowed to the princes.

"Sires. With your permission, I would consider it an honor to help carry the Crown Prince."

King Magnus was touched, and allowed this young man the opportunity to carry his son. The procession walked past the pews and to the outside. They carefully walked down every step to a cart that waited for them. They carefully placed the casket in the wagon, and each man mounted his horse. The wagon driver waited as the abbey emptied and helped the King and Queen mount their horses.

With the wagon before them, each noble member at the funeral followed closely behind. Every peasant and every town folk from Middlebrooke walked behind them. Five thousand people joined the procession out of Middlebrooke to a giant mausoleum just outside the city walls. It was here that only Alveun kings were buried. Because of the regard and station that Edward held, King Magnus felt he deserved the internment of kings.

As the men proceeded to lower the casket from the cart, they allowed every peasant to pass by the casket and express their farewells. Many peasants left flowers in the tomb as they paid their respects. When the last person had whispered their goodbyes, the royal family had their moment of grieving. Alexander went last and at the sight of his brother's body, nearly wept. He grabbed Edwards hand and quietly uttered that it should have been himself, and that he was responsible for everything.

He couldn't help but blame himself. He was lost. He hated Edward and loved him all the same. His selfish act to save Alexander's life was foolishness and yet the duty of a devoted brother. The weight of Edward's charge lay heavy on his heart.

When he finished grieving, the four men lifted the open casket and carried Edward into the mausoleum. A deep silence settled over the crowd as his body disappeared forever.

As they placed Edward's body in the tomb, the brothers stayed silent but their eyes showed full knowledge of the situation.

"And where was Calimus when bravery was needed?" Mattias finally mocked. "Where was the great son of Magnus? At the bottom of a bottle? Where you too engaged with the maidens to pick up a sword when your country needed you?"

"Let him alone Mattias," Alexander said softly, "There's nothing to be gained with this."

"Is that right? Can we count on him," Mattias pointed at Calimus, "For his loyalty and devotion? Or will he stay within the walls? Mark my words Calimus, you will fight for this kingdom. You will pick up your sword." Calimus hung his head in shame and fought back the tears.

"You disgust me. You're a disgrace."

"Let it go Mattias. Calimus did not kill Edward. They did. That's who we should focus our hate and anger on, not ourselves." Alexander offered his hand to Mattias.

"When I am King," Mattias bragged, "We will see where loyalties fall and how much certain people will do to ensure they stay within my favor."

"You're very sure of yourself," Alexander said coldly. "You stand next to your dead brother and claim his birthright. Have you no etiquette? Our father will make his decision."

"And an easy one at that," Mattias smirked. "The candidates are a drunk, a warrior, and an ideological cleric. Who would father choose?" Mattias laughed hatefully and walked out of the tomb leaving Calimus and Alexander in awkward silence.

"It's come to this," Alexander said softly.

"What's that?" Calimus asked.

"It's come to you to be King."

Calimus laughed then choked on his laughter. Alexander stood there silently and glared at Calimus until Calimus stopped laughing.

"I need a drink," Calimus stated flatly and he turned to leave the mausoleum.

"Calimus," Alexander called. "Drink up. For tomorrow, you will never touch anything stronger than water."

Alexander exited the tomb and wandered outside. King Magnus had stayed behind with the Queen and Bishop and the King made eye contact with him but stayed quiet. He shook his head sadly and said nothing as he limped away while he leaned upon his staff.

"Don't blame yourself Alexander," his mother said trying to ease his anguish.

"There was nothing you could have done," the Bishop added. "We have heard what happened. They are nothing but snakes who strike with cowardice from their holes in the earth."

"That's right, nothing I could do. Except stay home and never have brought this to our door. Father was right. I am to blame. For the good of the kingdom I should have left and never returned," Alexander said bitterly.

"For the good of the kingdom? Everything you have done is for the good of the kingdom. If you had not discovered this war, we would be much worse off." Caroline said firmly. She took his battered face in her hands. "Alex, you cannot dwell on this moment. You need to come together and not come undone. The heir is dead. You must position yourself to be the heir."

"I don't want that responsibility," Alexander whispered.

"Who then?" Malachius challenged. "Mattias? Calimus? You would entrust the fate of the kingdom and its people to your brothers?"

Alexander sighed. Mattias was a killer, and Calimus was a drunk. Either choice imperiled the kingdom, but challenging either one of them would lead to open conflict and war, something Alexander hoped to avoid.

"I will always fight for my Alex," Caroline said. "Your father will hear me whisper your name from morning till night. I swear that throne will be yours."

"You have the support of the church my son. We want a noble man of faith and character. You have our blessing."

"What you're both saying is treason," Alexander said. "The king chooses the heir, and I will abide by what my father chooses."

Caroline sighed. She smoothed his ruffled hair and smiled sympathetically. Her face was puffy, no doubt a result of tears for her eldest. With Edward's death, Alexander noticed for the first time that his mother seemed to age. He never noticed the wrinkles on her face or the grey in her hair. It saddened him to think of his mom as old.

"Sometimes," she said, "Doing what's right is doing what's wrong. You'll have to make that choice. But my support is and always has been for you. I love and respect you." She kissed his wound gently and left him there to ponder her words.

Alexander stayed silent. Talking was useless now but Father Malachius disagreed and insisted Alexander come back to the abbey under a matter of great importance. The streets of the town were empty. No one was at the market and no stalls were open. Everyone stayed inside as a sign of respect for Prince Edward.

When they arrived at the abbey, Malachius roused Father Peter and together they went down into the cellar.

"Bishop Malachius? What has happened to Katrina?" Alexander had suddenly remembered the little girl. He had not seen her since the battle. His concern had smoldered, but he suddenly burst forth in concern.

"I don't know Alexander. She disappeared after Edward died. Poor girl, orphaned like that. I wouldn't even know where to begin looking for her. I'm sorry, my son. You've lost a lot over the last week."

"You don't know the half of it."

"I know. But we have been able to find out something extremely interesting about the egg."

"The egg!" Father Peter yelped. "It's an incredible find!" Father Peter produced a cloak that wrapped around the egg. He took it out and placed it on the table in front of them. Alexander had not realized how big this egg was. It was larger than two of his fists together and was made of gold.

"If you look closely." Peter explained, "You can see cracks. The gryphon is trying to hatch."

Alexander examined it closely and swung a torch near it. The warmth of the flame caused an intense pecking to ensue. He kept the torch near it to ensure it hatched. Finally, a little shard of gold chipped off of the egg and a beak became visible.

Alexander handed the torch to the Bishop and attempted to break the egg. It was harder than it looked, but the gryphon continued chipping away at the shell with ease. Finally, the egg cracked in half and revealed a baby gryphon. The gryphon emitted a tiny screech and flapped its wings. It walked across the table and snuggled against the armor Alexander wore.

"It's the gryphon's blood! It senses it in your armor," Father Jean explained. "Maybe it believes you to be its mother!"

"Or father?" Alexander said crossly. He picked up the gryphon and held it. The gryphon became excited and squirmed out of his hands. He didn't let go fast enough and the little gryphon bit his finger.

"OW!" he yelped as he rubbed his finger.

"So, any ideas on what to do with the little guy?" Alexander was fascinated with the little gryphon and he brought his head down to gain a closer look at it.

Bishop Malachius suggested that he be taken to the monastery. Jean-Paul was perfectly located in the mountains to ensure the young gryphon would be safe against its enemies. If the gryphon stayed in the castle, its fate would be too difficult to predict. Then Father Peter asked to see Alexander's cut. Alexander showed it to him when Father Peter flashed a knife and slashed his hand. Alexander jumped back startled at the pain that was just inflicted.

Father Peter also cut a tiny piece of flesh on the gryphon's leg. The gryphon screamed in pain and tried to fly away. Father Peter held onto it and prevented the escape. He quickly brought it over to Alexander. Bishop Malachius took Alexander's hand and pressed it against the Gryphon's cut.

"What are you doing?" Alexander demanded.

"Think," the Bishop commented, "That if the blood of a gryphon can mix with armor, what could it do if it was mixed with your blood?"

"You're both crazy."

"We did tell you about the cup too. Did the cup work?" Father Peter peered up at Alexander.

"Yes."

"Then trust us," the Bishop commanded fervently.

Father Peter moved the gryphon away and stroked its head to calm it down. Alexander started to see spots in front of his eyes.

"Alexander, we will take responsibility for the gryphon and see its safe passage. There is one thing I need from you."

"What's that?" Alexander rubbed his eyes. The spots increased in number and he began to feel dizzy. He looked at his hands and tried to focus on their image. The spots eventually subsided and his vision returned to normal. A strange sensation tingled through his body that provided so much intense heat Alexander felt for a moment that his body would explode. It subsided and he looked back up at Bishop Malachius and Father Peter who had remained completely ignorant of his condition.

"Five of your brother's bodyguard survived the battle. Your father has sentenced them to death."

"For failure to protect to Crown." Alexander gingerly walked over to the table. The voices that he had learned to control with his armor had multiplied and become louder.

"Yes, but you were there. Did those men not fight as bravely as possible? Where were your men? Would you have your men executed as well?" Bishop Malachius appealed to the softer side of Alexander.

"It's the law. There's nothing I can do."

"There's something you can do. Protect innocent lives."

"You're asking me, a Prince, to break my father's law."

"Alexander, are you saying that man's laws are perfect and without need of rational questioning? Is it right for five men to die because traitors assassinated your brother?"

"What then, Bishop? What would you have me do?"

"Free them my son.... I must go quickly. I have men waiting outside of these walls to escort us safely to the monastery."

"Aren't you going up the stairs?"

"Every city has a secret that can save your life. Remember that Father Jean will be praying in the courtyard tonight. He can assist anyone who is in need."

He smiled at Alexander and without a sound left through a hidden door in the far corner of the room. Alexander was awestruck. He thought about what the Bishop had instructed him to do. Edward had stood the men down. It was Mattias's responsibility as garrison commander to ensure the protection of Edward. Would Alexander have his own men executed?

Alexander headed to his men's quarters and woke Farkas, Jack, and Fergus quietly. He instructed them to grab their swords and come quickly. Under the cover of darkness they carefully made their way outside the palace gate, to a small hut. Inside the hut, under some straw, was a trap door.

Due to the funeral, only two men sat inside the hut. Alexander confidently strolled into the hut, where he was stopped by the men.

"Halt. Sir. Prince Alexander! Please," the first guard stammered nervously.

"Don't worry. I'm only here to see the prisoners. Open please."

The guards looked at each other nervously.

"Well?" Alexander demanded impatiently.

"I'm really very sorry sir. We both are actually. But umm…the King has strictly forbidden anyone from going down into the dungeon."

"Even if let's say, someone wanted to break someone's nose? Or maybe one of them was to hang in despair?"

The two guards grinned.

"We really shouldn't sir," the second guard said. "If the King knew…"

"No, I see. And you two are simply the finest guards in the King's employ. So virtuous. I will let my father know of the excellent work you've done here. What's that?"

Alexander pointed at the ground and knelt down. He flushed three gold coins out of his sleeve into his palm and stood back up.

"Gentlemen, by God's blessing. I have found three gold coins here. Did one of you drop these coins?"

He held out his palm for the men to examine the three gold coins. They sweated profusely and licked their lips nervously. Finally they broke.

"Yes sir." The first guard said. "Thank you sir. Now if you'll follow us, we'll be happy to make your acquaintance."

The men brushed some straw aside and revealed a trapdoor. They opened it and one of them lit a torch. He climbed down slowly, and lit another torch to give light to the dungeon. Alexander and the second guard waited a moment.

"Okay," the first guard said. "All clear."

"Down you go then Sir. And please, not too long. If we're caught, our heads will be cut off too."

"Don't you worry," Alexander said. "I'll only be a moment."

The guard's eyes widened as he felt a sharp poke. Jack stood behind him with a sword pointed at his back.

"Do yourself a favor," Jack said. "Don't even breathe."

Alexander climbed the ladder downstairs and looked around. There were a few cells and each cell was surrounded by stone. The five men sat chained together in one cell as they waited for their death. Several rats scurried past Alexander's feet.

"There they are Prince. You can spit on them if you like."

"Prince Alexander," they murmured.

"We're happy to see you up and about!" The men nodded in agreement.

Alexander felt anguish that these loyal soldiers were about to be hung. They had done nothing wrong. They defended the Prince, most of them died for the Prince. Was this the end for excellent soldiers? Were they no better than those savages on the frontier?

Alexander quickly drew his sword and pointed it at the guard.

"Open the door," he commanded.

"Prince Alexander! Your father's orders! This is treason. You won't get away without the alarm being sounded!"

Just then Jack and Fergus came down the stairs with the other guard.

"I count to five and if that door's not open I'll slit your throat."

The guard quickly opened the door and worked to free the irons that held the men together.

"Friends, I've come to free you. You served my brother bravely, you don't deserve to die. But with this act, your lives now belong to me. Someday I will call upon you to repay this kindness."

"Our swords are yours," Kenric responded.

"Good. Take the guards swords, and take the guards with you. That way, any suspicion of treason will be directly at their feet. Take them with you to the abbey. Go into the abbey and find Father Peter. He should be conducting late night prayers. Tell him I sent you, and he will see you safely out of the city."

"Sir," the guard begged. "Don't do this please. I

have a family."

"You should have thought about your family before you thought about your greed. Now you're an outlaw. My blessings to you. And….if I hear any alarm raised from either of you….or anyone else for that matter….I will make it my personal mission to kill you and your family."

The guards were wide eyed at Alexander's threats, but they obeyed and moved up the ladder out of the dungeon. Fergus extinguished the torches and carefully closed the door once they were outside. The outlaws began moving through the shadows and carefully fled to the abbey.

"What will the future hold for us?" Jack asked once they were away and they were out of dungeon.

"Edwards's death was no accident," Alexander replied. "Everything these people have done has been incredibly well thought and planned. It's been a chess game for them and we have blindly stumbled through everything, they knew who I was in the forest. Their assault on the city was not in their nature, yet they did it to lure Edward and me into the fray. Edward's death….they knew how he'd react. They would have killed him regardless, but they wanted me to bear witness and to bear this burden for his death. All right, they've had their revenge…and now we must ask the one nagging question that's the key to all of this. Are the priests omniscient, or is there a traitor in our midst?"

Jack gasped. "It couldn't be someone in your guard?"

"You're right Jack," Alexander agreed. "It's someone else. It's whoever has been robbing Greystone for these years. The fact that Jacob and Duncan are working together tell me that our kingdom has more than external intrigues to worry about. This goes much deeper. I fear before long our country will lie in ruin." Alexander stopped and looked at Jack and Fergus' long faces. "Don't worry my friends, we will not let that happen, I swear it."

Alexander laughed and joked with Fergus and Jack for a moment, to allay their fears, and decided that all three of them should depart separately in order to return undetected.

All three successfully made it back without detection, and Alexander decided to cool himself with a walk in his garden. But he was not alone. A lone figure sat in the garden…as if he had waited for him.

"Prince Alexander," he said warmly.

"Abiyram. Your appearances remind me of rats with plague; uninvited and a pestilence."

"There's no need for impoliteness," Abiyram said with some sincerity. "I came to pay my respects for your brother."

"Am I to believe you cared about my brother," Alexander sneered.

"No, that's probably a stretch. But all of this could have been avoided if you would have taken my offer. The way in which he died, is not fitting. Your brother was a good man, he holds our respect. Please know that."

"I am to believe that you have feelings for my brother? Are you back trying to peddle me a bill of goods?"

"We are all human Alexander," Abiyram pleaded, "You treat us like animals and expect our reactions to be equal to a so called civilized kingdom. Your father murdered an entire city, and tried to extinguish my people from their own lands. Tell me, what would you do?"

"You make a compelling argument Abiyram, but you must forgive my lack of interest in your bloodlust. I will not join you in wreaking revenge on my father."

"Did your brother leave you any last words?"

Abiyram's words had weight to them. Alexander felt as if he was being tested.

"Why are you concerned with my brother's last words?"

"I think you know," Abiyram chuckled. "For a man who does not play court politics, you are extraordinarily deceptive at times. We would have worked very well together. I'm sorry but I have a new candidate now, and while a little difficult to work with, the dividends have been phenomenal."

"What do you want Abiyram? Is it your intention to bore me to death with your soliloquy? I killed a lot of your men today, and I'll continue to kill so many of them that I replace the Alveus water with your people's blood."

"And I believe you would Alexander, which is why you will enjoy peace on the frontier for some time. The death of my people was necessary, in order to weaken the kingdom. Tell me something Alexander, who does the crown look best upon? Calimus? Mattias? You? I think the next heir will make things even more fascinating."

"So that was your plan. Divide the country, let us devour ourselves, and pick up the pieces? I give you credit for the subterfuge. But you didn't count on one thing."

"What's that?"

Alexander drew in closer to the old man. "Whenever this ends, you won't be alive to see it, because my mission will be to find and kill you. Hang the crown. I just want you....unless....you hand over Jacob and Duncan to me. Hand them over to me and I will spare your life."

Abiyram laughed. "Oh Alexander, you're such an idealist. Do you really think I would sacrifice those two valuable pieces? You are so intensely rational and pragmatic. But, you chose your fate over your destiny. I do not know if our paths will cross again, and if they do not, I want you to know you have my respect, and my sympathy." Abiyram left Alexander in the garden and exited through the citadel gates. Amazingly, he moved passed the guards as if he was invisible while they simply marched back and forth.

He had underestimated Abiyram as nothing more than a bloodthirsty warrior and so had Edward. With every move and foray, Alexander felt more and more that he had become a fly trapped in a spider's web. He thought about his next move. It was obvious to him that his brother's death needed to be avenged. He needed to find Duncan and kill him. There would be no mercy for the thieves' guild, and he wanted to drive them from their hiding in the forest. Abiyram underestimated him also and in time Alexander would make him suffer for it.

Alexander sighed sadly and climbed his favorite tree and settled in quietly while he looked out over the quiet city of Middlebrooke. The city mourned for his brother and for the first time in his memory he heard the sounds of sorrow. He looked towards the stars and imagined that Jean, Edward, and Angelica were now among them and that they shone down on him. He promised himself that he would avenge their deaths and that he would someday be worthy of his brother's sacrifice. Right now, he planned to rest and recover from his wounds as he carefully and silently plotted his next moves. Abiyram had opened with his gambit, and Alexander had done everything that an educated man should do. In every situation, he had tried to do the right thing, and had taken the most logical course of action. He fashioned a new strategy and envisioned boldness, something that the Bete'szek would not expect from him and then, while they least expected it, he would strike at Duncan and Jacob and he would have his brother's death avenged.

Sleep well, he mused the stars, for the harbinger brings his retribution.

"I will have my revenge," Alexander promised.

THANKS

There are so many to thank; family, friends, and social media.

To God: Never will anyone steal the belief I have. The amount of times that you have shown up in the darkest of places with a word of hope for me can never be underestimated or forgotten. I never understood why, and now, I don't need to. Maybe I'm on the right track to finding peace.

Wyatt Huntingford: You are my pride and joy. I am incredibly proud to be your father. You are capable of so many things and whatever you choose you will be the best.

My Parents: Thank you for believing in my talents and for never giving up on me.

Stacy Marshall: you helped me put it all together. Without you, I'd still be talking about the manuscript I wrote that is sitting on my hard drive.

Dan Fowler at Red River Productions: What is all this you have done for me? From the one night where you challenged the paradigm of tradition, it's been a roller coaster since then.

Kell Horton and **Tony Calvano**: Thanks for being in my corner.

To all my friends from Oceanside, CA and my classmates from Vanguard University: You sharpened the creativity I have today. Thanks for watching the sketches, laughing at my jokes, reading my writings, but never cancelling our friendship. I might not be the easiest person to get along with, but I am the best person to get along with. ☺